MUSIC CITY MAYHYMN

A Detective Story

BILLY SPRAGUE

Out of the Bluebell Publishing

For my muses with faces
my children

Willow, Wyatt, Sawyer
you are my greatest story

He has told you, O man, what is good ;
and what does the LORD require of you?
but to do justice, to love mercy,
and to walk humbly with your God

Micah 6:8

In the balance of this life
we've got more love than time.

Joe Beck and William Luz
from *More Love Than Time*

Oh God, this is some shape I'm in

Jackson Browne
from *Sleep's Dark and Silent Gate*

CHAPTER 1

Monday night 11:40PM – Day 1

"Damn! Why can't people die at a decent hour? I gotta go."

Between the Scotch and the bent humans he hunted, Detective Max Malone should have been dead by now. For every person on the blue ball, staying alive means dodging the metaphorical bullet another day. Max had dodged real bullets and taken one to the shoulder. The way he saw it, life is just a dance of physics and impulse. Death is getting beat by the odds. Eventually, everyone loses. On this day in early May just before midnight, getting a code 10-64, deceased person, meant another dance was done. Someone's impulse trumped someone's physics.

Denying his own impulses and the appealing physics of the songwriter-waitress in his arms, Max got up and dressed. Going out the door he tossed her one of his go-to lines, "In Homicide, the hits just keep on coming." This time he added, "If you use that in a song, I get part of the publishing."

Per a new habit, en route to the scene Max sang his recently self-penned theme song, "Music City Mayhymn," one of the few songs he had ever finished. He felt especially clever about the alternate spelling of "mayhem." Nashville was full of clever songs and witty songwriters. Why shouldn't he have his own theme song? And if the aspiring songwriter he just abandoned two deft moves short of conquest could dream of a Grammy, why not him?

Under light rain he headed south out of Green Hills into the rolling equine estates of the A-list, the "rich and aimless," Max dubbed them. He thought he might use that in a song someday. On the narrow, winding roads around Nashville, you could hedge your bet against death in a bigger vehicle. So, he stacked the odds in his four-wheel drive F250 SuperCab complete with grille guard and side curtain airbags. The misspelled, wry boast of his personalized license plate on the front bumper, Alpha Romeo, was wasted on most of the younger women he dated, and whose impulsive physics he preferred. In fact, such impulsive physics cost him his marriage. That, and the Scotch.

The rain had nearly stopped, but the violent Spring storm still boomed as it retreated like a funeral procession to the northeast. Coming up behind two lumbering NES bucket trucks put a damper on his speed, but not on his Irish-Italian irascibility. He squinted in the glare of the yellow flashing lights.

"Son of a bitch. Not now!" Max hurled at his windshield. Glancing at the GPS on his phone he barely dodged the cones around a third electric service truck where a lineman was already at work thirty feet up. The physics of unusual darkness and NES crews suddenly lit a match in his mind. *Power's out. My bad. Note to self: Irritation impairs reason. Remind me to thank the next lineman I see.* Around the next curve, flashing blues of patrol cars marked the 10-20 of the call.

It was black dark. His F250 beams revealed the forensic team and his partner already on the scene. Caution instead of crime tape was going up. He hit the high beams. A tarp hung on the outside of an ornate security gate. *Probably tonight's loser.*

Max served up his routine Italian banter to his partner,

Detective Vince Wilson. "Cosa da, da Vinci? What a way to start the week, paisano." He remembered only a smattering of the beautiful language his mother spoke to him as a boy, but he always felt her delight when he exhumed a phrase.

Vince leaned close and volleyed back discretely with the perfect irritating moniker, "Curious circumstance, Sheamus." Using Max's middle name in public was taboo. Vince knew that and whipped it at him like a towel in a locker room.

Max returned fire. "Good call on the caution tape, cousin Vinny. Don't want to broadcast foul play until we know more."

Vince led Max around the gate, over a low, stacked-rock wall to where a photographer was finishing his work. A male, approximately thirty years old, hung on the inside of the gate, his black and white Converse three feet off the ground. The two detectives, flashlights in hand, stood looking up at the body.

"Impressive. This guy went out with some flare," Max said. "I've got that same pair of shoes."

Max Malone's cocaine was curiosity. The deceased bequeathed the detective a visually tragic drama to unravel, igniting his hunger for mental stimulation like an addict's craving. He felt his mind focus, redirecting his unspent ardor so recently intended for the willing waitress. To him, a mystery was as sexy as a beautiful woman. Resisting either was not the detective's strength.

"Don't I know this guy?" said Maximillian Sheamus Malone.

"Everybody knows this guy," Vince said. "Not a congeniality winner. A real jackass."

"Stronzo," Max translated.

"Yea, a real stronzo. Local rock and roller. Studio musician. Drug dealer. Coke, oxy and more recently meth. Stage name,

Fave. Real name, Abe Davidson. And get this, Shea-Max, this is daddy's front gate."

"Davidson Dream Builders?"

"The same." Detective Wilson began singing the Dream Builder commercial "It takes a whole lot more than wood and stone…" Max joined him at the hook, "Your love makes it home."

"Some dream home, huh?" Wilson said, returning to the business at hand.

"Suicide? Hoping to surprise dad on his way to work tomorrow?"

"Look closer. No rope. He's hanging by his damn hair. How the hell did he get up there? And we found around $90K in baggies in his coat pockets."

Can't Buy Me Love played in Max's head. *The Beatles, 1964, from A Hard Day's Night.*

Max had an encyclopedic memory for songs, especially the classics of the sixties and seventies. His mother played them daily. The detective traced his passion for great songs and fervor for justice to her love for music.

In his sophomore year of high school, Max traded in his sister Arianna's clarinet and some cash earned from working at a drycleaner for a mint 1970 Gibson J-45 sunburst. For a year, nearly every day after doing his homework, he spent many hours learning songs from the records of James Taylor, Bob Dylan and the Beatles. He discovered his mother's stereo would play 33.3rpm LPs at half speed, 16rpm. That dropped the song by an octave and slowed it down enough to hear precisely what the guitar parts were. One afternoon he came out of a music store after buying new strings. The guitar was gone. Someone must have seen the case lying in the back seat, found the door unlocked and helped themself to his prized possession. After all these years his fury still burned. At himself for leaving the car unlocked, and at the reprehensible perp. The receipt with the serial number was still in his firebox. He had it memorized in case he ran into anyone with a J-45. He never saw the guitar again. That incident planted the first seed of Max's mistrust for most human beings.

In his top floor music room, three rows of vinyl records stretched across an entire wall, alphabetized by artist. Many of them were his mother's. On the wall above the records hung a framed quote from Aldous Huxley:

> *"After silence, that which comes nearest to*
> *expressing the inexpressible is music."*

Part of the reason he had finished so few songs was the intimidation of those revered songwriters. How could he ever write anything that good? His prized 1970 Martin D-35 stood in a stand at one end of the collection. He splurged on it at Gruhn's Guitars, world famous for vintage instruments, thinking a classic guitar might help his songwriting. It took him a year and a dozen visits to decide on a model. One day, the very patient and affable guitar tech, Dan Greene, pulled out the D-35. He said Dan Fogelberg was coming by to look at it, so it must have some great songs still inside. Max put his money down and walked out with it. But he couldn't coax great songs from it. Every time he put a Fogelberg record on the turntable, he knew it was not the guitar's fault.

On the opposite wall were bookshelves, crammed with titles from Aristotle to Zafon. Max spent countless hours reading or listening to music, ruminating on cases behind the wall of windows that framed a view of downtown Nashville from his tall skinny perched on Love Circle.

Max braced himself for a hard day's night. He climbed the ladder placed by the paramedics. Sure enough, waist length dreadlocks clung to the steel bars like serpents, the matted mass suspending Fave's body. He made mental notes. *The driveway and bars wet from rain. Clothes damp, not soaked. Smells of alcohol and pot and something else, earthy, like a wet animal.*

"Broken neck?" Max queried from atop the ladder, lifting the dead man's arm and letting it fall.

"That's the prelim."

"Hasn't been dead long. Who called it in?"

"Girlfriend, groupie, probably customer. In the squad car. Brie Batson. Goes by BB. Pretty shook up. Looks like a music and meth fan. Says Abe called her to pick him up here."

Max knew his thorough partner had already begun a search of the area for evidence, but he enjoyed ordering him around. Climbing down he directed him.

"I know it's dark, Vince, but check again for footprints and tire marks, and hoofprints."

"Hoofprints?"

Max donned his best Sherlock accent. "Elementary, my dear Wilson. Anyone been up to the house yet? Told the parents?"

"Officer Hanover and her partner broke the bad news to Mr. Davidson. Apparently, Mrs. Davidson got a better offer a few years back. She and their daughter live in Hawaii. Two other officers assisting."

"Good, Hanover's good."

"She hasn't let on how it happened. Didn't want him running

down here. Not with his boy hanging like a piñata. Thought we'd leave that to you and your graveside manner."

Vince's sarcasm was not lost on Max. Telling a parent their child is dead and how, was more manageable for Max owing to his nearly complete lack of empathy. It gave him an objectivity that made him masterful at gleaning evidence early on. He found when nerves were raw, people revealed more than they realized or intended.

Max's keen mind, skills of observation, attention to detail and his emotion-free objectivity all served him well professionally and in mastering the art of barbeque, but in relationships they proved to be poor bonding agents. On the scene of a mystery, he was in his element.

Maximillian Sheamus Malone attributed his mental acumen and steady nerve to the genes and genius of his mathematician father, Liam Sheamus Malone, and to the atheism adopted in college when he threw off the Catholic, fear-drenched dogma of his childhood. In the same season, he embraced a devout Darwinian view of his own species.

Max telegraphed this in two assertions. One, a reminder stuck to the dash of the F250 was intended to temper his aggressive nature behind the wheel: "Survival of the fittest, biggest or least stupid." His dad taped it to the dash of his first car, a hefty 1984 Jeep Wagoneer. Dr. Malone drove a completely restored 57 Chevy, "real steel and full of V8 thunder." With their heads under its hood, professor Malone told him no son of his was going to die in a tin can, go-cart of a Karmann Ghia, the car Max wanted. The other declaration appeared on an apron, a gift from Vince, worn while presiding over his barbeque grill: "I like people. They taste like chicken."

Max would have displayed both personal proverbs on the rear

bumper of his rolling Ford fortress, but the department had policies against negative, aggressive, sarcastic, religious or political bumper stickers on police vehicles. Including irony. He had inquired. So far, Captain Haskins let Max's front personal plate slide on the thin rationale that he rotated them to make his vehicle "less identifiable." His other options: SMART CAR; two plates spelled backward for easy reading in a rearview mirror - EZIS LAUTCA (Actual Size) and RETAE SUIRP (Prius Eater): and, of course, KARMANN GHIA.

He ignored Vince's barb. "I'll have a word with the groupie and then head up to the house."

In just seven minutes Max extracted the following: the meth enthusiast's status as *part-time lover of Abe's*, which triggered the Stevie Wonder song in his head, *Part-Time Lover, 1985, from On Square Circle, reached #1;* also a steady customer of Abe; a rough sketch of a timeline; the fact that Abe sounded "furious and scared" on the phone; his dad was "infuriating"; Abe told her something "spooky" was going on; he demanded she meet him outside the gate or he would "cut her out"; and he insisted she get him out of there before he went "ballistic." *Mad at dad. Scared of what? Cut her out? not off?* He inscribed it all in a mosaic of mental tiles like a Rubik's cube.

Max preferred to drive up to the house, but the gate and body could not be disturbed. He set out on foot.

Stars reappeared through the tattered tail end of the storm. The night turned dead calm. Dark shapes of tall gables became barely visible over a rolling hill and the long, tree-lined drive.

Uninvited, the clean smell after the storm and soft, arhythmic sound of drops shedding from the trees thrust upon him a memory of his mother. She liked to walk in the woods after a rain, to "feel the new" she called it. She once made Max stop and listen to the drops, likening it to a music box winding down. *What did Zafon say about memories? Worse than bullets. Damn right. Like sniper bullets, Carlos. You never see them coming.* Just as he crested the hill, all the lights came on, snapping him back to the present. The Davidson dream home lit up like a movie set for the Great Gatsby, southern style. *Looks like someone is doing more than surviving at the top of the food chain.*

Like flipping a switch, Max willed his thoughts back into pregame mindset. He approached every case the same, reminding himself this one would be no different. Examine the physics - the evidence. Discover the impulse - the motive. Murder always involved both. Accidents boiled down to physics, poor judgment and/or the randomness of the universe. So far, this case seemed mostly about physics. The primary intrigues were the means and oddity of the victim's final resting place and whatever spooked the piñata. *Good one Vince.* As if on cue, "*Love is kinda crazy with a spooky little girl like you*" played in his head as he crossed the immense circle drive. *Spooky, 1968 by the Classics IV, later formed the Atlanta Rhythm Section.*

Mounting the Italian marble steps to the broad, castle-like front door, Max silenced the playlist in his brain by reciting to himself in Italian, like an incantation, "La verità è più forte del tempo." His mother, Sofia, etched this proverb on his young soul, "The truth is stronger than time." But that was only half of it. Her complete adage to him was:

*"La verità è più forte del tempo,
e il tempo è più breve dell'amore."*
Truth is stronger than time, and time is shorter than love.

Max worshipped his mother. She created delight in everything. He couldn't peel an orange without getting in the crosshairs of her memory. As kids she played a game with Max and his little sister, Arianna: Who can find a peeling shaped like a state or country or continent? It was like cloud watching, which she did with them as well.

Twice they decided their summer vacation this way. Arianna pulled off a piece that looked like Vermont. Max turned it upside down and said it could be New Hampshire. That summer they drove up from Virginia to see both states and then over to the coast of Maine. A second time, a sliver of peel looked like Tennessee. That summer, they drove across Tennessee to Memphis, ate barbeque at the Rendezvous and listened to the blues on Beale Street. On the way back thru Nashville, they had milkshakes at an old diner he now knew as Elliston Place Soda Shop. At the Ryman they saw Dolly and other Country artists. He still had a crush on her and most of her albums.

At the time, eleven-year-old Max said. "I wouldn't mind living here someday,"

Professor Malone wondered why none of the peelings ever looked like Ireland. So, the next summer they went to his ancestral home in County Westmeath, including Malone Castle, without the geomancy of the orange peel. He came home with a print of the Malone family crest bearing the motto: Fidelis ad Urnam, 'Faithful to the End.' The framed print currently lived in the closet of his guest bedroom with a dozen concert posters.

Whenever anyone asked Max what brought him to Nashville, he told them an orange peel. The story turned out to be a great pickup line with women, who became enthralled by the story, perceiving Max's devotion to his mother as especially sensitive - until they discovered the icy dispassion of the castle Malone within, shaped like Antarctica.

He came by his frozen heart honestly. Max was barely eighteen when his mother died of breast cancer. He watched her life and vitality slip away. She pleaded with him not to be angry with God. On her deathbed she told him, "This is not goodbye, il mio tesoro (my treasure). Only arrivederci. See you soon. We will have a very long hello." She loved the Psalms. Even near the end she spoke them aloud. "'Bless the Lord and forget not his kindness.' Thank heavens, Max, look how much he gave me in you and Arianna and your father. Il tempo è più breve dell'amore." Time is shorter than love.

Despite her plea, Max began to build his case against any God who would mismanage the universe in such incompetent and cruel ways. *Forget not his kindness? Seriously?* Look how much God took from them. She was only thirty-nine. Shiny and funny and a joy to all who knew her. During that dark time of grieving, "Til I Die" by the Beachboys 1971, became his personal anthem. "I'm a cork on the ocean…rock in a landslide…leaf on the wind." It was never a big hit. Just a B-side song. Like him. Until he became the youngest detective in Nashville history.

Shortly after her death, he tattooed her Italian gem of wisdom in a band around his right arm in mathematical notation: Verità > Tempo < Amore. The face of a clock represented the word "Tempo," its hands set at 7:17, the moment at dusk when Sofia died, the moment Max first felt the painful reality of having more love than time. Like the orange peel story, the tattoo also worked well at landing women. But only for catch and release.

Years later, after experiencing firsthand the darker pain of time outlasting love, in more than one failed romance, he now subscribed only to the first half of the adage, 'truth is stronger than time.' It suited his work, temperament and algebraic worldview. A few steps from Davidson's giant door, he repeated to himself, "La verità è più forte del tempo."

Before he could knock, Officer Hanover opened the door. Both were curt. Professional.

"Officer Hanover," Max addressed her, moving past her into the vaulted foyer.

"Detective."

"You clear the house? What have we got?" Pleasantries, especially in a work situation were not Max's strong suit. He had his game face on, already scanning the opulent interior. He noted Hanover's light perfume, *Este Lauder White Linen,* and a hint of *smoke, nontobacco.* In that order.

Officer Helen Hanover was very familiar with his style. If it appeared dismissive, that's because it was, especially when Max was on the scent of a trail. She had previously deflected his after-work invitations for a drink, except once, during which he said her name sounded like a nightly news anchor or motivational speaker. "Film at 11. I'm Helen Hanover." "Are you stuck in the same old, same old? Too tired to dream? I'm Helen Hanover and I'm here to help."

Glancing at her notes, Hanover didn't get right to it. This was a subtle and gratifying game she liked to play with the great Max Malone.

"Yes, sir. Cleared the house, guest house, garage and stable. Took a while. Look at the size of this place. You should see the collection of cars! Ferrari, Lamborghini, vintage Alfa Romeo and…"

"And Davidson?"

"Yes sir, sorry. When we walked up in the dark, Mr. Davidson and Ms. Andrews, his personal assistant, were lighting candles." *That accounts for the smell of smoke.* "They assumed we were from his home security service. He barked about why the backup lights hadn't come on and…

"Yes, got it. You touch anything? You're not gloved up."

"No, nothing, Sergeant."

"Move anything? Any outside doors or windows open?

"No. Yes, two. And No."

"Which doors?

"The guest house behind the pool and the main stable gate. Come to think of it, I closed the gate so one horse wouldn't wander out. I thought it was odd that…"

"Yes, alright," Max fast-forwarded her. "Where is Davidson now, and what does he know?"

"Mr. Davidson is in his study off the great hall. Drinking. Single malt Connemara. Neat. My partner is there. And Ms. Andrews. Attractive. Young. Mr. Davidson knows his son is deceased. But not how. I told him someone would be here soon with more answers."

"Good work," Max stopped short of saying thank you.

"I'm here to help, sir."

The reference hit the mark, as well as Officer Hanover's deadpan but non-sarcastic delivery. In fact, Max felt the tension between them ease. *Nicely played,* he thought.

"Lead the way," he said, gesturing with one hand, "to the stables first, please."

"Please?" Hanover noted. That was a first.

Passing through the great hall, Max hung back a bit, browsing the many pictures of Davidson's world. Hanover waited.

He had been in a few high-roller and celebrity homes around Nashville, for police appreciation and charity events his Ex insisted they attend. But none like the Davidson's estate. The vaulted, exposed-beam ceiling seemed designed to make those who entered feel small, like the cathedrals in which his mother found so much beauty and solace. *"How does it feel to be one of the beautiful people?* jangled in his brain. *The Beatles, 1967, from the song, "Baby, You're a Rich Man" B-Side single to "All You Need Is Love."*

"Do you like the Beatles, Officer Hanover?"

"Yes, sir. The stables are this way, detective."

Max lingered. Photos of horses and cars outnumbered those of people. Shots of show jumping, blue ribbons and trophies indicated some in the family were *excellent equestrians.* Max stopped in front of a large family portrait over a massive fireplace. He could have walked into it standing up. Against the backdrop of the mansion's stately entrance stood Davidson, wife, assumed, young Abe next to mom and sister by dad, each child holding the halter of two expensive looking horses, all flanked by a red Ferrari and what could be a rare 2600 GT Coupe Alpha Romeo, '66 or '67. A detail caught Max's eye. *Mr. and Mrs. not touching.*

Another record dropped in his head. *"You can't hide your lyin' eyes, and your smile is a thin disguise." Lyin' Eyes, Eagles, 1975, album, One of These Nights.*

"Does she look happy to you, Hanover?"

"Sir?"

"Does she look happy?"

Officer Hanover took a few steps toward the painting and humored the detective. "No, sir. How can you know? But if she was a victim of love, this is some kind of prison."

"Victim of love?"

"A song by the Eagles, sir."

"Yes, I know. From Hotel California, 1976." *She knows the Eagles. That song wasn't even a single.*

As they exited, Max radioed Vince.

"Meet us in the study in ten minutes. Davidson's assistant, a Ms. Andrews, is with him. You know the dance. Chasing a theory. Out."

Chapter 2

Late Monday night 12:45AM – Day 1

The Davidson stables looked like a Hilton for horses. On the far end it housed the other horsepower he collected, expensive cars.

"You say that gate was open?" Max inquired.

"Yes, one horse milling around in the main alleyway. I heard it walking on the cobblestones. It should still be there."

"Cobblestones?"

"Yes, you'll see. Very old school. Not very good on a horse's legs."

"You ride, Hanover?"

"Did a lot as a kid. Hope to have my own again someday."

"This horse have a saddle?"

"No, that's what I tried to tell you was odd. No saddle. Only a bridle. And…"

"Muddy hooves?"

"Yes, sir."

The horse clip-clopped to the gate like a puppy as they approached. It was a magnificent animal. Even Max could tell this was no kid's pony.

"I assume you can handle him?"

"Yes, sir. Glad to." Hanover passed thru the gate speaking to the horse in tones that made Max envious.

"Hello, beautiful boy. Storm's all gone now. You get a little spooked? Well, it's alright now." She extended one hand palm up under its mouth and then scratched the long face with the other. "Yeah, we're gonna get you back to bed with a snack. Good boy. What a beautiful boy."

Max watched as she ran one hand down the powerful neck to its wither, easily earning its trust, and secured the reins in her other hand. Without invitation Springsteen cued up in his head. *I just want someone to talk to / and a little of that human touch, 1992, from the album Human Touch.*

He took out a small plastic evidence bag. Hanover held the horse steady as he scraped a few hairs from its back with a pen. He took a few shots with his phone of the horse, its muddy hooves and surreptitiously, of Hanover. Her command and ease with the stallion enhanced her natural beauty and vitality.

When they first crossed paths on a case, Max noted Officer Hanover's appealing physics, even behind the regulation street blues and bulletproof vest. A gun on her hip only amplified it. She reminded him of Dorothy Malone, his dad's favorite actress, the early natural brunette years, less sultry but no less head-turning. Liam Malone claimed to be related to Dorothy, a distant cousin, proof that talent and good looks run in the Malone clan. Hence, Max's invitations for a drink after work, despite department guidelines against such liaisons. Their one drink got Max nowhere.

"Hanover, did I ever tell you how I got to Nashville?"

"You mean the orange peel story? No, sir. But I've heard about it. I'll put this boy away if you want to head back to the house."

Apparently, Hanover's skill with horses also extended to men. Max headed toward the gate.

"Good work, Hanover"

"Thank you, Detective."

On his way to meet Davidson, he passed Vince talking with Ms. Andrews in the great hall. *Wonder what else she 'assists' him with?* Entering the study felt like walking into the office of a university president or big country singer. High coffered ceiling of white beams, oil paintings and rich wood-paneling all around. The furniture, mostly leather, and appointments were clearly from places or countries a detective did not shop. A rolling ladder stood against shelves not filled with books, but awards related to business, fine cars and pedigreed horses. One section housed bottles of expensive liquors from all over the world. Hanover's partner, Officer Thomason, nodded. Davidson set down a drink, got up, and came around a giant desk.

"Mr. Davidson, I'm Detective Malone."

"A detective? Why? What's happened to my son?"

"Just routine in these situations, sir. This is only preliminary, but it looks like your son had a nasty fall from a horse. Was he in the habit of riding bareback in a storm?"

"He was a reckless fool, but an excellent horseman."

"Indeed. I saw the photos and trophies. Mr. Davidson, I know this is all very disorienting, but I need to ask, what were you two fighting about?"

"What makes you think we…"

"Your son called a woman to pick him up at the gate. She says he was very agitated about an altercation with you, that you were, in his words, "infuriating" and he was about to go "ballistic.""

Max believed in cutting to the chase. Oblique moves were not his style. Except with women. That's why he didn't like chess, preferred singer-songwriters to most poets and Hemingway to Faulkner.

"Money. What else?" Davidson added two fingers of scotch to his glass from a bottle on the desk.

18

"What about money?" Max asked, noting: *Connemara. Another point for Hanover.*

"He always wanted more, but this time he wanted a lot of money. Get this, he wanted a share of my holdings, his 'portion' he called it! Can you believe that?"

"Did he say why?"

"He went on and on about making a new start somewhere else, settle some things here and get out. Detective, I know my son. I know he was into some shady things, and I was not about to fund any of it!"

"Apparently, he took it badly?"

"He exploded. So did I." Davidson sat back down in his giant chair, behind his giant desk, in his giant house, and downed the Irish scotch in his crystal glass. He seemed to shrink. Max played a silent card, waiting for more.

"I asked him 'what's the hurry?' He was always in a hurry. He drove fast. Rode fast. Hell, he played guitar fast. Abe just lived fast."

Like you. Max kept that to himself, as well as the soundtrack in his head of *Life in the Fast Lane, Eagles, 1976, from Hotel California.*

"Like me, I guess," Davidson added.

"One more thing. Just routine. Do you know anyone who would want to harm your son?"

"What are you implying? Do you think someone…"

"No, sir, by all indications, it seems your son made a rash choice to ride one of your horses out in a storm. It's very likely all the lightning in the area spooked it down near the gate and three your son off, about the time the power went out. The medical examiner's report will tell us more."

"Can I see him?"

"Of course, but let me check." With a look, Max assigned Thomason to that.

He pressed again. "Mr. Davidson, are you aware of anyone who would want to harm your son?"

The shrunken tycoon poured two more fingers in his glass. "Unfortunately, that's probably a long list."

"Do you mind if we take a look at your son's quarters? Routine. I understand he lived in the guest house."

"Yes, go ahead. Haley, Ms. Andrews can show you the way. I need to call his mother." He downed the Connemara like a high-stakes gambler holding a bad hand.

"We won't be long, sir." As Max headed for the door, Davidson spoke.

"The last thing I said to him was 'Let's take some time and figure this out.' He screamed at me, 'I don't have any time to waste, dad' and stormed out."

Max caught site of Hanover through the door. She nodded.

"Mr. Davidson, officers Hanover and Thomason will escort you when you're ready."

Ms. Andrews led Max and Vince around a large pool to the guest quarters. She excused herself to assist Davidson. The door stood wide open per Hanover's report. Like everything in Davidson's world, the guest house was more than ample. It could easily accommodate a family of four. They gloved up and quickly surveyed three bedrooms. One stored at least twenty instruments in cases. One spacious bedroom functioned as an office and recording space, and third held a kingsize bed, unmade. There were two full baths. Abe was not tidy.

Max focused on the large office.

"Max, I got a happy meal on the kitchen table. Open bottle of Jack, baggie of buds, half-burned reefer and white residue."

"No one calls it 'reefer' anymore, Vince. Probably Abe's last meal. Bag some samples for the lab. Only for the lab."

"Shaemus, I wouldn't do anything to shame us." Max had heard that one more than a few times.

Opposite the desk, half a dozen guitars hung on the wall bracketing a recording workstation. Max knew something about great guitars. After all, this was Nashville. Three acoustics - Martin, McPherson and Olson on the left. Les Paul, Fender Strat and Tele on the right. *Nothing but the best. No surprise.* Cables snaked everywhere, connecting amps, foot pedals and a microphone on a boom stand.

"Vince. You should see these guitars."

"Thinking about taking a sample for the lab?"

"Can't lie. It crossed my mind."

An open shoe box lay discarded on the floor. *Probably held the cash Abe snatched for his midnight ride.* The accompaniment began in his head. *'We'll be ridin' Wildfire.' Michael Martin Murphy 1975, album, Blue Sky - Night Thunder.*

Max sat in the leather desk chair. No doubt in daylight the bay window looked out on an impressive view of woods or horse pastures and rolling hills. *How do you have all this and still have so little sense?* Surveying the scene, Max imagined the angry rocker's frenzied exit. *What spooked you, Abe? Why the money grab? Drug supply chain debt?* Max figured something in Abe's mess might lead to nabbing some bent humans. *Why the rush to get out?*

Nothing in the piles on the desk stood out. Unopened mail, song charts and crumpled papers with scribbled phrases, scratch outs and revisions, probably song attempts. *Been there, done that.*

A small trash can under the desk caught his eye. He had learned not to overlook a person's trash. If nothing else, it usually revealed fingerprints and sometimes DNA.

Another of his dad's pithy mottos scrolled into his mind. *Max, one man's trash is another man's treasure.* His dad's obsession to waste nothing fed Professor Malone's hobby of making junkyard "art" cobbled together in the workshop behind their garage. Many Saturdays, Max helped him create robotic creatures and random concept sculptures from hubcaps, windmill blades, electrical circuits and car and toy parts. They built a seven-foot model of the solar system with balls of different size and color perched on the ends of long metal rods taken from an airplane wing. Max was put in charge of painting the balls to resemble the planets. He put a red dot on the blue ball to represent where the Malone family lived. They pushed the rods into holes drilled in the heavy base of a rusty gas station sign. Moving one ball caused the planets to career into each other and swing about.

Young Max had remarked, "Thank heaven it's not really like that. We'd get thrown into space."

"Indeed. I was going to call it 'Chaos Theory,'" he remembered his dad saying, "but since your mother is always saying 'Thank Heaven,' let's call it that."

Dr. Liam Malone claimed one of his greatest breakthroughs in mathematics came while they were shaping a Mobius strip out of a metal STOP sign: Parameter Oscillating Tension Sequencing or POTS. It was an equation for determining stress that architects use to build more earthquake-resistant structures. Its application created an ongoing watershed for the family income and eventually the inheritance that enabled Max to buy the home on Love Circle, otherwise financially out of reach on a detective's salary. It was also

Max's first lesson in irony via his dad explaining the unspoken joke in making a symbol for infinity out of a "STOP" sign. He still had a strong affinity for irony. Most ironies. After his dad's death, his sister, still a true believer in eternal realities, chose the Mobius.

The sculpture of the planets currently stood in Max's music and book room, conjuring fond memories of visiting scrap yards and turning junk into whimsical art.

Compared to Abe's desktop, there wasn't much in the trash can. Max dumped the contents on the floor. A red ball of paper rolled away by itself. His inner DJ cued up: *and I think, it's gonna be alright, yeah, the worst is over now the mornin' sun is shining like a red rubber ball, 1966 by The Cyrkle. Little known fact - cowritten by Paul Simon.* Max picked up the red paper ball. It had been tightly compacted, *perhaps by an angry set of hands?* He unrolled it. One side red. The other white. Max cleared a place on the desk, spread the paper out, red side up. *Medium card stock. About 5"x7"* Handwritten in the middle of the card was simply:

Abe Davidson

He turned it over. The record in his head stopped like someone bumped the turntable.

You have sown poison and agony. Prepare to reap.
Put your affairs in order. Your life is required of you.
The Red Angels

It was not gonna be alright. And the worst was not over.

"Vince, get in here!"

CHAPTER 3

Tuesday morning 6:15AM – Day 2

The sound of the alarm started Max's daily routine. He sat up on the side of the bed. Felt for the slippers placed strategically where his feet first met the floor. They were there. Coffee beckoned. He made his first stop in the bathroom, relieved himself, dutifully washed his hands like Sofia trained him, and rinsed his mouth with a water pick like his father. He looked in the mirror to check on the recent invasion of grey hairs on the sides of his thick head of dark hair, a genetic gift from his mother. Sometimes when he looked at himself, he saw her eyes looking back at him, and his dad's straight nose and strong jawline. Some winters he grew a beard or goatee as luxurious as the one Liam Malone wore most of the time. Whenever he did, Vince called him Serpico or Rodrigo, from Dinero's character in the movie, "The Mission."

Per usual, he went to the northeast window to see what kind of day it was. Sunny and clear. That could change. It was Spring. He opened the window to a soft breeze. Birds chirped their morning correspondences. He normally didn't linger, but a troop of red cardinals caught his eye. *Red Angels*. Involuntarily, his mind retraced the scene at the Davidson estate.

Coffee shouted. He headed to the kitchen to start the brew. Early glow of sunlight bathed the room in golden hues, but it went unnoticed. The designer coffee maker began its familiar percolating sound. Max stepped to the front door and opened it. From behind the glass storm door, he watched more cardinals flit around the yard. Their chatter was as cryptic as last night's revelation.

* * *

Eight minutes in no traffic to the northeast, Jessie Bellaire pulled the silk sheet over her head to block the brazen sun trespassing the curtains. She fumbled for her phone on the nightstand, 6:22AM, threw off the covers and cursed the morning.

"Shit, why am I awake?"

She hit 'snooze' three times. Fog prowled her brain from the previous night's festivities. It resisted waking but prevented more sleep. In fact, she had not slept much in the last week, no matter how much she drank. She had tapped a connection to procure some oxy, a habit she kicked for the sake of control, but it provided only a small buffer to reality and little rest.

Even exhaustion from the vigorous sex she wielded like a wand over defenseless men failed to defeat the insomnia. And though she wouldn't admit it, sex of late had lost some luster. Even with him, the current target of her designs. This time, she had a very big trophy buck in her crosshairs, Tony Armstrong, head of Mergers and Acquisitions and major stockholder of enterprises in mineral rights, import/export and a name brand hotel chain.

The thought of her quarry made her check the nightstand. A slight breeze of satisfaction cleared the fog a little at the sight of the note. He always left a note.

See you tonight at the ranch. You'll get there ahead of me. Dress up. Pack for sun. Tomorrow we fly away!

All Yours

Jessie took particular delight in his salutation, "All Yours."

"Yes, you are, my dear," she said out loud. The next morning, they were to board Tony's private jet for a "business" trip to Cabo. The prize buck didn't know that Jessie's business was to extend her stay, indefinitely, on his dime, until his divorce was final. She could be very persuasive. This was a merger and acquisition, but for once Tony was not in charge.

Anticipation energized her enough to get her feet on the floor, walk to the French doors, open them and step out onto the balcony. She took in the view of Vanderbilt University from her luxury apartment high above 21st street. Jessie gloated. Only a few years ago, the university and sorority dismissed her for poor grades, excessive absentees and drug and alcohol infractions. Rumors of sex for grades with a married professor and graduate lab instructor could not be officially confirmed as a contributing factor. But what the professor paid for her exoneration helped land her on her feet. She took a visceral pleasure in the thought that being good on her back kept landing her on her feet. Who needs a degree in business when she already knew how to trade in the oldest currencies in the world, beauty and seduction?

Jessie learned early the power she held over men. It opened doors and wallets. Even as a preteen when she moved to music, twirling and performing the latest moves, she felt eyes on her, and liked it. At thirteen, in public places, she sensed men's eyes following her. At fifteen her mother, a striking serial heartbreaker herself, told her daughter most men are suckers for beauty and trainable, like dogs. They could be led around on a leash. She assured Jessie she could have any man she wanted, so aim high.

In high school, she began to wield her power. The day she walked into sophomore English at her new school, the boys who were there still remember it. To say Jessie was voluptuous is like saying the Grand Canyon is grand, until you see it, then grand won't do. Her long, jet-black hair, dark eyes, full lips, shapely everything else and pouty mystique earned her the title, Cleopatra. For three years, she ruled the school. Boys bragged and lied about sleeping with "Cleo." Only those she deemed useful made that list. Girls hated and envied her.

As homecoming queen her senior year, she and the top hunk paraded onto the football field at halftime, him a shirtless bronzed King Tut and she adorned like Cleopatra in sheer white linen, sans undergarments, complete with crown bearing a king cobra, its hood flared in strike position. Tut walked three steps behind her, being led on a golden leash attached to her scepter. When they reached the center of the fifty-yard line, the high school band struck up - what else? "Walk Like an Egyptian" 1986 by The Bangles. Jessie persuaded the band director to learn it. She could be very persuasive. The couple cut loose and danced. She twirled and gyrated like a Vegas showgirl. Every man in the stadium wanted her. All their wives and girlfriends wanted the cobra to bite her on the face.

Spring of senior year, she graduated from boys to men, secretly dating a thirty-year-old heir to the largest string of car dealerships in Austin. His boots and cowboy hat were not her style, but he had access to daddy's money.

Jessie learned if she took care of men, they would take care of her. The heir to the auto empire pulled some favors and got her to the front of the line for admission to the University of Texas and into a black BMW 1 Series convertible, with vanity plate as requested: IM CLEO. But Jessie's mother aimed higher. She maintained it would be many years before the Austin beau came into his inheritance. On Mother's Day, the two of them flew to Nashville. In three days, by unknown means, stage mom got beautiful daughter with average SAT scores accepted into Vanderbilt, the Ivy League of the South – to hunt bigger game.

The plan paid off. Jessie's power now provided the upscale apartment, a black Audi A5 coupe, clothes, incidentals and eccentricities. Soon, the payoff promised to be bigger than ever.

Jessie could smell victory. Tony had already separated from his wife. The thrill of the chase always strengthened her resolve and quelled any uncertainty. This May morning it refueled her. She was a fighter. Focused. Fearless. Nothing, no one was going to get in the way. She would not be threatened by Tony's business partners, lawyers, his brother, mother, two grown children near her own age, and certainly not by whoever scribbled the anonymous crank note stuck under her door a week earlier. *Put my affairs in order, my ass.* She wrote it off as probably one of Tony's associates or even his soon-to-be Ex playing cryptic hardball. *Impressive play though. I could use this someday. Report them for threatening bodily harm. People go to jail for that.*

Imperious, like the Queen of the Nile, she looked down at the people on the street heading for work or academia. With a fierce loathing for their scholastic smugness, for all the hoop-jumping posers down there painting inside the lines, and especially for *the f-ing Red Angels,* whoever they were, Jessie Bellaire declared, "This is the first day of the rest of my own damn life."

* * *

Twelve stories down and one block south on 21ˢᵗ, Max and Vince walked into their usual bagel place. They had slept little as well and were up early to brief Captain Haskins at 8:00.

"I see you changed your front plate. About time," Vince said.

"Yea, not that I don't enjoy helpful people telling me I misspelled Alfa."

"Probably time to confuse your fan. Oh, wait, that's me."

"Vince, don't you know by now you can't hurt me if I don't care?"

"Right, your not-so-secret weapon."

"So, it's agreed, we keep the note between us and the captain?" Max pressed.

"Agreed. It convinces him we gotta chase this. But ten to one this thing leaks. We need the lab to look at it. Do the routine. Where's the paper from? What kind of ink pen? Any fingerprints? Handwriting analysis. How was it delivered? The techs will have to read it."

Max was ahead of Vince. "I think I know the right guy in the lab. New young guy. New guys are eager to get on the inside of a hunt. Plus, we tell him if a leak is traced to him, we end his career before he has one."

"Fine, but what do we tell Davidson about maintaining a crime scene and snooping around?"

"Got that covered. Let's get a look at his security system. There was a camera at the gate."

"Got that covered," Vince sparred back. "I already asked Ms. Andrews. There's no footage. The lightning knocked out the whole system before the incident."

"Probably just as well for Davidson's sake. Imagine watching your son die like that."

"Max, that almost sounded like caring," Vince goaded.

Adopting a reasonably convincing Cary Grant accent, one of three he could do, Max responded, "My dear Wilson. Just because I don't have a heart doesn't mean I can't imagine having one."

"Touché. So how do we handle Davidson?"

"We tell the truth. We're following a lead about a credible threat made on his son from an unsavory in his circle, but emphasize his death appears completely accidental. Davidson said himself a lot of people would like to see Abe taken down a few notches, or worse. We're following that trail while we wait for the lab report. But primarily we're sifting through Abe's world to get a possible bead on bad guys in the drug chain."

"Right, that's good."

"Want to let me finish?"

"Are you ever finished? Are you finished with that?" Vince said, pointing to the other half of Max's breakfast bagel.

"Touché, but only because you're such a good listener." He slid the other half of his bagel over to Vince. "We tell him Abe's death could do some good. And it could. Getting bad guys off the street helps everyone."

"Yea, OK, that should work. I gotta tell you, Max. That's some kind of spooky note. Sounds so biblical. Like, 'God's been watching you, Abe, and boy is he pissed.'"

"Yea, the wording is no doubt part of the scare factor. And it worked. Scared him into making some fatal decisions, if that's all that happened."

Max's phone rang.

"Yes, sir, Captain. Well, that always sucks. Must be humans involved…. Yes, sir… Roger that… Damn!… en route, ETA about 7:25."

"Let me guess," Vince said. "Meet around back at Frothy on 12th. Order his usual."

"Right. He's stuck in traffic. And a heads up, reporters from the Tennessean and three TV stations are at the precinct wanting a statement about Abe's death."

"How do those vultures do it?"

"They eat roadkill for a living."

"Max, if they got wind of that note, it would be a circus!"

"And either spook or entertain the perp. This morning they've already broadcast live from Davidson's gate decorated with our tape and the officer posted there. One station is leading with 'Davidson's Dream House Nightmare.'"

"Holy crap!"

"Indeed. Let's go."

CHAPTER 4

Tuesday morning 7:28AM – Day 2

The only thing Captain Haskins disliked more than press conferences was lukewarm coffee. Max knew the gregarious manager at the Frothy Monkey, so per the routine, he and Vince got their own, prepaid the captain's usual - a large, add cream, not milk, to a medium tan, no sugar and a sprinkle of cinnamon - and Rachel would bring it to the side door ninety seconds after Max texted from his truck.

Max's mother had added cinnamon to her coffee as well. So did he. Some mornings, just shaking the cinnamon canister over his coffee and smelling the fragrance fired another memory bullet of her. This morning, he told Vince she once sprinkled it in his hair before school and said, "You watch, the girls will want to smell your hair." He had complained vigorously and tried to brush it out, but she was right. They did.

"Maybe you should try that with Hanover. Nothing else is working."

"Maybe you should try not to be such a stronzo."

The captain pulled into the rear parking lot. Vince took the back seat of the black Suburban, as usual, Max the front, with the coffee. It was piping hot and so was Haskins. Traffic jams sent him over the edge. His head tilted back on the headrest. He rubbed his forehead with two fingers, the front of his shirt already stained by the cup he spilled in the stop and go traffic.

Max handed him the coffee.

"Thank you. Gonna need this today. Ok, what do you got on? I want to be brief with those reporters. And why couldn't we do this over the phone? It was an accident, right?"

Max began, "That's what everything indicates. He and his dad had a big fight over money. Abe stormed out; we believe pretty high. He called a woman to pick him up at the gate, then rode a horse, bareback, from the stable as that storm rolled out last night. We think the lightning that knocked out power in the area spooked the horse, threw Abe onto the gate and broke his neck. The woman found him hanging there and called it in.

"Hanging on the gate? You mean by a rope?"

"No sir, he had very long dreadlocks. He was hanging by his hair."

"Lord have mercy! I hope we're the only ones with photos of that?"

"Yes sir. In fact, before I arrived Vince had the officers hang a tarp and made a good call to use caution, not crime tape."

"I saw that in the broadcast. Nice work, Vince. I can use that with the reporters."

"Thank you, sir."

Max continued, "Sir, besides a few officers and paramedics only the woman saw it."

"Get me a list of the officers and paramedics. This cannot get out right now, for the family's sake."

Dirk Haskins, for all his imposing leadership persona, was still a man very sensitive to the toll crime, violence and tragedy take on the people surrounding it. And on the community. In fact, he was very good with press conferences, sincere, courteous, thorough yet concise. Trauma was no stranger.

He was a boy from the boondocks of rural Louisiana. In his sophomore year of high school Haskins' only uncle, whom he greatly admired, was beaten to death on a hunting trip by two men who stole his guns and truck. The two were caught. Dirk saw his dad's agony and anger and grieved through his own. He sat through the trial, fastened on the remorseless faces of the murderers, watched the detectives submit evidence, and witnessed the legal twists and turns of the proceedings. Both murderers received life sentences. The unholy travesty of taking an innocent human life, a treasured, irreplaceable human life, ignited the young Haskins' drive for justice. His empathy for victims matched matched it.

"His boy's body in our lab?" the captain asked.

"Yes, sir, we hope to have a prelim this afternoon."

"And the woman? Girlfriend? She been interviewed?"

Vince jumped in, "Briefly, last night on the scene. She's kind of a girlfriend and groupie. Admitted to being a substance customer of Abe's. We advised her it's in her best interest not to speak to anyone. She's due at headquarters this morning at 10:00 for a follow up."

"Think she'll show?"

"We're sending a car for her. Hanover and Thomason."

"Good. Hanover has a good rapport with the lost groupie type." The captain looked at Max. At Vince. Then back at Max. "Well? We wouldn't be sitting here if that's all you got, right?"

"Indeed, sir."

"And do I want to know it before I address the press?"

"Not sure, sir, but we need you to see it to proceed. We found this in Abe's trash in his office." Max handed him the note in an evidence bag. He read the red side. Then turned it over.

"Holy crap!"

"That's exactly what I said, sir," offered Vince.

"We've got a vigilante angel out there."

"Angels, plural," Max clarified, "Unless that's meant to mislead."

"Now I wish you'd told me this after the briefing. But there it is. If the press got hold of this…"

"It would be a circus," Vince finished the captain's sentence.

Max, per usual, took the lead. "Sir, we'd like to keep this between the three of us for now and proceed with an investigation."

"Of course, of course," said the captain, rubbing his forehead again. "How will you explain to Davidson why you're there?"

Vince beat Max to the punch. "We've worked that out, sir." He explained Max's strategy wrapping up with his partner's own idea. "We tell him Abe's accident could do some good. Right, Max?"

Max responded, "Right. WE plan to go back there this afternoon. If you green light this, sir."

"Of course, good thinking and carry on. Keep me in the loop. What else do you need?"

"We have to keep a lid on this Red Angels thing, but we need the lab to take a look at the note. Do the routine analysis. What's your take on the new hire, Brickman? I'm gonna pull his file. Is he trustworthy for something like this yet or do we go with Dr. Jenkins?"

"Thor is a bona fide genius. Can't believe we got him."

"Thor? I thought his name was Joe?"

"His middle name is Thoreau. Early on his buddies started calling him Thor because of his mental superpowers. Get this, as a kid he used to work puzzles with the picture face down. Just by the shapes! Five hundred-piece puzzles! Lord have mercy, who does that?" It was just like the captain to know his team on that level. He made it a priority to get one on one periodically with each officer and staff member.

"I get a really good sense about him. That's why I hired him. Jenkins retires in June, so Dr. Brickman will be in charge. I'd go with Thor, no question. Get him inside this."

"Yes, sir, thank you," Max said. "We have a meeting with him this morning after we interview BB, Brie Batson, the women who called it in last night."

"And then back to Davidson's for the afternoon," Vince chimed in. "You want either of us at the briefing?"

"Thank you, but not a chance. You know these hound dogs. 'If nothing happened why the detectives?' In fact, come in the back way this morning."

"Yes, sir. Understood."

"Sounds like we all have a long day ahead. I'll keep this note in my office safe. Good work and stay safe out there. Red Angels. Lord have mercy, what next?"

"Indeed."

CHAPTER 5

Tuesday morning 8:30AM – Day 2

Vince sat at his desk directly facing Max, making a list of questions for Brie Batson. Max wanted him to take the lead in her interview. The open file in Max's hands bore the label "Dr. Joseph Thoreau Brickman."

"Vince, listen to this. Dr. Brinkman had a perfect SAT score. Full ride scholarship. BS double major in Forensic Science and Criminal Justice from Quincy University. Where the hell is QU?"

"Uh, in Quincy?" Vince opined.

"MA in Biochemistry from Vanderbilt, Thesis: Physical Matters of Belief – Quantifying the Biological Processes and Impact of What We Believe on Overall Health. Ph.D. in Clinical Psychology from Notre Dame. Dissertation: How a Belief System Affects Development of Moral Reasoning and Moral Intelligence – Practicum: Belief Therapy - A Course of Treatments to Find Health in Finding Meaning."

"I gotta add those to my reading list," Vince mocked.

"Seriously, Vince. He's twenty-nine! Does this guy have a life?"

"I don't know, but ten to one he has a library card."

"He grew up in Thailand and Paraguay. Speaks Thai, Spanish and some Guarani. Parents missionaries. Great. Another believer on the team."

"Be nice, Max. I'm Baptist and I barely hold your paganism against you."

"Noted. Only because you like my barbeque."

"Guilty. You know, you could use some belief therapy. And may I remind you we live inside the buckle of the Bible belt?"

"Indeed. You can't swing a dead Calvinist around here without hitting three born again Armenians."

"That's probably really funny, but I don't know why."

"Get this. Brickman's hobbies: Landscaping, grilling out, puzzles and reading."

"Hey, Max, a fellow griller and reader. You and Thor might become buddies."

Vince's desk phone rang. "Right. Put her in interview room B with something to drink. We'll be right there. Brie Batson. Let's go."

"Good morning, Miss Batson. I'm Detective Wilson and you remember Detective Malone from last night. Thank you for coming in."

"Did I have a choice?"

"Yes, of course. That's why we appreciate your willingness. You've been through a lot."

"I can't get the image of Abe hanging there out of my mind."

"That's understandable. A very traumatic experience. This won't take long. We just want to wrap up some loose ends to understand Abe's unfortunate incident."

Brie's nerves were showing. "I'm not in any trouble, am I? I told your partner here I use some drugs now and then."

"No, Miss Batson, not at all. For everyone concerned and especially for his family we want to get a better picture of what happened."

Vince walked her through a timeline of the evening, what time she got the call, when she reached the gate. Was the power out? Did you check on Abe or call 911 when you saw him? When is the last time you saw Abe?

Max took notes and unable to help himself, took over.

"What was your relationship with Abe?"

"We dated on and off but mostly I worked for him."

Max could see what Abe saw in Brie. Extremely attractive. Rough around the edges. But curvy edges. Torn jeans. Tight. Bare abs, taut, like a dancer or one of those hotties in a music video. *Your Body Is a Wonderland* invaded his mind. *John Mayer, won 2002 Grammy for Best Male Pop Vocal Performance beating out James Taylor.* He fought off the song.

"Doing what exactly?"

"I handle, handled, his guitar rentals, you know, like cartage. Abe has, I don't know, about thirty great instruments. Players all over town rent them. For recording mostly."

"So, you pick up guitars at the Davidson estate and deliver them to musicians?"

"Yea, I collect the rental fee and pick up the guitars when they're done. What does that have to do with Abe dying?"

"Miss Batson, it looks like Abe simply made a very rash decision that turned into a fatal one. Just a few more questions and we'll get you out of here."

"Good. I gotta wrap up a few things for Abe." Her voice quivered. "The least I can do."

Max pressed in. "What did you mean when you said Abe would 'cut you out' if you didn't pick him up?"

"We had plans?"

"Plans to leave town?"

"Yea."

"Together?"

"Yes," Brie broke down at this point. "He loves me… loved me… he asked me to run away with him somewhere, anywhere. He just wanted out! I can't believe he's gone."

Vince handed her tissues from under the desk. He and Max waited for the wave to pass. Then Vince spoke.

"I know this is not easy. We just have a two more questions."

Max continued, "When and why did Abe decide to leave town?"

"About a week ago. It was real sudden. He was rash like that. But this was different."

"How?"

"He loved it here, his life. Who wouldn't? Plenty of money, the horses, making music. He called. Said he was gonna hit his father up for his share of the family money and start over somewhere else. He said he loved me and asked me…he begged me to go with him." The tears came again.

Max paused a moment before posing the last question. "Miss Batson, one last thing. In cases like this, even when all indications point to an accident, we have to ask, are you aware of anyone who would want to harm Abe or might have threatened him recently?"

Brie's shoulders sank and her head dropped. "Lots of people. Abe could be such a prick. But no one in particular. Hell, I punched him a couple of times. But you had to know him. He was just so talented and wild and bright…like a comet."

"I'm sorry for your loss, Miss Batson," Vince wrapped it up. "For the sake of his family, we ask you not to talk about how you found Abe. Can you do that? For Abe. And his family?"

"Yea, sure. I can do that. For Abe."

"Thank you again. Here's my card." Max slid his across the table as well. "If you remember anything else, please call. The officers will drive you home."

After Brie left the room, Vince put a shot across Max's bow. "So much for letting me take the lead."

Max ignored it.

Vince was used to his partner's dance. "Some comet," he said. "More like a falling star. Gone and won't come around again."

"Indeed. You know, I don't think she knew she was a drug mule."

"What? Where'd you get that?"

"Studio musicians in this town don't generally rent guitars. They use their own instruments. I'd bet real money he fed her habit to deliver and never took her into the mansion to meet daddy."

"I can see that. Poor girl."

"Lunch? After we meet with our new Dr. Brickman?"

"Sure."

Max made his most frequent pitch. "How about barbeque?"

"How about not again? Tacos. SATCO. Quick, delish and on the way to Davidson's."

Max gave in. "Tacos it is. Good work with BB. I'm beginning to think that caring thing of yours is sincere."

CHAPTER 6

Tuesday morning 10:00AM – Day 2

Neither detective had met Dr. Brickman. It was only his second day on the job. They predetermined not to divulge the RA note card on this initial visit, rather, feel Brickman out first.

"Just because he's crazy smart doesn't mean he's trustworthy," Vince pointed out.

"Indeed." Max agreed.

"You're smart, Max, but I trust you because you're completely honest. Strike that, brutally honest."

"Good, my cover is working."

The detectives arrived four minutes early at Dr. Brickman's large office. It's size irritated Max. *How'd the kid draw this?* Vince stepped away to call his wife. The new Labtech/Medical Examiner arrived three minutes late. In that seven-minute window, by habit, Max did a cursory inventory of his office, building a profile of the young genius.

Open, unpacked boxes littered the floor, mostly books. Shelves lined one entire wall, partially filled with medical texts and reference books with ponderous titles, though one held murder mysteries including "The Postman Always Rings Twice", *saw the old black and white movie*; and "Red Light" by T. Jefferson Parker, *read the series, great writing but another damn good cops vs. crooked cops story.* Two small white drones mounted with cameras sat by themselves on a shelf. *High tech geek.* Three diplomas, *of course,* hung vertically on a wall beside a photo of a couple standing in a small group of Asian looking children, *his parents in Thailand,* Max presumed. A colorful woven blanket lay folded over the back of Brickman's high-tech, ergonomic desk chair. *Alpaca? Probably from his time in Paraguay.* A bamboo flute or recorder hung on a hook behind the desk. *Memento from Thailand? Wonder if he plays?*

A single low shelf beside the desk contained nine or ten titles, "Tom Sawyer," *read it,* "The Diary of Anne Frank," *read it;* "Man's Search for Meaning" by Viktor Frankl, *read it;* "Complete Works of Emily Dickinson," *prefer Bob Dylan,;* "The Closing of the American Mind," *tried to read it;* "The Sound and the Fury," *hated it;* Robinson Crusoe, *read it in high school;* "La Sombra del Viento by Zafon," *read it, in English. Apparently the young Dr. not only speaks but reads Spanish;* a box set of C.S. Lewis' "Space Trilogy," *Read it when I thought like a child. Allegory is no match for reason Dr. Brickman.*

We haven't even met and I'm already having an argument with him. Not a good sign.

By far the most surprising title on this shelf was "The God Delusion," *read it.* But the title beside it ambushed him with a direct hit. The last book Max could imagine being in an office dedicated to forensics on crimes and dead bodies was "The Velveteen Rabbit." This one fired a volley of memory bullets. His mother read it to him as a child. Just seeing the title on the spine disoriented Max like a blow. Something tried to rise within him, a pressure behind his eyes, like the last bubbles of a free diver desperate for the surface. He couldn't go there. By sheer will power he continued the inventory.

On one corner of the desk stood an antique microscope. Beyond it a medical book lay open to a detailed posterior view of the nervous system of the neck. On the other side were two books: one on landscape design and a large hardback about historic Nashville area homes.

A projected profile and visual image formed in Max's mind: *black slacks, polyester, white button down, wrinkled, no tie, pale complexion, weak lower back and neck from countless hours spent reading, researching and writing, maybe even a wrist brace from carpal tunnel, overall frail physically, gabby with technical terms, glasses, bifocals already at twenty-nine, unmarried* and most irritating to Max, *likely a believer, not Buddhist. Great.* The Doobie brothers mocked him inside his head with J*esus Is Just Alright, 1972 from Toulouse Street.*

An object cut short Max's cynical mental moment. Just behind the microscope - a red card, about 5"x7" stood in a clear plastic stand. Bending toward it he read the handwritten name:

Dr. Joseph T. Brickman

He drifted slowly around the desk toward Brickman's chair like he was trying not to spook a bird. In the same handwriting, on a white background was:

Science is a keyhole. Belief is the key.
We love you, mom and dad.

At the very moment Max seemed most like a snoop, Dr. Brickman bounded in.

"Very sorry I'm late. Uncharacteristic I assure you. Already diving into a case with Dr. Jenkins on the unfortunate Mr. Davidson."

"Is that a Shakuhachi?" Max pointed at the flute, trying to cover his intrusion behind the desk.

"It's a Thai version, sir. A Khlui."

Max's profile evaporated like a Tennessee morning fog. There was nothing frail or pale about Dr. Joseph T. Brickman. At about 6'1", 155 pounds, he had the sleek muscular physique of a runner or rock climber. Jeans, blue scrubs shirt, clear blue eyes, no glasses, thick, straight shock of blond hair like a surfer. Max only got three things right – no wedding ring, sandals, closed-toe Tivas, and a believer. *Guess he wears his geek on the inside.*

Vince walked in. Introductions were made.

"Max and I want to welcome you to the team. Don't we, Max?"

"Ah, yes."

"We've heard impressive things from the captain about you."

"Overstated, I'm sure. Nothing I can't debunk with a bungle or two," Brickman returned.

Healthy and humble, too? Max noted sarcastically.

"Since we'll be working closely together, we want you to know we'll have your back and assume you'll have ours."

"What Vince is trying not to say is, we know your credentials are up to the job, but there is a trust factor beyond what is required of regulations and policies. Naturally, you know we deal with very delicate matters. Leaks can be dangerous. Even deadly. The press can take a crumb and turn it into a feeding frenzy."

"Sir, I fully understand and I…"

"If I may finish. Public confidence in us can turn on a dime.

And that makes our job even harder. We hope we can rely on you."

"Detectives, I appreciate your directness. I think you'll find me to be the same. As I told Captain Haskins, I take my oath to uphold the law seriously, and beyond that, I am committed to a higher moral compass as well."

There it is.

"I'm sure I will make mistakes, so I look to your experience. And I welcome any course corrections from you."

"That's all good to hear," Vince said. "Thank you, Dr. Brickman."

"Please, call me Thor. It's from my middle name, Thoreau."

"Captain told us. My kids will love that. I'm working with Thor."

Max tried to head into current business. "We have a case right now that..."

"Hold that thought, Max." Vince cut him off. "One more thing. Thor, the reason we do what we do is we love our city. We live here. It's home. One of your degrees is from Vanderbilt, so now you're back. We look forward to working with you to keep it safe and make it even better."

"Yes, sir, I'm fully on board."

"If Vince is done with his press statement, we have a current case to wrap up. Sounds like you're already familiar with Abe Davidson."

"Yes, sir. First thing this morning, Dr. Jenkins and I began a workup."

"How soon can we get a report? The family has unanswered questions."

"We can have a summary by later this afternoon, barring any surprises."

"Good, here's my number. Don't pass it around."

"No, sir. Of course not."

Vince gave Brickman his card as well. "Let us know if you need anything. If you want to know about barbeque places, call Max. For the best tacos, I'm your man."

"SATCO was my go-to in graduate school," Brickman offered.

"We're headed there now, would you—"

"I'm sure you need to get back to Abe," Max interrupted, "Vince and I have another stop to make. Call me this afternoon with your findings." He stood to leave, paused, and pointed to the diploma from Quincy University.

"Why QU?"

"They have one of the largest cadaver inventories in the country," Brickman said.

Vince chuckled, "I chose a college for the inventory of babes."

Max pointed out the picture of the couple surrounded by Asian children. "Are those your parents?"

"Yes sir, taken in the village they served in Thailand."

"Still in the field?"

"No sir, the diocese brought them home a couple of years ago."

Catholic. Great. Max noted.

"Catholic missionaries?" Vince wondered, still sitting.

"Yes, sir, though not your traditional Catholics."

"How so?" Max inquired.

"They consider themselves Charismatic Catholics."

"Max was raised Catholic," Vince inserted, "though he's not very traditional anymore. Me, I'm Baptist. Where do your parents live?"

"Right here in Nashville. That's one reason I applied for this position."

"So, this really is your home now," Vince said pleasantly.

"Yes, sir."

"Let's go, Vince. I'll be looking for your call this afternoon, Dr. Brickman."

"Yes, sir. Thank you for coming by. I'm honored to be working with both of you."

* * *

As usual, Max drove to lunch and Davidson's. Vince climbed into the truck with his ukulele.

"Really, Vince? This is not a uke day."

"Every day's a uke day, Shaemus. You know it helps me think. Besides, I can play sad songs, too."

When Vince gave up smoking, the ukulele became his fidget object. Something to keep his hands occupied during stakeouts and surveillance. No one would accuse him of being a brilliant singer, but he could whistle as well as Bing Crosby and in just two years his command of the uke was better than average. He performed an impressive rendition of the theme song to "The Andy Griffith Show" at Max's birthday the first year he picked it up. His repertoire included Queen's "We Will Rock You" and a couple of show tunes. "O What a Beautiful Morning" from "Oklahoma" and "Tomorrow" from "Annie."

"Any requests?"

"Not show tunes."

Vince strummed a chord in a medium tempo. It went on without any changes. "Guess this tune. I've been working on it." He kept playing the same chord, with no changes.

"Stumped?"

Max was not. "It could be 'Walkin in Your Footsteps' by the Police but I'll say, 'House of Gold' by Twenty-One Pilots, 2013, from the album Regional At Best."

"No way! Right. My son just showed me that song. Max, you really should go on Jeopardy."

"Seriously now, two things. That's not a sad song, and what's your take on Dr. Brickman?"

"I'm with the captain. I get a good feeling about him."

"Of course, you do. Bright, polite, smart and another a believer in the ranks, though probably Catholic."

"Maybe. Two out of his three diplomas are from Catholic Universities. You're not the only one who does research, and his parents are Catholic. But that doesn't mean he still is. Look at you."

"Indeed. But he's a scientist and a believer. That's got to sit well with you."

"Max, you ever hear of Copernicus? Galileo? Pascal? Of course, you know DaVinci. All scientists. All Catholics."

"They didn't have much choice, but point taken. But Charismatic Catholic? Isn't that like cross breeding dogs and cats?"

"Max, he never once said 'have a blessed day' or 'Lord, have mercy' like the captain. I didn't see a big Bible on his desk. You afraid he's gonna do autopsies in a "Don't be caught dead without Jesus' T-shirt?"

"Nothing would surprise me around here."

It was 11:40AM by the time they found a parking spot and walked into the popular taco joint. On this beautiful spring day, young professionals, music types and students filled the outdoor seating and clogged the line. The manager, Robert, saw Vince and expedited their order. Max honestly liked the food almost as much as Vince. But he liked even more the classic rock that always played on the Muzak. He could name nearly every band, artist and song, and what year it released. Vince was always impressed, but had tired of the game. Max scored an outside table as two attractive coeds were leaving. Vince couldn't resist.

"Did you get her number?"

"Stronzo."

This time it was Vince who knew the rock song in the background. "Well, isn't this song appropriate?" Vince put on his DJ voice, "First caller to name this song, the band and year it came out, wins dinner with Music City's own, Max Malone."

"Hilarious. 'Walk Away', The James Gang, 1971, from their album 'Thirds' written by the lead guy, Joe Walsh, before he joined the Eagles in 1975," Max recited like an entry from Wikipedia.

"We have a winner. Table for one, please."

"Vince, did you happen to notice the note card on Dr. Brinkman's desk?"

"In all that clutter? No. He's still moving in."

"Same size, red on one side. White on the other."

"What? What are you getting at?"

"Hand-addressed to Dr. Joseph T. Brickman."

"Were you snooping around before we came in?"

"Profiling."

"Right. What was on the other side?"

"Same handwriting. 'Science is a keyhole. Belief is the key.'"

Vince played along. "Profound. Not sure what that means. Was it signed?"

"We love you, mom and dad."

Vince feigned intrigue. "Now that is sinister. A handwritten note from his mom and dad. Who should we arrest first?"

"Vince, it's not about what it said. It's about the card. I'd bet my barbeque sauce recipe it's the same card stock."

"Max, you can't be serious. That's a leap of reason if I ever heard one. Are you actually tying Thor's parents to the note sent to Abe Davidson?"

"Well, no, not exactly. But the cards definitely look the same."

"You really don't like Thor, do you? Have some more queso, Max. I swear it has medicinal properties."

Chapter 7

On the way to the Davidson estate, between Max's attempts to discuss the case, Vince played and whistled snippets of the Beatles' "Nowhere Man," and a song in a waltz feel Max did not know.

"That's nice. What's that?" Max asked.

"A song we sing at church. "Here's to the Day.""

Upon arrival, Ms. Andrews accompanied the detectives to the guest house. They had locked and sealed it the night before. She returned to her duties with Mr. Davidson. They gloved up.

"I'll start with the office and recording area, Max."

"Right. Keep an eye out for any kind of ledger or contact list and calendar."

"Miss Batson likely has a copy. Probably on her phone."

"And on his computer. Do we have Abe's phone?"

"At headquarters with his personal effects."

"I'll check out the guitar room."

"Ten to one there goes the afternoon. You gonna play them all?"

"Not all."

One minute later Max said, "Hey Vince. No ukulele. Imagine that."

"Stronzo!" Vince volleyed.

Three minutes into the search, acoustic chords emanated from the guitar room.

"Tom Petty?" Vince guessed right.

"Right. 'Free Fallin' 1989 from Full Moon Fever."

The chords stopped. Less than a minute passed. "Vince, come take a look at this."

By simply standing the butt of the guitar on the inside of the case, Max accidentally dislodged a panel in the padding, revealing a hidden void. Four baggies of white powder lay inside. He took a small taste on his pinky. "Cocaine. Let's call in a canine unit. It'll take forever to go through all these instruments."

"And probably more stashed around," Vince added.

"Indeed."

Over the next three hours, the drug dog sniffed out nine of the twenty-five guitar cases packed with drugs, seven more with empty compartments and two large stashes concealed in the walls. One appeared to be a former coat closet. The team emptied it to do an inventory. Together, both troves held over thirty bricks of marijuana, approximately two-hundred and fifty Oxy capsules, six quart bags of crystal meth and four kilos of cocaine.

Max stepped outside to call Captain Haskins to report and propose a plan.

The view was like the idyllic landscape paintings he saw on the family trip to Ireland. Afternoon shadows were lengthening. The new green of Spring blanketed the rolling hills, echoed in billowy clouds building in the southwest, bringing more rain to nourish the verdancy. White plank fencing rose and fell as if on waves instead of firm land. Half a dozen storybook horses grazed.

Without warning, the beauty summoned a deep misgiving in Max, "inquieto" his mother called it. According to her, it was a restless, unquietness intended to redirect our wandering souls to the only source of peace. In college Max discovered the go-to antidotes for his inquieto, drinking and women. Standing there, waiting for the captain to answer, he felt outside the beauty before him, a spectator viewing through a spyglass from a desert. He wanted a strong drink. *Damn, all this and it wasn't enough.* "I Can't Get No Satisfaction" kicked off in his head. *Rolling Stones 1965 from 'Out of Our Heads,' "and I tried, and I tried, and I tried, and I tried..."* Captain Haskins' voice in his ear cut off Mick Jagger.

"Yes, sir. I can hear you now."

"Sir, it looks like Abe was a very active dealer. We found coke, weed, Oxy and meth in his quarters. Street value above $300K."

"No sir, no warrant. Mr. Davidson gave us a green light. He wants the bastards more than we do."

"Yes, sir, got it in writing."

"A clever delivery system, sir. Abe rented out his collection of great guitars and stashed drugs in hidden compartments inside the cases. We're surmising Miss Batson delivered them around town, collected the money, picked up the guitars and returned them here."

"No sir. Not sure if she was aware. But likely. She's a user."

"Yes, sir, good idea. Surveillance much better than another interview. Don't want to spook her."

"No sir. As far as I can tell, Mr. Davidson smelled something foul but has at least plausible deniability. He's very cooperative."

"According to his assistant, he's holding up."

"Yes, sir, he's got a hell of a lot to process. Sir, we have a proposal. Leave the drugs in place and see who comes looking."

"I know... I know there's some risk, sir. But Abe's upstream is bound to miss the payments and want their inventory back. And maybe," Max lowered his voice, "Maybe one of them, or a customer with ambitions, wrote the note."

"Yes, sir. We'll link with Vice. Set up surveillance, including cameras…"

"Of course, sir. I'll clear it with Mr. Davidson. And sir, give a heads up to whoever you assign to Miss Batson that Abe's suppliers or customers may contact her. As you know, sir, the suppliers are more dangerous."

"Thank you, sir, we're on it." Max re-entered the guest house in full-on hunter mode.

"Vince, let's get Vice out here and why haven't we heard from boy wonder Brickman? "

"He called while you were on with the captain."

"What's he got? Never mind. I want to hear it from him. Dammit, you got his direct?"

"Should be on your phone. The last number you didn't pick up on."

Max made the call, pacing as it rang. The Dr. tried to answer with his name. All Max heard was "Doctor" and launched in.

"Brinkman, what have you got? I have Detective Wilson here on speaker."

Dr. Brickman had the sense to dive right in.

"The pattern of horsehair on the trousers confirms the deceased rode the horse you sampled. His bloodwork is a cocktail of cocaine, alcohol and pot. At levels that would have severely impaired him in a car or on a horse. Neck broken, low, between C6 and C7, caused paraplegia."

"Paralyzed, got it. Any blunt or other trauma not consistent with hitting the gate?"

"No. in fact, the blow didn't even break the skin, presumably because of his thick hair."

"Nothing extraneous to indicate foul play?"

"No sir."

"So, just lights out."

"No sir. He also had high levels of adrenaline, anoxic brain damage, eyes fully dilated and petechiae prominent on his upper eyelids."

"Anoxic, air cut off to the brain, got it. Petachiae, broken capillaries around the eyes, indicating strangulation. Got it." *I called it, gabby with technical terms.*

"Yes, sir. Burst capillaries on his upper eyelids."

"Meaning what?"

"Neither the blow nor broken neck killed Abe Davidson. The break paralyzed him. But he was still conscious. Unable to move. And had a panic attack. Unfortunately for him, it was not instant lights out. From the forensics and photographs, the cause of death is clearly asphyxiation. Probably slow. His own hair strangled him, and he couldn't do anything about it. Not a pleasant way to go."

"No one but the captain sees that report. Do you understand? Tell me what I just said."

"No one but the captain sees the report, yes, sir."

"Tell Dr. Jenkins the same. Strictly 10-36. And don't put it on my desk. Put it in my hand or the captain's tomorrow. Are we clear?"

"Yes, sir, perfectly."

The only words Vince got in were, "Good work, Thor."

"Thank you, detectives. I'm here to help."

Max ended the call. "Tell me he didn't just say that."

"Say what?"

"Nothing. Let's get Vice out here. I'll get Davidson in the loop."
By the time everything was photographed, catalogued and put
back in place, it was 6:15 PM. Vice was still positioning and
testing cameras.

"Let's go, Vince. Vice has got this. Green Hills is gonna be a zoo."

After dropping Vince at headquarters on Murfreesboro Pike, Max
didn't make his way back to Love Circle until after 8:00 PM. He
warmed some brisket, added a side of sweet slaw, and poured a
glass of wine. Since New Year's Day, he had limited his drinking
to one glass of wine, almost always with a meal, or a woman.
Tonight's vintage was a Chianti, Montepulciano d'Abruzzo, from
the region where his mother grew up. After eating, he settled on
the top floor in the music room with the remaining half glass, to
look out over the lights of the city and ruminate on the case, as
he often did. For music he debated between an instrumental,
"Feels So Good," Chuck Mangione, 1977, the remastered nine-
minute version, or "Sounds of Silence," *Simon & Garfunkel, 1965,
first cut on "Wednesday Morning 3AM."* Paul Simon won. "Hello
darkness, my old friend…" poured like a dark liqueur from the
Genelec speakers. Nothing but the best to listen to the best music
ever made, Max believed. He settled in. Paul and Art had just sung
the line about a vision planted in the brain when his phone
destroyed the vision, the moment, and the evening.

It was Vince. "Shit."

"Max, we got a 10-64, female, down a ways off Arno Road.
I'm rolling."

The address popped up in a text before he could ask for it. *At
least she had the courtesy of dying earlier in the evening.*

Chapter 8

Max saw the deer at the last instant. Barely felt the thud. The thought had just struck him, *What are the odds* he would hum his own theme song two nights in a row down a winding Tennessee country road to another death? The deer's last impulse was apparently to speed up. It misjudged the lethality of an F250 with a grill guard. And ignored the front plate warning about its actual size.

Max pulled over immediately, grabbed a flashlight. His reflex decision to check on the deer first, before the damage to his truck, was a monumental sign of life in his frozen heart. Max was not aware of his choice. Or its magnitude.

The doe was deceased. A pool of dark blood the size of a dinner plate expanded slowly from its mouth onto the asphalt. *Lights out.* "Thank heaven" rose automatically to his mind. But not to his lips. He did take note of that. His next thoughts shoved that one aside. *Wish I could get you in my smoker. Guess the coyotes will eat good tonight.* As he reached down to drag the carcass clear of the road, part of it moved. The fur on its underbelly rose and fell violently. Lumps came and went. This time, the G-word escaped his lips. "O my God!" *She's pregnant.* The rest of Max froze. His theory about accidents being merely physics, poor judgement and/or randomness failed him. Now two lives were in the balance. He had no idea one of them was his.

In a matter of seconds, the movements slowed. Ceased. Several convulsions and then nothing. Once again, Max felt like a spectator, this time not from a distance, but from a front-row seat viewing life and death right before his eyes. And he did nothing. There was nothing he could do. Not like the other time.

On a fishing trip to Montana for his fourteenth birthday, he and his dad watched a doe and fawn cross a field of high golden grass. The doe bounded effortlessly over a wire fence. The grass at the fence thrashed around. Slowing the car, his dad realized the fawn couldn't get through. He turned down a dirt road and parked. They approached slowly. The doe snorted at them, stomping a front hoof. The fawn bleated for its mother, struggled and kept trying to push ahead through the fence. Liam Malone spoke softly to both deer, walked to the fawn, knelt, secured it in his arms and backed it out of the hole in the fence.

He stood with the fawn snugly cradled in his arms and said to his son, "You gotta feel this, Max! This wildness."

He placed the fawn in Max's arms while the doe snorted and stomped. The fawn quieted a bit, but its brown eyes dilated with fright and flight. He felt its heart beating fast against his own. Together, they lifted the fawn over the fence. It hurried to its mother. The two of them stood looking at the two of them for a moment, then doe and fawn disappeared into the trees.

It was the high point of their trip. They told the story for years. The intimacy of that wild, unscripted moment translated to an awe that had since eroded in the trauma and debris of living, along with another casualty of childhood, his sense of wonder. For grown-up Max, awe and wonder were superfluous to survival. But he still remembered exactly how his dad described the fawn's predicament: "Taking a step back would have freed it. But fear and panic made it captive to the fence."

No one would be freed and safely reunited tonight. In this moment, awful displaced awe. Incredulity and indignation at the harshness of life suffocated wonder. Thoughts of succulent back strap dissolved like smoke into an enormous inquieto, more silent and still than the two deer in the ditch and deeper than the night sky. No song played in Max's head. Silence spoke the inexpressible. There was more work to do down the road, more death, and he couldn't take a step back.

Without inspecting the grill guard, he climbed back into the cab. GPS indicted two miles to the location. It seemed like twenty. He drove slowly, like a one car funeral procession. A vehicle tailgated him, honked and flew by in a no-passing zone. A real Alfa Romeo. Red.

A marquis on an old church irritated him. It read, "What does the Lord ask of you? Find out Sunday 10:00 AM." Max resented he knew the answer. It scrolled into his head in his mother's voice: "Do justice, love mercy, and walk humbly with your God. Micah 6:8" Sofia had it posted by her bed as a daily reminder. He watched her live all three. Early in his partnership with Vince, when this came up once he told him, "Look, I'm doing justice. As a batting average that's .333. That's big league." Vince called him 'Slugger' for weeks.

He turned off Arno Road onto a private drive. At the gate an officer from Williamson County in an unmarked car told him he was expected, instructed him to bear left, that the house was nearly a half mile over the rise. Max lost focus when the officer listed who was on the scene - detective Wilson, a few officers, paramedics and others. The officer opened the gate. Beyond the first curve he pulled over, turned off the engine. He didn't feel like doing justice tonight. He felt like drinking. But there was no choice. Till later. He would wrestle then with what just happened. Or not. For now, he found resolution in the sticker on his dash. *I was fitter, bigger and the least stupid back there. That's all. End of story.* He spoke out loud, "La verità è più forte del tempo," restarted his engines and proceeded.

CHAPTER 9

Tuesday night 10:15PM – Day 2

The country mansion at the end of the drive was lit like a national historic site. It resembled Tara, from Gone with the Wind, only bigger and built in this century. Beyond that resonance, something felt familiar to Max. Parking short of the circle drive where an officer and squad car were posted, he wanted to take in the panorama on foot, but the real reason was to avoid attention if there were traces of the incident on his truck. He didn't stop to inspect. A glance was enough. Blood splatter discolored the passenger side of the grill guard and head lamp. Ignoring it, he continued toward the business at hand.

Max's standard response at the sight of such ostentatious "houses" was a weak attempt to counterbalance the disorienting encounter with the deer still vivid in his mind. *Whatever the owner does for a living, he does a crap load of it.* He focused on visual details to replace the ones in his head. White brick. Black shutters. Large dormers on a third floor punctuated a red tin roof. The broad front porch and second-floor balcony extended the entire front facade, framed by large white columns, *classic sentinels of wealth and power*, he had read in a poem or heard in a song somewhere. *Ten to one, Vince makes a crack about the owner being a pillar of the community.* A drive-through portico on the right side of the mansion provided dry access in any weather. A dark car was parked there. Its Audi insignia reflected in the floodlights. The balcony above the oversized, double front door extended in a half circle like an elevated stage for a celebrity or politician to appear and greet supporters, or subjects.

Max nodded at the officer before passing a a distraught man sitting on a rock terrace of the circle drive. The man's face was buried in his hands. Another man sat beside him, speaking quietly. Neither looked up. A dark Mercedes coupe and a red Alfa Rome, *top-of-the-line Giulia Quadrifoglio*, were parked haphazardly, as if in haste. *Odds are the talker is the guy who passed me.*

The only odd architectural element was a giant sundial set in a circle of stone pavers in the middle of the circular drive. Max and his dad had built a small one out of junk. Because it looked up to the sun, his dad named it "Time's Up." The irony in this setting registered but felt thin tonight. On this much larger version, the upright steel gnomon was six or seven feet tall. The hour numbers on the dial were inlaid brass. On the far side from mansion, a compass was etched inside the dial, the letters N, S, E & W also in brass. The mansion faced due west. Four curved cement benches protected its perimeter from traffic in the drive.

Center stage, at the top of the steps, what looked like a pleated white curtain presumably concealed the deceased. *Not the work of paramedics.* A small pool of blood the size of a dinner plate had crept down onto the step below the curtain. Yellow crime tape cordoned off the main entrance and draped between the columns.

No sign of the forensics team.

Vince stood talking to an officer, who walked away and made a phone call as Max approached. The paramedics were wrapping up. They gave the detectives space.

"Vince, haven't we been here before?"

"Yea, three years ago. Officer appreciation day. But it was daylight, and we drove around to the back by the lake."

"Right. Giant tent, barbeque, kites and games for the kids."

"I remember you saying your barbeque sauce was much better."

"Sounds vaguely familiar."

"Do you remember who sponsored that event?"

"Vince, really? We need to get on with this," Max snapped back.

"Max, are you alright?"

"Fine. You were saying."

"The event was sponsored by the builder and the homeowner, pillar of the community, if you catch my meaning," he pointed to the columns. "Care to guess who built this place?"

Max didn't hesitate, "Davidson."

"That's why you're a detective."

"So, the rich hang together. Doesn't take a detective to come up with that. Now what have we got, Vince."

"You sure you're alright?"

"I'm fine."

"And the Oscar goes to…but OK. Female, deceased, a real hottie. Or was. Dressed in red negligee. And not much of it. Here's a twist. She had a crown on, shaped like a cobra. You'll see. The man in the suit is the homeowner, Tony Armstrong."

"She got a name?"

"Mr. Armstrong IDed her. Jessie Bellaire, age twenty-six."

"What else?"

"Don't have a full statement from him yet. He's married. Not to her. He and the young woman were meeting here to fly tomorrow morning to Cabo. She got here before him. He had meetings. When he arrived, he says she was lying there. Already dead. Looks like she somehow fell from the balcony. Severe head trauma. He tore down a curtain and covered her. And get this Max. Armstrong says when he drove up, he scared away a coyote. To put it delicately, it had just started scavenging one of her calves."

"Did I hear you right?"

"You did. A coyote."

Max took a couple of steps away.

"Seriously, Max, you OK?'

"Long night. Long day. Have you been inside?"

"Just a walk-thru to clear the house with Thomason."

"Is Hanover here?"

"Who else? They're taping the other entrances."

"How far out is forensics?"

"Five minutes. They went all the way down to 840 and over."

"Who's the man with Armstrong?"

"His brother. Arrived just before you. He's also his lawyer, James Armstrong."

"James Bowie Armstrong?"

"The same."

"I predict we won't get much more from Armstrong tonight."

"Unless we find evidence to detain him."

"In that case we'll get even less."

Forensics rolled up just as officers Thomason and Hanover came around the south corner of the mansion. Max nodded.

"Detective," both responded.

Oddly, Max said nothing. Vince took charge.

"Please, escort Mr. Armstrong and his brother into the house through the portico. Keep them on that end. We'll assist forensics and then be in to get his statement."

"Yes, sir," said Hanover.

Max spoke up, "You gloved up. Good. Spot anything?"

Thomason let Hanover answer. "A lot of windows open. Nice night for it. Open bottle of wine in the study. Louis Jadot. Nearly empty. Bags being packed in the upstairs master. A cell phone on a side table. Shattered wine glass on the balcony." She pointed up to it. "And a red wine spill, sir." She noticed Max didn't cut her off.

Again, he was silent. Vince jumped in, "We'll take it from here."

The detectives and forensic team waited till the officers with Tony and James Armstrong disappeared around the last column before they set to work. Max realized he left latex gloves in his truck. He asked a paramedic for an extra pair. His focus was clearly diminished.

Beneath the curtain, Jessie Bellaire was in death as she had been in life, a brutal mix of beauty and carnage. She was lying on her left side. But clearly, she had landed head-first. A gold-colored crown was imbedded deep in her hairline, the cobra's head bent, bloody and menacing, as if guarding its kill. Max surmised to himself that she fell forward, landed on the top of her head, then flipped over onto her side, but that was still conjecture. Her face was not bloody and if not for the surrounding gore, she could pass for Sleeping Beauty, serene under a deep sleeping spell, long black hair, ruby lipstick, dark eyeliner.

"You thinking what I'm thinking, Max?"

"If you're thinking 'Witchy Woman' by the Eagles, yes. 'Raven hair, ruby lips, sparks fly from her fingertips.'" He half expected

66

to find lightning bolts painted on her nails. There were none.

Vince took the music reference as a good sign. Typical Max.

"I can see that, but no," said Vince. "Obviously she was staging quite a welcome for Armstrong. A little buzzed. Anyone wanting to harm her could have pushed her off with a feather."

"If Ms. Bellaire was breaking up a marriage, that list is likely a long one, like Abe." *That means a hell of a lot of interviews.* On top of the Davidson investigation, that prospect was daunting.

The coyote bites on her left calf were deep, but not extensive. A small chunk of flesh appeared missing. Hard to tell how much in all the blood. If Armstrong had arrived twenty minutes later, it would have been far worse. Three steps down from the body lay a red stiletto with four-inch heels. Her right shoe. Her left foot was bare.

"Where's the other shoe?" Max wanted to know.

Vince was not exaggerating about how little the lingerie covered. Down Jessie's completely bare back was a tattoo. In fancy cursive between her shoulder blades were two large letters: F F

Below that, running sideways in the same font, but smaller, ran the words: Take It All.

"That may explain the license plate on the Audi, TIA. I ran the plate. It's registered to Jessie Bellaire."

"Good eye, Vince. Surely Armstrong knows what 'F F' stands for."

Still trying to cajole his somber partner, Vince threw out, "Ten to one, it's not Fred Flintstone."

Max was not amused.

Further down, in the small of her back, in the tramp stamp region was a small purple blossom.

"That seems tame for this one," Vince said.

"If I'm not mistaken, that's a Nightshade blossom or Belladonna. Italian for 'beautiful woman.'

It's one of the most poisonous plants on the planet."

"So, a long way from tame."

"Many think it's what Juliet drank. Ten to one Brickman can identify it."

"You really should audition for Jeopardy."

"Let's let the photographer have this area and take a look at the balcony."

"What about Armstrong?"

"He'll keep. If he's complicit, let him sweat. Either way we may not get much with his lawyer present."

On the balcony they found what Hanover reported.

"Careful, Vince," Max said. "The spill pattern of the wine and glass may help determine her final movements."

Max's curiosity and skill kicked in. *Facing the driveway, wine splatter and shattered glass exclusively to the right. No footprints in the wine. None leading away.*

"Over here, Max." Two large pots holding blossoming forsythia branches framed the doorway onto the balcony. *Fake flowers,* Max noted cynically. Inside the pot, also on the right, the beam of Vince's flashlight spotlighted a red stiletto. Vince leaned in to retrieve it with his pen.

"Leave it for photos, Vince." Something looked odd. Max inspected it more closely. "Look, Vince, broken heel. It's barely attached to the shoe."

"You thinking what I'm thinking?"

"If you're thinking 'Lady in Red' by Chris De Burgh, no."

Another good sign to Vince. The Max he knew was back on his game.

"But if you're thinking Jessie Bellaire may have been the victim of a broken shoe. Then, yes."

Reviewing the Rubik's tiles in his head, Max began to sketch a scenario. A soundtrack crescendoed in his head as he pictured it, *"Will it go round in circles? / Will it fly high like a bird up in the sky?" Billy Preston 1973 from My Life Is Music.* It was ripe with irony, just the way he saw the world, irony as a mirage mocking any meaning in the universe.

Max talked out the sequence like a director. "Picture Miss Bellaire here. She's feeling like the Queen of the world. Even has a crown. She's in a great mood. Had two, probably three glasses of wine. Maybe she dances around in circles anticipating Armstrong's arrival, the amorous night ahead, the luxury trip tomorrow. Exhilarated and buzzed, she dances up to the railing, glass of wine in her right hand. Maybe she toasts her good fortune, shifts her weight to her left foot. Snap! goes the heel. In an instant, she reels to the left, spins right, wine and glass fly to the right. It happens too fast to grab the railing with her left hand. She topples head down over the railing, broken shoe flies off into the pot. Headline: Beautiful lady in red has a head on collision with a planet speeding around the sun at 67,000 miles an hour."

It was very convincing. The last part about the planet struck Vince as odd, but Max had been a little odd tonight. And he wasn't done.

"Vince, if that's what happened, Jessie Bellaire's titanic plans were not sunk by an iceberg, but by the broken heel of an f-ing stiletto."

"It's a tragedy for sure."

"No, Vince. It's absurdity. Chaos prevails again."

His partner didn't know what to say. After a moment he proposed, "Thor can piece all this together and do a computer model of that scenario."

"Right, if the physical evidence leads there. But that theory doesn't get us off the hook. We still can't rule out the possibility of foul play. We don't know enough. Let's have a talk with Armstrong while forensics does their thing up here."

"Keep this theory to ourselves for now?"

"Indeed. Don't want to show these cards. Until we know more."

"What about Thor?"

"No, especially not Brickman. Let him put his fresh 'genius' eyes on all this. Let's go."

The Armstrong brothers sat like beleaguered frat boys in the formal dining room at one end of a table that sat fourteen. Two glasses and a bottle were between them. Wild Turkey Honey Sting. Their economic choice surprised Max. *That's my speed and price range.* Hanover and Thomason had been monitoring them from the massive kitchen. James was on the phone when the detectives came in.

Hanover spoke first. She addressed both detectives, but looked at Max. "Is there anything else we can do for you, sir?"

Max asked them to assist forensics. The officers exited.

He had called it. J. B. Armstrong made the interview a short one. But Tony wanted to talk, insisting he had nothing to hide. He repeated what he told Vince, adding that he was divorcing his wife; loved Jessie, and they were starting a new life together. Max had him detail the timeline and whereabouts of his day. Before he could answer the question, if he was aware of anyone who might want to harm Miss Bellaire, his counsel deflected it. If a more formal interview was requested, they would be glad to comply, but right now, his brother was in shock. Max asked for a list of all staff, caretakers, and anyone who had access and security codes to the property. J.B. wanted to know when Tony would have access to the house again. Standard procedure, two days, unless further notified. Vince inquired about Miss Bellaire's relatives. Tony knew her mother lived in Austin, Texas. He thought her first name was Jacqueline or Jazmine.

There was no reason to detain Tony Armstrong. The detectives collected cell numbers and addresses in town and apprised them a search would continue based on probable cause. Tony's willingness to cooperate fully was evident. As the Armstrong brothers got up to leave, Max had one more question.

"One more thing. The tattoo on Miss Bellaire's back. What did F F stand for?"

Vince was quick to soften the question, "If that's too personal you don't have to answer."

J.B. advised that but Tony responded, "No, it's alright." Clearly still shaken, like a man with the wind knocked completely out of him, he said, "It changed, depending on her mood and the situation. I'm not sure she ever told me the real meaning. I think she wanted it to be a mystery."

Vince, always the ameliorator, wrapped it up. "Thank you for your cooperation. We know this is beyond difficult."

Max advised him not to leave town. Two minutes later, the Alfa headed out the drive carrying both men.

They spent the next two hours combing through the scene with the other officers, conferring with forensics, looking for any signs of ingress or egress, anything to indicate someone else had been on the property. They found none, at least in the dark.

Hanover approached Vince while Max was going through Jessie's car.

"Sir, if I may ask, is detective Malone alright?"

"Long night last night. Long day today. Another one tonight."

"I've never seen him this subdued."

"Looks like he might be human after all, right?"

"Yes, sir."

At 1:00 AM they called it a night. Cleopatra was not going to Cabo. Her body was headed to a metal tray in the medical examiner's cooler. Vince to his sleeping family. Max to the solitude of Love Circle. The street blue officers still had shifts to complete. Two would remain all night at the mansion. Walking to their vehicles, Hanover spoke to Max.

"Be careful on these roads, detective. We've all been putting in long hours."

He acknowledged her simple kindness with a casual salute and, to her surprise, "You, as well."

* * *

At home on Love Circle, Max went straight to a hall closet, took down a shoe box and removed a fifth of Wild Turkey 101. Determined to break his New Year's resolution, he grabbed a glass and fought gravity up the stairs to the music room. He often brushed a hand against the sculpture of the planets and set them in motion like nine wobbly pendulums. It helped him ruminate on cases or just wind down as their swaying slowed and they returned to stasis. Tonight, he bent the rod supporting the blue ball and sent it careening into the others like a malicious cue ball. While the planets collided, he stood in front of the rows of vinyl. Last choice of the day: what music to put on.

Few voices consoled him like James Taylor's. His choice tonight: "Never Die Young." He had the studio album from 1988 but preferred the version on "One Man Band," the live acoustic concert with Larry Goldings on piano, 2007. Removing it from the sleeve, he cleaned it, placed it on the turntable carefully, like a priest dispensing a communion wafer. He hit 'play,' then 'pause' on the remote. Set the turntable to repeat. Opened the bottle, poured two fingers, downed it, poured two more. He sank into the recliner, remote in one hand, glass in the other. The nine planets rocked pell-mell in the corner in search of equilibrium. The Nashville night skyline front and center, he hit 'play.'

The needle dropped, followed by the familiar scratching sound. It had the effect of time travel. The music poured into him like the whiskey. JT's guitar was 90 proof, aged and mellowed. His voice was trustworthy and *smooth as a gravy sandwich*. JT became Max's therapist and tormentor. The whiskey his truth serum. It disarmed him. The music made it possible to get it all out, hold nothing back. JT sang, "They were glued together body and soul." To Max, it wasn't so much what James said. It was what he sketched that couldn't be spoken except in the music. And the music now synced over the image in his head of the furry lump fighting for life inside its dead mother. "Never do let them fall prey to the rust and the dust and the ruin that names and claims and shames us all," JT dared hope. But the admonition fell in vain

73

against Sofia's suffering and death and the fate of the unborn fawn. And in vain for Max, too. He felt rusted. Ruined. Unclaimed and Ashamed. Two fingers disappeared. He poured two more.

What he did not feel was guilty. *It was an accident, dammit.* If he had a soul, it felt like a cocktail, one part regret, one part recrimination and two parts justification. *Sure, I was in a hurry. What was her damn emergency?* The whiskey in the glass disappeared. He poured more. He threw his dad's words at it. *If she'd taken a step back, one step back, she'd be alive, bedding down for the night under the stars. But no. Fear and panic made her captive to the outcome.* Max was too blind, stubborn and well on his way to drunk to apply those words to his own captivity. He emptied and filled the glass again. JT sang on about taking to the sky and forsaking the ground.

A tragedy? Seriously, Vince? Hell no. Chaos prevails. It's modern fiction and Bohemian Rhapsody all rolled into one. Nothing really matters. The good, the bad and the otherwise – everybody loses. The whiskey took the wheel. He tossed back another one. This time, he spilled some fumbling with the glass.

JT counseled, "Let our golden ones sail on, sail on/To another land beneath another sky."

Hell, even Solomon said it would be better if he'd never been born. He raised his glass as JT sang "Hold em up, hold em up."

Max spoke a dark toast, "Here's to the sooner the better," and drained the glass.

His thoughts spiraled down like the whiskey. *Everybody loses. Exhibit A your honor: the young and*
beautiful Jessie Bellaire. Exhibit B: the young and talented Abe Davidson. Exhibit C: the young and priceless Sofia Beatrice Malone.

74

The rant in his mind went silent. In his gut he knew nihilism couldn't apply to his mother. But absurdity could. She mattered. And she died too young. He protested aloud, "Too damn young." And then the crux of the matter erupted much louder, "Where was your God for all of them, Vince? Where the hell was he?" He downed another one and slammed the glass on the side table like the final angry punctuation on a summation to a jury from a drunken lawyer defending a broken-hearted little boy.

At 2:07 AM the bottle was more than half gone. Between sips, Max mumbled his last thoughts of the long day: "Sofia Malone, cause of death: cosmic apathy; Jessie Bellaire, brought down by exuberance and gravity; Abe Davidson, died of fear; Jane Doe, KO'd by an F250. And the winner is: Unborn fawn, cause of death: life."

JT faded. So did Max. The empty glass dropped from his hand and rolled onto the floor. The scratching sound began again, followed by JT's valiant lament about the inexorable passing of time toward an inescapable exit, "We were ring-around-the-rosy children/They were circles around the sun…"

* * *

Max woke up in the recliner. In the same clothes. The music had stopped. It was morning. Someone was banging on the door downstairs.

CHAPTER 10

Wednesday morning 7:00AM – Day 3

On this third day of his new job, Dr. J.T. Brickman arrived at his office an hour and a half before official hours. If nothing else, he was dedicated. Historically, this made him a star pupil, brought him top honors and job offers from all over the country, but also made him a little too eager to please. Detective Malone's text at 11:00 PM alerting him that another case "needs your immediate attention in the morning," ignited both motives. But he had others as well, to begin a case independent of Dr. Jenkins, not to undermine his superior on the threshold of retirement, but to get the work-up staged and ready to proceed without delay. And not the least of motivators, to underscore his competence and reliability with the detectives. His morning did not go as planned.

* * *

Getting no response at Max's front door, Vince went around to the back deck. The sliding door was locked. He banged on it. Nothing. Max was home. His truck was in the drive because it wouldn't fit in the garage. Vince climbed the staircase to the top floor. The morning sun illumined the music room. No Max. He called again. This time Max answered.

"Cosa da, da Vinci? You're up early."

"I've been banging on your door. We've got a situation at headquarters."

Max lied. "Just getting out of the shower. Give me ninety seconds." He splashed water on his face and wet his hair at the sink, stripped out of yesterday's clothes and threw on sweats, t-shirt, slippers, left a towel around his neck and headed to the door. Vince blew past him.

"Did you sleep? You look rode hard and put up wet."

"Yea some. Want coffee?"

"No, thanks. Did you hit an animal last night on the way home? There's blood and fur on your grill."

Shit. I meant to wash that off last night. "Yea, on the way out. A deer. That's why it took me so long."

"Bet the deer was the loser on that one."

"Yea."

"I hate that feeling. Nothing you can do."

"Not a damn thing."

"Max, I need to ask you something. Did you toss back a few last night?"

"What?"

"I saw the glass on the floor upstairs. I'm a detective. And your friend. I thought you got rid of the hard stuff."

"It's been four months. I kept one bottle for a special occasion."

"What's the occasion, Thirst-day?"

"Nice one. The last thirty-six hours haven't exactly been Beaujolais days."

"You got any left? In case today becomes a special occasion?"

"Vince, I get it. I'd offer you the rest but you're Baptist, right?"

"Intermittently. And you know I rarely drink before breakfast."

Max went into the kitchen and fired up his shiny new Italian espresso machine. Like his barbeque, he prided himself on better-than-good coffee. His dad had made it a science. This machine, a high-tech, nearly automatic work of art, made it far less effort. It began grinding the beans. Vince tried to talk over the noise.

"No coffee for me. Max, Thor is freaking out. He tried to reach you then called me."

"Wait a second." The grinding stopped. "What did you say?"

"It's Thor. He's freaking out. He tried to reach you, then got me. We gotta get to the station."

"So, boy wonder hit a wall? That didn't take long. What's the crisis?"

"I don't know. He insists on talking to both of us, with the captain."

"So, depending on traffic we got a few minutes. You go ahead and I'll finish primping."

"No, I'll wait for you. And I will have some of that coffee. It smells great."

"Suit yourself. Straight up. No cinnamon?"

"No, thanks."

Max topped it off with a squirt of whipped cream anyway, handed it to Vince and said, "Perfect will have to do."

"Thanks. Get a move on, Max."

"Make me one. Hit 'double.' Then 'grind. 'When that's done hit the green button." He headed to get dressed. "And don't forget the cup."

* * *

At the station, they went first to the captain's office to brief him more on Monday night's scenario.

Vince insisted they walk and talk, considering the urgency of Dr. Brickman's concerns.

The captain asked. "Do you think she was pushed, or just another bizarre accident like Davidson?"

"No way to rule out either yet, sir," said Max. I have one theory, but we need more eyes on it, full forensics and follow up. There's security footage to go through and a list of people to interview."

"Vince, any idea what's got Dr. Brickman so worked up? Something about Davidson? or this Bellaire case?"

"No idea, Captain. None of us knows him very well yet, but he sounded frantic on the phone."

They arrived to find Brickman pacing behind his desk, one hand in the pocket of his jeans, the other worrying his full head of surfer hair. The visual of him so amped up launched Freddy Mercury in Max's head, "He's just a poor boy from a poor family," Queen, 1978, *Bohemian Rhapsody from "A Night at the Opera."* Brickman spoke before anyone else could and the music faded under his panicked tone.

"Thank you for coming. I'm so sorry to start the day like this. Detective Wilson I know I must've sounded pretty rattled on the phone. And I am but there's..." The captain jumped in.

"Thor, take a breath. Whatever it is, just lay it out. Let's sit."

"Thank you, sir." There were only three chairs. Max stood. Unknown to the others, his hangover required him to lean against a bookcase. Captain Haskins set the table.

"Now, what's chasing you around the room this morning?"

Brickman propped his elbows on his desk, rubbed the knuckles of one hand inside the other and began. He told them straight up that he knows, rather, knew the woman brought in last night. Jessie Bellaire was a student of his at Vanderbilt, in a bio lab he taught as part of his graduate school duties.

"Lord, have mercy," said the captain.

Vince, the empathizer, weighed in, "So, you rolled the body out of the cooler, uncovered her and wham? 'I know you.' That would freak anyone out."

"Yes, sir. But there's more."

"Girlfriend?" Max injected.

"No, sir, not at all, sir."

"A fling?"

"No, sir, absolutely not."

The captain refereed. "Max, let him tell it."

An hour ago, the confident, competent young Dr. Brickman could not have known that a head-on collision with his past lay in wait on a metal tray in the morgue. Now, he teetered on the edge of editing the story in the best light or full disclosure.

Max wondered three things: if this personal matter would wreck the meteoric rise of the young boy wonder; if Brickman would tell the whole story; and could he trust it? He knew something about partial versus full disclosure and life-changing meteors, especially in his defunct marriage.

Vince, though sympathetic, wondered if this might sideline a great asset to their team for a while and make their job even harder. Cases were stacking up.

Captain Haskins, the most circumspect of them all, which is why he was Captain, withheld judgement until he heard the rest of the story.

For Thor, as a scientist, full disclosure was a nonnegotiable for reliable findings. As a man of faith it was a nonnegotiable for reliable character. He chose. He revealed that the University had agreed to expunge his academic record. He told how from the beginning of the lab class Miss Bellaire had been very flirtatious, arranged selfies with several of the students to show her mother how cute her lab instructor was. She edited them to make it appear only she and Thor were in the pictures and posted them on social media. Unknown to Thor, Jessie's mother had counseled her to get involved with him only to a point that it helped her grade. Jessie had hinted at that to Brickman, inquiring if there was anything she could do for "extra credit." Near the end of the semester, one night as he was shutting down the lab, she came back dressed only in a white lab coat, open down the front, intending to seal the deal. He admitted it was the most seductive temptation of his life, but he was about to be engaged. He bolted for the door, leaving his backpack and all the lights on and doors unlocked.

"Wait a minute," Max interrupted. "You're telling me you didn't touch her, kiss her, nothing?"

"Yes, sir. I know that's hard to believe. She was beautiful, as you saw."

"Go on," the captain said.

Thor continued. The next day in another class he taught, she delivered his backpack in front of twenty students, implying he left it at her place. In it was a note begging him to talk with her. The note sounded desperate, saying she didn't know if she could go on without him, that all her grades were suffering because of their unresolved relationship. It had overtones of self-harm, so he agreed but insisted on talking by phone. She attempted to tighten the trap by threatening to report their "affair" to the University. Jessie was not aware Thor recorded the phone call. Not admissible in court, but highly beneficial and exonerating in case he needed it. Thor was not aware she was having an actual affair with a married, tenured professor, whom she pressured into a much better grade than her work warranted. Just before posting her failing grade, Thor went to his department heads in a pre-emptive move detailing the whole saga exactly as he was telling them now, including the recorded call. He posted her failing grade.

Within two weeks, a disciplinary panel summoned Jessie. They dismissed her from Vanderbilt not only for failing grades but failure to attend classes, breaches of drug and alcohol rules and even a stack of parking tickets. The professor retained his position, but volunteered to lead a study abroad program for the next semester. Behind the scenes, rumor was he paid Jessie to absolve him of any impropriety.

For Thor, there was collateral damage. His girlfriend got cold feet. No engagement happened. The dean hoped Thor would continue his studies to a doctorate level, but the dynamic in his department cooled toward him. He applied to Notre Dame to pursue a Ph.D., completed his master's degree at Vandy the next semester and moved on. He had no idea what happened to Ms. Bellaire or if she were still in Nashville. Until this morning.

Thor's audience went silent. The captain breathed a huge sigh and Vince beat him to the first words, "Lord, have mercy indeed."

Max, the only remaining pragmatic cynic in the room, followed up with, "For clarity, I have a couple of questions. Where were you last night between 7:00 and 8:00 PM? Did you push Jessie Bellaire off the balcony? Sounds like you had motive."

"Max, dammit, that's out of line!" Vince blasted back.

The captain rocked back in his chair, shook his head and looked at the ceiling.

Brickman responded, "No, it's alright. I understand, detective. I was with my parents. We had dinner at a Thai restaurant in The Gulch. I bought them dinner to celebrate my new job and I have the receipt. We spoke Thai with the waiters. We even took a photo."

"If you're done, Max," the captain took over. "First, Dr. Brickman, I commend you for your candor. Thank you. Tough situation. Extraordinary. I suspect if any of us had to face our worst moments, the body count would be a lot higher."

"Amen," Vince said with a glance at Max.

"Here's how this is gonna go down. Dr. Brickman, I want you to concentrate today on evidence at the scene. Take someone from forensics if you like, and I'll have Lieutenant Casey assign Thomason and Hanover to you for the day. She's got a good nose for this stuff. Dr. Jenkins can examine the body, report his findings."

Thor, visibly much calmer, responded, "Yes, sir. Thank you, sir."

"Vince, you and Max find out where Miss Bellaire lived and head over there. See what you can turn up."

"Yes, sir. Good plan, sir," Vince said.

"Already got her address last night from Mr. Armstrong, sir," Max said with a glance at Vince.

The captain put on his sternest tone. He always meant business, but the detectives knew when he shifted into that voice there was no equivocation. They called it his southern Gandalf voice.

"Let me make one thing perfectly clear. None, nothing, nada, not one inflection or inference from this conversation leaves this room. If I get the slightest hint of it from anywhere, I'll have your nads in the deep fryer. Are we clear?"

A unison, "Yes, sir" followed.

"Are we clear?" he repeated with a look at Max. Another unison affirmation followed.

Thor added, "Thank you, Captain. Thank you, detectives."

The captain dismissed them with his usual, "Keep me in the loop. Remember, this is a team sport. Let me know what you need and be safe out there."

Chapter 11

Max and Vince drove separately to Jessie's apartment at 21st and Grand. Max arrived first, made the manager aware of the situation. He asked to see the lease. The manager made a call to Mr. Armstrong for verification. His brother answered, gave the OK. As the call ended Vince joined them. He instructed the manager not to speak to anyone about the situation because Ms. Bellaire's mother in Texas was being located and notified. The manager sent them on up to the twelfth floor and would follow.

Waiting for the elevator together neither spoke. The doors opened. They entered. Max hit 12. When the doors closed Vince broke the silence.

"Sometimes you beat everything, Max. The kid's pouring his heart out and you treat him like a suspect. Really?"

"Just investigative protocol 101. Wouldn't be the first time a perp hid in plain sight. He had more reason than anyone for her to take a flying leap."

"First, if that was the case, he deserves an Oscar. If what he told us is the gospel truth, and I have no reason to doubt it, his integrity is off the charts."

"Come on, Vince. A woman that hot comes on to you like that and you head for the door? Who does that? Especially at his age."

"Just because you and me might fold like a tent in a tornado doesn't mean there aren't men who wouldn't."

"Name one."

The elevator stopped. Doors opened. They stood in the hall waiting for the manager.

"OK, Joseph. in the Bible. Handsome guy like Thor. His boss's wife kept after him to do the deed. He's not havin' it. One day no one's around. She grabs him by his coverall thing or…"

"His cloak. I know the story."

"Yea, his cloak and he leaves it behind to get away. Like Thor's backpack. She framed him for rape. Sounds a lot like this girl."

"Yea, Ok. That's one in twenty-five hundred years, a Biblical icon. But plain men just aren't wired to be faithful."

"A lot of men, I'll grant you that. Not sure it was a good idea that God made us so, so driven."

"'Horny' is the word you're looking for. Or maybe it's just the primal urge of natural selection. Ten to none, Vince, in that situation men will be animals. Period."

"Well, apparently this guy may be cut out of different cloth. Hell, even his name is Joseph. Pretty crazy."

"Well, pardon me if I'm naturally suspicious of crazy."

"And he's damn smart, too. Recording that phone call was brilliant. Saved his bacon. He smelled deceit. Even at his age. Admit it, Max. He's really good."

"Yea, I'll give you that." *Maybe a little too good.*

The manager arrived. Max asked if anyone had been there overnight. No one had. The cleaning staff put the place in order between 4:00 and 5:00 PM the day before, per Ms. Bellaire's request. He requested to see the security footage from the last few days and advised that the apartment would be off limits except to officers until an inquiry was complete. He intentionally avoided the word "investigation."

The manager unlocked the door and returned to the elevator. Once the doors closed, they gloved up.

"Talk about up town," Vince said as they entered the posh apartment.

The vaulted ceiling came only with the corner suite. Top to bottom every square foot was like a showroom for interior design. The palette of the entire apartment was various hues of sage and white. Chic, eclectic with some traditional southern pieces. A vintage natural wood hunt board bearing a wine carafe and crystal decanters of whiskey sat behind an art nouveau, velvet sofa. White bookshelves bracketed and spanned the top of the pass-through from the kitchen. They held only a dozen or so books, wine and cocktail glasses and fancy collectibles. A long pine blanket chest with dovetailed corners served as a coffee table. In the middle of it, white marble coasters with compasses etched in them surrounded a brass sundial. Two side chairs covered in brown and white cowhide brought in a touch of Texas. In one corner of the main room stood a seven-foot obelisk made of white stone covered with hieroglyphics. A cowboy hat hung over the top.

"The lease is in Tony Armstrong's name. The manager says he paid all the bills."

"For a kept woman she was kept very well."

"Indeed."

"I'll take this room and the kitchen. Why don't you start in the bedrooms, Max. Familiar territory."

"Ouch. Friend."

Vince quickly apologized, "I'm sorry, Max. That was low. I told you I'm an intermittent Baptist."

"Forget it. Probably deserved. Look at that view."

Max opened the French doors and stepped out onto the balcony. Vince joined him, in the same spot Jessie Bellaire gloated twenty-seven hours ago.

"How ironic," Max opined. "She gets kicked out of Vanderbilt a few years ago and winds up here, in the lap of luxury with a bird's-eye view looking down on all of them."

"Hey look, Max. You can see SATCO from here. And there's our bagel spot. You good with tacos two days in a row?"

"Maybe we should broaden our horizon. There's hot chicken minutes away in nearly every direction. Let's see how this goes first."

Jessie's bedroom was nearly as big as the living room. Same sage carpet, four-poster white bed covered by a sage brocade spread, plush pillows and two nightstands, both white. Two things caught Max's eye.

Along the wall opposite the foot of the bed was a hunter green, contoured yoga couch. *Indentions in the carpet. Probably moved for access.* In this setting Max knew its other role. He wondered if Vince had ever seen one.

Vince yelled from the living room, "All these books are photography of Texas landscape or Egyptian Archeology."

"She was from Texas. Who knows about the Egyptian fetish?"

The other more curious bedroom item hung above the headboard in a white frame, a state of Texas license plate that read: IM CLEO.

"Vince, I'm gonna run a plate. Hey, come in here. Any idea what this is?"

"What plate?" came from the other room.

Max called it in. He pointed to the green tantra chair when Vince came in holding a big book. The Baptist surprised him.

"Oh, a tantra sex chair. Julie and I had one of those before kids." He walked over to it and sat down. "Ours wasn't real leather. This is a high-dollar one. Oh, that plate. Hey, I thought this was a two-bedroom apartment." He got up and returned to the living room.

His joke foiled, Max continued the search.

In the drawer of one nightstand Max found the last note from Tony. *Sounds like two nights ago.* He informed Vince. "There's a note from Armstrong in the drawer of a nightstand. A bunch of them. This one sounds like two nights ago. Confirms their travel plan."

"Roger that. So that part of his story sticks."

The luxurious bathroom yielded nothing but luxury. *Where's the closet? There's got to be one.* He opened a door next to the bathroom. The second bedroom had been converted into a walk-in closet. Cubby holes stacked six feet high under a long shelf extended down the left wall. Each one held at least one pair of shoes. Shoe boxes filled the long shelf above. On the right wall two built-in dresser drawers book ended a dressing table and giant mirror with track lighting overhead. In the middle of the room was a complete circle of clothes racks, mounted on a mechanical track, packed to capacity.

"Vince, I found the second bedroom." He pressed a pedal switch on the floor. The hanging clothes circled the room like a train set under a Christmas tree.

Vince said, "Julie and I never had one of those." He returned to the front room.

One surprise still awaited. As Max rounded the ring of clothes, the back wall revealed a row of diverse outfits or costumes:

cheerleader, prep-school outfit with plaid skirt, nurse's scrubs next to a white lab coat, the shirt only of police dress blues, with handcuffs and more. Once he could see the far corner down to the shoe wall, a full body mannikin came into view. It was dressed in an exotic costume of sheer white material with gold trim. One hand gripped an ornate scepter. *This girl's imagination finally got a budget to match.*

Max's phone rang. He headed to the living room.

"Hey, Vince. Got a hit on this plate. Could be the key to the FF tattoo."

Vince was holding an open book. "I'll see your license plate and raise you a high school yearbook. I think I found the source of the FF. You go first."

"You're on. The tag linked to a BMW in Texas registered to Jessie Bellaire and a Finn Fielding, titled from a Fielding Fine Rides, Austin, Texas. Ten to one she dated Finn, and he bought her a car."

"Not bad. Not bad."

"Elementary, my dear Wilson."

"Now, look at this Sherlock. This is her high school yearbook, senior year."

The two detectives stood side by side to look. Vince had fingers in three spots in the book.

Under her senior picture the name read, "Jessie 'Cleo' Bellaire." "Apparently her nickname was Cleo. And look why. She was homecoming queen." Vince turned to another page he had a finger in. "Look how she dressed for the ceremony."

"Cleopatra. Cleo. That costume is in her closet back there. All but the cobra crown."

"There's more." Vince opened the next bookmarked spot.

"See this picture with two of her girlfriends? Look how they signed her yearbook. 'FF Forever, Sasha' and 'Femme Fatales take it all, Lacie.'"

"Bam! Vince, you found the golden ticket. That's gotta be it. No wonder she left it a mystery to Armstrong."

"Why give away the con?"

"Exactly. And how many people around Tony saw through it and tried to warn him? That's our suspect pool."

"Exactly."

"Wait till you take a look at the erotic bait in her closet. He couldn't see through the heat she generated."

"Exactly."

"And like most men his compass was in his pants."

"In this case, no doubt. But I've heard you put it cruder."

"You're welcome."

"Score one for da Vinci. Lunch is on you, Sherlock."

Just as Vince claimed his victory something dropped out the book onto the carpet. A red envelope. Both bent down to look. Handwritten on it was simply:

Jessie Bellaire

Max picked it up in his gloved hand. He looked once at Vince. Pulled out a red card. Turned it over. On the white back side, they read silently:

You have sown treachery and wickedness. Prepare to reap. Put your affairs in order. Your life is required of you.

The Red Angels

CHAPTER 12

Wednesday morning 11:00AM Day 3

En route to the Armstrong mansion Thomason and Hanover nearly collided with a buzzard, one of more than a dozen fighting over a carcass by the side of Arno Rd. The officers arrived at 10:45 AM, twenty minutes before Dr. Brickman, per Sergeant Malone's request.

Earlier, Hanover was surprised to get a direct call from Max. He was on his way to Ms. Bellaire's apartment as part of the "inquiry," he called it. He informed her that the captain decided to put Dr. Brickman in the field today. Max expressed concern that this was the young Dr.'s first time on a scene for the department and since she has more experience, he asked her to observe and help him in any way. She assured him she would. At first it seemed slightly odd the way he asked her not to tell Dr. Brickman he reached out to her. He explained he didn't want him to operate under any undue pressure. That seemed reasonable to her, and not just professional, but possibly a hint of care for Dr. Brickman, at least she liked to think it was. She was wrong, and unaware of the detective's unease about Brickman. What piqued her curiosity was Max's reminder not to leave Brickman alone on the scene, per protocol and again, in case he needed anything. She was well-versed in investigative protocol. She chalked it up to the detective's dogged style and fastidious attention to detail. Again, she assured the Sergeant she and Thomason would assist Dr. Brickman.

At the end of the call, Max gave her an oblique compliment, passing along the captain's comment about her "good nose for this stuff." She was pleasantly surprised. Max stumbled a bit trying to say that the captain was usually right about these things, but it came out, "The captain usually has a good nose about a good nose." He chalked up his awkward phrasing to a lack of sleep. Reciprocating, she let him off the hook by saying it was good to hear the captain liked her nose - for investigative stuff. Max was unaware of her aspiration to one day be Helen Hanover, Detective, not news anchor or motivational speaker. But she had a good enough nose not to use this moment to clarify that.

* * *

Dr. Brickman encountered the same gang of buzzards. They were so thick and aggressive he had to hit his brakes and drive around them slowly. Through the contentious black mob, he could barely make out what remained of a deer. This was not the visual he needed after the way his morning began in the morgue. It conjured a similar scene with his parents in Paraguay. A dead burro by the side of a dirt road had become the entrée for a dozen giant Buitres Rey, King Vultures. It was a gruesome sight for a boy. His father's words repeated now in his head. "Some of nature's ways appear grotesque, but are part of the balance of things, just as some of God's ways are far from gentle, but part of the holy balance of his justice and mercy."

The officer posted at the gate knew Dr. Brickman was expected.

He welcomed him to the force and opened the gate. Before leaving his office, Brickman had spent two hours studying the photos of the scene as objectively as he could. But physically driving onto the property seemed to multiply the pull of gravity on his body. He parked on the near side of the circle drive, unloaded three cases of gear onto a rolling hand cart and walked toward the house, pausing next to the shadow cast by the gnomon of the giant sundial. Though the cloudless spring day was far from warm, he could feel the weight of the sun on his face. He checked his watch. Eight past eleven. The shadow fell on the dial just past the Roman numeral XI. This had the effect of centering him. He reminded himself *the sun is dependable. There is holy balance in the universe. Justice and mercy. Life and death.* The officers watched him take a deep breath and his cheeks puff as he blew it out, like a diver returning to the surface. He spoke something too soft for them to hear. "Science is a keyhole. Belief is the key." He looked down for a moment, then crossed himself. Hanover and Thomason looked at each other. Brickman headed for the front steps where the officers stood. Introductions were made. His first statement was to thank them for their help. And he went further.

"I've got a lot to learn about all this so please feel free to weigh in at any point. You'll see things I don't."

"Yes, sir. Thank you, sir." His humility enlisted them immediately.

"You were both here last night, is that right? And had the first look at the premises?"

"Yes, sir."

"Good, that will help a lot."

"Where would you like to begin, sir?" Hanover asked.

"From my study of the photos, I'd like to go to the balcony.

But first, please, give me the three- minute version of what you each saw." He took out a notebook and began to scribble. His pen trembled slightly. Hanover noticed.

Thomason began. He described the scene, the sequence of events, where Mr. Armstrong met them, the location of the body, checking for any sign of life, finding none, clearing the house with Hanover, discovering of the open wine bottle, the paramedics arriving, followed by two other officers. He assigned one to the gate on Arno Rd, the other to wait with Mr. Armstrong while he and Hanover cleared the house.

Dr. Brickman asked what state Mr. Armstrong was in, not just what he said but what he did, where he walked or sat, who he called and when, any sweating, tears, unsteadiness? Hanover filled in those details. She was thorough, adding the name of the wine, how much remained in the bottle and the curtain Mr. Armstrong tore from a front window to cover Miss Bellaire's body. She described Armstrong's state down to his pale color and shaky hands and how he collapsed onto his brother when he arrived.

"So, both of you would say he appeared sincerely devastated?"

Hanover affirmed that. "Yes, sir, completely distraught. It was a horrifying way to find someone you care about. He was miserable and clearly in shock." Thomason agreed.

"Just one more question. Did either of you overhear any of Mr. Armstrong's conversation with his brother, either on the phone or after he arrived?"

"No, sir. Officers Calton and Weber might have. As I said, I believe Mr. Armstrong made the call to his brother before we arrived. Thomason and I escorted them to the dining room while detectives Malone and Wilson investigated the scene, but we gave them some space from the kitchen. His brother talked to him quietly. We heard Mr. Armstrong cry out a couple of times, basically in disbelief that this was happening."

"Thank you. This is all very helpful. Officer Hanover, will you, please, lead me to the balcony? And Thomason, remain below on the steps?" They agreed.

Brickman unloaded two cases from the dolly. They all gloved up. Hanover carried one case and led the way upstairs. As they ascended, he sighed again deeply.

"Are you alright?"

"I'll be fine. A little first-time jitters, I guess." Only Brickman knew this was not the whole truth.

He seemed for a moment so much like a boy dressed up in man clothes that Hanover wanted to hug him. Instead, she put her hand on his arm and said, "You'll do fine. I've heard remarkable things about you, about your expertise."

"Thank you."

Near the top of the stairs, she had to ask.

"Dr. Brickman, tell me if I'm out of line but are you Catholic? I saw you cross yourself out there."

"Yes, well, I was. I grew up in the Catholic faith. Missionary kid. Old habit." Then he told part of the truth. "I stopped out there for a moment because for whatever reason, someone's life ended in this place. That's a solemn and sacred thing."

"Yes sir. It is." Hanover felt buoyed at the prospect of another person of faith might have joined the force. She noted how much older he sounded than he looked and it moved her that he cared about someone's demise whom he didn't even know. She made a note to tell this to Sergeant Malone. She was wrong. And right.

In this moment, Dr. Brinkman's innate and nurtured capacity for compassion melded with a personal angst about the victim and his history with her. Even the best nose would be hard-pressed to sniff that out at this point.

Max, of course, when told, would not buy it. Years spent unmasking the truth carved the belief in his core that no one is who they seem. *How can you really know someone unless you see them under extreme pressure and dire hardship?* Like his saint of a mother, whose shining spirit grew brighter as the cancer took her life. But even she defied her father's wishes to marry an Irishman, and worse, a protestant. It broke his heart and cost them years of silence. Max believed all saints and sinners are capable of anything given the right levers. He had no idea how much he and Dr. Brickman and Officer Hanover agreed on this. To Max, the only remedy for endemic and acculturated duplicity was justice, truth winning out in time. Dr. Brickman and Officer Hanover aligned with Max on this global human condition, but they subscribed to a different cure.

Hanover watched the young Dr. methodically unpack his case in the sitting room off the balcony. A tape measure, a type of laser gadget, what he called an LDM, laser distance meter, evidence bags, a magnifying glass, head lamp, a bottle of water, a small plastic cup, a sketch pad of graph paper and three hardback books with paper jackets, an anatomy book, a pictorial of Tennessee mansions and a third about landscaping.

Before even approaching the balcony, he sketched a floor plan of the various avenues of egress, then studied each route on his hands and knees with the large magnifying glass and head lamp looking for any signs of foot traffic or debris potentially tracked in or out. Anything "extraneous or out of place," he told Hanover. To her, he looked like a Beach Boy playing Sherlock Holmes.

Next, Brickman laid out six photographs on the threshold of the double balcony door, pictures of the balcony floor, closeups of the spill pattern of the red wine and broken glass. Both were still there as they had been the night before. In a row above that he placed three photos of Jessie's body on the steps below, minus the curtain, taken from three angles over the railing. He turned these face down. Below the spill shots he laid out five photos of Miss Bellaire holding a glass of red wine, very much alive. She was wearing the red negligee and the unmistakable cobra crown. The poses were playful and provocative.

This caught Hanover completely by surprise. "Where did those come from?"

"Her phone. Selfies sent to Mr. Armstrong perhaps minutes before her fall. By the backgrounds you can see she took them in sequence from downstairs up to this very spot."

"What does this show you?"

"First, based on the wine remaining in the bottle and the level in the glass, it looks like this was at least her third. Dr. Jenkins is doing the toxicology, so we'll know her blood alcohol level soon."

"That makes sense."

"Beyond that, the photos, together with her texts under the pictures like "I've started dancing without you," indicate she was having a quite a good time, celebrating the moment. She was exhibiting the kind of freedom that can animate anyone feeling exuberant, a little buzzed and unwatched."

"She certainly was beautiful."

Thor paused his exegesis for a moment before responding, "Yes, she was." Then continued, "All this paints a picture of what led up to such a horrific turn of events."

With the regular tape measure, he determined the height of the pot where the broken shoe still remained. With the LDM he took readings from several places to the top of the railing. He pulled a chair to the center of the open double door, sat down and began to sketch.

"Officer Hanover, feel free to sit. This will take a little while." She was far from bored and took a seat.

After nearly fifteen minutes he walked to the railing and asked Thomason if he wouldn't mind, please, assuming the position of the body. For this he held a grim photo in his hand, directing Thomason into the exact spot and posture. The photo distressed Dr. Brickman. Hanover noticed.

When he was satisfied with Thomason's position, he set the photo face down again. Using the LDM he took more dimensions from the railing to the reclining officer. He returned to the chair, made more sketches, picking up one photo and then another. Twice he got up, stood by the railing and turned around a few times, his right hand out as if holding an imaginary drink, sat again and resumed sketching. It was another ten minutes before he spoke again.

"Officer Hanover, I don't mean to be personal but how tall are you and your approximate weight? Jessie, uh, Ms. Bellaire was nearly 5'10" about 132 lbs."

"I'm 5'9, in full gear about 148."

"So, close to Ms. Bellaire, in street clothes or, uh, swimsuit? Four-inch stilettos would make you both over six feet tall. Have you ever danced in stilettos, officer?"

"No, I tried on a pair once."

"And what was your experience?"

"It was like walking on stilts on a railroad track."

"I can only imagine. Would you mind standing at the railing for a minute? Facing outward."

"No." She moved to the railing.

"Wait a minute." He grabbed the three large books and placed them three inches from the railing. The paper jackets were shiny. "Steady yourself with the railing and stand on these, please, carefully."

Hanover saw where he was headed. "You want to get an idea of where the top of the railing hit Ms. Bellaire's torso, right?" She carefully stood on the books.

"Right." He returned to his chair. "Let me take a few measurements and one quick photo."

The longer she stood the more precarious she felt. If they were not there on such serious business, the view of the rolling green hills would have been beautiful.

From the water bottle he poured the plastic glass half full. He stood, approached Hanover and said, "Now, I'm going to stand to your left, by the railing. Let go with your right hand and hold this glass of water. Put your weight evenly on both feet."

"I am."

"Good. Now when we're set, and not till then, I want you to let go of the railing with your left hand, and on my count shift all your weight to your left foot. I'm right here."

He yelled over the railing to Thomason. "Officer, will you get the video camera from my other case in the foyer?" Thomason disappeared below into the house.

Hanover tensed all over. Her heart rate elevated. With only one hand on the railing, she could feel her lower back stiffening to remain steady on the books.

"All right. Thomason, are you ready? Now, let's do this in two steps. Step one: Let go of railing. Then on my count shift your weight to your left foot. Shall we count three for both steps?"

"Go on three or one, two, three, go?" Hanover wanted to clarify.

"Which would you prefer?"

"One, two, three, go"

"All right, how about one, two, three, let go. Then one, two, three, go, for the second step"

"Yes, got it. What about Thomason? Is he in place?"

Brickman counted. "One. Two. Three. Let go." She did.

"One. Two." The top book slipped to the right out from under her. Hanover's weight followed it. She felt the rush of panic as she spun to the right and leaned helplessly toward the railing; her right arm swung behind to counterbalance; the glass dropped from her hand as she spun; both hands grasped for the railing but missed; her left waistline pressed against the top of the railing; simultaneously her head and upper torso headed over it; her left foot snapped backward involuntarily. At that moment Brickman caught her firmly in his arms. It all happened in a flash. Thomason shouted from below, "OK, I'm ready."

"Breathe, officer. You're alright."

Hanover's eyes were dilated. Her heart pounding. She felt a rush of relief and anger. "What the hell! Why didn't you wait for Thomason?" She stepped away from the railing, visibly shaken.

"I am so sorry, officer. I apologize. I had to trick you a little into a real experiment."

"You pushed the book, didn't you?"

"Yes. You had to perceive real danger in order to respond reflexively, without thinking."

Hanover took a moment to process and catch her breath. "Like she did."

"Precisely. Again, please; forgive the subterfuge. You were in no real danger."

"But only you knew that!" She took two more deep breaths. Her natural wit kicked in as a counterbalance. "Ok, sure, no harm, no foul. I've fallen for guys for worse causes."

"Thank you. You're a good sport. And look on the plus side. You'll have a better nose now for which guys to be wary of."

"I thought I already knew which ones. All of them."

Dr. Brickman apologized again. He pointed out that the spilled water and cup landed exactly on the pattern of the wine and broken glass. After taking more photos, he packed up, saying he wanted to speak briefly with the other officers later, perhaps at the station, but had all he needed for now from the scene. Hanover carried a case back down the stairs with Brickman. He thanked both officers again and expressed what an honor it was to be on the same team.

Hanover left thoroughly impressed, and more motivated than ever to become a detective. Dr. Brickman met and exceeded his press. She only knew one other cop with that kind of deductive instinct, and she was plenty wary of him.

CHAPTER 13

Wednesday afternoon 1:15PM – Day 3

"I don't mind Frothy two days in a row but this better be good." The captain's tone was not pleasant. "I've got reporters camped at my door. One of them got wind Abe was dealing drugs out of daddy's house."

"Probably from a rat jumping ship, sir. Or Abe's competition." As he and Vince climbed into the suburban Max handed him his coffee - real cream, two sweetener packs, dash of cinnamon.

"Same pack mentality, sir," Vince chimed in from the back seat.

"Agreed. They're addicts for news maybe, but they have their job to do. Now, detectives, before you justify this clandestine powwow, I have three things. Brickman found the contact info for Ms. Bellaire's mother in her phone. She's been notified in person by local authorities in Austin. Poor woman. Hardest job in the world knocking on those doors."

"Yes, sir. Never easy," Vince agreed.

"Second, I just came from lunch with an old friend on faculty at Vandy. Science department. He backed up Dr. Brickman's story. All the professors admired him, saw his genius. Offered him a full ride and stipend to do his Ph.D. but Notre Dame did, too. He says the University behaved honorably, tried to contain the story but things like that tend to leak. He understands how Thor could've felt some awkward vibes after what happened."

"That's good news, sir," Vince said, then looked at Max. "Looks like we've got a heavy hitter on our team, right, slugger?" Max ignored the comment.

"And third, sir?"

"I just got a call from Dr. Brickman. He has a "compelling theory," his words, about Ms. Bellaire's death. Says according to initial evidence it looks like a freak accident. He'll have a presentation for us tomorrow morning with lab results."

Max, looked back at Vince. "Sir, we've just come from Ms. Bellaire's apartment. Dr. Brickman doesn't have all the evidence."

"What did you find?"

"We connected a lot of dots. So far, Mr. Armstrong's story holds up. They planned to leave town this morning. But Ms. Bellaire wasn't showing all her cards. We think she was playing him. And someone knew it." He handed the captain the card in an evidence bag. He read both sides.

"Oh, my dear God." There was no need for 'Indeed' from Max. The captain tapped the card against the steering wheel and went silent. "What the hell is going on?" Then he did what captains do. Took action. "This is going to take a small, tight task force to keep these notes on the down low. Who do you want to bring in?"

Max pushed back. "Sir, Vince and I agree. Let's not spook whoever's behind this. So far, the Red Angels don't know that we know. That's to our advantage. If we show our hand, they may change their MO and go silent."

"I get that. But what if more of these things are in the works? We might avert one."

"Ten to one, Captain, this kind welcome publicity," Vince said. "And they're three steps ahead of us."

"Vince is right, sir. They thrive on sensation and spreading fear. The best way to avert another one is to find this pious bastard."

"You have any reason to believe it's just one person?"

"No, sir. Nothing. But posing as more than one might be a distraction."

"We can't soft-shoe this! We may have a serial judge, jury and executioner out there!" The detectives could sense the captain's tone ramping up toward his southern Gandalf voice. "What do you suggest?"

"Vince and I keep digging, sir. As far as anyone else knows, Abe and Ms. Bellaire's deaths are officially accidents. We aren't investigating, just completing inquiries to give some closure."

"I want specifics. Where will you begin?"

"We focus on how, when and who delivered the notes. So far, there's only one envelope, no postage or postmark. Probably delivered by hand. Maybe slipped under her door. There's a lot of security footage in the days leading up."

Vince jumped in. "Ms. Batson said Abe's behavior changed about a week before his death."

"Right. Someone delivered these, sir. Someone saw something or a camera did."

"Good. What else?"

Vince stayed on the offensive. "We quietly build a suspect list, see who had access to buildings and properties."

"And motive," Max tag teamed. "There's even a guy in Texas we think Ms. Bellaire may have snared and discarded before she came to Nashville."

"What about the notes themselves? Someone with zealous religious views or Bible knowledge had to write those."

"Or wants us to think so, sir." Max rarely took anything at face value.

"But we need them analyzed," the captain argued. "The handwriting. Is it the same on both?"

"Doesn't appear to be, sir."

"Dr. Brickman might turn up something about that and the paper, like where you can get it."

"Yes sir, but not yet," Max insisted. "All hell will break loose if this gets out." The captain's report from the Vandy professor did not ease his misgivings about Brickman.

"Alright." The captain took a sip of coffee. The detectives' answers seemed to mollify him. "We keep a lid on the notes for now. But I want answers. And I want them yesterday."

"Yes, sir."

"Lord, have mercy, what next?" He sipped. No one spoke. "Thank you, detectives. Be safe out there. Let me know what you need. And thanks for the coffee."

Max and Vince decided to split up for the rest of the day. Vince headed to Davidson's under the guise of the ongoing drug sting and providing closure. His actual mission was to look for an envelope, get panoramic security footage six to eight days prior, and find out who has access to the property.

First on Max's list was a call to Finn Fielding in Texas, then back to Jessie's apartment. He planned to tell the manager Jessie's mother had been notified, ask to see the guest registry and security footage of the building entrance and Jessie's hallway, to determine a timeline, all to help wrap up the "inquiry." While logged in he would check the hard drive archives for Jessie's hallway going back about a week. If anyone from the cleaning staff were available, he

Billy Sprague

could casually engage them, find out any inside skinny. Max had
learned the invisible people among us often see things we miss.
Traffic was already getting heavy. Max sat through a green light
once at Wedgewood and 21st. He was hoping to make the second
one. A faded blue 1950 something chevy pickup in front of him
displayed the kind of bumper stickers on the tailgate that drove
him nuts. 'God is my co-pilot.' The big dog beside the long-haired
driver at least made that one amusing. 'Don't be caught dead
without Jesus,' *Nothing makes converts like cleverness.* One sticker
advertised 'BreathtakingPipes.com Recorders, Flutes, Penny
Whistles'. *Hippy musician, no doubt.* Under that was, "Lord, make
me an instrument." Another declared, 'God loves you, and I'm
trying to.' *Well, if there were a loving God at least that's honest.*

What incited the most dissonance in Max's antipathy toward
God's flock was the contrast between that sticker and the one beside
it, a contrast apparently lost on the driver. 'It is mine to avenge. I
will repay." Deut. 32:35. *Loving and wrathful. Just the kind of God
the world needs.* And, of course, one sticker had a call to action and
extended an invitation: "Honk if you're a HOLY MESS! Meet me
and Jesus this Sunday at COOL SPRINGS CHURCH." *First
chance I get.* Vince had attended there a few times. He said the staff
and volunteers wear t-shirts that say, 'I'm a holy mess.' The church
sprung up in the last five years and exploded into thousands
attending every week. *One of those rock and roll, hip and holy places.*
Max had seen the sign out front and their promos, "Tattoos,
Doubters and Traditionals Welcome." Vince assured him you
don't have to show your tattoos to get in. Or your doubt.

The driver of the truck was playing with his co-pilot and didn't
see the light turn green. Max nearly honked. *No way.* While he

fumed through the red light, a second time he called in the tag. A
Jubal Biggs cited three times for driving too slow on the freeway.
No warrants. Max let it go. He had more pressing business.

He parked at Jessie's building. Before going in he intended to
find a number for Fielding Fine Rides in Austin, Texas, then
wondered if Jessie's phone might list Fielding's cell number. *Is it
in the evidence room or Brickman's office?* He called the officer at
the evidence desk. The phone was there. Brickman had logged it
out and back in. *Good boy.* He decided Finn Fielding could wait
till tomorrow.

The building manager was genuinely empathetic. He explained
the policies and login for guests, the stringent security measures
for their caliber of residents, and showed him around. A bank of
mailboxes lined a wall around a corner from the front desk. Max
noted the position of a box labeled 'Bellaire.' The manager left
Max alone with the video archives. After twenty minutes of
viewing only the feed from the mail room camera and Jessie's
hallway he realized this would take time. In order not to arouse
the manager's curiosity, he made a judgment call to download the
archive from those two cameras onto a thumb drive starting seven
days prior to Jessie's death. Better to view it in his music room
with a glass of wine. He guessed Vince would do the same with
the footage at Davidson's. Just as he left the building Vince
phoned.

"Anything?"

"Bingo. Red envelope. I was just about to wrap up. Earlier I
went thru a pile of envelopes in the guitar room. Probably from
the payments Miss Batson couriered around. But no red envelope.
Went into the big house to the room that houses all the security

equipment. Fifteen cameras besides the three Vice set up. It would take forever to go through it all."

"Vince, the envelope. Where did you find it?"

"Yea, sorry. So, after I downloaded footage from the three main cameras covering three days, about the time Abe starting acting funny, and… "

"Vince! The envelope!"

"I'm getting there! I circled back to Abe's place and something said, 'There has to be an envelope so no one could read the note except the one who opened it.' Then I asked myself, "What would I do with an envelope after I read such a crazy note?' Nothing. Who cares about the damn envelope, right?"

"Vince, you're killing me. Where was it?"

"You know the trash can under the desk where you found the note? Beside it on the left is a wooden filing cabinet the same height. It matches the desk, but there's a crack between them. I moved the filing cabinet and bam! Red envelope."

"Any postage or postmark?"

"None. Just like the other one."

"Vince, both of them were hand delivered."

"You're welcome."

"Great work, Vince. Was Davidson curious why you were there?"

"Not at all. He's very subdued and compliant. Poor man. Can't imagine losing one of my kids."

"Indeed." Max and his Ex never had kids. One miscarriage. As the years passed, when he thought about his own childhood, he wished they had. But as things turned out maybe it was best they didn't.

"What now, Max?"

"I did the same thing you did with the footage. Downloaded from two cameras. One in the mail room and one in her hallway. Guess we'll be doing the same thing tonight. I'll scroll through it at home with a glass of wine."

"Ah, the hall and the mailroom. What a sad love story," Vince joked. "I hate to spoil it for you, Max, but they never get together."

Maxed laughed out loud. He couldn't remember the last time he laughed. Vince laughed, too.

"Whoo. Good one, Vince. I needed that."

"What are paisanos for, right?"

"Indeed."

* * *

By the time Max pulled into Love Circle it was nearly 9 PM. Long shower. Pulled pork with sides of coleslaw and red potato salad. He drank water and made an espresso. Poured one glass of Chianti. Left the bottle in the kitchen, grabbed his computer and headed up to the music room to watch *The Hallway and the Mailroom.* He laughed again. *What soundtrack goes with this movie?* He chose guitar master Tommy Emmanuel, "Live One" 2005, and set it to begin on an exquisite instrumental called "Questions." He settled in the recliner.

Tommy played. Max slid the thumb drive into his computer, saw the icon appear on the screen. Instead of clicking it open, he searched the internet for the scripture on Jubal Biggs truck, Deuteronomy 32:35. *To get the context,* he told himself. *If Vince could see me now.* He found the entire verse:

"It is mine to avenge; I will repay. In due time their foot will slip; their day of disaster is near and their doom rushes upon them."

The gravity and irony of the passage, with the specificity of how Jessie Bellaire died, rang loud and clear. As usual, Max archived it on a tile in his mental Rubik's cube, a manageable distance from his heart. That distance would soon prove inadequate.

He double-clicked the thumb drive icon, searched a file, a date, and hit play. In five minutes, he was nodding off. He dreamed he was in a long corridor. A lady in white pushing a cart walked away from him. She bowed low. And slipped an envelope under a door.

Chapter 14

Thursday morning 6:15AM – Day 4

Max's alarm went off at the usual time. Except for the brief dream, he slept so well he only made a single espresso. For twenty minutes his head felt as clear as the beautiful Spring morning. The weather report called for thunderstorms in the late afternoon, but his storms began much earlier.

Sitting in the usual morning traffic the tiles of the Rubik's cube collator in his head tumbled. The details of the current caseload rushed at him like hailstones from the clear blue sky. He trudged and cussed the traffic, and the thought of sitting through Brickman's presentation at 8:00. He called Vince. No answer. Left a VM.

"Vince, I tried to watch The Hallway and the Mailroom last night. What a snoozer. In fact, I fell asleep five minutes in. I guess no revelations yet from your home movies? Had an odd dream. I think it was a dream. Tell you at boy wonder's presentation."

Max was the last to arrive at Brickman's office. He was four minutes late, not because of traffic, but because he ran into Hanover. She wanted to brief him on her observations of Dr. Brickman. He said he could meet closer to lunch, *doesn't hurt to try*, that he was on his way to a meeting with the captain and he and Vince had a week's worth of work to do this morning. She had a session at the gun range, teaching. *Did he just hint at lunch together?* He said he heard what a good marksman, or woman, or shot she is. *Damn that was awkward.* She parlayed it into a "give me a call" to set up a meeting. *Uh, oh, wonder how he took that?* He liked the sound of that and said he would. *I certainly will.*

Entering the meeting Max lied, "Traffic. Did I miss anything?"

"No. Dr. Brickman was showing us the project he's doing in his back acre. Take a look."

A photo filled a large screen high in a front corner of the office. It showed an unfinished crisscross pattern where bricks were being laid. The serpentine paths resembled two elongated figure eights stacked on each other. Another set of smaller figure eights ran across the upper, larger pattern to form a giant cross.

Vince pointed out, in his helpful, instructive tone, "Max, Dr. *Brick*man is laying the *bricks* himself. The brick layer is Dr. Brickman."

Max patronized his partner. "No wonder you're a detective." Vince took it well.

"I'm just beginning," Dr. Brickman said. "It will have lots of seasonal flowering plants, native bushes and grasses and dogwood trees in each of the central spaces."

The captain quizzed Max, sure he would not guess Brickman's design. "What does it look like to you, Max?"

Max took a moment. He said, "Obviously, the paths form a cross, so I'm inclined to say a prayer or meditation garden. But I'm torn..." Max paused, capturing his audience. His first impression of the pathways was the intertwining serpents on the ancient medical icon of the Hippocratic oath. But he remembered the card on Brickman's desk, "Science is a keyhole. Belief is the key." He also retrieved a tidbit from an old Rubik's tile stored away from the family trip to Ireland. *All cathedrals have a cross as the footprint.* He wondered if Brickman's Catholic upbringing influenced his landscape design. He finally relieved their suspense with, "I'm torn between the intertwining serpents on the medical icon of the Hippocratic oath and the double helix of DNA."

Brickman was delighted. "That's amazing, detective! Yes, it's both! I'm having a stone carved with the Latin motto of the oath, Primum Non Nocere."

Max immediately translated, "First, do no harm."

"That's right, detective. I'm also having a metal plaque inscribed with my parents' reminder when I headed into science. It's here on my desk." He showed it with pride, "Science is a keyhole. Belief is the key."

"Profound," said the captain.

Dr. Brickman kept talking like a professor, "The overall shape of the garden is a cross because all cathedrals are laid out like a cross. This is an open-air cathedral."

"I did not know that," Vince said. "Did you, Max?"

"Yes."

The captain applauded, "Well done, Max. You never cease to amaze me."

"I keep telling him he should try out for Jeopardy, sir," Vince said.

Max suddenly hoped Brickman 'show and tell' with the card might strike a resonance in the captain with the two identical sinister cards. If it did, Captain Haskins showed no sign and steered the meeting to the business at hand. He turned it over to Dr. Brickman, who handed each of them a binder.

For the next fifteen minutes, the young scientist led them through photos, sketches and a lab report, much of it displayed on the screen as well. Per the scene at Tony Armstrong's mansion, he showed in great detail how he searched every route onto or away from the balcony for signs of "extraneous debris." The result. No findings. Photos and diagrams illustrated the spill patterns of the wine and broken glass. He described Ms. Bellaire's emotional state via the selfies and her physical condition. As the toxicology revealed, though not legally drunk, the level of alcohol in her system without a doubt impaired her motor skills. Brickman walked them through Tony Armstrong's state related to him by Officers Hanover and Thomason. He gave high marks to the officers for their valuable input and assistance, especially Hanover, who helped with a reenactment of Ms. Bellaire's demise. He showed pictures of the water spill pattern aligning with the wine stains. As he described Hanover's role, Max became angry.

"Are you telling me you tricked her into a near fall?"

"Detective, I assure you she was never in any danger," Brickman insisted.

"Sounds like she didn't know that and that was your damn purpose!"

The captain had to referee. "Max, I've already spoken with Hanover and Dr. Brickman together about this earlier. She's good with it and actually commended the Dr. on his unorthodox method. Now, let him finish."

Vince was the only one in the room who attached the measure of Max's defense of Hanover to his interest in her beyond professional. He intended to point this out later in another setting. It was ripe fodder for one of his favorite pastimes, making Max squirm. But behind that was Vince's higher goal, getting under his partner's hard shell.

Dr. Brickman saved the most impressive piece for last. He cued a CGI reenactment of Jessie Bellaire's last moments on earth. Though an animated figure, it was shapely, clad in high heels and carrying a wineglass in her right hand. As the video began, she came up the stairs with a phone in her left hand, presumably taking and sending the selfies to Armstrong. Even the crown was on her head.

The Captain and Vince were both thinking, *wow, Brickman certainly has computer skills.*

Max thought: *I know where this is headed.* And he did.

The figure of Ms. Bellaire set her phone down, where the officers found it. Twirled around on the balcony and raised her glass. The camera view shifted to a close-up of her left foot as the heel broke, then immediately back to a rear shot of everything Hanover experienced, except the fall. CGI Jessie tumbled in slow motion, the camera following her over the top of the railing. It switched to the wine spilling, the glass breaking, Miss Bellaire's left shoe flipping off her foot and landing in the decorative pot. The final sequence, in slow motion, followed her toppling over the railing, flipping once and landing on the top front of her head, settling on her left side.

When it was done the room grew understandably quiet. Until Vince, in a measured tone, blurted out.

"Max, that's exactly what you visualized Tuesday night. Captain, Max walked thru the exact scenario that night. Tell him, Max."

They all looked at him. Waiting.

Max looked at Vince, as if to say, *but we know more than Brickman knows.* He felt the trap close. On one hand, he would appear dismissive and attempting to steal Dr. Brickman's thunder. That would also risk conveying envy or pettiness. He couldn't have that. On the other hand, his corroboration would affirm the "accidental" nature of the incident that was now in question after finding the note, and a previous one. Brickman was clueless about both. The choice between straightforward and vague was clear. He chose the latter, hoping Brickman didn't have the savvy to sense it. He would be wrong.

"Yes, Vince, I did and as you recall, I also said that was a preliminary theory, that it doesn't rule out foul play because we don't know enough yet. Remember that?"

"Yes, I remember that." Vince caught Max's drift and played along. He had plenty of practice at that over the years. "But Thor, you illustrated that theory extremely well. Didn't he, Captain?"

The captain caught both of their drifts. That's why he was a captain. "Yes, really impressive, Dr. Brickman. Truly. This kind of asset is exactly the reason we're so glad you're on the team."

"Thank you," Brickman said. But he wondered why all this incontrovertible evidence wasn't yet resulting in a conclusive cause of death and a resolution to the case.

"Here's the way this is going to play out." The captain headed toward winding it up. He addressed Dr. Brinkman, "Has anyone else seen this computer model or the binders?"

"No, sir."

"Good. Let's keep it that way. Understood? None of that leaves this room. If we're clear let me know."

Three 'yes, sirs' followed.

"Good. Here's the page we'll all be on." Captain Haskins was as uneasy about Brickman not being fully in the loop as Brickman was unaware that he was not fully in the loop. Based on who knew what and didn't, he had been strategizing his summation. Like Max, he chose to be vague but was even worse at it.

"Unless and until, uh, unforeseen further evidence surfaces, we will maintain an inquiry status with the public and in the department, based on a probable cause of death as a senseless accident, though in our ongoing inquiry, as always, we will follow any lead that may arise, since we are still in a very early stage...of the inquiry." In his head that went way too long. Normally he was a man of short, straightforward sentences. Max noticed it, too. *He used the word "inquiry" three times. In one sentence.* "Dr. Brickman, again, truly impressive work. Please keep these binders, photos and video under lock and key for now. Thank you."

Subdued, Dr. Brickman assented, "Yes, sir, of course."

"Really remarkable, Thor," Vince agreed enthusiastically.

Max threw in a lackluster, "Indeed."

The captain signaled the meeting was over. "Gentlemen, be safe out there. Let me know what you need." The detectives exited with him.

Dr. Brickman stood for their exit, then sat and remained in his chair. *That didn't go like I figured.* Having made countless presentations in graduate school, sat for critical reviews of his papers, critiques of experiments and faced stony demeanors in many oral exams, he had learned not to take it personally. Almost. After several moments of pondering, he spoke the obvious out loud, "They know something I don't."

On the way back to their desks the detectives briefed the captain on their progress, especially the discovery of the other envelope, which Vince recounted in the same vivid details he told

Max. Just as they were explaining the unviewed security footage, the front desk officer approached.

"Excuse me, Captain. Detectives, there is a woman out front, a Ms. Adele Jacobs, says she has an urgent, confidential matter to discuss. Says she'll wait."

Max responded, "Put her in interview room A. And tell her we don't have much time."

"How about room B?" Vince suggested, "Much less intimidating."

"Yes, sir," the officer said. "And Captain, a quite forceful woman is out front demanding to see you. Jazmine Bellaire. Says she's Jessie Bellaire's mother, from Texas."

CHAPTER 15

"Ms. Jacobs, I'm detective Wilson and this is detective Malone. Would you like some coffee? It's not as bad as the police brew you've probably heard about. Or some water?"

She accepted water. Vince stepped out and returned quickly, leaving the door open slightly. He set a chilled bottle in front of her and took a seat across the table by Max. She thanked him, unscrewed the cap and took three swallows. Her hands trembled slightly as she replaced the cap, then returned them to the top of her purse on her lap. She looked at her watch, fidgeted with a charm bracelet, cleared her throat and pushed her long hair out of her eyes behind her ears, as if she hadn't taken the time this morning to make herself presentable.

Max had already begun his mental profile: *Early forties, no wedding ring, two children, working mom, late for her job, attractive though in her present state, frazzled, clearly afraid of something or someone. This is likely about her Ex or troublesome boyfriend.*

Vince began. "How can we help you, Ms. Jacobs?"

"What I have to say must be confidential. I don't want anyone to know that I'm the one who told you this."

A very loud voice, female, came from the hall in the direction of Captain Haskins office. Vince got up and closed the door.

"Sorry. If this is about a potential crime, can I assume it is?"

120

"Yes."

"Then, first, you are not legally obligated to talk to us. But it's safe to speak freely, that's why we're here."

"But what about testifying in court? Would I have to do that?"

Max fielded that issue. "Only if you receive a subpoena and even then, a deposition is an option, privately before a judge and lawyers for both sides."

"But what's to keep them from revealing my identity?"

"In certain cases, a judge can seal your testimony to prevent it going public, let's say, in case it put you in danger from a defendant. In extreme cases there is a witness protection program."

Vince buffered Max's explaining with, "But we're getting way ahead of ourselves." He pushed gently. "Ms. Jacobs, do you feel like what you have to tell us may put you in danger?"

"Yes. But I don't know who that might be."

Vince slowed her down. "Let me assure you, we will take every precaution to protect you and your rights. Take a moment and then tell us what's troubling you." She took two more swallows of water. Steadied a little, she told them her story.

"Ten days ago, my Ex died."

"I'm sorry to hear that," Vince said.

Max surprised Vince by adding, "Very tough on your children."

"How did you know I have children?"

"Your bracelet. Two? Boy and a girl?"

"Yes. Thank you. It is very hard."

"Go on, Ms. Jacobs."

"Don, Donovan, was the foreman at a warehouse. They distribute cleaning supplies. You need to know Don could be very difficult. He pushed his guys hard. He was hard on everybody.

Early on I just thought he was really strong and decisive, but I finally couldn't take it. But that's another story. Anyway, Don had a way of rubbing people the wrong way."

Vince wanted clarification. "Was he ever physically abusive to you or others?"

"No, not to me. Never. But he picked some fights with guys over the years."

"So, the confrontational type. Go on."

"Yes, but he also went behind peoples' backs. He couldn't keep his mouth shut. He blabbed things that hurt people whether he knew it was true or not. I think he even made things up to hurt people. He'd say, 'Some people just need to be cut down to size.'"

Max was thinking, *I hope she can cut this story down to size. We've got a lot of work to do.*

"Even at church I'd hear him whisper to people, 'You didn't here this from me, but…'" Anyway, two years ago our church split.

Must be humans involved, Max thought, his impatience growing.

"The pastor changed all the signature cards at the bank to spend money the way he and his supporters wanted to. Don sided with the pastor. It got very ugly. The church split. And besides ours, two marriages broke up. But we had other reasons, too."

Max had listened longer than he cared to without hearing the point of her story. He attempted a fast forward.

"Ms. Jacobs, what does all this have to do with why you are here? Are you thinking someone might have wanted to harm Mr. Jacobs?"

"Yes. A lot of people. I'm sorry to say I wanted to hit him over the head in his sleep a few times. But I didn't. That's not what this is about."

"Then what is this about?"

"I found out the day before he, before he died, Don fired someone on the spot for storing something in the wrong racks. And that wasn't the first time. With Don, you towed the line or you were gone. Another time..."

"What happened that day, Ms. Jacobs?" Max redirected her.

"Don was closing up the warehouse. The fire department figured as he was putting a forklift away a pallet of bleach got knocked off a rack onto a pallet of ammonia - that was stored in the wrong place!" She spoke the last part with defiance as if defending a man she clearly did not admire. "Do you know what happens when those things mix?"

"Chloramine gas. Very toxic." Max answered.

"Max, that must have been the hazmat call off Harding near the airport."

Max was aware of it. Thomason told him he and Hanover worked it, but he didn't offer that. He wanted Ms. Jacobs to get to the point. He had an idea how to do that.

"That's the one." Ms. Jacobs lower lip began to quiver. Vince reached for the tissues always kept under the table. "The fumes killed him. They said he couldn't get out in time."

Vince handed the tissues to her and intended to give her a break, but Max forged ahead strategically, and unconscionable.

"Ms. Jacobs. Do you get a bigger settlement if it was an accident or foul play?"

"Max!"

Ms. Jacobs flared. "Damn you! What kind of question is that? I have no idea. How dare you! I came here because yesterday I went over to his house to prepare some things for the funeral, and

I found this!" She pulled a white card-sized envelope out of her purse, slammed it face down on the table and sobbed.

It was not Max's finest hour. But her point soon became crystal clear.

"I apologize for my partner, Ms. Jacobs."

Max said nothing. He reached for the envelop but Ms. Jacobs snatched it away.

"I want your guarantee my identity will kept out of this! And my kids!"

Vince tried to reassure her and told her the truth, "Ms. Jacobs, like I said, we are here to look out for you and your rights. We can't give you a full picture until we know what we're dealing with here."

She gathered herself and continued, "No matter what I thought of Don, he's my kids' father. I just want to know what really happened."

"I can guarantee you we want the same thing." Vince's empathy won her over. She released the envelope.

Max picked it up. Turned it over. No postage. No postmark. Just a handwritten name:

Donovan Jacobs

The look Max gave Vince said, *are you thinking what I'm thinking?* Vince was. It took great effort to remain stoic. Both resisted taking a deep breath.

"Well, open it! What are you waiting for?" She aimed her agitation at Max.

He slipped a plain white card from the envelope. Mr. Jacob's name was on one side. Vince leaned in. Max turned it over. It took even more effort to remain measured and professional as they read:

You have sown discord and corrosion. Prepare to reap.
Put your affairs in order. Your life is required of you.

The Red Angels

Silence.

Ms. Jacobs broke it.

"Well?"

Max finally responded. "You did the right thing coming here, Ms. Jacobs. My next questions are very important, if you want to remain off the radar. Has anyone else seen this note? Or have you spoken to anyone about it? Think carefully. Anyone?"

She shook her head. "No. No one."

"Are you sure?"

"Yes. Yes. I was too scared."

Vince sympathized, "Of course, that's only natural given the situation."

Max piggybacked. "And actually that's good, Ms. Jacobs. Not sharing this information is very much in your favor and ours."

Silence again. The detectives would have to improvise. That was not new, but the situation was unprecedented.

Vince began. "Detective Malone is right. You did the right thing bringing this to us. We know it was difficult. Normally, at this point we would step out of the room to confer with each other, no one else, just he and I. But we want you to have complete trust in us, so we're not going to do that this time."

"Thank you."

It was Max's turn to solo. "Ms. Jacobs. It's understandable that this has rattled you, as it would anyone in your, in your…"

"Grief," Vince filled in the blank.

"Yes. As investigators, we know that broadcasting this kind of evidence can make it fifty times more difficult to solve the case. Because the perpetrator knows we have a trail to follow and are on it." He looked at Vince, "Right, detective?"

"Exactly."

"So, what do I do? I mean, what do you want me to do?" Ms. Jacob directed at Vince. But Max answered.

"Something very simple, but difficult. For your sake and your children."

She waited. So did Vince.

"Nothing," Max said.

"Nothing?" Ms. Jacobs was confused.

"Yes. I know that's hard to hear. But for now, go about your usual routine. Go to work. Pick up your kids. Make dinner tonight. And do it again tomorrow. Right, detective?"

"Right. In the meantime, we are required to bring our Captain into this. He's a fierce advocate for victims of crime and a better man than either of us. You can trust him."

She nodded.

"Good. Now, Detective Malone and I will begin what we call an inquiry, not an official investigation, to avoid tipping off the perpetrator. We'll get the hazmat report and things like security footage. What else, detective?"

Max took over. "We need your help with one other thing. It will give you something to do besides nothing, which is very important as well. Start making a list of people Mr. Jacobs rubbed the wrong way, especially the more volatile ones, say, over the last two years - with as much contact information for them as you know."

Vince added a caution, "Do not contact or call any of them or snoop around, like trying to find the man Mr. Jacobs fired. That's our job."

"Ok." Having unburdened it all she wilted like a plant in summer heat.

"Drink some more water, Ms. Jacobs. It's a lot to process," Vince said in his characteristic compassion. Tears welled in her eyes again. He handed her another tissue.

Max waited a moment before continuing. "Ms. Jacobs, get that list directly to us, say, later tomorrow afternoon."

"Or even Saturday," Vince suggested.

"Yes, or by then. Put it in a sealed envelope with only our names on it, Wilson and Malone." Both officers slid their cards over the table. "Can you do that?"

"Yes. I can do that."

"If we're not here leave it with the officer at the front desk. We'll let him know to expect it."

"Alright." All the air had gone out of her.

Vince did what he did so well. "Ms. Jacobs, you were very brave to bring this to us. I can't imagine
how long last night was for you, wrestling with this. I am sorry for your loss, for you and your children. When is the funeral?"

"Thank you," She directed that only to Vince. "Not till next week."

He assured her again, "We will do everything we can to bring resolution and beyond that, some closure. That's why we do what we do. It will take some time. So, be patient and hang in there."

"Thank you."

He asked if she needed a moment, he would walk her out. She was ready to go. Late for work. He escorted her all the way to the street and returned. Interview room B was empty. Good thing. He was planning to take Max's head off. Instead, he got a text from him, "Meet me and the captain out back. His suburban. Early lunch. SATCO on me."

CHAPTER 16

Thursday morning 11:10PM – Day 4

Vince and Max were quiet on the ride to lunch. They listened to the captain download the drama of his meeting with Jessie Bellaire's mother. Naturally, she was devastated by her daughter's death. But beyond that, she became completely unhinged and expressed it in rage, particularly toward Tony Armstrong. The captain told them it was very telling how much she knew about him. She planned to sue him into poverty. She would own every hotel, mineral right, all his holdings, the estate in Lynwood Downs, the home off Arno Road, everything, even his private plane.

"She even knew he owns a Gulf Stream G280!"

She demanded to take her own investigator to the scene and aimed her ire at the police for not doing enough, even railed about the heartless way they contacted her. If she found out the police were negligent in any way, she threatened to sue Nashville. Of course, the captain peppered his description of the encounter with 'Lord, have mercy.'

"Sounds like she lost more than a daughter," Max surmised.

"Yes, it was obvious she lost the gravy train, too. The way she carried on I wondered which one she's more upset about. Lord have mercy, she was a sight."

Along the side street by SATCO, the Captain finessed the suburban into a free parking spot even though there were two metered spaces open directly across the street. He hated to pay for parking almost as much as he hated tepid coffee. As he turned off the engine he said, "Vince, you're awful quiet. What was the meeting about with that lady, Ms. Jason?"

"Ms. Jacobs," Vince corrected, "Her Ex was killed in that chemical spill ten days ago on east Harding."

"Oh, right. That was terrible. What did she want?"

Neither detective spoke. Vince finally did.

"Just show him, Max."

Max took the card out of his jacket in a clear evidence bag.

The captain erupted. "No! Not another one! Dear God, Almighty." In anyone else's mouth it would have been an exclamation bordering on cursing but coming from him it was genuine prayer.

Max tried to give the short version of Ms. Jacob's story, but Vince kept interrupting to elaborate. The tension between them became obvious. The captain finally had enough.

"Did you two have a fight at recess? What's going on?"

They both spoke. Vince deferred. Max explained his abrasive tactic with Ms. Jacobs, his right foot bouncing up and down involuntarily. He came as close as he ever got to an apology. "I admit it was not a kind calculated risk, and certainly not what Ms. Jacobs deserved."

The captain's tone carried what he expected, "Well, Max, that's in the ballpark of an apology, but the other audience for it is not here."

"Yes, sir. I will, sir."

Captain Haskins put an elbow on the center armrest and leaned his face into his interlocked fingers. He took a deep breath.

Didn't say a word. Just breathed. Max and Vince thought he really might pray or start the engine and head back to the station. Finally, he said,

"We're here. I called the manager and told him we're coming. Let's eat. We're gonna need it. Cause we're going back to my office and we're not leaving till we have a damn good plan for this. And lunch is on Max."

They sat outside. Chit chat was impossible. The sky a cloudless blue. People came and went around them. Greeted each other. Talked and laughed. Oblivious to the storm clouds the officers were under. Classic rock provided the soundtrack to a classic spring day. Max's mind couldn't help itself. *Like a Rolling Stone by Bob Dylan 1965 from Highway 61 Revisited.* Vince thought about challenging him to play the 'name that song game' to engage the captain. But he didn't. Besides, everyone knew that song.

Instead, Vince said, "Forecast calls for thunderstorms later today."

"Sure couldn't tell it sitting here," Max responded.

The captain had nothing to add about the weather.

Max's name came over the speakers. He retrieved their food. The deck got more crowded.

A slight breeze picked up. Someone higher up the chain of command cued "Free Fallin." Officers Hanover and Thomason came up the steps to the deck as Tom Petty sang, "She's a good girl / loves her mama / loves Jesus and America, too."

Officer Hanover greeted them. "Hello, Captain, detectives. Perfect day for this place."

Only the captain responded, "Yes, it is. So far. Storm on the way, I hear." The officers continued inside to the growing line. After only a moment Hanover returned and spoke to Max.

"Thomason knows my order by heart. Detective, can I have a few minutes for that report? If that's alright, Captain?"

She caught Max completely off guard. He said they had to get back to the station 'pronto.' He never used the word 'pronto.'

"Go ahead, Max," the captain said, "but make it quick. We've got a lot of ground to cover."

The two of them stepped out, beyond the crowd and noise.

"She's a fine officer," the captain said, "Wants to do what you guys do. I believe she could."

"Yes, sir."

"Something going on between those two?"

"No, sir. I know he respects her, as an officer."

"Come on, DEE-tec-tive. Pretty woman like that? A loner like Max. But he is a hard nut to crack. I'm sure she's deTECTed that."

"Yes, sir. Good one, sir."

Out on the sidewalk, Max told Hanover if this was about Dr. Brickman it could wait.

"No, detective, I'll fill you in on that another time."

"Then what is it?"

"I had an encounter at an incident about ten days ago and it got me thinking about the Davidson and Bellaire cases. But I certainly don't mean to walk on your turf."

Max, the detective, was all business on the outside. But Max, the man, glanced furtively at her dark hair, her mouth, her hands. He moved downwind of her to catch a hint of her White Linen perfume.

"No worries. What happened?"

"A man died in a chemical spill at a warehouse."

"I remember. Thomason told me you guys worked it with Hazmat."

"Right. We were maintaining part of the perimeter. A few people were hanging around and I heard a guy say he heard the fatality was the foreman, a man named Jacobs."

"Go on." Max was all in.

"This other guy rips on Jacobs, saying how the 'bum' had it coming. I pulled him aside and asked why he thought that. He went into a whole litany of things…"

Max lost track of her story for a moment enjoying her use of the word 'litany.'

"I'm sorry, go back to 'litany of things.'"

He must have appeared distracted because Hanover said, "We can do this later, detective."

"No. go on, I was just… never mind, please, go on."

"I'll make this quick. This guy claims nobody got along with Jacobs. He was a brawler, a liar, a contentious SOB and even part of breaking up a church this guy used to attend."

Max was intrigued. This corroborated Ms. Jacobs' profile of her Ex but he still didn't see a connection to the other cases.

"Ok. But how do you connect that with Davidson and Ms. Bellaire?"

"This is gonna sound a little out there, detective. But I've heard you say a case has to be looked at from many angles."

"Yes, and really, I'm intrigued. More than you know."

"I know you're not a religious, that is, you operate from other than a God point of view, I'm saying that badly, I'm sorry."

"No, that's pretty accurate. No need to apologize. Go on."

"Well, here it is. A few days later, on the 6th I was reading Proverbs 6 because our church is going through Proverbs this month, and anyway, a verse jumped out."

That's actually very charming, reading chapter 6 on the 6th. Max thought.

"It described exactly the kind of man that guy at the warehouse said Jacobs was, and what happened to him." She had already pulled up the verse on her phone. "I'll just read part of it detective, so bear with me."

"I'm listening," said Max, the detective. Max, the man, watched her lips as she read.

"'A troublemaker and a villain, who goes about with a corrupt mouth, who plots evil with deceit in his heart, he always stirs up conflict. Therefore, disaster will overtake him in an instant; he will suddenly be destroyed – without remedy.'"

Max made the connection himself. "So, I can see it wasn't much of a leap to think that's what happened to Abe and Miss Bellaire."

"Yes, sir, it may be nothing, and I know it comes from left field, but that's not all."

"Ok, I see how those connections can be made, and I want to explore this some more, and soon, but I need to get going."

"I know, I'm sorry. Detective. One last thing. Our pastor at Cool Springs Church has been in the Old Testament. Last week…"

Max interrupted, "Wait, do you go to that holy mess church?"

"Yes, well, that's what some people call it but it's the Cool Springs Church off Moore's Lane.

I also work security and traffic some. Why?"

"Nothing. Go on."

"Real quick. The pastor used two stories to illustrate Psalm 73. But that's not important now. One story was King David's son Absalom. He rebelled and died running away on a horse when his long hair got tangled in the branches of a tree!" She paused for effect. It worked. That story rang a bell in Max's Catholic training. Now it rang louder than ever. *David's son, Absalom. Davidson/Abe. No, it can't be that glaringly tidy.* But Hanover was not done.

"And the other story was about Jezebel, a wicked lady. She died when she was thrown from a balcony. And her body was eaten by dogs!"

The Rubik's cube in Max's head started spinning. The tiles flashed by like note cards in a tornado. An enlarged picture of the zealot killer they were potentially dealing with began to take clearer shape in his mind. It took him a bit to harness his thoughts. Max, the skeptic, was a long way from all in but couldn't deny the clear line drawn through Hanover's observations. Max, the man, was more drawn to her than ever and understanding why. This was a bold, incisive move coming to him, of all people, advancing a biblical MO for these cases and yet completely unaware of the three prophetic notes.

Uncharacteristic for the great Max Malone, he stumbled over himself.

"Officer Hanover, I think all this is not nothing. In fact, I think you could be, I mean, it could be quite something."

"Thank you, sir."

"And no, you did not walk on my turf. In fact, you may have connected some crucial dots, and, uh, opened a window I sensed might be there but wasn't able to, uh, to color outside the lines of my own perspective. I'm not even sure what that meant. But thank you."

Vince rescued him, "Max, we packed your lunch to go. Come on. Captain's in the car. Good to see you, Helen."

Hanover apologized again. Max said, "No need. And I want to hear your take on Brickman, too."

"Yes, sir. Thank you."

He and Vince hustled to the suburban. The wind was gaining strength.

"Bet that storm's sooner than later," Max said on the way.

Vince had no response. They got in.

"That took longer than expected, sir. Sorry."

"Forget it. Probably important, right?"

"Yes, sir. It was."

They caught the red light at twenty-first.

"Good cop, Hanover," the captain said to Max.

"Yes, sir."

"Beautiful woman, too, wouldn't you say?"

"Yes, I suppose so, sir."

Vince held his tongue. But Max could feel his opinion from the back seat.

Max changed the subject. "Sir, I think it's time we put a team together on this."

A gust of wind rocked the suburban slightly and sandblasted the left side with dirt and debris.

Change was in the air. Max Malone had spoken two apologies, one sincere 'please' and a genuine 'thank you' all in less than an hour.

"Here it comes," Vince said from the back seat.

CHAPTER 17

Thursday afternoon 12:30PM – Day 4

By the time the three arrived back at headquarters, the storm reduced the blue sky to a narrow band on the northern horizon. Rain hurled loud drops the size of silver dollars on the windshield. The wind blew strong enough to make opening a car door perilous. Just as they entered the building the sky opened up.

"That's gonna be a frog strangler, as my dad used to say," the captain said.

Vince followed suit. "My dad used to say, 'Better call Noah, reserve another seat.'"

Max's memory bank served up something from his mother. "My mom would say, 'Kids, looks like the Lord wants us to read a book today.'"

Vince couldn't resist, "Another reason you'd win big on Jeopardy. Literature for 800, Alex."

The captain took the helm. "My office. Ten minutes."

"Yes, sir."

The turbulent storm going on outside mirrored the beginning of their strategy meeting. The main contention was whether to include Dr. Brickman in the task force. Max squared off against Vince and the Captain. He argued Brickman was untested in a team setting and an unknown factor in highly confidential matters. For Max, brilliance did not outweigh those factors. Again, Vince was the only one in the room aware of Max's added resistance owing to Brickman's risky experiment that blindsided Hanover. Even Max Malone did not have the cojones or the evidence to state openly his vague suspicions about Brickman's history with Jessie Bellaire or the card on his desk with the uncanny resemblance to the three death threats. Max lost. The captain prevailed.

They all agreed the primary concern was keeping a tight lid on the notes. The nature of that threat in the community would spread like a forest fire and adversely hamper the investigation.

"And can you imagine?" the captain added, "Ms. Bellaire's mother camping out here with lawyers!"

Max contended strongly that Hanover and Thomason should join the task force. They had proven track records and were present at both scenes. The other two agreed. Max also relayed that in his conversation with Hanover at lunch she had some insights worth hearing. He thought it best the details come from her.

"So, that's six of us," the captain said. "Vice will continue to monitor the drug angle at Davidson's but remain outside this loop. Are we on the same page so far?"

"Yes, sir," Vince responded immediately.

The captain looked at Max to get a "Yes, sir."

"Lord have mercy, boys, we've got an uphill road ahead of us."

"No shit," Max muttered. The captain gave him a look.

"No shit, sir."

The captain called the next move. "Take fifteen. I'll reach out to Dr. Brickman and the officers. Let's reconvene in Conference B as soon as Hanover and Thomason can get down here. Vince, commandeer that room for the afternoon. Kick out anyone you have to, on my orders."

"Yes, sir, I'll take care of it."

But the meeting would have to wait. The detectives didn't get to their desks before a tornado warning was issued across Davidson County for the next hour and a half. They all remembered the tornados that struck in and around downtown Nashville. Vince called his family to make sure they sheltered in place. Under the guise of the impending meeting, Max called Hanover to check on where she and Thomason were weathering the storm. They were hunkered down in the parking garage across from SATCO. He carried it off professionally but ended the call with 'stay safe' and immediately felt awkward. Caring didn't come naturally. The captain directed all personnel to the basement briefing room till the warning lifted. He intended to prep them for deployment in the storm's wake. Outside the wind and rain swept the streets clean of debris, pedestrians and almost all traffic.

Max went by his desk to grab the raincoat he kept there. He headed outside to move his truck closer to the leeward side of the building to minimize the risk of any damage. Ten steps out of the building it began to seem like a bad idea. The rain raced vertically across his path. He held onto a railing to keep from being knocked down by a gust, made it to the truck and moved it a half dozen spaces to a more protected corner of the building.

Just as he got out to dash into the back of the station, he felt a bright flash and deafening BANG! A thirty-foot light pole crashed onto the open spaces his truck had occupied. *Ha! Damn lucky. Cheated death again.* He felt a defiant euphoria as the storm raged, though it sounded strangely muffled. His ears were ringing. Eric Clapton sang in his head, "Let it rain, Let it rain. Let your love rain down on me." *1970, his debut solo album.* The rain intensified.

The entrance back into the building was almost invisible in the torrential downpour. He felt a little disoriented. A gust knocked him off balance. He fell. Someone forcefully grabbed him and walked him under the portico, swung the door open and they were inside.

"Detective, are you OK? Man, that was close." It was Dr. Brickman.

"Yea. I think so. My ears are ringing. What were you doing out there?"

"Just got back. I was eating take out in my car waiting for a break to dash back in. Saw you move your truck. Then the flash. Wow!"

"Yea, I've never been that close to a strike."

"I nearly parked by your truck for protection, but that pole would've flattened my Karmann Ghia. Looks like we both dodged a bullet."

As soon as the worst of the storm passed, calls came in from all across the city. Beat officers scattered to check for injuries and direct traffic around downed trees, power poles and swollen streams. All other staff and officers returned to their desks and called their families. Power outages and flooding affected a few areas. It was still nearly four hours till dusk so better an outage with some daylight left. Everyone breathed a sigh of relief. Music City seemed to have dodged a bullet, too.

The captain called Max and Vince to his office. A 10-64 had come in off West End at 20th Avenue near a construction site. Max requested Hanover and Thomason meet them there. The captain said he already made that call. A team was en route. The detectives drove separately. Vince wanted to get home as soon as he could after.

Max hummed his theme song. Then stopped. In light of all that had happened in the last four days the tune made it feel too much like a TV cop show. This was real. Life and death. All week long had been real. And surreal. The bizarre cases and proximity of the lighting strike opened a place inside him. Something he tried to bury with his mother, a window he still sensed was there but refused to open. It always came accompanied by the same song. "The Long and Winding Road," *the Beatles, 1970, from Let It Be, their 20ᵗʰ number one, released a month after the band broke up.* The pathos in Paul McCartney's voice in his head threatened to undo him. He had to fight it off or it would put him off his game. He had to be 'on.' Paul wouldn't let up, "Don't leave me waiting here / lead me to your door." It wasn't inquieto. It was more focused. A longing he drowned in a river of Scotch many times. To shake it off, he called Vince to see how close he was. The window closed.

"Just walked up. Looks like you're right, Max. The hits just keep on coming."

"I'm ninety seconds behind you."

The storm still rumbled. A light rain fell, though the wind had spent itself. The streets were still nearly empty. Max spoke his centering mantra as he pulled up, "La verità è più forte del tempo."

It was a familiar scene - an area cordoned off with yellow tape - officers on the perimeter - Vince and a photographer talking. A white plastic sheet covered a body just off the street in an alleyway. Hanover and Thomason stood at each end of the sheet holding large umbrellas, each with a foot on it in case the wind picked up again. The only thing different was the shape of the sheet. It looked like a triangular pup tent draped over just one waist-high tent post.

"What have we got, Vince?"

"From ID on the body, Sydney Sera, 54. Deceased. Recovered his brief case twenty yards downwind against a fence. County building inspector. Tracing a tag now we believe is his."

"Anything to indicate what he was doing here?"

"No, maybe his phone will tell us more."

Max didn't want to think what he expected Vince to find in the briefcase.

"Any visible cause of death?"

"That's a yes. Look for yourself."

Max greeted both officers as he walked between the sheeting and the side of the building to keep passersby from glimpsing the body. He invoked a fundamental about detective work he liked to call "Maxims." Hanover and Thomason had heard this one many times.

"Alright, take it from the top. Let's start with what we've got."

He squatted to lift the edge. The officers assisted. Max had seen a lot of things, but this week kept making the top of the list. Mr. Sera was lying face up. A piece of rebar protruded three feet from the middle of his forehead. His first thought, *wow, bullseye*, he kept to himself. The tiles in Max's Rubik's cube began to multiply. Usually, he kept them to himself as mental notes. This time, for whatever reason, he spoke them out loud.

"Shouldn't there be a much larger pool of blood behind Mr. Sera's head? Rain and wind likely washed it away. The small pool still here looks like his heart kept beating till after the heavy rain stopped." It reminded Max of a nimbus on medieval icon paintings of martyrs, except the light rain pushed the blood in six or seven short streams like spikes on a crown. He kept those thoughts to himself. "The wind and rain were strong when this happened, or just after. Mr. Sera couldn't have been conscious for long." In Hanover's presence he couldn't help adding, "But Brinkman, the boy genius, will tell us more."

Hanover smelled the sarcasm, but Max's verbal assessments emboldened her to speak. She remained professional. "Detective, the rebar went all the way into the asphalt. Not sure how far."

"Thank you, officer. That took a great deal of force." This came from a man who avoided 'thank you.' And who just avoided a lightning bolt that could have delivered a similar fate to the one he was viewing.

Max stood and looked up the wall of the building. "Vince, this building doesn't look under construction."

"It is on the other side. Scaffolding, crane, a covered pedestrian walkway. Looks like a refurb. One of those small, hip hotels going up everywhere."

"Maybe Mr. Sera was here for an inspection. I'll get the builder's info, find out if a crew was here today before the storm. Let's see if we can get up there within the hour. Hanover and Thomason, canvas the immediate line-of-sight buildings, please. See if anyone saw anything."

Max walked around the corner, and up the sidewalk twenty yards to look up at the construction side.

"Is it just me or did anyone else hear Max just say 'please?'" Vince asked Hanover and Thomason.

"I got a 'thank you,' too," Hanover bragged.

"Of course, you're his favorite." Vince quipped.

"Whatever, sir," Hanover protested.

"You know he just missed getting struck by lightning down at the station."

"What?" Hanover asked with genuine concern.

"He went out to move his truck away from some light poles. Lightning knocked one down. He wasn't thirty feet away from the flash."

"Is he OK?"

"Says he is. Maybe a touch of shock therapy knocked some common courtesy into him?"

"Ok, that's a little funny but seriously, is he OK?"

Max returned. "Dammit, shouldn't Brickman be down here? Where the hell is forensics?" The sound of a VW engine punctuated Max's outburst.

Vince confided to Hanover, "See, he's fine,"

Dr. Brickman parked his Ghia in front of Max's F250 and hurried to the scene.

"So sorry, traffic rerouted, and our team is spread a little thin. What have we got, detectives?"

Vince filled him in. Max walked around to the construction side and put a call in to the builder on the sign. The rain let up. The sounds of traffic on wet pavement increased. Over the next ninety minutes the investigation proceeded. Hanover and Thomason canvased the neighborhood. No one saw anything. Half a dozen people heard crashes they assumed was flying debris. The photographer did his thing. Brickman scoured and mapped the scene. He took a few samples. There were a number of faint bloody footprints, but the rain had spread blood over a large area. Max even tracked some around the corner. Brickman requested shots of the soles of everyone's shoes.

The project manager showed up. He led Max, Vince, Brickman and the photographer four flights up to the roof in hard hats. They found evidence of wind damage, materials scattered randomly, including scraps of rebar. Two of Brickman's team showed up and freed Mr. Sera's body. They managed to transport him to the precinct morgue with the rebar in place. The preliminary consensus was a freak accident caused by the storm. Max informed the captain. He assigned Vince and Hanover to break the news to Mr. Sera's wife. Max, relieved, headed back to the station to file a report. Vince thanked him for taking care of that.

"No worries," Max told him. "I'd rather do a report than make that call."

It was nearly dusk. Another day. Another dance was done.

Walking to his truck Max stopped to envy Brickman's car. *1970, Pacific blue. Original color. Black cloth top. New, but they wore out. Mint interior. Sweet.* The carryout bag still lay in the passenger seat. *Thai Satay. That's on Elliston. Just three blocks from here.* Max's interior Rubik's cube resorted. A question etched itself on a tile: *Any rebar in Brickman's landscaping?* He walked back over to Brickman and Vince.

"Dr. Brickman, maybe sometime Vince and I could come see your landscape project."

"Of course, that would be great. Maybe this weekend?"

"Vince, you in?

"Sure. Let me check what's going on at home."

"Good, lunch Saturday? I'll bring barbeque. Vince, you're in charge of beer. And bring your ukulele."

Max headed to his truck.

Vince looked at Hanover. "Is it just me or did iceberg Malone just act sociable, and normal?"

"Maybe that lightning strike warmed him up a bit," Hanover jested.

Not to be out-quipped, Vince said, "I think I'll call him 'Sparky' for a while."

CHAPTER 18

Thursday Evening 6:10PM – Day 4

Max hit 'send' on the email with the report on Mr. Sera's death attached. He rocked back in his chair, closed his eyes, and exhaled, "Damn, what a week." *And it's not over.*

The captain had already called him about rescheduling the task force meeting for Friday morning at 10 AM. He directed Max to create a timeline starting with the call on Monday night from Ms. Batson about Abe Davidson to the conversation with Ms. Jacobs Thursday morning. *This morning. This week feels a month long.*

The captain informed the detective of his plan to reveal the Red Angel cards to Dr. Brickman, Hanover and Thomason. He wanted Max to read the timeline, without commentary or theorizing, rather than put it on a screen in powerpoint. Max was to make only two copies, one for himself and one for the captain. And put it directly in his hands before the meeting. No digital or paper trail. Also, this way no one could read ahead. No one would have a copy to leak or misplace. And no taking notes. The cards, any other evidence and both copies of the timeline were to be locked in the captain's safe.

At the top of the meeting the captain would heighten the gravity and security by asking everyone to turn off their phones and collect them till the meeting was over. He would require them to put away pads, pens and computers. If Max knew the captain at all, he knew he would tell them they *have been chosen for this based on their character and skill.* The captain would advise the three new team members that once they see this evidence, they will understand its sensitive nature. Last, he planned to put the fear of God in everyone about confidentiality and the dire consequences for anyone who broke that code. Then hand the meeting over to Max.

It was obvious to Max the captain had put a lot of thought into this. He remembered and appreciated again why Haskins was Captain. And the captain was not done.

He expected a deluge of questions after Max finished. But before any Q&A he would address protocol for the evidence. If anyone needed access, like Dr. Brickman for forensic analysis, the check-out and check-in times would be closely monitored. Evidence, photographs photocopies, sketches, nothing left the premises. Anything checked out must be returned to the captain or Max.

Q&A would follow. After lunch, which would be brought in. He expected a long strategy session including action items assigned to everyone.

If Max knew the captain, either somewhere near the beginning or at the end of the meeting, he would remind them all of their *sacred oaths and the high calling of protecting and serving the people of Nashville. He'll thank us, genuinely and profusely. And end with 'Be safe out there. Let me know what you need.'*

When the captain's long call was done, he said, "Got it, Max?"

"Yes, sir. Got it all."

"Max, you're a great cop."

"Thank you, sir."

"So are the others. But between you and me, we're gonna need some outside help on this one."

Max didn't know how to respond.

"I know you're not much on the God factor, Max, but I'm hoping for some divine intervention."

"I understand, sir. I'll take any help we can get."

"Get some rest, Max. Lord have mercy, it's been a hell of a week."

"Yes, sir. You as well. See you in the morning."

Max leaned his chair upright intending to create the timeline before heading home. But there was something he wanted to do more. It took a few moments to silence the risk-averse voice in his head, which wasn't completely successful, but He called Hanover anyway. He wanted to hear her assessment on Brickman before tomorrow's meeting. But that wasn't the real reason. He wanted to see her. To hear her voice. Watch her lips move. He wanted to follow her thought process and the line of her neck down into her collar. He wanted to know her. Anything about her. Does she have a pet? What kind of music she listens to. What happened to her marriage? Anything. He knew to be with her, really with her, was futile. A man like him. A woman like her. But like he told the captain about the case, he would take anything he could get.

She answered. "Detective Malone, hello, sir."

I'm in her contact list. Well, of course.

"Officer Hanover, I'm calling for two reasons. The captain has scheduled a meeting tomorrow morning for several of us and…"

"Yes, sir, I just got a text from him about it. In Conference B at 10:00 AM. I hope this isn't about what happened at the Armstrong house. Dr. Brickman and I squared that away with the captain, sir."

"No, not at all. But that brings me to my second reason for calling. Before the meeting I'd like to hear your full take on Dr. Brickman. He and I haven't gotten off on the best foot."

Why did I say that? Totally unprofessional.

"If you like, sir, I can do that in the morning before the meeting."

"No, that won't work. The captain assigned me something I have to take care of during that time. I'm just leaving HQ. What about now, or I mean, in the next half hour? If you're done with your shift."

"Yes, sir. I need to stop by my place to feed the dog and let him out for a bit. And get out of this uniform."

She has a dog. I've never even seen her out of uniform.

"This would only take about fifteen minutes."

"Alright, what about the Commodore Grille on West End? A songwriter friend of mine is playing there tonight. I was gonna head over. She's really good."

She likes singer-songwriters.

"I don't want to interrupt your plans."

"No worries, sir. She doesn't start for a while."

"Alright, let's say forty-five minutes?"

"That works, sir."

Max used the next few minutes to begin the timeline for the meeting, but he found it difficult to concentrate. *After Brickman I can ask her about her dog. Or maybe ask about the dog first. No, less professional. Brickman first. Then the dog. What am I? In high school?*

He wrote a few lines in the timeline.

Wonder if she's eaten? Probably not. Should I offer? No, best get in and out.

He wrote a few more lines.

149

What if she mentions food? No way. Not gonna happen after last time. News anchor and motivational speaker? Am I really that stupid?

After fifteen minutes he had only written two entries. It was time to go. *Don't want to keep her waiting.*

Traffic crawled way too slow for an Irish Italian. He was tempted to use his siren and lights tucked in the front grille. But resisted. He arrived before Hanover. He thought about having a drink to calm down. *No, alcohol on my breath? With my history? Wonder what she knows about my history?*

Just as the hostess asked, "How many?" Hanover came through the door. He knew it. She was even more beautiful out of uniform. Her dark hair was down. Jeans. White button up. Buttoned all the way up. Blue sweater around her shoulders. Max forced himself not to look her up and down. But he added her profile to his profile of her.

The hostess repeated her question. "Two," Max replied as Hanover walked up.

"Detective."

The hostess asked, "Bar or table in the listening room?"

"Listening room," Hanover answered. And then said to Max, "Is that alright? I want to get a seat in case it fills up."

"Sure." He would have agreed to anything.

The hostess seated them. A waitress introduced herself and asked about drinks.

"Water with lemon for me," Max said to her. Then to Hanover, "I've got more work to do at home. Bloody Mary with gin for you?" That was the drink she had last time.

"That's a Red Snapper," the waitress said.

The drink was part of her growing profile in Max's head: Believer. Beautiful. Confident. Compassionate. Sharp mind. Good shot. Divorced. Dog owner. Bloody Mary with gin, Red Snapper.

"Yes, sir, please."

"We're off the clock. You can relax on the 'sir.'"

"Sorry, habit. And sounds like you're still on the job, sir." She said pleasantly.

"Yes, this whole crazy week has been 24/7."

"Isn't that the truth? I've never seen anything like it." She omitted the 'sir.'

The drinks came. The waitress asked if they were ready to order.

"Not for me," Max said, "You go ahead."

"Detective, eat something. The music doesn't start for more than a while. You're just gonna warm up whatever at home, right? This way you can get right to work."

"Well…"

She suggested, "The Hugo salad with grilled chicken is great, good burgers and the bourbon salmon rocks."

"I don't want to take much of your time," he lied. He wanted all he could get.

She stuck out her hand to shake his and said, "Detective, I'm Helen Hanover. How can I help?" They both laughed at the reference. His second bona fide laugh of the week. Both ordered the Hugo salad. He added 'balsamic vinaigrette' to her profile.

It only took a few minutes for Hanover to share her observations about Brickman, all glowing.

She described him as thorough, brilliant, respectful, inclusive, innovative, and remarkably mature for his age. She capped off the accolades with, "Thank heaven we have him."

Hearing one of his mother's common expressions coming from Hanover's mouth detoured him for a moment. He regained his thought and asked her point blank about Brickman literally setting her up for a fall.

Their food came. She ordered another Red Snapper, then briefly described what happened.

Max listened and ate. When she came to a pause he wanted to know, "So, in your mind is he trustworthy?"

She said the experience actually built her confidence in him, and then quipped, "But not in men in general." She laughed.

What a great laugh. "I can understand that. We're a cagey, devious lot."

"So are women, detective. Exhibit A, Jessie Bellaire."

He resisted revealing what he knew to confirm why Hanover was so on target about Ms. Bellaire, but that could wait till tomorrow's meeting. Instead, he pushed back.

"That's an extreme, broad brush to paint all women with."

"Yes, I suppose so. But without redemption we all have some Jezebel in us. Or for men, maybe a prodigal son, like Abe Davidson. I should know. I married one. Whoa, sorry to go so heavy."

There it was. Her core view of things. And an inkling of what happened with her marriage.

Max didn't know which one to respond to. He inclined toward avoiding the personal issue, a habitual function of the carefully monitored distance he maintained between his heart and his head. But something less rational, desire, allowed simple human curiosity to win over clarity about the downside of human nature. Even as the risk-averse voice in his head warned she might turn the same topic on him, he went there. All this mental machination happened in the time it took Hanover to raise her glass, place her desirable lips on the rim, sip twice and set the glass back on the table again.

"Not my business, but where is he now?" *Simple interrogative, good.*

"Here in town. He's a musician. Songwriter. Had some pretty big cuts after our divorce. Even some radio hits. Basically, he decided he had to live his own truth, whatever that means, and apparently our marriage wasn't part of that."

Now that Max had played the personal card, he didn't know what to say next. He had so little practice in the last twenty-five years. He thought about asking what the hit songs were, then decided against that. *Too much about him.* He thought about saying something understanding and simpatico like, "O, one of those Sinatra "I gotta be me' guys." But the fact-checker in his head said, '*Hey Max, duh, that's you.*' A sentence formed in his heart and was heading for his mouth, 'It must be tough hearing those songs on the radio." He had some experience in his twenties with that, having dated a young singer who became quite famous. But feeling the pressure of his silence building he blurted out something with solidarity in it instead.

"What a load of shit."

Her laughter relieved the pressure. Hanover raised her glass and toasted, "I'll drink to that, sir."

Max felt like he did when he hurried home to show his mother an 'A' on a test. He had made Hanover laugh. This created a momentum inside he should have reigned in but didn't. This was real human interaction. He galloped full-on into the other issue.

Though Max's core views of redemption and human nature

diverged from Hanover's, her words about a Jezebel or Prodigal in all of us rang with some truth, just like her observations of the cases this week. He responded by putting a core view on the table.

"As for a Jezebel or Prodigal in all of us, that's fascinating, especially in the week we're having."

"No kidding."

Max's head took over. "Seems to me the propensity for darkness in some people is why we have a job. Why some of us are driven to do justice. We might actually agree on the basic premise." He tried to soften the landing with a deep southern accent, but as soon as it came out, he regretted it.

"As a friend of mine says, 'for whatever reason, most people are no damn good, present company excluded.'" He felt his nerves tighten.

Hanover was unflappable. She lifted her glass and leaned forward on the table. "Detective, I'll go even further. Left to ourselves none of us are very damn good." She took a drink.

He immediately heard his mother's voice in his head. He started, as usual, to keep it to himself but something about Hanover, something safe about her made him say it out loud.

"I know where you're coming from." He leaned forward on the table because the room was filling and growing louder, "My Italian mother used to say to me and my sister Ariana, "I miei tesori, my treasures, God made us and what he makes is good. But we are 'rotto dal peccato' broken by sin." literally, 'rotted by sin.'"

"She called you 'my treasures? How beautiful."

"Yes, and she finished that with, 'But the Lord, 'benedicilo,' bless him, took care of that on the cross.'"

"Exactly. I couldn't put it better than that. She must have been quite a woman."

"Yes, she was."

"I like that 'benedicilo' expression."

Max liked the sound of it in her mouth.

They ate for a bit in silence as people filed in searching for empty seats. Three songwriters took the stage and began a sound check.

Max insisted on paying the bill. Two people Hanover knew asked if they could sit in the other two chairs. Max excused himself, thanked her, apologized for taking so much of her time, said he would see her tomorrow at the meeting, and left. He still had to complete the timeline and make two copies. On the short drive to Love Circle he added to Hanover's profile: 'unflappable', 'safe', 'forthright', 'great laugh' and 'thank heaven.'

At home he grabbed his laptop and the bottle of Wild Turkey. There were about five shots left. Maybe more. In his mind having dinner and a real conversation with Hanover certainly qualified as a special occasion. He headed for his recliner in the music room, poured one drink and downed it. In twenty-five minutes, he completed the timeline, without "commentary or theorizing." He poured another drink, sat it on the side table and got up to put on some music.

Quoting his mother to Hanover made him miss her. He had the perfect song for those times. He found the LP, "Baby, I'm-a Want You." He cleaned it, carefully set it on the turntable, hit pause, repeat and placed the needle over the space before track four. Instead of sitting down he stood at the sliding glass door that led to a small balcony. Drink in one hand. Remote in the other. The Nashville night cityscape lit up before him. He hit play. The scratching sound surrendered to the smooth, clear voice of David

Gates singing "Everything I Own, *1972 by Bread, written by Gates for his dad after his death.*

"You sheltered me from harm / kept me warm / You gave my life to me / Set me free." Thoughts of his mother and Hanover overlapped. On the Rubik's cube in his head, except for 'good shot', 'divorced' and 'Red Snapper', their profiles aligned remarkably.

He downed the whiskey, sank into the recliner and poured another one as Gates lamented, "I would give everything I own / just to have you back again." He finished the bottle. It finished him. The last thing he heard was, "Nobody else could ever know / the part of me that can't let go."

CHAPTER 19

Friday morning early – Day 5

Max woke up in his bed but couldn't remember how he got there. The digital clock read 7:21AM. *What happened to the 6:15 alarm?* He smelled perfume. Estee Lauder White Linen. Someone with dark hair lay next to him under the sheet. Naked. It was Hanover. He knew it. She was even more beautiful out of uniform and clothing. He didn't deserve her and yet there she was. She rolled over to him and whispered, "Good morning, Sheamus. I want you."

The alarm went off. Max woke up in his bed but couldn't remember how he got there. He was alone. The digital clock read 6:15.

He sat up on the side of the bed. *That's gonna make it more awkward than ever around her.* He tried to shuffle the Rubik's tiles in his head to make sense of what he was feeling. But he couldn't. It defied order and logic. The naysayer in his head tried to fool him by pretending nothing passed between him and Hanover last night and to doubt if she was wondering if anything did. The voice argued the futility of his attraction to her. This triggered Michael McDonald in his head, *What a Fool Believes, 1978, The Doobie Brothers from Minute by Minute.* Michael took the view that to a fool, "What seems to be is always better than nothing." Max argued with the singer. *No, Michael, something happened.* He knew it was not nothing and he couldn't reason it away. And he knew why he hoped there was something. Helen was good. Like his mother. In so many ways. And a true believer.

He knew something else, too. He was more lost than ever. He felt something looming, something he had escaped many times. He sensed his day of disaster nearing, his doom about to rush upon him. Death was an occupational hazard. Until her, the impossible possibility of her, he had welcomed it for years. A melody floated into his head, "Till There Was You" *originally 1950 by Meredith Willson, Beatles released it in 1963.*

It took a long hot shower, a double espresso and a call from Vince about the meeting to restore the distance Max maintained and preferred between his head and heart. Until now. Until her.

He left Love Circle thirty minutes earlier than usual. On a day like this he didn't want to take any chances of being late. He had learned in his line of work something always comes up. Two large manilla envelopes lay in the passenger seat. Copies of the timeline. One for Captain Haskins. One for him. The RA notes were in the captain's office safe.

To avoid slowdowns on 440 he tacked over to West End and up. Wedgewood was blocked by crews clearing storm damage. Just as well, as traffic slowed passing the Commodore Grille, the time with Hanover replayed in his head.

To other commuters it was just another building. Not to him. Not since last night. Despite the impending heaviness the day held, he entertained himself thinking someday it should be a stop on the bus tour for tourists. He role-played a tour guide in his head, "Early in the 21st century detective Max Malone became more human in this place. The brass heart on the table marks the exact spot on that Thursday night. Feel free to sit a moment where he did with the lovely Officer Helen Hanover who became a detective and later a motivational speaker. The bartender will serve Red Snappers. It's included in price of the tour."

He made himself chuckle. On a day like this, in a week like this, a chuckle was some kind of miracle. He understood more than ever why young lovers carve their initials into the trunks of trees that have stood the test of time, and years later return as old lovers to sit and remember. Odds were, the Commodore Grill would someday be demolished or completely renovated by a new generation of developers, lovers and memory makers.

For the present it was a seismic shift to have a new bright spot in the landscape. Max had lived in Music City long enough to watch it explode and expand, see new buildings replace old landmarks. In spite of the all the changes it could still be a ghost town of old memories for him. Dead bodies and the agonizing sobs of loved ones haunted the map all over the county and beyond, none more so than the sites of his own brushes with death. A place just off eighth near the old Melrose theatre harbored the grim specter of being shot by a domestic abuser. Max killed the man in the exchange. He knew he came close to his name being added to the memorial to fallen officers on the front of the new headquarters building. He had known some of those officers. Attended their funerals.

Personal ghosts were everywhere, too.

Almost everyone has a young love that didn't work out. Before he met his wife, Max fell in love with an aspiring Country singer, a Nashville native who attended Vanderbilt. They fell in love late nights at Dalt's restaurant on White Bridge Road over malt cake and cold milk and parking under the stars off Highway 96.

Ghosts. Her honesty and tenderness and the way she looked at him brought down all his defenses. She even wrote him a song called "God Told Me" after she declared to Max she heard God tell her he was going to be her husband. He had stopped believing in God before then, but she was a true believer, beautiful and seriously talented. He had long forgotten the melody, but still remembered the chorus: "God told me, you're gonna be my man / we'll take the highs and lows hand in hand / Make me a better woman, be my better man / Baby, baby, just believe and you'll see, God told me."

Three months later her heart did a one-eighty. She went back to an old boyfriend, a rising songwriter whose songs helped her career take off. Max was already a beat cop. He could see they were a strong musical match. Work occasionally took him by the place on Music Row where she told him, in her honest, tender way that she was marrying the former boyfriend. Her not wanting him to hear about it from anyone else affirmed all the more why she was so desirable. And why he fell so hard. He took the news without protest, like he understood, like a scalpel wielded well. But he didn't understand. He wondered but didn't ask what her God had told her about marrying the old boyfriend, and how could she trust God's voice this time. Ghosts.

The next summer he actually attended their wedding at a church on West End. At the reception her new husband removed her garter and shot it at him like a rubber band fight. The garter of that ghost still lived in the back of his top dresser drawer. Ever since then he heard her on the radio or the Muzak while buying groceries or at restaurants. A singing ghost. At a bagel place years later in Green Hills, across from the famous Blue Bird Cafe, they ran into each other. She started to say she was sorry for the hurt and confusion of that time, but a fan interrupted before she could finish. Ghost.

Not long after that Max still remembered exactly where he was when he heard the news of their divorce. That night, lying beside his new wife, Jennifer, in an already troubled marriage he started a song in his head,

> I heard the news today your love is over
> Can't stop my brain now as I lie here in the dark
> Wish there was some way I could offer you my shoulder,
> I really do
> But that might be a little too close to my heart.

In a rare creative flash, he finished the song the next day titled, "The Way You Made Me Need You." But never recorded it.

Max rebounded by dating a series of women. He knew they were remarkable but was unable to trust his heart to any of them. Sometimes a call took him to a neighborhood where they hung out or made love, or past places where he broke up with them with lame lines like 'the brakes are on in my heart, and I don't know why." Ghosts.

And, of course, there was the fiery romance with his younger wife, the 1920's cottage with a porch swing in Richland Hills, the night at the Baptist hospital when she lost the baby, the rocky years, the brewery on West End he frequented many nights after their fights, the law office in Green Hills where he signed the divorce papers and wrote a big check. Ghosts. Max even had a country song with the title "Ghosts, Everbody's Got 'Em." Still unfinished.

But now. Hanover was reanimating the city for him, like Spring did every year across the rolling hills. The peculiarity of Max's profession, dealing in death, was always more dissonant in Spring. The crocuses and daffodils handed off to the forsythia, followed by the redbuds and dogwoods, the lavender-pink and white lace of the forest. Now, in May, all manner of blossoms signaled a return to life. *New steps on old paths* he heard someone say, maybe in a song. He knew he was getting way ahead of himself. But he couldn't fight the thought: *So, this is what hope feels like.*

Driving north on West End by Vanderbilt it felt like the moment in the "Wizard of Oz" when black and white turned to technicolor. Or when the nightmare of Pottersville gave way to the humble glory of Bedford Falls in "It's a Wonderful Life." What was stirring in him made him concede, if only to himself: *If there isn't a God there ought to be for things like this.*

An NES crew repairing fallen lines from the storm detoured traffic just after Vanderbilt over to 21st. The Irish Italian in him slammed the steering wheel and cussed. But he was ahead of schedule, making good time. He took a deep breath and decided to stop for a bagel at the place he and Vince frequented across from Vanderbilt. Passing the spot on the sidewalk where Hanover talked to him just yesterday about the Jacobs incident shifted him into case mode. He lucked out on an open, metered space, popped three quarters in and looked at his watch. 8:15. *Plenty of time.* He grabbed one envelope.

He didn't order to go, thinking he would let the traffic ease and go over the timeline and details from the surreal week - ruminate on death while the world came alive around him. From where he sat, he could look up and see Jessie Bellaire's building, and the balcony he and Vince stood on just two days ago.

As he ate, a beautiful woman came in with a man in an expensive suit. Max profiled them. It's what he did. *Luxurious, long, dark hair, airbrushed looking make up, snug black dress, late forties, single, about 6' tall in two-inch heels, cleavage prominently on display. Someone's well-kept woman. Him? Not in charge enough to be her sugar daddy. Bet he's her lawyer or investment broker.*

The woman was not subtle or soft-spoken. She gave the suit an ultimatum the whole place could hear, "You get me in there or I'll hire someone who can!"

The suit responded quieter, but Max heard him loud and clear, "Ms. Bellaire, the manager is stuck in traffic. Let's have coffee and wait till…"

Max didn't need to hear more. He headed for the door. The guy behind the counter said, "Thanks detective. Be safe out there." He didn't look back to see Jessie's mother get up and follow him. He hurried to the truck and sped away. In his rearview mirror he could see her standing on the sidewalk waving both arms, but in a few seconds he was around the corner. The stark reality of the last four days bore down on him. Even in Spring death stalks the living.

He was fully engaged again.

Max took every shortcut he knew to get to work. It was 8:45 when he reached headquarters. Brickman's Ghia mocked him in the morning shade of the captain's suburban. A crew was loading up the downed light pole and preparing to set another one. He looked for Hanover's silver 4Runner. It wasn't there yet. He got a text from Vince, "Hey Sparky, delivering kids to school. In traffic. ETA about 9:20. Keep you posted."

'Sparky.' Crap. Now I prefer 'Slugger.'

Max grabbed the two envelopes, entered the building through the back and went straight to his desk. He made a separate list of details for every entry on the timeline, to clarify things during Q&A. He considered making copies of the reports from the week, then decided he could pull those up if needed. He got up once to go to the bathroom, careful to put the documents back in the envelopes and take them with him. Dr. Brickman came in. He joined Max two urinals over.

"Big meeting today, sir," he said. "You always bring your work to pee?"

"Yes, I mean, no. Yes, big meeting, lots of ground to cover."

"Yes, sir. We still on for tomorrow at my place?"

"Yea."

Max took his time. Let Brickman wash his hands before doing the same.

"I look forward to being on the team, sir. See you in a few."

Max nodded.

At 9:30 the officer at the front desk rang to say someone was there with the package he was expecting.

Ms. Jacobs. That was quick. He walked to the front desk. No one there. The officer handed him a large, thick manilla envelope labeled only, 'For Detective Malone'. From the way it went the day before he was surprised Ms. Jacobs addressed it to him and not Vince.

"Who brought this?" Max asked.

"A young man about fifteen or sixteen. We can inspect it if you like."

"That won't be necessary. Where did he go?"

"He said a lady gave him twenty bucks to bring it in. As I called you, he left."

"Well, we've got him on video if we need it, right?"

"Yes, sir."

Max returned to his desk. *Good timing.* The information from Ms. Jacobs would become part of the evidence. It was thicker than he expected. He opened it dreading how long her list might be. There was a cover letter. It began:

> Detective Malone,
> My name is Sydney Sera. I'm a building inspector for
> Davidson County.
> If you're reading this, I am probably dead.

Vince came around the corner. "Max, what is it? You look like you just got horrible news."

Max gathered the package and the other two envelopes and said, "We can't do this here. Follow me." He started toward interview room A but didn't want to take the time to turn off all the mics and cameras and make sure no one was behind the mirrored window in the observation room. He led Vince out back to the parking lot. They climbed into his truck.

"Max, what is it?"

"This just came to the front desk. I assumed it was from Ms. Jacobs. It's not. I only read the first lines." He held up the cover letter and read it out loud.

> Detective Malone,
> My name is Sydney Sera. I'm a building inspector for
> Davidson County.
> If you're reading this, I am probably dead.

"Ho-ly crap," Vince said, drawing it out.

I have good reason to believe my life is in danger. I am deeply ashamed to admit this, but for the last three years I have been taking payoffs from a large construction company to falsify inspections. This enabled them to cut corners, increase their margins and secure large bonuses, millions, by meeting or beating deadlines.

My motive does not justify the wrong I've done and the harm I've contributed to.

My dear wife, Sarah, is battling cancer. Her medical bills for surgeries and treatments would have ruined us. The builders paid them somehow through a non-profit.

I rationalized it all until three workers were recently seriously injured in a collapse.

One of them is paralyzed for life. I have sons, too.

The injured workers are suing for damages. Which they deserve. Next week I am scheduled to testify on behalf of the construction company, to lie under oath that they complied with all codes. At this point I still intend to do that, but only under compulsion and fear for my life.

I am scheduled to meet with the builders this week to coordinate testimonies. They know how anxious I am about it. And how scared I am of God's retribution, though I'm not much of a religious man anymore. Last week I received a note threatening my life. It's also in the package. Obviously, they mean business.

I kept detailed records of the dates, job sites and violations: skimping on rebar, using a concrete mix of an insufficient PSI to bear the loads, floors poured too thin, cheap steel lintels over openings, footers dug too shallow, etc. Several contractors are complicit as well. It's all in this package including a thumb drive. In the event something happens to me, I have instructed a loyal friend to deliver all this immediately to you. He also has a letter for my wife to be delivered later, confessing everything and asking forgiveness from her and our children.

If only I had chosen another way. Believe me, I am devastated by my actions. But I know what I deserve. I can only ask God to have mercy on me and my family whatever happens.

In the event I am not around to see it, I beg you to see that justice is done and those young men get the help they deserve.

A weak and broken man, Sydney Sera

"Can you say, 'indictments by lunch'?" Vince said.

Max pulled the documents out of the packet. Invoices, material lists, receipts, a calendar, code forms and a thumb drive. But no threatening note. He checked again, handing Vince each document. Neither said it but they were scanning for a red envelope. Halfway into the pile he found a white envelope, the size of a greeting card with 'Sydney Sera' handwritten on the front. In red ink. He glanced at Vince then pulled the card out. White with a red foil border. 'Sydney Sera' in red ink on the front. On the other side, also written in red:

You have sown deceit and corruption. Prepare to reap.
Put your affairs in order. Your life is required of you.

The Red Angels

An hour and a half earlier Max had been driving down West End with helium in his heart, seeing the world in a new way. Now he slumped listlessly like a losing boxer in the corner after the tenth- round bell.

"Damn! Vince. That's four in four days. What the hell is going on?"

"Do we tell the captain now?".

"No time. The meeting's in five minutes. We'll have to break it to everyone there."

Max's phone rang. It was the captain.

"Yes, sir… Yes, sir, I'm here… Vince is with me… Yes, sir, I'm ready… I understand. Good idea, sir. I can do that… Yes, sir. See you in a few minutes."

"What was that about?" said Vince.

"Yesterday the captain asked me to create a timeline of the three cases for the meeting. He's going to start things, of course, but now wants me to save the RA cards till the end of the timeline. Break it to the team all at once."

"Now we have four! God help us."

"Indeed. And amen.

CHAPTER 20

Friday morning 9:57AM – Day 5

A herd of details about the meeting stampeded through Max's head. The one he kept trying to lasso was whether to sit beside Hanover or across the table. If across, he could glance more naturally but be farther from her. If beside her, more subtlety would be required but proximity had its allure. He leaned toward the latter. He arrived five minutes early to find Thomason sitting next to her. There were six chairs, one on each end. Two on each side. Brickman headed around the end of the table by Hanover. Max suddenly seized upon the clear advantage of taking the chair on the end adjacent to Hanover. He made a beeline for it hoping Brickman continued to the other side. *Where he belongs.* At that moment the captain came in, stepped directly in Max's path and stood behind the end chair.

"Max, why don't you take the seat on the other end for your overview."

"Yes, sir." He handed the captain a manilla envelope. The captain set it on the table with another he brought in. *The RA notes, no doubt.* Max took the seat at the other end, set the thick packet on the floor and fidgeted with the thin manilla envelope in front of him.

Brickman sat across from Hanover. Vince had no choice. He came in thirty seconds later and took the remaining seat.

"Good morning," Captain Haskins began. "We are going to be here for a while. Three items: One. I've taken the liberty to have lunch brought in. Salads with grilled chicken and three choices of dressing on the side, Ranch, Italian and Balsamic Vinaigrette. There is a case of water over by the coffee. That aroma you're smelling is a blend from Paraguay courtesy of Dr. Brickman."

Suck up, Max thought.

"Two. Please, turn off your phones and put them in this basket." All complied. The captain set the basket on the table by the coffee and water.

"Thank you. And three, please, put away any notepads, pens and computers. Max and I have some documents we will need." He took a moment till the team stowed everything on the floor or in cases.

"And you better grab some water or coffee now."

The captain took his seat as Hanover got up. She went over to the side table, retrieved six bottles of water and set one in front of each of them. Max wasn't about to drink the Peruvian blend.

"Thank you, officer Hanover. I trust you are all getting the idea? I want your undivided attention. What we are here about today requires the strictest confidentiality. You are here because you have been closely connected to the incidents of this week. Beyond that, you have been selected for your skill and character to be part of a select task force related to…"

Max knew where the day was headed and had heard the rest of the captain's opening remarks the day before. He tuned in and out, alternately watching Hanover listen to the captain, catching snippets of the captain's speech and trying to spot a trace of anything about Brickman to further jaundice his profile of him.

After a few minutes, the captain turned up the intensity.

"The evidence we are about to view cannot, will not, be photographed, photocopied, sketched or taken off the premises. Anyone checking out evidence may not leave the premises before checking it back in with me or Max. Are we clear?"

'Yes, sirs,' all around.

"I know you have a lot of questions. Please, hold them until after Detective Malone runs us through the events of this crazy week. After that, here's how the rest of our day looks. Evidence will be presented. Followed by Q&A for as long as it takes. Lunch. Reaction. Input. Clarification. And we're not leaving here without a plan with a substantial list of action items for each of us. Before I hand it off," *Here it comes.* Max called it. "Let me remind all of us of our sacred oath and high calling to protect and serve the people of Nashville. Thank you, for bringing your skill, character and devotion to this task force. Detective."

Max and the captain simultaneously pulled timeline sheets out of their envelopes. Max began reading:

"Monday 11:17 PM

Dispatch received a call from a Brie Batson about a body at the gate of the David Davidson residence off Moran Rd. and Old Natchez Trace. Officers including Hanover and Thomason, forensics, Detective Wilson and I responded to find Abe Davidson, 31, deceased, hanging on the inside of the security gate. Abe's father admitted heated altercation over money. After search of premises and brief investigation preliminary cause – horse riding accident – drug and alcohol use indicated.

Tuesday @ 10:30AM

Detective Wilson and I interviewed Brie Batson. Discovered she and Abe dated. She carted rental guitars around town for him. Abe Davidson was planning to leave town in a hurry with Ms. Batson. She verified an altercation the night before over money between Abe and his father. We prevailed upon her not to talk while the inquiry proceeded for the sake of the family.

Tuesday @ 1:30PM

Detective Wilson and I searched Abe's quarters. With the help of a K-9 unit discovered a mid-level drug stash of cocaine, Oxy, meth and marijuana. Street value @ $300K. Evidence of distribution in guitars cases around the city by Ms. Batson. Still undetermined if she was complicit. With the Captain's authorization in coordination with Vice, we put a sting operation in place with the goal of flushing out the upstream sources. That operation is ongoing.

Tuesday @ 5:45PM

Dr. Brickman delivered results of toxicology and cause of death for Abe Davidson. Cocaine, alcohol and pot at debilitating levels. Broken neck resulting in paraplegia, paralysis of all limbs. But the cause of death was asphyxiation. He was strangled by his own hair."

The captain broke in, "There's an example of the need for absolute confidentiality. Imagine his father hearing that bit of information on the news. Heartache on top of heartbreak. Understood?"

oc5dducyucsht

Contrite 'yes, sirs,' responded.

"Go on, Max."

"Tuesday 8:46PM

Dispatch received a call from a Tony Armstrong about a female, fallen from a balcony at his residence on Arno Rd. Officers, including Hanover and Thomason, officers from Williamson County, Detective Vince and I responded. Forensics arrived shortly after. Discovered Jessie Bellaire, 26, deceased from apparent head trauma due to a fall from the balcony. Mr. Armstrong was on the scene, distraught and cooperative. His brother and lawyer, James Armstrong, arrived to console and counsel him. Preliminary assessment: undetermined cause. After a brief interview with Armstrong, he was released. The scene secured for further investigation.

The captain spoke up again, "People, that was all in just twenty-four hours. Monday night to Tuesday night."

No one said a word. Max waited. A nod came from the captain to proceed.

"Wednesday," he paused, took a drink. It was really a move calculated to see if Brickman showed any nerves anticipating whether Max would include the confessional meeting Wednesday morning about his relationship with Miss Bellaire. Brickman took a drink, too. He appeared calm. Max continued.

"Wednesday @ 10AM

Detective Wilson and I searched Miss Bellaire's apartment at 21st and Grand Found love notes from Mr. Armstrong that confirmed his story they planned to meet Tuesday eve at his country place. Then fly out of town Wednesday morning. Discovered some background on Ms. Bellaire. Pulled some security video to view ingress and egress. As yet unviewed.

Wednesday @ 11AM

Dr. Brickman investigated Armstrong residence aided by Officers Hanover and Thomason. Gathered data and discovered no conclusive evidence indicating foul play.

Thursday @ 8AM

The Captain, Detective Vince and I met with Dr. Brickman. He presented his findings from the Armstrong scene, including a CGI rendering of his theory of events around Miss Bellaire's death. His determination: freak accident caused by the combination of a broken high heel and a tipsy woman. Dr. Jenkins toxicology and autopsy report are pending."

Hanover was the only one who wondered why Dr. Brickman was not conducting Ms. Bellaire's forensics. She concluded perhaps the captain wanted to get Brickman into the field. His next comment confirmed that.

"Max, pardon me again. Dr. Brickman did extraordinary work out in the field on this one. Go on."

"Thursday @ 10AM.
Detective Wilson and I interviewed a Ms. Jacobs..."

Hanover gave Max a look of incredulity. Her lips formed an unspoken, "What?" He could feel her look. He paused but didn't look up and kept reading.

"...Her husband was killed in a chemical spill off Harding ten days earlier. Though it appeared to be an accident, her husband, in her words, "had a way of rubbing people the wrong way," so she had some concerns about the way he died."

At this point Max called an audible the captain did not expect. No one expected it, including Hanover.

"Sir, with your permission, Officer Hanover has some insight into Mr. Jacobs' death that will tie some things together in a way that will become even more apparent later. She reported this to me at lunch yesterday."

Vince knew his partner would not go down a random trail for no purpose, even to give Hanover a spotlight.

Brickman thought, *I knew it. They do know something I don't know.*

Thomason was lost. He didn't see any connection between these cases or what the task was in this task force.

The captain looked at Max, then at Hanover. He said, "I'm all ears."

Hanover laid it out exactly as she had done for Max - overhearing the man at the hazmat scene unloading on Mr. Jacobs; the Proverb, which she quoted in full, describing a man like Jacobs and his end. The others thought that was very interesting but when she likened Abe and Miss Bellaire's deaths to King David's son Absalom and Jezebel, lights began to go off.

Vince, of course, connected the dots but so did Brickman and he spoke first to Hanover. "Are you saying, there may be a vigilante zealot or group of zealots behind these deaths?"

Before the room could break out into a free for all, the captain regained the helm.

"People, no comments. No speculation. No Q&A yet. You'll get your chance. Thank you, Hanover, extraordinary police work. Max, was that all you had on the timeline?"

"Yes, sir, except that you intended to have this meeting yesterday afternoon, but the storm blew in." Max looked at Vince. They both knew there was more. He looked at Hanover. There was a new connection between them, forged in something foreign to both of them – trust.

"Right. Well, this might be a good point to take a bathroom break," the captain suggested. "I'll check on getting lunch here a little early. And then we can dive into evidence and Q&A."

"Sir," Vince had a question. "If we're likely to be here through dinner I'd like to let my wife know."

"It's likely. But use your desk phone. And all of you. Talk to no one, not even each other, on this ten-minute break. Are we clear?"

Five unison 'yes, sirs' affirmed it.

"And I mean ten minutes."

Five more 'yes, sirs' stepped in line.

CHAPTER 21

Friday morning 11:30AM – Day 5

When the meeting reconvened, five coffee mugs ringed the table. Everyone but Max retrieved their own from a desk or patrol car. Thomason and Vince had Titans travel mugs. Hanover's read simply, "Breakfast Wine," which Max thought delightful. Brickman's cup quote went philosophic. It bore the image of Rodin's sculpture, The Thinker, contemplating a twist on Descartes' famous maxim. "I think and drink coffee, therefore I am a human bean." The room was as quiet as a chapel. The only sound was the gurgle of the coffee maker brewing a second batch. Captain Haskins drank from his customized cup presented by all the detectives bearing the words, "Lord, have mercy on the boy from down in the Boondocks." He restarted the meeting in his southern Gandalf voice with a stern warning.

"Officers, if I have not sufficiently put the fear of God in you about confidentiality let me try again. If a single fact, an inference, a hypothetical, leaks from this meeting, someone will not only lose a job, but likely a career. Are we clear?"

Four 'yes, sirs' blended with Vince's "Crystal, sir."

"Detective Malone has evidence to present that he and Detective Wilson have gathered. I'm not sure how to describe it. So, I won't try. Detective."

Before Max could utter a word, someone knocked at the door.

Lunch had arrived. The captain made the call to eat first over some general Q&A before heading into what he knew would be a hailstorm of issues. Max and Brickman sparred over a dressing for the salads. Max won.

There were a lot of questions already, about the drug sting, Jessie Bellaire's background, Ms. Jacobs' suspicions. A lot of talk centered on whether foul play was involved in any of these cases. By the gravity of this meeting no one could avoid that implication. And if so where to begin building suspect lists. The captain kept the conversation from running too far ahead on assumptions. At one point he tried to divert some energy by asking Vince how his son's soccer team was doing. That provided only a few seconds of diversion. This was a group curious and hungry for the main course. In less that fifteen minutes the table was clear again. Coffee cups refilled. There was no putting it off. The captain turned the meeting back over to Max.

"There's no best way to do this so I'll read a few other entries in the timeline." He took a drink of water and began, attempting an even tone.

"Monday night, technically Tuesday @ 12:50AM at the Davidson residence. Detective Wilson and I not only found evidence of drug use in Abe's quarters, we also found a note Abe apparently received about a week before his death, which we believe accounted for his erratic behavior.

Tuesday morning @ 9:30AM we revealed this note to the captain."

Billy Sprague

"Captain, I believe you have that note. If you would read it and pass it around."

Dirk Haskins, normally the rock in any storm, was clearly nervous. Even Brickman, the newest in the room, picked up on it. The captain looked in his big envelope to choose the right note. He fumbled a moment. To avoid confusion, he had labeled each note with stickers on the evidence baggies: D for Davidson, B for Bellaire and J for Jacobs. But inside the envelope from an angle the D and B looked similar. He did not want to pull out the wrong one or reveal more than one note at a time. Once he was sure, he showed it to the team. Abe Davidson's name was clearly visible. Instead of reading it, he deferred to Max, handed it to Hanover, on to Thomason, who passed it to Max.

There are a few moments in life that overwhelm, when the capacities of mind and soul are forced to expand with shocking suddenness beyond normal daily parameters. For some on the team, this was one of those moments. More were coming.

Max prefaced reading it.

"As you can see, it's a handwritten note. Addressed to Abe Davidson. It's crumpled because we found it in a trash can by his desk. On the other side, also handwritten, is this message." His right foot began to bounce. He took in and exhaled a deep breathe. "'You have sown poison and agony. Prepare to reap. Put your affairs in order. Your life is required of you.' It's signed, 'The Red Angels.'" Several sighed heavily in disbelief. No one spoke. They had no pens or pads to scribble their tension. Thomason and Dr. Brickman white-knuckled their coffee cups. Hanover tapped the ends of all five fingers together in front of her face. Minds shifted between idle and overdrive. Max passed the note to

179

Thomason. He and Hanover viewed it together. She extended it back toward the captain. He pointed to Dr. Brickman, who took it, looked at both sides, read it silently then passed it to Vince, who handed it back to Max.

"Permission to speak, sir," Brickman asked the captain.

"Not yet, Dr. Detective Malone isn't done."

Max read more from the timeline:

"Wednesday @ 11:45AM the day after Miss Bellaire's death, Detective Wilson and I searched her penthouse apartment at 21st and Grand. The manager confirmed Tony Armstrong paid the bills. Detective Wilson uncovered valuable background on Miss Bellaire from her high school yearbook. Her nickname was Cleo, short for Cleopatra. As Homecoming Queen, she dressed as Cleopatra in the same snake crown she died in. As we were looking at her yearbook, an envelope fell out."

Max looked at Captain Haskins. Steady again, he produced a similar note in an evidence baggie. He showed the team the name on one side, 'Jessie Bellaire.'" Mute incredulity gripped the team. This time he commented before reading it himself.

"As you can imagine, the detectives and I were dumbfounded by the note to the Davidson boy. Wednesday afternoon they brought me this one. It says, 'You have sown treachery. Prepare to reap. Put your affairs in order. Your life is required of you.' Also signed, 'The Red Angels.'"

He passed the note around the table to stupefied faces. Incredulity battled with a tsunami of questions on the minds of Hanover and

Thomason. Brickman appeared ready to run around the room. His feet and legs involuntarily bounced under the table. He had to scoot back his chair to stop vibrating the coffee in every cup.

The captain tried to calm the rising tension with two of his best assets, authenticity and affirmation.

"Lord have mercy and holy crap, right? Under the circumstances you're doing great. Remarkable, really. I was blindsided, too. We all are. Hang on a little longer and we will sort our way through this." The Rock had returned. "Max, go ahead." Dropping the formality of titles helped the atmosphere. The captain didn't calculate that. He came by it naturally.

Max continued the timeline:

"Thursday @ 10:00AM interview with Ms. Jacobs."

He clarified, "The wife of the man Officer Hanover referred to earlier." Hanover gave him a steady gaze and head nod that said, *Go on. I understand why you couldn't say anything yesterday.* He continued reading.

"Ms. Jacobs was more than concerned, actually suspicious, about her Ex-husband's death in the chemical spill. Nine days after his death, she was going through some of his things at his place to prepare for the funeral. She found a threatening note that alarmed and scared her. She brought it to us."

"No way!" Thomason blurted out.

All heads turned toward the captain. The element of surprise was not a factor anymore. Anticipation of another bizarre revelation created a state of stupor.

The captain presented a third note. Addressed to Donovan Jacobs. He read it without comment: "You have sown corrosion and discord. Prepare to reap. Put your affairs in order. Your life is required of you. The Red Angels."

Silence, as the note traveled around the table. Even Brickman knew this was not a moment to speak. Finally, the captain took a soft, measured tone, the one they only heard him use after an officer was injured or killed on duty or someone on the force lost a loved one.

"It's a lot to take in, people. I've never seen anything like it. Before we move into Q&A and strategy, I want you to take a minute. Imagine these notes going public. The media frenzy. The copycats. A flash flood of lawyers and reporters. Here, and at the homes of the families affected. At your own homes. Beyond that, picture the fear spreading through this city, our city. We cannot allow that to happen. It may at some point, but right now we need to do our jobs, our duty, to the families, this community and the law. How do we best protect and serve? That's the decision the detectives and I were faced with the last few days. On my authority we've kept a tight circle on this. Now you are in that circle. Understood?"

Nearly whispered 'yes, sirs' responded.

"Are you with me?"

Same response.

"Now...". Max interrupted him.

"Captain."

"Yes, Max."

"Sir, Vince and I have one more item."

"Sure, but I have a couple more things first. We are damned lucky, strike that, we are blessed to have these two detectives on our force. I am sure the Lord handpicked them for this assignment. And that goes for the rest of you, too. Thank you, Max. Vince. Thank you, all. The last thing is this. Back in Louisiana we have a saying, 'Lache pas la patate.' All but Brickman had had heard him use it many times. "Don't drop the potato. Hold on no matter how hot it gets. Go on, Max."

Vince and Max took the compliment heads down. Both knew the captain thought he was wrapping up to move on. Max quickly debated whether to head straight into the Sera matter, abruptly announce there's another note or ramp up to it. He chose the ramp.

"Ms. Jacobs is the only person outside this room who has seen one of these notes. She is desperate to remain anonymous for her sake and her children. We convinced her that keeping it to herself is in her best interest and best for the case, in order not to spook the person who wrote it. She seemed amenable to that, don't you think, Vince?"

"Yes, attention is the last thing she wants."

"We instructed her to do nothing. Go about her normal routine. Let us investigate. I gave her an assignment to make a list of everyone over the last two years who had an altercation with Mr. Jacobs."

The captain spoke, "Good move. Gives her something to focus on, feel like she's helping. And that generates leads on possible suspects. Good work. Keep her close and in the loop. Now before we…"

"That's not all, sir."

The captain leaned back in his chair and said, "Sorry, go on."

"We asked Ms. Jacobs to bring the list back to us in a couple of days. To put it directly in our hands. We advised the front desk a package was coming. We were thinking maybe by Saturday." He reached down, retrieved the thick envelop, set it on the table. "This morning at 9:30 this packet arrived. The officer on duty said a teenager delivered it. A lady paid him twenty dollars to carry it in. The boy left immediately."

The captain, ready to move on, spoke up again, "Good, now we have a solid resource, which we will get into after…"

"Sir." Max cut him off. The ramp up was over. "The package is not from Ms. Jacobs."

"Then what is it? We have a long day ahead. Cut to the chase, detective."

"Yes, sir. Yesterday, after the storm, five of us responded to the site of Mr. Sydney Sera's death off West end at 20th. This morning, an anonymous friend of his delivered this package." The others stared like spectators at a horrible car wreck. They watched Max pull out the cover letter. From all that had already occurred, they reflexively tried to ready themselves for another shock. There was no avoiding it. They were like riders on a roller coaster, locked in and the car had left the station. Try as they might, they couldn't fully ready themselves for another overwhelming moment.

Max read the opening of the letter. 'Detective Malone, my name is Sydney Sera. I'm a building inspector for Davidson County. If you are reading this, I am probably dead." He read the entire letter. Every word was the clicking of a roller coaster climbing to the precipice. They all knew where this was headed. When Max reached the lines, "Last week I received a note threatening my life.

It's also in the package. They mean business," the roller coaster paused at the peak before the plunge and stuck there. The exhilaration of a roller coaster makes the terror worth it. This ride lacked the exhilaration. Max finished the letter, pulled out the note. There had not been time to put it in an evidence bag.

"Sir, there wasn't time to let you know."

"I understand."

Max held up the card. It had a gold foil border, He showed the team the name written in red, 'Sydney Sera.' He turned it over and read: "You have sown deceit and corruption. Prepare to reap. Put your affairs in order. Your life is required of you. The Red Angels."

Someone had to talk the team down. Get their feet back on solid ground. They expected that to be the captain, so, Hanover's voice surprised them. What she said surprised them more.

"I know who's next. Captain, can we take a fifteen-minute break? And I'll try to explain."

He looked at her and honestly at a loss said, "Fine. Fifteen minutes, people. Talk to no one. Not each other. Phone no one. Back here with notepads ready."

CHAPTER 22

Hanover was the last to return to the conference room. Four minutes late.

"I apologize, sir, and everyone. I needed to search some things and didn't have my phone."

"No worries," the captain said. She took her seat next to him across from Brickman. In front of her she set a yellow pad, pen, a black marker and a worn Bible with a handful of bookmarks visible. Everyone waited for the captain's lead.

"Helen, I think we would all like to hear what's behind your statement. And where it leads."

"Yes, sir. Bear with me. All this just came together in my head after the last note to Mr. Sera.

I think it could help determine a strategy. May I use the whiteboard, sir?"

"Yes, of course, it's time we get some of this out so we can look at the pieces we have."

Hanover went to the board behind her and drew a line down the middle.

Max couldn't take his eyes off her. *This is so gutsy. I hope she tricks Brickman into falling on his surfer boy face.*

"Max, Detective, sir, I've heard you say many times, 'Take it from the top. Let's start with what we've got.'

186

The flattery paled in comparison to hearing her speak his first name for the first time. He was likely to believe anything that followed.

"Set aside the manner of the four deaths for a moment. Dr. Brickman, when you used the term 'vigilante zealot' or group of zealots, what led you to that?"

"The biblical language of the notes. It's right there."

"Exactly. So, in my head I started at the top with 'You have sown, prepare to reap.' That's repeated in each of the notes. We can begin there to create a profile of who we're looking for." She picked up the Bible. "Scripture is full of sowing and reaping. Sowing good and sowing not good, and the results. Here are two." She opened to a bookmark and read, "Galatians 6:7 and 8, 'Do not be deceived: God cannot be mocked. A man reaps what he sows. Whoever sows to please their flesh, from the flesh will reap destruction; whoever sows to please the Spirit, from the Spirit will reap eternal life." She turned back to the board and across the top left wrote:

We reap what we sow

She flipped to another bookmark: "Job 4:8 and 9, 'Those who plow evil and those who sow trouble reap it. At the breath of God they perish; at the blast of his anger they are no more." She added to the top of the board:

We reap what we sow; Sow evil & trouble,
reap trouble & death

187

"What comes next in each note?"

"'Put your affairs in order,'" Vince answered.

She turned to another bookmark. "2 Kings 20: verse 1, In those days Hezekiah became sick and was at the point of death. And Isaiah the prophet the son of Amoz came to him and said to him, "Thus says the Lord, 'Set your house in order, for you shall die." She turned to the board and added:

We reap what we sow; Sow evil & trouble,
reap trouble & death Get ready

"Next?"

"'Your life is required of you,'" said Thomason.

"This phrase comes from a story Jesus told about a rich man who thought he had enough stored up to eat, drink and be merry for a while. I won't read the whole thing. Luke 12: 20 'God says to him, you fool, this very night your life is required of you.'" She turned and added:

We reap what we sow; Sow evil & trouble, reap trouble
& death Get ready; You are about to die

The captain pushed a little. "Well done, officer, but where and who does this point to?"

"I'm getting to that, sir. I think this will point us in two directions, to the sort of person or persons, who would write these warnings, and their targets."

Vince couldn't resist, leaned toward Max and said, "Quite the Bible refresher, huh?"

"Indeed." Max answered him, not taking his eyes off Hanover. The captain kept things moving, "Proceed, Helen."

"Thank you, sir. Let's look at two things at once. The manner of deaths and what each victim sowed." She turned to the board. Down the left column she wrote:

Hung by the hair: sowed poison/agony
Fell from balcony: treachery/wickedness
Impaled by rebar: sowed deceit/corruption
Inhaled toxic gas: sowed corrosion/discord

Max was not the only one who noticed that Hanover had remembered all of this detail without taking a single note. *She is beyond remarkable. Top that, boy wonder.* Max was unaware of Brickman's photographic memory that enabled him to excel in academia or that it rendered moot the captain's edict not to copy evidence.

Hanover continued, "You've already heard what I told Detective Malone, how the first two deaths have uncanny resemblances to famous deaths in the Bible, King David's son Absalom and Jezebel. Mr. Sera's death does, too." She turned to another passage. "Listen to this. Judges 4:21, 'As he lay sleeping from exhaustion, Heber's wife Jael took a tent peg, grabbed a hammer, and went silently to Sisera. She drove the peg through his temple and into the ground, and he died.' Pretty eerie, right?"

Thomason surprised everyone by speaking up. "What about Mr. Jacobs? How does his death fit that pattern?"

"Good question, Marvin. That led me back to the Proverb I showed detective Malone. This month our church is reading a chapter of Proverbs every day." As she spoke, she turned to it. "Proverbs 6:12,14 and 15 describes Mr. Jacobs' situation. 'A troublemaker and a villain, who goes about with a corrupt mouth, who plots evil with deceit in his heart – he always stirs up conflict. Therefore, disaster will overtake him in an instant; he will suddenly be destroyed without remedy.'"

Until now, Brickman had kept his tongue. He finally spoke up, more than a little skeptical. "So how does all this inference and resonance possibly tell us who is next? We've got no hard evidence yet that any crimes were committed. How can we even know there is a next?"

Max hoped this was the setup for the smackdown. He should have known Hanover was too gracious for that.

"Exactly, Dr. Brickman. No hard evidence. And only part of an MO. If we had a better picture of the MO, we might get a little ahead of this, right?"

"Yes, of course."

"I went back and looked at what the rest of chapter six includes. And more puzzle pieces came into focus. Listen to this starting at verse 16: 'There are six things the Lord hates, seven that are detestable to him: haughty eyes, a lying tongue, hands that shed innocent blood, a heart that devises wicked schemes, feet that are quick to rush to evil, a false witness who pours out lies and a person who stirs up conflict in the community.' Seven things. Let me put them on the board and see if you see what I did." To the right of the middle line, she listed them in a column:

We reap what we sow; Sow evil & trouble, reap trouble & death Get ready; You are about to die

	Haughty eyes
	Lying tongue
	Hands that shed innocent blood
Hung by the hair: sowed	Feet quick to rush to evil
poison/agony	
Fell from balcony: sowed	
treachery/wickedness	Heart that devises wicked schemes
Impaled by rebar: sowed	
deceit/corruption	False witness
Inhaled toxic gas: sowed	
corrosion/discord	Cause conflict in community

"When I saw this list, I asked myself, we have four victims, what were their offences?"

It was almost like Jeopardy. Max hit the buzzer first. "I get it!"

"Yes, of course," Vince said.

"Oh my. That's brilliant, officer Hanover," Brickman conceded.

All Thomason could muster was, "Wow."

Captain Haskins let Hanover have the moment and spell it out.

"Which of our victims had a heart that devised wicked schemes?"

All answered, 'Miss Bellaire.' Hanover wrote the initials 'JB' between the two columns.

"Which one bore false testimony?"

'Sydney Sera' came the answer. 'SS' went in the gap.

"Who stirred up conflict in the community? Obviously, Mr. Jacobs." 'DJ' went by the seventh offense.

"And finally, the first victim we encountered. Who was quick to rush to evil?" She added 'AD'.

We reap what we sow; Sow evil & trouble, reap trouble
& death Get ready; You are about to die

		Haughty eyes
		Lying tongue
		Hands that shed innocent blood
Hung by the hair: sowed		Feet quick to rush to evil
poison/agony	AD	
Fell from balcony: sowed		
treachery/wickedness	JB	Heart that devises wicked schemes
Impaled by rebar: sowed		
deceit/corruption	SS	False witness
Inhaled toxic gas: sowed		
corrosion/discord	DJ	Cause conflict in community

"Captain, if this is the MO of the Red Angels, it's likely we can expect at least three more deaths and notes. We don't know the targets' names, but we know their offences, according to the Red Angels. It's a place to start."

The entire team could not have been more wowed. Max's admiration turned to awe. He knew he would not, could not have seen all of that. And he knew why, but before he could articulate it to himself, Brickman did it for him.

"Science is a keyhole. Belief is the key."

Precisely, Max thought, *she's poetry and reason in motion.* For the first time in a while a song struck up in Max's head, *She Blinded Me with Science, 1983, Thomas Dolby, from Blinded by Science.*

"What's that Dr. Brickman?" Captain Haskins asked.

Billy Sprague

"Sir, as Officer Hanover demonstrated so well, we've been looking for physical evidence when a belief system is the real trail to follow."

Vince and Thomason concurred. Everything in Max wanted to say 'amen' about Hanover but he suddenly felt alien and uncredentialed in their realm. They all believed. That was their window on the world, the lens through which they viewed everything.

Max was used to living on the outside of that sphere. Divorced, philanderer, atheist cop in a southern culture still largely imbued with Christian cosmology, theology, family values and morality, at least in principle though not always in practice. He knew well the reactions from people when they found out he was a cop. From politely guarded to open disrespect.

Now, when he wanted more than anything to draw nearer to Hanover, he felt her recede to a distance he could not cross. He was an exile on the outside of belief. Not that he blamed the others. He didn't. He had exiled himself. What surprised him was the faint but steady pulse of envy. The same envy he felt toward his mother, who believed to the end in the face of agony and death. It still made her brave and heroic in his mind. And by comparison made him a cardboard man, two-dimensional and flimsy, with only bravado and eloquent bullshit to battle suffering and stare down mortality.

In Max's college days The Welsh poet, Dylan Thomas's most famous poem became his battle cry. "Do not go gentle into that good night, Rage, rage against the dying of the light," More and more that seemed to him like the tantrum of a soul shriveled by bitterness against the very force bent on liberating it from fear of the darkness into the light. As a student, when he learned Thomas' mother was a

193

true believer, like Sofia, he admired the poet even more for throwing off religion in any form. Now, many years later, a creeping hollowness drained all the valor from what had seemed valiant then. The captain noticed Max's silence. "Max, what have you got to say? Where do we go from here? Anyone?" Captain Haskins could have imposed a next step on the task force. He had a couple in mind. But he didn't. He trusted his people and entrusted the next move to them. That's why he was Captain.

Brickman beat Max to the punch. "Let's focus on the three remaining offences."

Max was reluctant to agree with Brickman. But he did. "Exactly my thought," he said. "That points us to possible targets, but without specifics, 'a lying tongue' could be the weatherman. We can't just warn every liar to stay off the streets."

Trying to lighten the mood Vince said, "That would at least thin the traffic out." This produced mild chuckles but didn't advance their task.

Max continued. "As Hanover pointed out we have two directions, the sort of person or persons, who would write these notes, their mindset, and their targets. Let's spitball a while then maybe split up to look at both."

That was the impetus the captain was looking for. "Vince, you and Marvin take downstream. Let's define those targets. Get as specific as we can. It may be we can advise some in each zone to beef up security based on, say, chatter on the streets. Max, you and Helen look upstream…"

The captain kept speaking, but all Max heard was he and Hanover would be working together. He was still in exile, but the distance closed some.

"… build a profile of who uses this kind of language. Talk to some clergy. Find out where these cards can be purchased, how they were delivered, view security footage. Theo, assist both teams in any way you can. Run some tests on the cards, ink, handwriting, and continue to work the scenes for anything that points to tampering or foul play. Hell, check Davidson's horse for fingerprints if you have to."

"Yes, sir. I'm on it." Brickman stood up and as if about to leave the room.

"Hold on, Dr." the captain said. "Didn't you hear Max? We're gonna spitball this together and not come out of here until we have action items in both directions." Max savored the embarrassed rookie look on Brickman's face as he retook to his seat. *I'd pay to see that again.*

The captain was in his zone, "Ok, break out your notepads. Think like a Red Angel. First, pardon my Cajun but who are the biggest sack of shit liars in town?"

"Politicians," Thomason blurted out. That sparked a small chuckle. The second of only three all day.

"Easy target." The captain said, "Start a list. Next, let's start another list of who, in the view of the Red Angels, have hands that spill innocent blood? Third, Helen, what does 'haughty eyes' mean in that verse?"

She looked down at the text, "In the margin notes it says, 'not just prideful, but someone who looks down on others, feels superior, is condescending, overbearing and obnoxious."

Vince tried levity again, "That sounds like me at my son's soccer games." That drew a polite chuckle. The last one for the day.

Max wasn't laughing. All he could think was, *That's me.* And wondered if anyone else was thinking the same. It troubled him most if Hanover made that connection.

For the next hour the three lists of potential targets kept expanding. The range was impossible to narrow except everyone agreed, when it came to spilling innocent blood, pious Red Angels would certainly rank abortion providers at the top of their hit list. But other suggestions made that list as well: gangbangers and their stray bullets, or judges too lenient on criminals who upon release commit assault or worse. All conceded, in the haughty eyes category there was no shortage of arrogant, condescending, prideful targets around the area. As for lying tongues, politicians topped everyone's list, but could include used car salesmen and waiters who don't report tips on their taxes.

"Don't we all lie in one way or another?" Max argued. To his own surprise he admitted lying to Vince two days ago on the phone about just getting out of the shower. But he did not confess the lie about traffic making him late for the first Brickman meeting instead of the real reason, running into Hanover.

"By the way, Max, I knew that," Vince said amicably. "But I didn't send you a note threatening your life for it."

Hanover shook her head. She admired their relationship. She offered, "Maybe we should focus on chronic offences, the ones sown over time. Not the generic 'all have sinned and fallen short of the glory of God' category."

"We're all in that boat," Brickman said. "But apparently not just anyone can be on the Red Angels' list."

Thomason summed up what everyone was thinking. The categories were so broad there was no end of targets. In his view, "The chance of picking the next target has the odds of the lottery."

Undeterred, the captain changed course. "This is a good start," he said, "Now that we know what we can't know, let's take it from the top. Start with what we've got?" he said, looking at Max.

"Yes, sir," Max responded. "Upstream, whoever wrote the notes is a much smaller group."

"Still needles in a haystack," Thomason pointed out.

"Then all we need is a magnet," Brickman surmised.

What the hell does that mean? Max thought.

The captain sat back in his chair. "I knew we had the right people around the table. Before we dive into that, any suggestions for supper? We'll order in again."

CHAPTER 23

Friday afternoon 3:57PM – Day 5

Eleven minutes in medium traffic to the northwest of headquarters, as the task force futilely made lists of possible Red Angels targets, the first person on the list of lying tongues, a politician, exited her office accompanied by advisors and handlers. Her ears should have been burning. Agnes Brown-Hyden, State Senator from a Memphis district, was about to hold a press conference. Under duress. She avoided it by simply letting time pass, hoping better angels would prevail. They had not.

The Senator's heels clicked steadily across the marble floor. Flanked by her staff she strode into the foyer just outside the Senate chamber to face a phalanx of cameras, lights and reporters. A less than friendly press, many of them familiar faces over the years, expected answers about a complete reversal on a campaign promise. This recent one-eighty was one of many in her political career, which earned her the derisive moniker, 'Spineless Agnes.' Protestors outside held signs: "Spineless Agnes has more positions than a porn star." They chanted, "Spineless Agnes, what's she hidin'? Spineless Agnes, NO MORE HYDEN! The Senator could see some of the crowd through the glass doors, hear the noise and chants, feel the hostility. Officers lined the entrance inside and out.

Just before she headed to the podium with notes in hand, she stopped short and spoke to her media consultant.

"You haven't been off the phone since you got here. I need you to focus. Pep talk. Tradition you know."

"Hang on, Cannon," her consultant and brother held the phone to his chest. "Sorry Agnes, checking in with my sons. You've got this. Just stick to the script." He seemed off. Nervous. He was never nervous.

"I'm fine. You awright, Sammie? What happened to 'nevah let 'em see you sweat'?"

"Right. You're right. Just a lot of pressure. See you after. Steaks waiting at Morton's. Remember, you're a survivor."

"And yor my genius." She held up the statement in her hand, drafted by him. "I'll sell evry word uh this."

She was indeed a survivor. Senator Brown-Hyden began her public career as a Democrat. When her district was redrawn and the power in the state shifted, she became a Republican. In her most recent victory, she retained her seat as an Independent. By a slim margin. The chameleon act enabled her to remain in the public eye and on the public payroll for nearly thirty years. Presidents and Governors came and went. Agnes survived them all.

She had more than a knack for politics. She possessed impressive verbal and recall skills and knew how to surround herself with highly capable people. In the trenches she became adept at navigating controversy, pivoting, spinning, dodging political bullets, and firing her own with deadly aim, especially in campaign season.

Early on she claimed to be a direct descendent of John Brown, the abolitionist. An actual descendent debunked that. Agnes offered a sincere explanation based on a letter, recently "discovered," from her Grandmama, who as a young suffragette took the surname to honor John Brown, and never told her granddaughter the real story. That was plausible enough for the voters. Via her charisma and persuasive tongue, Agnes survived and won another term.

For years she ran on the claim that she made possible the expansion of runways at the Memphis airport, which helped FedEx grow into a giant, pumping millions into the Memphis economy. The truth was very different. FedEx was already thriving before Agnes graduated from high school. She did have one suspicious tie to FedEx. Shortly after an 11,000 foot, one-hundred-million-dollar runway went in, expressly to expand FedEx in 2000, she bought a mansion on a public servant salary in upscale Germantown, but maintained an apartment inside her district.

Agnes Brown-Hyden stepped confidently to the microphone prepared to smile and assuage the voters' ire about why she changed her view and vote, departing from her voting record on the issue. This challenge was not new. She began in the soft, down-home style she adopted in such emotionally charged settings. She liked to think exaggerating her southern accent diffused tensions and disarmed resistance.

"Good aftahnoon, Aih have a statement and, of khos, will be happeh to take yor questions aftah." She took a drink of water. "When Aih was a little girl growin up along the Mississippi we saw the river change khos many times. Likewise, the rivuh of ouwa culcha continyas to change khos. Mah constituents change with the times. And so have Aih." She took another drink of water but missed her mouth slightly. Water dripped off her chin. Her closest handler was the first to see the shaky hand as Agnes reset the glass. "Ahcordingly, mah vyooth," pause, "mah views on some ithooth,," pause, she swallowed hard and spoke slowly, "change with theirs, sometimes aftah theirs," yet another pause, "sometimes beflor, be-beflor." The entire press corp focused on the slurs. Cameras clicked. The Senator blinked repeatedly, looked down to find her place in the text, took a breath to speak. She didn't get out another word.

At the back of the room there was a commotion. Someone collapsed on the floor. A cry went out, "Is there a doctor in the house?" Senator Brown-Hyden was rushed down a back corridor to a waiting car.

* * *

Supper arrived at conference room B at 4:55PM. Max suggested barbeque, but the captain wanted to keep it light, avoid sleepiness. He made the call. Calypso Café. They closed at 4:00 but, of course, the captain new the manager, who delivered the meal himself. Turns out it was Brickman's favorite. *Jamaican hippie food* according to Max, but good. He gave the corn muffins high marks.

Captain Haskins aimed to be done by 8:00PM. Brickman brewed a fourth pot of coffee. They ate mostly in silence followed by a ten-minute break. When they gathered again the remaining objective was action items for each officer based on the afternoon strategizing.

"I have some very odd news," the captain began. "There's been an incident. Senator Brown-Hyden, has been hospitalized with a stroke."

Her name was on every pad on the table. Even Brickman's. He heard her name pilloried back in graduate school. No one said it but everyone leapt to another Red Angels scenario.

"When did this happen?" Hanover asked.

"A little over an hour ago. She started slurring some words in a press conference at the Capitol. They got her immediately to the Stroke Center at Centennial."

"Is she expected to live, sir?" Max asked.

"Yes, for now."

"Thank heaven," Hanover said,

"But she's paralyzed on the right side of her body. And can't speak. The video from the Capitol has gone viral."

Tensions eased only a little.

"There's more," he went on, "Her brother and media consultant, Gunner Brown, was in the back of the room. He collapsed at nearly the same moment. Died on the spot."

"Holy crap!" Vince said.

"The Senator's office and the Governor want a complete autopsy immediately. His body's already in our morgue. Dr. Brickman, it's gonna make a hell of a long day for you but with Dr. Jenkins out can you assist the county examiner?"

"Yes, sir. As soon as we're done here."

"I think you better go now. They want to confirm that it's natural causes. Get ahead of rumors. We'll wrap up here and I'll get you whatever you need."

"Yes, sir." Brickman exited.

Max hadn't heard 'the phrase' yet. He waited for it. The captain delivered, "Lord have mercy. Their poor families." *There it is.*

* * *

Samson Gunner Brown first made a name for himself as a teenager playing bass on Beale Street. His love for his hometown turned into a passion to join the revitalization efforts. One speech in front of the city council changed the course of his life. He argued that the history and culture, the music, not just Elvis, but the civil rights history and the great food could all be promoted and developed to take the city to the next level, make Memphis a go-to destination for people from all over the world. He talked about the battle between the preservationists and the developers. He argued eloquently that culture would have to work with capital; investors had to prioritize the culture. He plagiarized most of this from articles he read. He would later say he "collated" the prevailing arguments. But his trademark statement was original: "The Mississippi river changes courses, but it's always the mighty Mississippi. Memphis can change, but still be Memphis and mightier." Verbal skills ran in the family. The very next day, a media/marketing company hired him. The river remained his favorite metaphor. And it carried him to his first fortune.

When his little sister, Agnes, ran for office, Gunner opened his own Media/PR firm, launched primarily by contracts with her campaign. He soon brought on other clients. He gained another fortune, two sons, Cannon and Colt, and lost two marriages. Through it all he consistently marketed, collated, embellished, amplified and sometimes invented his sister's story through many campaigns. He often wrote or edited her speeches. He was the one who "discovered" the letter from their Grandmama revealing the "true" origin of the Brown name.

He and Agnes had a good long ride on the political train from Memphis to the halls of power at the State Capitol. But now, on this Friday afternoon, for Gunner Brown the last stop was the basement morgue at Police Headquarters on Murfreesboro Pike.

Dr. Brickman was the first to attend to the body. He spoke to the county examiner on the phone who had taken a long weekend at Cherokee Lake in east Tennessee. He was en route but still hours away. They agreed Brickman should begin.

Thor knew the protocol and procedure. All seventeen steps. It took time. He filled out what he could of the autopsy form: name of deceased, 'emergency contact' he left blank, 'time of death.' blank, 'cause of death,' also blank, date, time and signed his name. He started at the top of the checklist.

1. Photograph the body inside the body bag. Check.
2. Collect evidence, hair, nails and blood samples. Label all. Check.
3. Remove the body from the bag and undress it. Check.

Transferring a body from one table to another was difficult for one person but Brickman was strong. And well-trained. Gunner Brown's naked body lay on a metal examining table. His tailored suit, Zegna dress shirt, Gucci belt, socks, white undershirt, boxers, Kiton Brogue Two-Tone Wingtips, and Droz wristwatch all lay neatly on another metal table.

He must be wearing $10K, Brickman thought. The watch was worth that.

Dr. Brickman only made it to step 4 - Inventory and photograph personal effects. He inventoried and photographed all the items except the last one.

* * *

In conference room B columns of action items were growing on the reverse side of the whiteboard. Hanover stood, marker in hand to add more. Team initials topped each column. W/T - Wilson and Thomason. M/H - Malone and Hanover. Vince knew how satisfying that was for Max. The Captain and Brickman had their own columns. They had been at it for over an hour when Dr. Brickman burst through the door in his blue scrubs and lab coat.

"From Mr. Brown's inside coat pocket, nearly missed it." He tossed a white, gift-card size envelope face up on the table. It landed closest to Max. The handwritten name 'Gunner Brown' was clearly visible in black ink. No one moved.

"Is that?" the captain didn't finish. Brickman cut him off.

"Yes, another one."

Captain Haskins leaned both elbows on the table, buried his face in his hands. He took one long breath, exhaled and said, "Max, read it."

"Better let Dr. Brickman, sir. He's still gloved up."

Brickman obliged. The card was cream white. Gold foil border on both sides. Black ink.

You have sown lie upon lie. Prepare to reap
Put your affairs in order. Your life is required of you.

The Red Angels

Without a word Hanover flipped over the whiteboard, added what they knew, the initials GB and took her seat.

We reap what we sow; Sow evil & trouble, reap trouble
& death Get ready; You are about to die

		Haughty eyes
Collapsed suddenly: sowed lies	GB	Lying tongue
Fell from balcony: sowed		Hands that shed innocent blood
treachery/wickedness	JB	Heart that devises wicked schemes
Hung by the hair: sowed		
poison/agony	AD	Feet quick to rush to evil
Impaled by rebar: sowed		
deceit/corruption	SS	False witness
Inhaled toxic gas: sowed		
corrosion/discord	DJ	Cause conflict in community

Max finally broke the silence, "And then there were two."

The captain bypassed commentary. He opted for action. "Here's how we're going to play this. Sorry, gang, but we gotta work this through the weekend. Forget downstream. No way to predict a next move. I want everyone, except Dr. Brickman aiming upstream. Theo, thank you for moving quickly on the note. I know you bent the evidence protocol a bit by bringing the note here, but don't sweat it. Please, get back to the autopsy. We need to know cause of death. After that you can help look into the card stock, ink, and handwriting."

"Yes sir, thank you, sir." Heading for the door he addressed Max and Vince, "I guess no barbeque at my place tomorrow, detectives. Another time?"

"Sure," Vince said. Max nodded. The 'kid' was proving competent but remained on Max's radar.

"Wait, Dr. Here's your phone." The captain returned all the phones.

"W/T, focus on the cards. Do an internet search. Find these card styles and where they can be bought locally. Tomorrow visit a few shops. Vince, you have some footage from Davidson's place, right?"

"Yes, sir."

"Scour it. Go by Mr. Sera's office. And this is delicate, talk to his wife. We don't know how much she knows yet. If she has the letter he wrote her yet."

"Yes, sir."

"M/H, view whatever footage you have. Go by Jacobs' warehouse tomorrow. I'll reach out to Capitol security now and get you access. Someone delivered these notes. The one in Brown's suit could've been handed to him at the Capitol earlier today. And find a pastor or priest, confidentiality an absolute. Only reveal as much as you need to. Get a view on who might want to play God."

It was a daunting task for twenty people. The captain knew how much he could push. "It's after 7:30. Good work everybody. Let's call it a day for now here. Do what you need to do. Progress reports by phone in the morning by 10:00. Let me know what you need. And be safe out there."

Vince requested he and Thomason take the cards for forty-five minutes for research.

"Granted. But not at your desk Vince. Stay here or sit in a car. Bring the cards directly to me in my office in forty-seven minutes."

"Yes sir." They remained in the room to work on their laptops.

The captain made a call. Capitol security gave him a green light to send someone over.

"I'll drive," Max said to Hanover.

"Ok, meet you out back. I need to make a couple of calls first."

CHAPTER 24

Friday evening 7:50PM – Day 5

Max hurried to his truck in the fading daylight. He removed some folders and a bagel wrapper from the passenger seat. Drove close to the rear entrance. Parked. And waited. *Engine running might seem impatient.* He turned it off. He was as nervous as a high school kid. His right foot bounced up and down. *Didn't see this in my day this morning.* A completely non-classic rock melody came into his head, "Beauty and the Beast." Just the hook line. He had no idea what year or who sang it. But he knew which part he was playing.

Hanover came out the door. He started the engine. She walked in front of him through the headlights. The Disney melody played again in his head. She climbed in, buckled up and said, "Wow, I think I can see Kentucky from up here, sir."

Max was impressed. *She's funny.* Three responses fought for his mouth, the first one an attempt at humor. (A) *Yea, size matters in traffic.* (B) *Do you like trucks?* And (C) *Did you get your dog situated?* The first two he had used many times on women he dated. He went with (C).

Hanover was impressed. *Only a detective could've guessed that.* "Yes, my neighbor knows I have crazy hours sometimes."

Two remarks presented themselves in Max's mind. (A) *That's good, my neighbors wouldn't piss on me if I was on fire, unless there*

was barbeque on the grill, or they thought I could fix a ticket. Or (B)
That's good. He went with the latter. But didn't know why he
added. "I have a neighbor up the hill who's a big country artist.
Plays his music louder than I do."

"Do you like his music?"

"It's actually pretty good. It's not the Eagles, but who is?"

"Nobody."

Getting across Friday night downtown traffic was going to take
more than eleven minutes to get to the Capitol. Tonight, Max
didn't mind. In fact, he chose a more congested route. Pedal party
bars and Uber drivers were out in force. There was a lull in the
conversation. Max went blank. Hanover broke the silence by
asking about the sticker on his dash. He told the story. She
chuckled at the irony of Dr. Brickman driving the Karmann Ghia
Max always wanted. He added "enjoys irony" to her profile.

"So why don't you like Dr. Brickman? Besides the Ghia."

"Is it that obvious?"

"Doesn't take a detective."

"He's growing on me."

Hanover asked, "Does it work?"

"Does what work?"

"The sticker from your dad. Does it slow you down?"

"Not enough." He noticed she had dropped the 'sir'.

Another lull.

"Sir, the other call I made. I hope this is all right. I called my
pastor."

"Of the holy mess church?" He tried to make his tone light,
but Max lived in the sarcastic lane so much he wasn't sure he
pulled it off.

Her slight grin was a good sign. So was her response, "Yes, sir, we messes tend to stick together."

"What did you tell him?"

"Just that we have an unusual case involving some biblical and spiritual overtones. That our detectives are looking for some input that might help."

"Good. That sounds good. Do you think we can trust him with this?"

"Yes, sir, I have no doubt about that, but I asked him if a different pastor could meet with us tomorrow."

Tomorrow. Max savored the thought of being with Hanover three days in a row. *That beats going to Brickman's.*

"Look out!" Hanover shouted. She braced herself with one hand on the dash. The other grabbed Max's right arm. He braked hard. A pedal bar full of singing, drinking young women slid by on the right into their lane.

"Idiots" Max blurted out. He managed to muzzle, *just like that deer.* He knew how close he came to nailing the girl on the end seat with the same spot on the grill guard. She flipped him off, then returned to singing with the rest of them at the top of their lungs, "Life is a highway, I'm gonna ride it all night long."

"They think they're bulletproof," Hanover said, "We all did."

"We never were."

"No. Thank heaven we survived."

Crossing Broadway on 5th Avenue they caught the red light a few cars from the corner. On their right, in a sea of pedestrians stood a tall man turning a double-sided white sign on an even taller pole. It read: "Be Ready." In block letters on his white shirt were the words: "Are You? I am." Displayed on the front of his black bill cap in white letters was the name "Jesus." The most prominent thing about him was a big smile.

Hanover said, "Hey, I know him!" The light turned green. As Max moved forward, she rolled down the window and yelled, "Hey, Daniel. It's Helen."

"Helen, I know you're ready."

"10-4. Great idea Daniel." She gave him a thumbs up as they went by.

"Let me guess. He goes to your church."

"No, he works at a mission I volunteer at sometimes."

She's Florence Nightingale with a badge. He couldn't resist a pun.

"Seems like an 'outstanding' guy."

She laughed that free laugh he loved and said, "I see what you did there."

Traffic trudged on. They crept along immediately behind the pedal bar for another block.

Max said almost without thinking, "'Life is a Highway', 2006 Rascal Flatts from the movie Cars, but originally by Tom Cochran, 1991, a Canadian artist."

"You know a lot about music, sir."

"My mother played music all the time. I have most of her records."

"My dad was a DJ."

"No kidding?"

"Nope. At several big stations. Kansas City. St Louis."

"What kind of stations?"

"Rock. Pop. R&B. They promoted a lot of concerts. I got to see everyone. Clapton. Zeppelin. The Stones. Doobie Brothers. Stevie Wonder. And my favorite. Paul McCartney. I have a lot of autographs. Probably why I married a musician."

Max was more enthralled than ever. The rock DJ in his head said, *Ask her, moron. Go on. Sure, it's lame but do it. Say it. I'll show you my records if you show me your autographs.* Hannover's next statement evaporated the lame cliché.

"That was all before I knew the Lord."

There it was. The chasm. Just moments ago, she physically touched him for the first time, but now she was light years away. Or he was.

Several responses cued up in his brain. *When was that? So, how'd you get religion?* Or something clever like, *So now you don't like music? Lame.* He chose silence.

After another lull, he steered it back to business.

"What were you saying about this other pastor? Who is he and why him?"

"He pastored a church on music row for a long time. Very loved and revered. Knows scripture inside and out. People, too. And still loves them." She chuckled.

"Uh, huh. Let me guess. He's a holy mess?" She chuckled again. *Made her laugh again.* Max thought he could get used to that sound.

"I've heard him say that, yes. I think he may have started it. He's in his eighties but has more energy than I do. And he's part Italian. Don Giachinto. If that helps, sir."

"Sounds like a godfather."

"Well, a lot of people consider him their spiritual father. Full disclosure, sir, I went to his church for a few years. He baptized me."

"Sounds like your history with him might help. I'm game. See if you can set it up."

"Yes, sir. My pastor is on it."

The security guard at the Capitol was expecting them. He knew Hanover and was obviously glad to see her.

"Hello, Helen, how you been?"

Hanover made the introductions. She and Officer J. Large graduated from the police academy together. He was very chatty as he walked them to the communications center.

"Crazy stuff around here today. I hear the Senator's gonna survive."

"That's what we hear, too."

"But not as a Senator. The buzz around here is she's done. Any word on what dropped Gunner Brown?"

"Autopsy going on right now," Hanover answered.

"Were you there?" Max asked. Hanover enjoyed watching Max pickpocket Officer Large for information.

"Yes. Not six feet to his left."

"Did he say anything, do anything out of the ordinary?"

"He seemed edgy right before."

"How so?"

"I'd seen him around here a lot. He had a swagger. Very confident. Today he kept looking around, rocking back and forth on his feet. Might've been the protestors made him nervous."

"Good observations, officer. What did you hear?"

"The Senator was speaking. She slurred some words so everyone was glued to her when I heard this 'AH'! Mr. Brown grabbed his chest with both hands. His head went back, and he said, 'O, God, not now!' He dropped like a rock. Like someone cut the strings on one of those, you know, one of those... "

Hanover and Max finished his sentence simultaneously, "Marionettes?"

"Yea, a marionette. Several of us worked on him but he was gone."

In the communications center Officer Large set them up to view the footage from 1:00PM through the press conference. There were ten screens and three times as many cameras monitoring various areas.

Max asked, "Which of these cameras cover the street entrances and where the Senator and Mr. Brown parked? And her office door and corridor."

The officer eagerly dialed those up, showed them how to toggle between different feeds, fast-forward and reverse. It was not Max's first rodeo. He had watched more nondescript footage than the Hubble telescope but far less inspiring.

"Well, I'm clocking out so when you get done check out with the officer where you came in."

Hanover thanked him.

"See you at church Sunday, Helen?" *They're everywhere*, Max thought.

"Maybe, we might be working." *That would be four days in a row,* Max contemplated.

"Understood. Here's my card." He handed it to Hanover, "in case you have questions. We should have a drink sometime." She didn't respond. He left them alone.

Max couldn't let it lie. "So, Officer J. Large. He makes Barney Fife look like Michelangelo's David. How did he pass the physical?"

"Triathlete. Ninja beast in hand to hand."

"People can sure surprise you."

"Yes, they can. Sir, have you been to Florence to see the statue of David?"

"No. On my bucket list."

"Mine, too."

"It's not far from where my mother grew up."

"You should go."

Max couldn't let up about officer suggesting they have a drink. "Seems you and Officer not-so-Large have a lot in common."

She laughed. That was his intent.

"You're both cops. He goes to church. And drinks."

"Nice guy. Nice try. The play button is right there, sir."

For twenty-five minutes they skimmed through nearly two hours of images of people in suits bustling by. Max spotted a tall woman striding down a corridor flanked by two lawyer types. He paused the image. "That's Jessie Bellaire's mother," he told Hanover. "Wonder who she's suing."

In the footage of the parking garage at timestamp 3:13PM, Hanover spotted Gunner Brown exiting his grey Mercedes. He hurried toward the elevators. The feed lost him around a corner. Another camera picked him up less than thirty seconds later, walking slowly, head down, reading something. He turned around and hurried back in the direction of his car, as if looking for someone. The paper in his hand went into his breast coat pocket.

"Scroll back to what he's reading, sir," Hanover said. Max rolled it back, paused and zoomed in on the image. The gold border around the card was unmistakable.

"Someone in that blind spot handed Brown the note! Now we're getting somewhere," Max said. He switched to exterior cameras on that side of the building and rolled it back two minutes. At timestamp 3:17PM the back of a figure in a gray hoody and sweatpants exited the parking garage heading toward

215

Charlotte Ave. Max rolled back the feed fifteen minutes to see if the figure entered by the same route. They saw Gunner Brown's grey Mercedes enter at 3:09PM.

"There!" Hanover said.

The same hooded figure ducked under the security gate as it closed and entered the garage. In this shot, though in dim light, a face with a thick, dark beard in sunglasses appeared.

"Not much there to go on," said Max. "We need to see if there are other city or business cameras on the street toward Charlotte Avenue." Max downloaded the pertinent footage into a thumb drive.

The guard checked them out of the building. They walked around to the garage entrance and headed toward Charlotte. They counted four cameras mounted on buildings that might provide a view of the street. Turning back toward the capitol a man with a backpack approached them. Except for his spotless gray hoody and sweatpants, he was likely homeless. He had no beard.

"O, sorry officer. I was just gonna hit you up for some change."

Hanover reached into a pouch on her utility belt and handed him a Chic-fil-A coupon. "Nice hoody and sweats, sir."

She's Mother Teresa in street blues, Max thought.

"Thank you, officer," the man said, "I found 'em this afternoon folded nice and just layin' back there in the alley. Honest. God works in mysterious ways."

"Yes, sir. He does. You be safe out there."

It was nearly 10:0PM.

"You've got a dog to retrieve," Max said, "and we've got our work cut out for us tomorrow."

They talked mostly music on the way back to the station. Max dropped her at the silver 4Runner. Before she got out he said,

"Officer Hanover, I don't know what your plans are in the department but if you ever want to pursue it, you've got detective instincts."

"That means a lot coming from you, sir. Thank you. Honestly, I've been considering that for some time."

"Well, as the captain says, let me know what you need."

"Goodnight, detective. Stay safe out there."

* * *

The entire task force had a late night. Brickman and the country medical examiner turned the lights off in the lab at 2:30AM. Vince and Thomason returned the RA notes to the captain at 9:04PM. They had searched the internet, made a list of a few stationery stores to check on Saturday, then scoured the Davidson security footage till nearly midnight. The captain put on a pot of coffee in his office, reviewed Max's timeline, the five RA cards, Sydney Sera's confession letter and documents. He made notes, a list of unknowns and action items till 11:40PM, locked everything in his safe and trudged home. His head hit the pillow next to his wife at 12:25AM, but sleep didn't come for another hour.

Hanover retrieved her dog from the neighbor, changed clothes and walked him for fifteen minutes. She put a kettle on, drank a cup of chamomile tea and savored the encouragement from detective Malone. At 11:45PM she knelt at her bed beside her rescue dog, an Irish Terrier, and prayed. For the families affected by the deaths this week. For the team. Max topped her list. Her last thoughts wandered to how it might go with Pastor Giacinto. Picturing him with Max made her smile and eased her mind like the chamomile tea. *God does work in mysterious ways.*

* * *

Max arrived at Love Circle Max exhausted but too keyed up to sleep. The Rubik's tiles from the cases kept sliding by. The only trouble now was one out of three flashed something about Hanover. He poured a glass of Chianti, climbed the stairs to the music room and went straight to the artists beginning with the letter E. Eddie Money. Ella Fitzgerald. Elton. Elvis, Emmylou Harris. and there it was, his mother's original 45. He cleaned it, set it on the turntable, hit pause on the remote and walked to the sliding doors. In the soft night lights of Music City, even his ghosts seemed at rest.

He calculated since Monday night he had seen, spoken and worked with Hanover every day. Tomorrow would make day six. The only trouble was he knew the possibility of her was impossible. *But dreaming is free, right?* He didn't make the connection in his mind, but the blue feeling telegraphed it - dreaming is a first cousin of hope. He hit play. The song voiced his unspoken desire. He wanted Hanover in his arms. He wanted her and all her charms. To taste her lips like the Chianti. Phil and Don summed up his quandary, "All I Can Do Is Dream." *1958 The Everly Brothers, #1 on all Billboard singles chart, recorded on Music Row in two takes, Chet Atkins on guitar.* Bone-weary and mellowed by the music and wine, he mumbled along, "Only trouble is, I'm dreamin' my life away."

At 2:35AM he woke up in the recliner, filed the spinning 45 away and went to bed.

CHAPTER 25

Saturday morning 7:15AM – Day 6

Max started his Saturday morning as usual. Slept in an hour. Twenty minutes on the elliptical listening to music facing the view across Music City. He put on Steely Dan. "Deacon Blues." 1977 from "Aja." *Too dark.* He replaced it with "Reelin' the Years," just to hear the energy and brilliance of the guitar solo by Elliot Randall. *Recorded in one take. 1972, from "Can't Buy a Thrill."* Shower. Double espresso. Cinnamon raisin bagel from Star Bagel. Toasted. Cream cheese with apricot jam. One boiled egg. Lots of pepper, just like his dad.

At 8:35AM he took his laptop to the balcony off the music room. He scanned security footage from Jessie's building beginning eight days prior to her death, monitoring the maildrop in the lobby and her hallway. He watched her come and go. A different outfit every time. Armstrong came and went, too. The second night he stayed all night. It felt odd to watch Jessie so much alive, so oblivious to the sudden stop just ahead. *Like most of us.* The adage 'ignorance is bliss' came to mind, but he said out loud, "Ignorance is blistering." *Sounds like a rock song. Better write that down.* He had a special folder on his desktop for nuggets that might turn into songs. He added it to the untouched trove of raw gems.

As he clicked 'Save' a tiny yellow dot landed on his screen. Thinking it was pollen or dust, he moved his index finger to remove it. The dot moved two inches, as if blown by the wind.

219

But there was no wind. He tried again. The dot moved away. He looked closer. The dot was crawling. It was a tiny round bug with yellow wings. Immediately, an expression of his dad's popped into his head. "Earth is like a flying iota."

When he and his dad were building the model of the planets, Liam Malone, mathematician, tried to give his son a scale of the universe compared to our solar system. He talked in terms of a light year being an inch and how many billions of inches were involved in the span of galaxies and between them. "And multiply that by a billion billion. Then double that a billion times." Max was just attaching the small blue ball representing earth to a metal rod, with a red dot showing where they lived on the planet. Dr. Malone said, "Son, our planet is a tiny dot, like a flying iota. You and I are on that iota with billions of other people." He described the mathematical probability of one iota sustaining the complexity of life in the immensity of a mostly uninhabitable universe. "And yet here we are. Son, I don't have enough blind faith to believe we're an accident. Some people do, but the math doesn't add up."

Max missed being called, "son."

In college he formed a band called "The Flying Iotas," an acoustic trio modeled after America or Crosby, Stills and Nash. The other two band members played better than Max, but were average singers. So, he sang lead on most songs. They fought a lot over original songs. It lasted a year.

Max followed the yellow bug to the top of the screen and spoke to it. "How do you ever find another bug to make more bugs? I know how you feel." With one breath he launched it into the universe.

When he looked back at the screen Tony Armstrong was leaving the apartment. Timestamp, Wednesday, 5:35AM. Max wrote on his yellow pad: "Wednesday AM. Six days before. Tony leaves apt." He hit fast-forward. Nothing till 10:33AM. Jessie left the apartment. He fast-forward, then immediately rewound. 10:38AM the back of a woman in white pushed a cleaning cart down the hall. She dropped a roll of paper towels in front of Jessie's apartment. The woman knelt to pick it up. When she did she slipped an envelope under the door. *Bam! Gotcha!* Max rewound and watched it three more times. *So, I didn't dream that!* The cleaning woman went directly to the elevator. He never saw her face. He rewound. If she came off the same elevator, he could get a look at her face. She didn't. *Must have come out the service elevator beside the camera. Or from cleaning the apartment next door.*

It was 9:42AM. His first impulse was to phone the captain. But he dialed Hanover. He hung up before it connected. *Slow down. Cominciando dall'inizio.*

There she was again. Sofia. In his head, the sound of her voice. 'First things first,' literally, 'commence from the beginning.' He heard it almost daily his entire childhood. *Cominciando dall'inizio.* Homework before play. Brush your teeth before school. Before bed. Pray before eating. Kiss mama before leaving.

* * *

The captain didn't have to wait till 10:00AM for updates. At 9:15AM Brickman phoned with the autopsy report: Catastrophic systems failure. Heart. Central nervous system. Like someone unplugged him. No elevated serum enzymes in the blood as a precursor. No arterial blockages. No clots. No aneurism. Gunner Brown appeared to be in perfect health. Brickman likened it to an electrical malfunction. Circulation stopped immediately. Blood pressure plummeted. In Brickman's words, "Just bam! Tick and no tock. Maybe fifteen seconds of clarity. Tops. And lights out."

* * *

At 9:28AM Vince called the captain from a specialty paper store in Green Hills. He and Thomason found two card stocks that could be matches. Bigger news than that, the security footage from seven days before Abe's death showed a walker, female, in black and gold sweats, hoody and sunglasses stop at the Davidson mailbox just before sunset. According to Vince, she looked both ways then placed something in the Davidson mailbox by the gate. Twenty minutes later Abe's Maserati pulled up, Abe got out and retrieved the mail. He appeared to sort out his own and replaced the rest. A red envelope was clearly visible in his hand.

"Great work, both of you," the captain told them. "So, as Max likes to say, there are definitely humans involved. These are not just acts of God."

"No sir. Have you been thinking that, too?" Vince asked.

Captain Haskins conjectured, "Except for the notes, haven't we all wondered? Maybe that's what these people want us to think. Keep me in the loop. Be safe out there."

* * *

At 9:44AM Max dialed the captain. As it rang his mind still conjured the sound of Sofia's voice telling him, 'First things first, il mio tesoro.'"

"Max. Are you there? Can you hear me?"

"Sorry, yes, sir. We caught two breaks on delivery methods. Definitely humans involved."

"That's what I just said to Vince not ten minutes ago." The captain filled Max in on the autopsy report, the card stock and the jogger at Davidson's. Max described the parking garage exchange and the cleaning lady at Jessie's door.

"Great work, Max. Tell Hanover I said so, too."

"I will, sir. By the way, sir, you know she's got the makings of a detective."

"You should tell her."

"I did, sir. Last night."

"Good. And good stuff, Max. We have some actual trails to follow."

"Yes, sir. Hanover is trying to set up a meeting with a Pastor she trusts. Might happen today. We're going by Jacobs' warehouse. And back to Jessie's apartment to see if the manager can identify the cleaning lady."

"Great. If you need Brickman for anything, reach him directly. We may all need to meet here later today. Keep me in the loop. And be safe out there."

"Yes, sir."

As he dialed the number for the manager at Jessie's building, Hanover's number came up on the screen. He took her call.

"Good morning, Hanover. Get much sleep?"

"Not enough, sir. Hard to shut off my brain."

"Same here. I just spoke with the captain. Autopsy report is in. Vince and Thomason caught a break or two. And I did, too, just a while ago on Jessie's security footage."

"That's great, sir. I got a call from Papa G, that's what a lot of people call him. Pastor Giacinto can meet with us at 11:15 this morning. He's doing sermon prep till then."

"Where?"

"At Cool Springs Church. Does that work for you?"

Max had not set foot in a church except for funerals in decades. He would have met her anywhere.

"Sure, that works."

"I live in Crieve Hall. Aren't you on Love Circle, sir?"

She knows where I live.

"Want to drive down together? Bring me up to speed on everything?"

"Uh, sure." *Does she want me to come to her house?*

"Ok, do you know the Cracker Barrel at Harding and 65?"

"Yea, Vince and I go there sometimes."

"Good, let's meet there, say, 10:45?"

"Perfect will have to do."

"What's that, sir?"

"Something my dad used to say when he showed me how to do something in our workshop."

"Nice. I like that. See you there, sir."

"Wait, Hanover, how do you like your coffee? I have a killer espresso machine."

"Don't go to that trouble, sir."

"No trouble. Touch of a button or two."

"Does it make a latte?"

"The best."

"OK, thanks. If it's not too much trouble, do you have any cinnamon?"

CHAPTER 26

Max parked in the Cracker Barrel parking lot five minutes before Hanover. She pulled in, climbed up into the F250 and buckled in. Her latte was in the cup holder.

"See what you think," Max said, pointing to it.

She took the lid off the insulated cup. It was still steaming. She blew on it once. "Mm smells good."

As he watched her take a sip the thought came, *I envy the rim of her cup.* He didn't know if he heard that somewhere or made it up in the moment. *I should write that down.*

"Well?"

She nodded and said, "Thank you, sir. Perfect will have to do."

Max laughed. An actual free and easy laugh. From a place where real laughter was an endangered species. His Antarctic heart thawed two degrees. The song that began in his head made him laugh more, disproportionate to Hanover's witty remark. He heard JT singing, *Lord, have mercy on the frozen man, 1991, from New Moon Shine.* He headed out of the parking lot.

"What's so funny, sir," Hanover asked.

"Nothing. Do you like James Taylor?"

"I've seen him three times. He signed his autograph, 'Lovely Helen, you've got a friend.' I gave him my phone number, but like most guys, he never called."

"Seriously?"

She took another sip. "Absolutely. He led me on. I don't think we were really friends. I was eight and still very trusting."

Max played along. "Ouch. That's tough. First heartbreak?"

"No. Peter Frampton. I used to kiss his autographed poster at bedtime."

"Tell me you still have it. It would be worth a lot to the right collector."

"No, I threw it away after I met JT. Big mistake." She took another sip.

She's a riot! Max's thawing continued in the warmth of natural, light-hearted human conversation.

He mentally fumbled for a segue back to business. Fortunately, Vince called to touch base. He and Thomason were on their way to a third stationery shop.

"Let me put you on speaker, Vince, Hanover is here. I was about to brief her on my call with the captain."

"Sounds good. We're listening," Vince confirmed.

Max chronicled all the recent developments, especially the revelations from security footage.

"Still a lot of legwork to do but three out of five confirmed delivery points is a strong start."

"Yea must be humans involved as you say. The captain even quoted you. Except for the notes he admitted he was beginning to think these are all acts of God."

"Not on my watch," Max volleyed.

Vince laughed. "Of course not. Where you guys headed?"

"We're going to quiz the manager at Jessie's building about the ID of the cleaning lady. And swing by Jacobs' warehouse. Ask

some questions. Unless you and Thomason want to take that.
We have one more stop to make."

"Where's that?"

Max had avoided the detail about the meeting with a pastor
to avoid a predictable ribbing from Vince. He let Hanover answer.

"Hanover here, sir. Good morning to both of you. Per the
Captain's request I was able to set up a meeting with a pastor I
know to get some insight on this thing."

"Who's that? Anyone I know?"

"Don Giacinto. We're meeting him at Cool Springs Church."

"Papa G! Max, he's amazing. You're meeting with him and
going to church? Hanover, I've been trying to get Max to church
for years. What's your secret?"

Maxed called it. *He's predictable as sunrise.*

Hanover played them both, "Perfume and the Holy Spirit. But
mostly the captain's action item."

"Now that's funny!" Vince was enjoying himself, "Two things,
Hanover. First, good one. And second. Don't be funnier than me.
I'm still his partner."

"Yes, sir. I'll try to avoid that."

"Hey Max, this card search is a bust," Vince segued back to
business. "No way we can trace who bought cards where, except
online purchases. And that's a long shot. Why don't Thomason
and I stop by the warehouse for you guys?"

"10-4. That would help us out."

"O, by the way Max. At the last shop we met Dr. Brickman's
mom. Really sweet lady. She works there two days a week."

Silence.

"Max, you still there?"

"Roger that," Max finally responded. The captain also said we may all need to have a face to face at HQ later today."

"10-4. Keep us posted. Hey, Max, don't get baptized without me. Out."

CHAPTER 27

Saturday morning 11:15AM – Day 6

Max and Hanover walked into Cool Springs Church under the sign: Tattoos, Doubters and Traditionals Welcome. Max qualified as the first two. Technically, his Catholic upbringing made him all three. He estimated the lobby could hold a thousand people. There were two coffee bars. A long welcome desk stood against the wall between the doors to the auditorium, 'I'm a Holy Mess' T-shirts displayed behind it. The wall to the far left looked like the side of a wooden ship with a wide gangway. The sign above said, "Children Board Here." The wall to their right held a framed, black and white mural of a shirtless man's back, flexing his muscles. Upon closer inspection it was composed of hundreds of pictures of tattoos pixelated to create an image of strength. *Dad would love that. Probably name it something clever like, 'I ink, therefore I am.'*

Max chuckled.

"What's so funny, sir?" Hanover asked.

'Nothing' poised on his tongue, but the way Hanover looked at him made him say what was on his mind.

"Just picturing my dad seeing this and thinking he would title it something witty like 'I ink, therefore I am.'"

"That is funny. Did he have tattoos?"

"Yea, one for my mom, and me and my sister Ariana's initials."

"Do you have any, sir?"

"Yea."

"Then you're definitely welcome here."

"You?"

"Yea, a couple of small ones. We'll have to swap tattoo stories."

"JT's initials?"

She laughed. He had done it again.

They entered the auditorium. Except for the huge wooden cross in the middle of the stage between two giant electronic screens, it felt more like a concert venue than a church building. No windows, flat black steel girder ceiling, stage lights, trusses, line array speakers, TV cameras, one on a long boom, all made it a far cry from the ornate cathedral full of color, art, height and light he attended as a boy. The cynical moderator in Max's head said, *What kind of God, who supposedly made the universe, shows up in a monochrome black box?* Theatre seating in a semicircle sloped down to a massive, stage, all black but for a shiny set of drums.

"How many people does this seat?" Max asked.

"I think around twenty-five hundred."

From the right, a tall, older man with a white, close-trimmed goatee walked slowly onto the stage, bald head down, reading from an electronic pad in one hand. The other hand, fingers spread, lay on his chest. His long sleeve, black crew neck and dark slacks made his head and hands appear to float. In the sea of black he seemed spotlighted, but only a few house lights lit the room. He was unaware of Max and Hanover standing in the back.

"Papa G," Hanover called out as she headed for the stage.

The pastor raised his head, set the pad on the podium. A broad smile spread across his face.

"Helen Hanover, bless my soul!" For a man in his eighties, he moved easily down the steps and up the aisle toward them. She continued toward him. Max held back. Pastor Giacinto approached her, his arms spread wide.

The pulse of envy returned in Max. No one had greeted him that way since his own father on trips home from college. Or his mother, on her knees in the morning as he ran into her arms when he was small. The embrace of his lovers was not the same. Those carried only desire. Not elation at who he was. All the fancy stage lighting in the room could not outshine Pastor Giacinto's face.

"I didn't know it was going to be hug a cop day," he said as he wrapped her up like a man reunited with a fawn he had once rescued.

"Pastor, I want you to meet Detective Malone."

"I'm very pleased to meet you, detective." His handshake was as generous as his greeting to Hanover.

"Likewise," Max managed.

"Are you teaching here tomorrow?" Hanover asked.

"Yes, Pastor Ben asked me to fill in. Will you be here?"

"I hope so, but we may have to work. Are you continuing the series?"

"Yes, 'Roads to Faith,' my title is 'Doubt Doesn't Have to Be a Detour,' but that's all you'll get from me now."

He got right to the point of the visit. "I'm very intrigued by your request about a case with spiritual or biblical aspects. No one's ever asked me to consult on such a thing." The gravity in the pastor's tone tempered his enthusiasm. That went on a Rubik's tile in Max's head.

"Let's get some privacy in Ben's office," he said, and led the way.

As they walked up the aisle Pastor Giacinto momentarily put an arm around Hanover's shoulder and a big hand on Max's. Having lived most of his adult life with little physical human contact, particularly from men, he chalked it up to *Italians are touchy feely.*

"Tell me about you, detective? Would you mind if I call you by your first name? I'm Don or Pastor Don or Pastor G. Papa G to some like Helen here."

"Max."

"Max Malone. Strong name. Is Max short for Maximillian?"

"Yes, sir."

"Let me guess. Malone. Father Irish?"

"Right again."

"You don't altogether look Irish. Some Mediterranean in you? Like me?"

"My mother was Italian."

"Hey, Giacinto. Me, too, paisano. But on my father's side. My mother was German. Your mother chose Maximillian?

"Yes, sir."

"She expected great things of you. Who chose your middle name?"

"My dad."

"Opposite for me. My mother chose Oscar, her father's name. It means 'Divine strength but also, for some reason, a friend of the deer.'"

Max had a private moment. *Probably not a good time to bring up my recent deer encounter.*

"I'm still grateful my parents realized before they left the hospital how those initials would do me great harm in school, D.O.G. So. they flipped it to Oscar Donaldo Giacinto."

"Thank heaven," Hanover said. "I like Papa G a lot better than 'What up, Dog?'"

The pastor laughed loud. Max wanted to but enjoyed the hilarity between them.

"Mind if I ask you your middle name, Max?" Pastor said.

He hesitated. "I don't use it much. It's old Irish. My partner, detective Wilson, breaks it out now and then."

Hanover surprised him. "I already know it, detective. It suits you. Your dad chose a great name, sir."

She could do no wrong.

"It's Shaemus."

Pastor G knew exactly what to say next. "Max, that's the Celtic version of James. The only reason I know is I met several men named Shaemus on my trip to Ireland. It means 'one who follows.' You follow clues, follow trails for a living." The broad smile dominated his face again. The personal attention and affirmation were so foreign to Max, he was at a loss. Pastor G heaped on even more.

"Maximillian Shaemus Malone. Now that's a name." As they got to the door of the office, Pastor Don turned and looked directly into Max's eyes and said, "Max, your parents sent you out into the world with a destiny. So, did mine."

The pastor's graciousness and his own curiosity directed Max away from the purpose of the meeting. He thought of resisting but decided to ask.

"What part of Italy? My mother grew up in Tuscany north of Abruzzo."

"My father's people farmed and fished in the Adriatic in east Abruzzo. I've been there. Incredible beauty. And people. Have you been, Max?"

"No. We wanted to." Max regretted saying too much. He covered it with, "We got to see where my dad grew up in Ireland, though."

Pastor G tread lightly. He simply said, "Well, you must go. Lord willing. Now, I'm sorry for diverting us but I often doubt if a detour is a detour."

"I see what you did there," Hanover volleyed back. "Is that part of the message tomorrow?"

"Caught me." He invited them to sit. Hanover pulled out a yellow pad to take notes. The pastor pulled the rolling chair from behind the desk, grabbed three bottles of water from a small fridge, but didn't sit. Instead, he walked around and stood behind their chairs. Before Max knew what was happening, he heard Pastor G say, "Before we begin let's ask the Lord for his help."

Hanover immediately bowed her head and closed her eyes. Max knew. He glanced. He felt a hand on his shoulder. The pastor's other hand rested on Hanover's. Max knew. He glanced. He bowed his head but didn't close his eyes. Pastor G was hard to resist. Like Hanover.

"Heavenly Father, we praise you for ordaining this day, this meeting. Things are not always clear here, Lord, but you've made it clear what you want. Justice, mercy and to walk humbly with you. Jesus, thank you for showing us mercy when we deserve justice. Help us trust your wisdom in doing both. Holy Spirit, nothing is beyond you or out of your sight. Guide Max and Helen and their team. Give them sight beyond their eyes, through the evidence and beyond it to the heart of this matter. In the name of Yeshua, Amen."

He came round, sat in the desk chair and said, "*Cominciando dall'inizio.* First things first. Max, did your mother ever say that to you?"

Max could see why people called him Papa G. "All the time, Pastor."

Papa G smiled, "Good then. Let's begin at the beginning. How can I help?"

CHAPTER 28

As Max and Hanover explained the delicate situation to Pastor Don, Dr. Brickman sat in his office at headquarters. The five notes lay in order on his desk. Two red. One with a beveled border. One without. A third all white. A fourth white with a narrow red foil border. The fifth was cream white with gold foil border. He had less than an hour remaining to return them to the captain's office.

After a visual inspection under bright light and a magnifying lens, he discovered only two subtle marks.

One card touted the use of recycled paper. The macabre irony struck Brickman like the zany humor his parents introduced him to in Monty Python movies. He actually spoke out loud in a mock British accent, "This announcement of your impending doom is written on environmentally friendly paper." He chastised himself for the levity but chalked it up to exhaustion and coroner's humor, a humanizing defense against the somber matters of his profession.

Another card revealed the manufacturer, the largest card producer in America. Neither mark narrowed the odds of a source or author.

None were glossy enough to capture a fingerprint.

One red card, the one to Abe Davidson, had a subtle stain the size of a pea. He took a small scraping to examine later in the lab.

Four notes were written in black ink. One in red. The writing utensils varied. Three ballpoints, one fine tip felt marker and one fountain pen.

None of this supplied any specific direction or help.

Brickman was no expert on handwriting. He had taken one graduate semester in graphology and studied it out of personal interest online with an expert mentor with the FBI. The handwriting on each card appeared to be unique. Four writers used simple, printed styles, perhaps to make identification difficult. One Red Angel wrote in a natural, more personal cursive.

As he reached to adjust the magnifying lens his 'I think and drink coffee therefore I am a human bean' coffee cup tipped over, fortunately, away from the cards. The spill ran under the microscope. He snatched up the scope, and the framed card sitting behind it. The one from his parents. The spill missed the card. He moved it. Coffee dripped from the base of the microscope. He stepped to grab tissues from a bookshelf, cleaned the microscope, wiped up the spill and put it back in its place. When he sat back down his parents' card stood beside the first red RA card to Abe. He picked both up. One in each hand. The card stock appeared to be identical. *What are the odds?* The handwriting was not even close. *Of course.* The RA card was a printed style. His parents, in cursive.

If he had a portent, it remained buried below layers of other concerns.

An exercise his FBI mentor taught him clicked into mind. *That would be good practice.* He counted the recurrence of each letter in both, vowels first, beginning with 'a.' He counted two lower case 'a's in his parents' card: seven 'a's, six lower case, one upper, in Abe's card. He reminded himself a sampling ratio of at least 2 to 1 assures a high match. A lesser ratio meant no similarity.

Next, he counted the most frequently used vowel in the English language. He found nine lower case 'e's in his parents' card: ten 'e's in the Red Angel card, also all lower case. Nearly a 1 to 1 sample ratio. To his surprise, the 'e's seemed eerily similar. The loops nearly closed and upright. *No way.* He checked more closely under the lens. Even the type of pen, a fine felt tip, seemed the same. *That just can't be.* Brickman wrote it off as a fluke or his own lack of expertise. Still, he examined them more closely under the light and lens.

Just as an exercise, he told himself, he partially broke the captain's rule about no photographs or photocopies of the cards. He photocopied both cards, cut out all the words with the letter 'e' in them. He placed them in two columns in random order on his desk. Words from his parent's card on the left. Abe's card on the right.

Key	reap
Science	Angels
the	Prepare
Belief	required
We	Red
keyhole	life

He photographed them, uploaded the jpeg, and attached it to an email to his FBI handwriting mentor without mentioning the letter 'e'. He wrote:

I know it's the weekend. Time sensitive case. ASAP can you tell me if there is any match between the columns, remote or close, and if close, where and with what percentage of certainty? Thank you. I owe you, big time.

Brickman put all the scraps of copy paper into his shredder. He returned each RA card to its evidence baggie, placed them all in the manilla envelope and headed for the door to return them. His computer dinged. An incoming message read:

Got it. Understand. Everything is time sensitive at the FBI.

Give me an hour.

Some good barbeque will make us square.

He had six minutes till the cards were due back in the captain's hands. Brickman called his mother. She didn't answer. He left a message.

"Mom. I know you're at work. Have you had lunch yet? I can meet you in about an hour. Call me. Love you."

* * *

While Brickman poured over the RA cards in his office Vince and Thomason were touring the warehouse where Donovan Jacob's died. It was fully operational again. They could find no sign that the chemical spill ever happened. The new manager, promoted in the absence of Jacobs, walked them through. He confirmed Donovan was an equal opportunity abuser and bully. It didn't take much to set him off.

"I understand Mr. Jacobs fired an employee the day of the accident," Vince said. "We'll need to speak with him, just routine."

"Yea, Choppy Ambler. I'll call him to the office."

"He still works here?"

"Yea turns out he didn't screw up at all. Our supplier labeled the containers of bleach wrong."

239

"So, Jacobs was restacking them ?" Thomason asked.

"That's what we figure, but he didn't know that. He must've bumped some containers off the palette. It happens. He was a hothead, and it was closing time, so not hard to imagine him being in a hurry. That's when things can go south. And they did."

The manager led them back to the front office. He left to find Mr. Ambler.

Vince said to Thomason. "Sounds like humans involved at every level."

"Yea, but how do humans orchestrate all that?" Thomason responded. "Wrong labels from somewhere else. Bad timing. Careless driving? And the RA note. We still don't know when or how Jacobs got it."

The manager returned with the rehired Mr. Ambler.

"Mr. Ambler, I'm detective Wilson. This is officer Thomason. Thank you for meeting with us."

"Sure. I already talked to the insurance people. I still can't believe what happened."

"These things are never easy," Vince began. "We just have some routine questions to wrap up the inquiry. Potentially part of the Hazmat report." *It could be,* Vince justified. "Can you tell us about that day?"

Mr. Ambler walked them through it, how he did what he always did. Unloaded product from a semi, took it on a forklift to the assigned aisle and bin, according to the labels. Recorded it in the log. Jacobs found a discrepancy between the log, invoices and labels and went ballistic. Fired Choppy on the spot.

"How long have you worked here, Mr. Ambler?"

"Two years."

"We understand Jacobs could be pretty hot-tempered. You seen that before?"

"Yes, sir. Many times. He ran a tight ship."

"That day, when he fired you, did he say or do anything odd or unusual, something you hadn't seen before?"

"I'd heard him go off on guys, but he really came unhinged."

"How so?"

"I can't describe the look he gave me, but he got right up in my face and screamed, 'You're not gonna be my f-ing red angel of death today. No way! God's got my back. Nice try.' It was intense."

"Did he threaten you in any way?" Vince said.

"No. I just went straight to my car and headed home to tell my wife I got canned by that asshole. An hour later my wife and I hear he's dead. Does that count as odd, or what?"

"Yes, sir. That's odd," Vince agreed. "Here's my card. If you think of anything else, please call."

As they headed to Vince's car the captain called. He needed them to be ready to aid Vice in a drug sting related to Abe's stash.

* * *

At the same time, back at police headquarters, Captain Haskins was finding more questions than answers. He rarely worked Saturdays unless the caseload required it. His wife, Miriam, had lived with a cop long enough to know that life is adjustable. He blocked all calls on his cell, except from her and the task force to focus on the evidence and coordinate the team.

It didn't take long for a knock on his door. The Vice commander came in with a breaking situation. He showed the captain a video of two men arriving at Brie Batson's apartment earlier in the morning, and her leaving with them. In the footage Ms. Batson appeared nervous and under duress. Thirty minutes later they showed up at Davidson's place. BB told Davidson's assistant they were friends of Abe's. The men offered their condolences. Brie told her Abe had some of their guitars. Vice had instructed Ms. Andrews to play along if anyone requested access to Abe's quarters.

Sure enough, as Max predicted, the men went through the guitar cases opening the secret compartments. BB protested and appeared genuinely surprised by the drug stashes. The thugs were not pleased at how little they found. They roughed up BB demanding to know where Abe kept the main inventory. She had no clue. They looked all over the place without discovering the hidden stashes. Frustrated, they packed a small amount of cocaine and oxy into one empty guitar case.

Vice followed them back to Brie's apartment, ready to intervene if she appeared to be in danger. They dropped her off unharmed. Vice tailed them to another location where a raid was staged and ready to launch. All the commander needed was the captain to give the green light. Vince and Officer Thomason were closest for back up. The captain reached them, but Vince advised against it.

"These guys don't sound like the big fish, Captain. If we nab them the games over. I think Max would agree."

Reluctant, the captain agreed. Better to wait. He called off the raid. Vice understood and complied.

This was a part of the job Dirk Haskins enjoyed most, getting bad guys and their poison off the streets of the city he loved. He was chomping at the bit to get face to face with the thugs and pressure them for information by inferring their connection to Abe's death. But he knew he couldn't hold them longer in connection to that without arousing interest, especially from the press. Those interrogations would have to wait. But their time would come. The evidence was irrefutable.

The duty officer rang. "Sir, sorry. There's a Dr. Clay Guryon to see you. He tried to call. He says your wife told him you were here."

CHAPTER 29

Saturday morning 11:25AM – Day 6

Max spent the first ten minutes with Pastor Don thinking more about what not to say. He felt awkward requesting complete confidentiality from a pastor, especially Hanover's pastor, but *humans are humans* he reasoned. Of course, Pastor Don understood and agreed. Max indicated there was more than one case but didn't say how many. He revealed the similar occurrences of prophetic notes and their general content, emphasized how that would play in public, particularly in the media. He confirmed there was visual evidence of the notes being delivered by separate, distinct individuals. The longer he talked he found it difficult to withhold anything from Pastor Don. To get himself out of the spotlight, Max credited Hanover for making the first breakthrough in the case. He asked her to describe how she traced the language of the notes to four or five places in the Bible. Pastor Don lit up like a proud father.

"I am not surprised. Helen, I am so proud of you! Psalm 119 says 'I have more understanding than all my teachers because your words are my meditation.' Max, you better keep an eye on this one."

"Yes sir," is what Max said. *O, I have been,* he kept to himself. One of his mother's favorite songs floated into his head, "You're just too good to be true / Can't take my eyes off of you" *Frankie Valli and the Four Seasons, 1967.* Sofia sang it to his dad just to embarrass him.

Max explained that if the notes hadn't turned up these deaths would have been considered tragic accidents. He thought, *acts of God*, but left it unsaid. It did not fit his MO of the universe. After a few more minutes of listening to Max talk around the core issue, Pastor Don summed up and asked a direct question.

"So, Max, you have more than one, perhaps several deaths, each accompanied with a similar prophetic, biblically based note. You haven't told me much about who died or how. This is going to sound like a strange question coming from a pastor, but in your view did these people deserve the warning and the sentence?"

"They certainly did in the minds of the Red Angels, sir."

"How about in your mind?"

"Uh, well, the more we find out about the victims, yes, sir, they all sowed, as the notes put it, what they were accused of."

"Can you tell me, in general terms, what the accusations were?"

Max had less and less reason not to trust the pastor. He glanced at Hanover. Her look and nod said, 'Whatever you think.' He made a 'first things first' decision, deciding to reveal the first three victims 'crimes' without their names. 'Sins' was the first word that came to mind, but that didn't fit the MO of his universe either. Pastor Don listened intently to Max's description of Abe, Jessie and Donovan's "offenses" then asked another question.

"So, the only suspects you have are these anonymous Red Angels, and you want me to help narrow your search for them?"

"Help create a profile," Hanover clarified.

"That's right. Yes, sir, you see, the mystery is we have virtually no evidence at the scenes pointing to any specific suspects but because of the notes and security footage we know humans are involved."

"Max, I can't help but notice you haven't used the term 'acts of God' even as a legal term."

The pressure Max felt not to reveal himself as an unbeliever ramped up two of his other well-honed skills, intellectual prowess and evasion. "No sir. Again, the notes clearly point to a perpetrator or group of perps. We're just trying to build a profile and MO to focus our search."

"'Focus our search.' I like that, Max. In fact, that's part of my message tomorrow. How doubt doesn't have to be a detour. Doubt is an honest way to focus our search for meaning and ultimately God." Pastor Don gazed steadily at Max and let that soak in.

Max felt blindsided. The Pastors' completely matter-of-fact delivery rendered powerless Max's usual defenses, which normally manned the inner walls of Castle Malone - reason, logic and verbal firepower. A twinge of fear that Hanover had leaked Max's unbelief to the pastor tried to sound the alarm but failed. There was no salesmanship. No evangelical agenda. Simply unconditional honesty, man to man. Vince was right. This was an amazing person. What Pastor Don said next put 'amazing' it in all caps.

"Max, I think I can narrow your search. What you've described to me sounds likely to be a Proverbs 6 MO."

Max immediately looked at Hanover, not realizing his mouth was hanging open.

Hanover spoke up, "I didn't say anything about that, detective. Have I, Papa G?"

"About Proverbs 6? No, not a word. Max, this whole church read that chapter on May 6 as part of reading a chapter a day through Proverbs."

Max and Hanover spoke at the same time. She deferred to him.

"I know. Helen, officer Hanover, told me about that. She," he hesitated but there was no reason now to withhold the obvious. "She proposed to our task force that the Red Angels are targeting people guilty of the seven things in that chapter that God hates." He immediately regretted using the term 'task force.'

Pastor Don picked up on it. "Benedicilo! Helen, again, I'm not surprised. Max, can I assume there are less than seven deaths, and your task force is trying to get ahead of the next one?"

"Yes, sir."

"So, as you say, you believe there are humans involved targeting what God hates?"

"Apparently."

"Max, have you considered two scenarios could be true simultaneously?"

"What do you mean?"

If it were possible, Pastor Don's voice became even softer, kinder. He said, "Max, I don't know if you are a man of faith or not. But I assume you have faith in the law. In justice, science, your mind? Or that your gun will work when you need it, right?"

"Yes, sir."

"You're probably brilliant at what you do." He glanced at Hanover. She nodded. "You like to solve things. The cases you take on. They're like puzzles."

"Yes, sir, I do."

"You deal in 'who done it' scenarios, evidence, possibilities, and motives, right?"

"Yes, sir." Max braced himself for a full-on gospel pitch. It didn't come. Instead, Pastor Don's questions kept circling around the case.

"Have you ever found the answer you're looking for is invisible till you ask the right question?"

"Yes, many times."

"Me, too. To give you a peak at my message tomorrow, doubters often resist asking the right question. For instance, a first things first question. Doubters often only ask, 'what' created the universe? The question casts the evidence in the light of only one window and ignores any other possibilities, forces or motives. But asking, 'Who' created the universe? Could point to a completely different answer that fits the same evidence. Does that make sense?"

"Yes, I see that." Max tried to suppress what came to his mind but something about Pastor Don's reasoning beyond reason had the similar effect of truth serum. He blurted out, "Like science is a keyhole. But belief is the key."

Pastor and Hanover both laughed. Pastor Don said, "Yes! Max, that's marvelous. May I borrow that for tomorrow?"

"It's not mine. I saw it somewhere. Feel free."

"Thank you. Max, you haven't told me, but you know what killed each of these poor souls. You assume the Red Angels are to blame. But you don't know how they did it. And you suspect there will be more. Is that about right?"

"Yes, sir."

"I'd say this is an unusual case."

"None of us have ever seen anything like it, pastor."

"Do you think there is any possibility the evidence in this case may color outside the lines of your normal perspective?"

"There is very little normal about it, for sure."

Hanover added, "And most of it has happened or come to light in the last five days."

"Extraordinary," Pastor Don said. "What if you took a different approach? What if there is a possibility you haven't considered?"

"What are you saying, Pastor? That there's an evil genius Moriarty behind the Red Angels?"

"Sounds like you've considered that. But no. Hang with me. Are you familiar with a thing in scripture called a 'word of knowledge?'"

"Generally." Max knew more but didn't want to telegraph any familiarity with scripture or his roots in it.

"There are many instances in Holy Scripture where God gave people messages to deliver containing information they could not have known. The Spirit of the Lord told the Apostle Peter that Ananias and Sapphira lied about their offering. When confronted, Ananias fell down dead on the spot. His wife, Sapphira, came in later, lied about it, too, and she fell down dead."

"Wait, pastor, are you saying the Red Angels are only messengers, but God is the hit man?"

"No, not the 'hit' man, but, Max, all lives are in God's hands. I just saw on the news this morning a State Senator had a stroke at exactly the same time her brother collapsed and died during her speech at the Capitol. Looks like she may survive, though severely impaired. Whether God causes or allows things he is aware of everything."

Neither Max nor Hanover responded. Pastor Don read the silence. He didn't miss a thing.

"Wait, did one of them get a note?"

Max sighed, "I'm supposed to say we are not at liberty to discuss that." But now they all knew the answer.

The kindness in Pastor Don's voice returned. "Max, the

mystery you may have is that God can give life. Take life. Spare life. He can give and take away in any way he chooses or allows."

"Pastor, surely you're not saying, if we wind up with seven bodies and seven notes, from seven different people, completely independent and unaware of each other, using nearly the exact same wording, that they may have delivered the notes, but had nothing to do with the killings?"

"Max, I'm saying all things are possible with God, and whatever MO he chooses, he is just and merciful. To put it in your terms that's part of his profile. Benedicilo."

The Italian expression heard so frequently from his mother triggered a subterranean outcry that rose from deep within Max. It originated inside the stony, clenched fist in his chest about her death. In his mind it was still inexcusably unjust and unmerciful. And according to Pastor Don, God was completely aware of it. He realized he was gritting his teeth. Swallowing hard, he forced himself to breathe a few steady breaths until the pressure behind his eyes leveled off. He would *not* unleash a torrent of rebuttals and rage. Not in front of Helen and Pastor Don. And certainly, no tears. The last time he cried, sober, was at Dr. Liam Malone's funeral. He felt a hand on his arm. It was Helen's.

"Max, sir, are you alright?"

"Uh, yes. Fine. Just a lot to take in and frankly, not what I expected."

"Max, I understand," Pastor said. "The dots Helen connected open a different window on the same evidence. A window you and your team didn't expect."

"Indeed." Max moved to wrap it up. "Thank you for your time, Pastor Don. Could you write down your number and a couple of references for 'word of knowledge' and the passage where that couple died from lying. I'm not sure where this leads us but…" Pastor Don cut him off.

"Max, go where the evidence leads." He kept talking as he went to the desk and scribbled what the detective requested. "You're after justice, it's what you do. That's a Godly pursuit." He finished writing and returned to the seat facing Max. "May I say one more thing to you, not about the case? and ask one more question?"

"Alright," Max said, "but I have one more question, too.

"Of course, go ahead."

"Pastor, have you ever received a 'word of knowledge.' About something you could not have known?"

"Yes, many times."

"With names, details and accusations?"

"A few, for some who needed to be confronted. But, Max, there is an overlap in scripture about words of knowledge, discernment and words of wisdom. Sometimes they come as persistent or urgent impulses. Sometimes like counsel, and in some cases as more specific revelations."

"Would you call the Red Angel notes 'words of knowledge?"

"As much as you've told me, yes. Yes, I believe they could be."

Pastor Don turned to Hanover and said, "Helen, could you give Max and me a couple of minutes?"

"Sure," she responded.

"But don't leave. I want to hug a cop again."

She laughed and said, "We rode together." She stepped out of the office.

Here it comes. The gospel pitch. Max readied himself to deflect and exit as quickly as possible.

Pastor Don paused as if honoring Max's permission and out of a reverence for what he was about to say. For Max the pause was long enough to feel awkward. The compassion on the pastor's face and the tender way he addressed Max threw him completely off balance.

"Maximillian Shaemus Malone, it's OK to be angry at God."

Max had to look away. He didn't know what to do or say. To stay calm he breathed through his mouth. Pastor Don let his statement hang in the air, then said it again.

"Whatever the reason, Max, it's OK to be mad as hell at God."

The words took on the shape of a key. No one had ever inserted those words into the heat-tempered deadbolt of Max's vault where he stored and expanded his case against God. It didn't matter if the pastor's words were a word of knowledge, discernment or word of wisdom, the distance between his head and his heart felt threatened. It began to shrink. Inside he ran desperately around castle Malone searching for a defense. Denial, Rebuttal, Deflection and Obfuscation were not there to repel the tenderness of Pastor Don's direct approach. The castle was temporarily undefended. At the last second, from a dark corridor, Delay handed him an out.

"Pastor, that sounds like a topic for another time."

Pastor Don was courteous but undeterred.

"Max, you're in good company. Moses, King David, many of the prophets and the disciples, were all angry at God. Some of them furious. I was adopted and grew up with an anger like thick concrete around my hurt from being abandoned by my biological parents."

Max had no words. Pastor Don could tell he had touched a raw, deep nerve. Out of care and wisdom, he offered Max a soft place to land.

"I know you've got a lot on your plate right now, but my door is always open, Max. And you've got my number."

Before the last sentence fully left the pastor's mouth, Max's phone buzzed. It was the captain. He was never more relieved to be saved by a call.

"Excuse me, Pastor, it's the captain. I need to take this."

"Of course."

"Yes, sir. At Cool Springs Church with Hanover and a pastor. Sir? Pastor Don Giacinto. Yes, sir, I will. Yes, sir. We can be there in twenty minutes." He ended the call. "Pastor, we need to go. Captain Haskins says to tell you hello."

"I've known Dirk a long time. A fine man and good brother." Max agreed. They stood. The pastor was still not done.

"Here's my question, Max. I know you're in full-time pursuit of this case but, time permitting, would you consider coming here tomorrow for a service? I'm teaching as you know. Maybe Helen could meet you here?"

Three responses queued up on the tip of Max's tongue. "Not a chance." "It all depends on our captain." And "If Hanover's coming I will." The call from the captain made response number two the obvious choice.

"It all depends on the captain."

"Of course. I understand." They joined Hanover in the foyer. Without asking, Pastor Giacinto bowed his head and prayed.

"Lord, give us eyes to see your evidence, ears to hear your voice and the will, humility and strength to follow wherever that leads. Amen."

He gave Hanover a bear hug, Max a strong handshake. Pastor Don looked him in the eye and said, "Pax vobiscum."

'And also with you' came immediately to Max's mind from his Catholic upbringing, but not to his lips. Peace seemed as far away as all the masses he attended as a kid and as impossible as ever being with a woman like Hanover. All he could muster was, "Thank you, Pastor."

Normally, Max would have given the pastor his card, but he wasn't sure he wanted to give him that access. So, he didn't.

As he and Hanover walked out under the welcome sign Max said to her, "The captain just called. He wants us all at the station immediately."

"What's up?"

"He just said something very important's come up. He didn't say what, but I could hear it in his voice."

They climbed into the F250. Max was quiet. They were headed north on I-65 before Hanover spoke.

"Guess we better go straight there, get my car later?"

"Alright." Max liked the sound of that.

After a few seconds Hanover asked, "So, what do think of Pastor Don? He's something, huh?"

"Yea, he's a force. I can understand why people are drawn to him."

A long ten seconds passed.

"If you don't mind me asking, sir, what did Pastor Don ask you? You don't have to say, of course."

"No, it's fine. He asked if I would come to a service tomorrow to hear him teach. I guess he didn't want me to feel any pressure in front of you. And, uh, he wondered if you might meet me there. I guess he didn't want to put any expectations on you either."

"I see. What did you tell him?"

"That it all depends on the captain. He understands we're slammed with this case."

"Right."

Five unsettled seconds passed. Max was about to say he would come for Pastor Don's message but not for the music. But Hanover played the next card first.

"Sir, I know church is not your thing, but I would meet you there. Pastor Don really is an amazing teacher. Such a great heart and mind. And the musicians and songs are the best and…"

"Ok."

"Seriously?"

"Sure, maybe a little light through another window might help with this case. But probably not for the music. Does that happen first?"

Three quick seconds passed. Hanover laughed.

"What's so funny?"

"I'm picturing the look on Detective Wilson's face when he finds out you're going to church tomorrow."

Max laughed, too. "Well, I'm sure as hell not telling him."

Fifteen untangled seconds passed in calm. Max felt a slight pax vobiscum in his chest. And behind his eyes.

Hanover added, "And tomorrow is Mother's Day."

Max had forgotten that in the chaos of the week. His sister always called him midday every year.

"They always do something special to honor mothers. I can only imagine how you miss your mom."

Max's brush with pax vobiscum evaporated.

CHAPTER 30

Saturday morning 11:30AM – Day 6

Dr. Clay Guryon stepped into Captain Haskins office like a visiting dignitary. He had the hawkish good looks of Robert Redford with the black hair and charisma of Elvis.

"Long way from the boondocks, huh, Dirk?"

Clay and Dirk met in first grade. Grew up dirt poor together. Attended the Abundant Life Church of God together. Baptized on the same day in the eighth grade on the last night of a tent revival. They felt guilty about discovering anatomy via Playboy magazines Clay stole from an older cousin. After the revival, Clay lied to Dirk about throwing them all away. He kept a few for further study. They played on the basketball team. Fished together. Drank their first beer together. And a lot more after that. As lab partners in biology Clay told Dirk while dissecting a frog, "I'm gonna be a doctor."

Clay was the first one Dirk went to when his uncle was murdered. In their junior year, Clay "borrowed" his stepdad's 1965 Mustang. He picked up Dirk and said, "Hop in and buckle up." He lost control rounding a curve too fast in the rain. The car was totaled. They both walked away with only a few bruises and cuts. Clay's stepdad added more of both to his hide.

They double dated to the Senior prom. Dirk and his steady girl, Sandy, made out under the bleachers in the gym while Clay practiced anatomy with his date outside on the fifty-yard line. Dirk knew because Clay bragged about how he "scored." They graduated high school together.

Both went to LSU. So did Dirk's high school sweetheart. She studied nursing. Dirk majored in Criminal Justice and Psychology. Clay went pre-med. The summer after their sophomore year Dirk took a paid internship at Angola prison where the two men who killed his uncle would spend the rest of their lives. One had softened, found Jesus, and asked for Dirk's forgiveness. He gave it. The accomplice was still hard as nails. When Dirk came back to LSU in September, Sandy broke his heart. A month later she was dating Clay. The next summer she married him. Clay became a doctor. Sandy a nurse.

Dirk moved away, went through the police academy in Nashville and took a job as a beat cop. Soon after Clay finished his internship, he divorced Sandy and married a young intern. Clay moved to Nashville twelve years after Dirk for an opportunity to run his own clinics. He was currently engaged to wife number four.

The childhood friends had seen each other on less than a handful of occasions around town. The last time was in passing at a Preds game. Their paths and boondock values diverged a long time ago.

"Let's take a drive," Dr. Guryon said.

"I'm swamped, Clay. Why do you think I'm here on a Saturday? Besides, I remember how you drive."

"Thirty minutes, Dirk. Official business. Don't want to talk about it here. And you're gonna love my new ride."

"Thirty minutes."

In the parking lot Clay's Bentley stood out. Like him. Continental GT. Azure purple with a gold tweed top. LSU colors.

"Hop in," Clay said.

The camel color leather seats smelled and felt like money.

Dirk quipped, "It's no 65 Mustang but I guess it gets you down the road."

"Yea, buckle up."

"Hey, no Earnhart moves today, Clay. I'll haul your ass in for reckless driving and assault with a killer car."

Dr. Guryon headed east on Murfreesboro Pike. At the on ramp to I-24 east he pushed the captain back in the seat a bit. He took the exit onto 440 west and opened it up. In seconds the speedometer hit 95.

"Shut it down, Clay." He did.

"It does zero to a hundred in 3.7 seconds."

"Point made. We going any place in particular?"

"Yea, not far."

Clay turned north on I-65 toward downtown, exited at Wedgewood, turned north on 8th. When he took a right on Chestnut Dirk guessed. "Fort Negley?"

"Exactly. You can see all of downtown from there."

"Clay, I don't have time to walk up there."

"Me neither. I'm a big contributor to the Parks and Rec. I called ahead." Clay pulled up to the gate. He rang the Visitor Center. The attendant came out and opened the gate. Dirk didn't know that was possible. The Bentley glided up the hill. Clay parked facing a panorama of downtown.

"Nashville's bustin' at the seams," he said.

"Yes, it is." Captain Haskins wasn't interested in small talk.

Being in the same car with Clay after all these years was not bringing out his better angels. "What's on your mind. Why the surprise visit?"

"Dirk, I know we don't agree on many things anymore. I respect what you do. What you've done with your life. I know you don't feel the same about my work."

"Honestly, I've always been puzzled how two people with the same roots can make such different choices."

"I'd expect you to put it so tactfully. Well, old boondocks buddy, here's the reason for showing up unannounced." But he didn't get to the reason, not directly.

"In your line of work, Dirk, I imagine you've received some death threats?"

"A few." he had the captain's full attention.

"Well, I get several a month. Sometimes one a week. It comes with the territory. I live with professional security at home and at the clinics. I even upgraded the windows in this car to polycarbonate glass. Practically bulletproof. I have to take precautions."

"Let's cut the crap, Doctor." Dirk spoke the word 'doctor' with a sneer. "You knew the risks going in. You and I see this from completely different places, but have you forgotten I was in charge of a perimeter for your security at the courthouse the first time you beat a case against you for a partial birth abortion? Because that's my job. So, why come crying to me now?"

Clay's clinics provided the lion's share of the abortions in middle Tennessee. Charges were brought twice against him for partial birth abortions he performed. The plaintiffs argued neither abortion met the high bar of the state code regarding risk to the mother's life. His high-dollar lawyers and medical experts won acquittal both times. He avoided a class C felony conviction and revocation of his medical license. He became the face of abortion providers in middle Tennessee and a visible target of pro-life advocates in Tennessee and beyond. Balloons filled with red paint periodically stained his house, his clinics and even his car while leaving a restaurant.

"This is why I didn't want to talk in your office, Dirk. You get so emotional about this. You always did."

Dirk unloaded both barrels on him. "Listen, fancy gator bait, I don't need an excuse to get passionate about tearing a living baby to pieces, or that my once best friend still thinks it's like dissecting a frog and gets f-ing rich on it!" He thought about asking how many abortions it takes to buy a Bentley with bulletproof glass, but he knew there was a lot more history behind his anger at Clay. His better angel bit his tongue for him.

"Dirk, for God's sake! I have other investments and businesses. And I will not have this college debate again."

"For God's sake, really Clay? If you looking for cover or sympathy you've come to the wrong place."

"Not why I'm here, Dirk. I need your professional help. And it is your job, dammit! Hell, I'm used to the protestors and their anonymous threats. But I got one this week that scared the hell out of me." He reached in his breast coat pocket and pulled out a white envelope. Dirk called on all his restraint to calm down and put on his officer of the law face.

Dr. Guryon showed him the front of the envelope. 'Clay Guryon' Hand printed. Nothing else. He pulled out a plain white card. Again, 'Clay Guryon' on one side. He turned it over and read it aloud:

You have sown death and despair. Prepare to reap.
Put your affairs in order. Your life is required of you.

The Red Angels

"Lord, have mercy," the captain said, for more reasons than Clay could imagine.

"What the hell do you make of that?" Clay tried to hand the note to him. Dirk became a policeman.

"Lay it on the dash, with the envelope," he told Clay. "If there are fingerprints or DNA you've compromised that."

For the first time in their long relationship the captain could sense genuine fear behind Clay's airbrushed bravado. His childhood friend had never been afraid of anything. Gators. Snakes. Cliff jumping. Not even his violent stepdad. Dirk took momentary gratification in seeing his fear. But knowing what he knew about the finality of the other cases, his Clay's obvious fear took the edge off his anger, and even loosened the grip of his long-harbored disdain for what he had done to Sandy and who he had become. The dissonance pressed down on Dirk. He couldn't tell Clay how serious this threat was. Dr. Guryon's next statement confirmed withholding that information. He was as obstinate now as he had been about stealing his stepdad's Mustang.

"Dirk, you gotta find whoever's behind this. I want these pious sons of bitches caught. Otherwise, I'm gonna take this to the media and do a scorched earth campaign on the religious community like this town's never seen. You thought my two trials were shitstorms? Imagine this in the news."

The captain knew this was a delicate moment - legally, professionally as well as personally. It pitted duty and ethics against best strategy. This could come back around to a 'who knew what when' scenario.

"Alright, Clay, I can see why this upset you enough to come to me. I take this kind of thing seriously, of course."

"I do too, now. For the first time I'm leaving town over this. Tomorrow morning for Mother's Day I'm taking my fiancé and mom to breakfast. She's losing some memory, but she remembers you, Dirk. I think she always liked you more than me, by the way." He was back in his bon vivant mode.

"Give her my best."

"I will. I'm taking her to Pancake Pantry, her favorite. The manager's a friend. He's bringing us in through the back to avoid the line."

Same old Clay, Dirk thought. *Always working an angle. I wonder if his mom knows what kind of doctor he really is.*

"Tomorrow afternoon Victoria and I fly to New Orleans. Staying through Memorial weekend. Will that give you enough time to put someone behind bars?"

"That's impossible to say. But you have my word, I'm on it."

"Thank you. That means a lot, bro."

'Bro' nearly set Dirk off again. They were not bros. Hadn't been for a very long time. With some effort he kept his composure and pressed forward.

"I need to ask you a few more things," the captain said. "Where and how was the card delivered to you? Has anyone else seen it or have you told anyone else? And I'll need to keep the card. Forensics can do surprising things to find a useful clue or two.

And one more thing: Let *me* reach out to you with progress reports."

Clay assured Dirk he wouldn't bug him. The captain knew that was not likely. The note had shown up in a stack of birthday cards on Thursday from Clay's staff. He didn't know how it got there. He opened them at home. No one else knew about it. He balked hard about leaving the card, but Dirk's integrity and investigative reasoning prevailed. The captain picked up the card and envelope by the edges and put them in his coat pocket.

They descended the hill. The attendant opened the gate on a new chapter in their relationship. On the drive back to police headquarters they talked about the whereabouts of some classmates. Dirk kept wondering how to throw Clay a rope of some kind. As they pulled into the lot at headquarters, he took a shot at it.

"Clay, what if this is some kind of wake-up call?"

"Are you serious?"

"Dead serious. You ever have any second thoughts about what you do? We grew up in the same church and…"

"Let me stop you there, Dirk. We might have been born on the bayou, as the song says, but I left all that swamp religion behind. We got out, bro."

There it was again. *One more 'bro' and I'm gonna launch on your sorry ass.*

"Besides," Clay went on, you ever known me to back down from a fight?"

"No."

"You damn right."

The captain composed himself again. He opened the car door.

"Clay, all I'm saying is maybe do some soul searching down in New Orleans."

"I'll try to work that in between the beignets and fais do do."

"I'm serious, Clay. We're not kids anymore. We both sowed stuff we don't want to reap."

"I can't believe you'd care if anything happened to me."

In spite of Dirk's distaste and even deeper enmity toward Clay, an urgency welled up in him. If this played out like the other cases this might be the last time they ever spoke. Anything left unsaid he would regret for the rest of his life. Instead of getting out, he closed the car door.

"What else?" Clay said with an edge. "You got something to say, say it."

The captain took a deep breath to collect himself. He looked at his childhood friend and spoke the hardest words he ever uttered. And the last thing his childhood friend expected to hear.

"Clay, I forgive you."

In the quiet, all the bluster drained out of Clay. They weren't Doctor and Captain. They were just two boys from the boondocks. Two men on different roads.

Clay finally spoke. "You always were a bigger man than me. That's why I knew I could count on you now. Whatever happens, Dirk, whatever you do, Lache pas la patate, bro."

"I'm on it." The captain got out, closed the door and watched him glide away. He spoke his signature line. "Lord, have mercy," this time completely as a prayer. Before the sleek Bentley left the lot, he began calling the task force to meet at the station. Immediately.

CHAPTER 31

Saturday afternoon 12:50PM – Day 6

Conference room B was locked when Max and Hanover arrived. Per Captain's order. Not even the usual Saturday cleaning staff had access since the Task Force began Friday morning. The information on the white boards was too volatile. They headed to the break room for coffee where they found Vince and Thomason on the same mission. Vince wasted no time goading Max.

"I want to hear about Pastor Don and whether you got saved, but first, how's your new partner working out?"

Max volleyed back. "It feels good to have a much better shot around, but her singing isn't anything like yours. Thank heaven." Even Max surprised himself by using his mother's expression.

"'Thank heaven?'" Vince picked up on the phrase. He put on his best Irish accent. "Don't you mean your 'lucky stars', Shaemus?"

Only Max didn't know Thomason knew his middle name. He had so many Rubik's tiles swirling in his head he ignored Vince's out-of-bounds barb and deflected.

"Thomason, did Vince break out his uke on you?"

"No, sir. He drove, so it stayed in the back seat. I hear he's pretty good."

"Palatable. His whistling rendition of "We Will Rock You" will rock you to sleep. Hey, I need to stop by my desk. See you in there." Max exited.

It was 1:30PM before every chair was filled. They each took the same seat as the day before.

Dr. Brickman arrived last. "Sorry, I was having lunch with my mom."

"No worries," said the captain. "Everyone got here ASAP. Thank you. I know we're all stretched very thin this week. And it's not over yet." He took the five RA notes out of the manilla envelope and arranged them in a single row in front of himself. "I want to hear what you've found. Then we're going to review each case. Save your security footage evidence for that. We will probably order dinner in again. But first." He took a sixth card from his breast coat pocket in an evidence bag and placed it in the middle of the table, face down. He tossed a pair of latex gloves beside it. The room went quiet as a grave.

"Number six walked into my office today. Still very much alive. Let's start with who. Max, show us the name."

Max gloved up. Removed the envelope. Held it up for the task force to see the name.

"Clay Guryon," the captain said. "Dr. Clay Guryon. Ring any bells?"

All of them were well-aware of Guryon's history and reputation in Nashville.

Vince blurted, "There's got to be a hell for guys like him."

"Detective Wilson!" The captain erupted. "That's unbecoming of an officer and even an intermittent Baptist. Everyone, keep your opinions and theology to yourself. Vince just cast the first stone. Anyone else?"

"You're right. I'm very sorry, sir." Vince was genuinely contrite. "My apologies to everyone."

Officer Marvin Thomason felt the same anger as Vince for a different reason. He and his wife, Shannon, had been trying to have a baby for three years. Without success. They recently considered adopting. Regardless of theology, it was inconceivable to him that some would routinely do away with so many unborn lives when thousands like him and his wife want so much to become parents.

At Guryon's name, Dr. Brickman's mind summoned two memories: a few girls from his days at Vanderbilt who used the services of one of Guryon's clinics, and a paper he wrote for a medical ethics graduate course.

For Thor, every life was sacred. Of highest value. Reflecting that view were two prominent tattoos which the team had yet to see. On his right upper arm covering his entire deltoid, a large Bethlehem star shone over the outline of a village. Below were the words: "Til He appeared..." On his left deltoid, a large cross stood against the backdrop of a rising sun. Under it were the words: '... and the soul felt its worth.'

For him, men of science, especially those untethered from faith, like Guryon, were merely sad, appalling and still asleep in the light. He knew so many colleagues and friends who considered themselves liberated, 'woke' in the new Orwellian jargon, from the vast darkness of the unknown by the flashlight of reason. He found it an absurd loop that many of them held the view that matter evolved consciousness, could study matter and conclude that matter in the form of an unborn human does not matter. For that intellectual reason alone, he considered the wide acceptance of abortion, the height of nihilism.

He put this view in the graduate ethics paper called, "Does

Some Matter Matter Less to Some?" Thor argued that especially in a country which ignited from the proposition that all people are created equal and endowed by their Creator with certain, immovable, non-negotiable rights, apparently some can be denied those rights. Slavery certainly bore that out until a bloody civil war codified the founders' ideals into the fabric of the culture. Likewise, the blood of millions sacrificed in WW2 repudiated the Nazi's extermination of Jews and others viewed as having lesser value. In the matter of abortion, Dr. Brickman maintained some matter clearly still matters less to some. He took the position that faith and reason, combined as the founding fathers had done, together open a grander vista to the full light of reason and true enlightenment. As he put it in his ethics paper, "Reason is a flashlight. Faith is the sun."

On the sunrise end of Thor's outdoor garden cathedral in process, he had already placed a quote from C.S. Lewis next to a sundial, "I believe in Christianity like I believe in the sunrise, not because I can see it, but because by it I see everything."

It was beyond reason, but within the realm of free choice, Thor wrote in the paper, that otherwise brilliant people preferred the flashlight to the sun, but he understood how such a narrow perspective through the keyhole of science could misinterpret a sacred living being as mere tissue, just as a blind man might mistake an elephant for a rope by touching only its tail. This was an illustration learned from his time in Thailand. Without an Imago Dei view of every human, a Godless, "we are only matter" approach is only logical, and results in a very different human valuation and societal ethic. But if there is more to matter than meets the microscope, it matters, and 'matter only' logic becomes diabolical and deadly.

The ethics paper was the first time he used his parent's counsel about science being a keyhole. His professor, a woke medical man, did not take kindly to science playing a diminutive, secondary role to faith. Thor, received an F, for "denigrating reason and anachronistic thinking." He appealed his final grade in the class to his advisory panel based on unfair treatment compared to the standard applied to other students. The woke professor got a wake-up call from his peers. The failing grade was rescinded and changed. It was the only B Thor had in graduate school, but it did more to forge his tenacity than any 'A'.

Hanover felt no judgement of Guryon. Internally, she was busy resisting an old shame and reminding herself of the grace and mercy she found to overcome it. She was the only one at the table able to have an abortion. And had had one. In her pre-Jesus groupie days, at one point it presented the best option to carry on with her life. Besides, the musician boyfriend was not marriage material. But the scar that remained on her soul was part of what brought her to faith in Christ. Papa G called it a "redeeming scar." He told her the Lord would turn it into compassion for others, especially young women. It did. 'Protect and Serve' was not just a motto for Hanover. She rested in that grace now as the discussion continued. Though another thought unsettled her. What would Max think if he knew?

As soon as Vince voiced his condemnation of Guryon, the song *You Must Be Evil* kicked off in Max's head. *Chris Rea, 1989, from The Road to Hell.* Like Thomason, Max and his Ex, Jennifer, wanted to be parents. They had only been pregnant once, but at about four and a half months, something went wrong. Even with his faith in God shattered, the wonder of the ultrasound was something he still held at bay in his memory. It brought too much pain. The joy of having a child bore an echo of watching his mother carry Ariana. Max was only five, but he remembered feeling Sofia's growing tummy, putting his ear against it and talking to Arianna. Sometimes the baby moved when he spoke to her. Sofia read parts of a psalm to Max about God knitting Arianna's unformed body together in her womb and being "fearfully and wonderfully made." When Jennifer lost their baby, all the echo of that wonder and the anticipated joy of seeing his own child petrified into the already formidable barricade around his heart.

So, momentarily, Max was all in with Vince. *This bastard deserves whatever's coming.* He was mentally gripping a second stone when another sniper memory shut down Chris Rea. In his junior year of college, a good friend got pregnant. She didn't want the boy to know. She came to Max for three hundred dollars. He knew what it was for. In his calcifying view of life, the world and mankind, he gave her the money. A week later, she returned it. Couldn't go through with it. The girl told everyone she transferred schools but actually dropped out and gave up her baby boy for adoption.

Even if that innocent blood was not on his hands, Max lived torn between knowing that child was a grown man out there somewhere, probably with kids of his own, and the haunting awareness that he had valued that man's life at three hundred dollars.

Max Malone, the white-knuckling atheist, knew the 'cast the first stone' story. He dropped his. But another anxiety unsettled him. What would Hanover think if she knew? He glanced at her, but looked back at the card in his hand.

In his mind, the chasm between them doubled. A song floated into his head. Jennifer sent it to him just before she asked for a divorce. "Sometimes I feel like I'm looking up at you from the bottom of the Grand Canyon, so small and so far / from the Grand Canyon with a hole in my heart." *Grand Canyon, 1992, Susan Ashton from the album Angels of Mercy.*

As all these unspoken ruminations simmered around the table, Captain Haskins related a short version of his long relationship with Clay. He finished with their conversation at Fort Negley, culminating in Dr. Guryon's threat.

"In Clay's words, if we don't catch "these pious sons of bitches" he will take the note to the media and, again, his words, 'launch a scorched earth campaign against the religious community like this town has never seen.' Max, read the card, please."

Max removed the plain white card from the envelope. He read the familiar words:

You have sown death and despair. Prepare to reap.
Put your affairs in order. Your life is required of you.

The Red Angels

The dissonance of adding a victim to the list who was still living traveled around the table.

Hanover got up and stood at the whiteboard. She said what everyone was thinking.

"Sir, should we add Dr. Guryon yet?"

"Yes," the captain came back immediately. "He's been targeted. Just leave out cause of death. People, we have to do everything in

271

our power to make sure that blank remains empty." Everyone knew the odds of that were heavily against them. Even witness protection, which the captain had considered, only guaranteed the case would blow wide open, ignite Clay's threat and make him an even bigger target.

Hanover added Dr. Guryon to the board. The captain asked Dr. Brickman to tell what the autopsy revealed about Gunner Brown's cause of death.

"Catastrophic systems failure. Lights out," Brickman said.

Hanover amended that item on the board as well.

We reap what we sow; Sow evil & trouble, reap trouble
& death Get ready; You are about to die

		Haughty eyes
Catastrophic systems failure:	GB	Lying tongue
sowed lies		
? : sowed death/despair	CG	Hands that shed innocent blood
Hung by the hair: sowed		
poison/agony	AD	Feet quick to rush to evil
Fall from balcony:		
treachery/wickedness	JB	Heart that devises wicked schemes
Impaled by rebar: sowed		
deceit/corruption	SS	False witness
Inhaled toxic gas: sowed		
corrosion/discord	DJ	Cause conflict in community

"One thing may be in our favor," the captain said. "Clay and his fiancé are getting out of town tomorrow to lie low while we sort this out. He's taking his mother and fiancé to Pancake Pantry at 8:30AM tomorrow morning for Mother's Day. His flight leaves at 2:00PM. I want an unmarked car at his place tonight. All night. Work it out between you. Since this is the volunteer state, I'll take the shift from when we're done here till midnight."

'Yes, sirs,' followed all around.

The captain wasn't done. "I know the manager at the Pantry. Max and Helen, I'll get you a table. If a waiter spills anything on Dr. Guryon, I want you there."

Max couldn't have been more pleased. A breakfast date with Hanover. Captain's orders.

Hanover was pleased and relieved. Avoiding the long line at the Pantry presented a sweet perk. But even better, barring any complications, breakfast at 8:15AM meant she and Max could still make church at 10:30AM.

Vince couldn't resist. "Captain, since this is the volunteer state, wherever Guryon's dining tonight Julie and I can cover him."

"Big of you, as usual, Vince. But you're dining here with us tonight. Tomorrow, you and Thomason, in two cars, keep eyes on him from the Pantry till he's on that plane."

Max, the skeptic, couldn't muzzle the irony taunting him that if what Pastor Don said was true in these cases, that God was the perp, leaving town was no protection for Dr. Guryon. Naturally, he kept that thought to himself. Not doing so would risk giving credence to a realm he knew the others assumed Max denied.

Two chairs down Hanover contemplated the same irony. She also wondered how Max would report their interview with Pastor Don. How would he present the choices between a clandestine band of religious zealots directed by a maniacal mastermind or the sovereign Lord of the universe behind it all? In her view the evidence pointed more and more where Pastor Don described. When she remembered how Max put it to Pastor Don, God as the "hit man," she failed to contain a slight, involuntary chuckle.

"Helen? a revelation?" the captain asked.

"No, sir. Nothing. Sorry, just trying to get my head around all this."

The look of calm confidence she gave Max began an inner struggle in him between the whole truth about their conversation with Pastor Don, and a "Maxified" version that would pass muster in Hanover's view of it. He feared even a hint of spin or discrediting the pastor on his part would erode her view of him, whatever that was. Besides that, Pastor Don arrived independently at the same MO Hanover did. Amid his quandary, he felt a rare potential elation of her belief in him already making him want to be better than he knew he was. But how could he lie to himself, capitulate now and let years of entrenched and cultivated disbelief buckle like cardboard in the welcome rain of her affirmation, no matter how sweet the soaking might be? By the time the captain asked them to report, he would have to decide. The captain gave him a momentary reprieve.

"Vince, Marvin, what have you got?"

Vince reported the card stock search was a bust. Several of the RA card types were available locally, but impossible to know who purchased what, when, except online, which would take an inordinate amount of time. Their visit to Jacobs' workplace yielded better intel. The new manager confirmed Jacobs was, quote, "an equal opportunity abuser and bully." An error in labeling caused dangerous solutions to be stored improperly. But the real find was the statement Jacobs made to the man he fired that day, a Choppy Ambler.

"Thomason wrote it down," Vince said. "Go ahead Marvin."

"Mr. Ambler said he'd seen Jacobs go off on a lot guys in the two years he worked there, but that day he really came 'unhinged' as Mr. Amber put it."

"Alright, alright, skip to what Jacobs said to Mr. Ambler," Vince said, pushing Thomason to get to the point.

Thomason reacted amiably, "Detective Malone, is this how he is with you?"

"Obviously, you're not feeding him enough tacos," Max counseled.

The captain knew the pressure they were under. He countenanced some banter. But he wanted results, especially with the sword of Damocles hanging over Dr. Guryon. He weighed in.

"Alright, when we break let's order tacos. SATCO work for you, Vince?"

"Yes, sir."

"Everyone else good with that?"

'Yes, sirs' all around.

"Good. Marvin, proceed."

"Yes, sir. According to Mr. Ambler, Jacobs exploded in a way he hadn't seen before and shouted
at him. Quote, 'You're not gonna be my f-ing red angel of death today. No way! God's got my back. Nice try.'"

"Great work! Thank you," said the captain. "So, we know Jacobs read the note, and it obviously affected him."

"Yes, sir," Vince said. "Mr. Ambler was at home with his wife when he got the news about Jacobs'
death. The labeling error and Jacobs' state of mind created the perfect storm for what happened."

Thomason added, "If I may, sir, at the time it appeared clearly to be an accident, so the only follow-up was done by their insurance company."

"I assume the cleanup is complete?" The captain asked. "So, the scene is not likely to yield anything else?"

"Yes, sir." Vince said.

"Thank you. Good work."

Max braced himself to be next.

"Brickman," the captain said, "You're up. The cards and handwriting. Go."

As expected, Brickman was precise and thorough about the paper stock, trademarks, types of ink and pens. He even brought a laser pointer to highlight some of the finer details on the cards arrayed on the table, down to the small stain on Abe's card, which he had not yet analyzed. In a word, he was, to Max, boring and seemed distracted, certainly less engaged from the eager-to-please golden retriever from earlier in the week. Brickman's only revelatory fact was the handwriting on all five cards was positively the work of five distinct individuals. *Or a brilliant deceiver intent on making it appear so*, Max thought.

Theo immediately said, "Or a very clever person intent on throwing us off just one trail." Dr. Brickman suspected the handwriting on Dr. Guryon's card would not match any of other others. He qualified his findings by acknowledging he had some handwriting training in graduate school from an expert mentor at the FBI. But there were sufficient variations to come to the conclusion: different people wrote the five cards. He paused. Reviewed his notes. Turned a page, then turned it back to the captain.

"Is that all, Dr. Brickman?"

"Uh, yes, essentially, sir, in relation to hard evidence."

Max smelled more. He threw out an unusual challenge. "Dr. Brickman, why do I feel like you're pleading the fifth chapter of hesitations?"

Brickman was silent. Hanover smiled. Thomason laughed, "Sorry, sir, but what is that?"

The captain and Vince knew. They had heard it from Max many times. Vince answered Thomason.

"It's something his dad used to say to Max and his little sister. It works great in interrogations. Tell him, Max."

"Whenever my dad could tell we were not telling the whole story he would say that. It was his way of telling us, 'I know there's more. You can tell me anything.' In his Irish accent it was very persuasive."

Hanover thought that was the most endearing thing she ever heard from a man, especially from a father to his children. Early on, she thought her own father was the most poetic dad ever. He told her things like "love is a flower and you're its only seed." "You're my tiny dancer." "Try to be once, twice, three times a lady." It wasn't till she was a teenager she realized he stole it all from song lyrics. Her power DJ Dad once told her after a heated argument with her mother, "Helen, I don't care what Helen Reddy says. No man wants a roaring woman!" She remembered a lot of roaring going both ways.

To hear such an original gem from Max's father made her one degree less wary of him and two degrees more intrigued.

Max added, "I can use the accent if you like, Dr. Brickman." And he did. "So, laddie, why do I feel like yer pleadin' the fifth chapter o' hesitations, eh?"

They all had a much-needed laugh. Even Brickman.

"OK, there is something else," Brickman said. He described

how sitting at his desk examining the cards, he noticed the card stock of Abe's note looked identical to the one in a frame on his desk from his parents.

Max glanced at Vince, gloating in vindication.

He told the team that his mother works in a specialty paper shop in Green Hills, so he had lunch with her earlier, just to see if she remembered anyone who purchased those kinds of cards. Turns out they sell a lot of them. Thor became very forthcoming about his parents' charismatic style of Catholicism, revealing that his mother had experienced certain revelations, particularly in the mission field - revelations related to discerning spirits of oppression and illnesses. As a boy he saw people healed and even a few barren women able to conceive children after she prayed for them.

No one around the table was bored now. And then his honesty stunned them all.

"Actually, I didn't want to, but I started to wonder if my mother may have written the note to Abe."

Max shot a "never doubt me" look at Vince.

Brickman apologized to the captain as he described how he stretched the evidence rule a bit by photocopying the handprinted note from Abe and the one in cursive from his parents. How he cut out random words from each and sent them to his mentor expert at the FBI. He assured the captain he shredded the copies and leftovers.

For the first time, a seed of respect grew in Max for Brickman. Still, he thought, *Unless this is the most ingenious, elaborate CYA, I gotta hand it to this kid.*

"Well?" the captain asked. "Have you heard from your FBI guy?"

"Yes. While I was at lunch with my mom. No possible match."

Max was about to ask to see the FBI report when Brickman

slid it onto the center of the table from his stack of papers. The captain picked it up. Viewed it. Passed it on around the table.

Vince leaned toward Max and whispered, "Who's the stronzo now?"

The captain took the floor. "Dr. Brickman, I think we might all agree, I have rarely seen such a rigorous pursuit of the truth in the face of personal risk. We are fortunate to have you. Blessed, actually. I know you needed to find out, but, son, next time come to me if you think we need to color outside the lines."

"Yes, sir. I will. Thank you, sir."

As impressed as Max was, he had a couple of lingering questions for Brickman.

"Sir? I have one more question for Dr. Brickman. Two actually."

"Make it quick and germane, Max. We need to take a short break," the captain directed.

"Yes, sir." The questions Max wanted to ask Brickman were whether he was familiar with the concept of a 'word of knowledge' in scripture, and does his mother or anyone in her circle ever receive them with the specificity of the RA notes? But reading the room, he chose two other questions.

"Dr. Brickman, do you prefer brisket or ribs?"

Everyone chuckled in relief.

"Love both. If I have to choose one. Ribs, sir."

"Noted. Second question: wet or Memphis dry?"

"Wet, sir. The messier the better."

"Indeed."

The captain instructed the team to write down their order for tacos. "Max, you and Helen are up next." He released everyone for a twenty-minute break.

CHAPTER 32

Saturday afternoon 3:30PM – Day 6

As the task force went to the break Hanover tried to get Max's attention but he was out the door two steps behind Brickman. She was hoping to discuss how he wanted to present their conversation with Pastor Don.

Max followed Brickman to the men's room. They stood two urinals apart in silence. Max finally said, "You get it."

"Get what, sir?"

"Follow the evidence. No matter where it leads."

"Yes, sir."

"Even if you don't want to go there. You had to be sweating bullets waiting for that FBI report."

"Yes, sir. But I had to know."

"Exactly."

They finished their business. Washing their hands, Max said, "I need your opinion on something."

"Yes, sir."

"Your office in two minutes."

Between the questions about brisket or ribs and Detective Malone's request for his opinion, Brickman felt like he had just come through a rite of passage. He thought surely he was part of the team now.

Max headed to his desk to create a new folder. There was a

packet with a note from the duty officer saying it had just arrived. He also wanted to give Brickman time to savor what had just happened. Max calculated that between Brickman's noble, and genuinely impressive display in the meeting, his congeniality about brisket vs ribs and now a request for Brickman's opinion, the boy wonder ought to be back in his golden retriever mode by the time he got there. He was right. Before Max sat down, Brickman was wagging his tail.

"How can I help, Detective? Whatever you need, sir."

Out of a new folder marked simply "RA" for effect, Max pulled out a white page of copy paper with handwriting on it. The top was cut off cleanly. Like the letterhead had been removed. Max leaned onto the desk toward Brickman and spoke like they were engaged in espionage.

"I need to know if there is any resemblance in this handwriting to any of the RA notes. We don't have time for your FBI connection."

"Of course, but I'll have to get all six cards from the captain."

"I'll make that happen. And I need to know by tomorrow."

"Yes, sir. I'll do level one and two analyses. A/B vowels and then consonants in this sample with each card. Should take about an hour and a half."

"Great. And just to make sure, check to see if the handwriting on Guryon's matches any of the others. I'd say probably not. But take a look."

"Yes, sir. Good idea."

Brickman took a closer look at the page. "These are all scripture references and biblical names. If I may ask, sir, where is this from?"

"I'm gonna have to plead the fifth chapter of hesitations on that. I want you to come at this blind, completely objective. If there's no match, no harm no foul."

"I understand, sir, of course."

"We better get back. You know the captain."

Just after they reconvened tacos arrived. Max welcomed another delay to report. He passed the few moments of reprieve listening to Vince talk about where Julie wanted to take the kids on summer vacation. But he furtively watched Hanover eat and converse with Brickman and the captain. While Max half-listened to Vince and the table cleared of taco debris, a song in his head provided the soundtrack. "Romance and all its strategy / leaves me battling with my pride / but through the insecurity some tenderness survives…". *Sometimes When We Touch, Dan Hill, 1977, from Longer Fuse.* Just as Dan Hill was about to launch into the chorus, the captain's insistent voice called the meeting back to order.

"Max, Vince, are you with us? People, I know it's been a long day. Lord, have mercy, this week seems like two months. I can't tell you how impressed I am with your fortitude, and how much I appreciate what you bring to this team. Now. Max, Hanover, what have you got?"

Max chose. He showed the packet that had just arrived, revealing it was from Ms. Jacobs. He stalled, referring briefly to the breakthroughs from security footage at the Capitol and Ms. Bellaire's apartment, saying he would detail those later in the case review time. Then he cleverly covered his cowardice in chivalry.

"Officer Hanover arranged a meeting earlier today with her pastor and friend, Don Giacinto."

"A great man, Pastor Don. Good choice," the captain threw in.

"He certainly makes an impression. Hanover's strong relationship with him made it happen. Since you regularly endure the sound of my voice beyond the daily recommended dosage, I'm going to let her describe that meeting."

"Amen," Vince agreed.

Hanover didn't hesitate. "Yes, sir." Without missing a beat, she began. "Our purpose was to gain insight from a seasoned pastor into the MO of the Red Angels, to build a better profile."

Max watched Hanover summarize the hour and a half meeting with Pastor Don into seven or eight minutes. While the others listened, Max built more into his profile of her: cogent, articulate, focused, engaging. She made certain to clarify that Detective Malone walked a fine line between describing the cases, but not revealing too much. But she pointed out that Pastor Don's keen intuition sensed exactly what they were getting at. The only time Max interjected was when Hanover underplayed the fact that Pastor Don arrived at the same scripture, the MO of the same seven targets in Proverbs that she already deduced.

"Pastor Don heaped major kudos on her at that point."

"Well deserved," the captain said.

She described what Pastor Don said about the concept of a "word of knowledge" in scripture, how messages and information are given by God to be delivered by people who couldn't know the information any other way. She left out the part where Max called God a 'hit man.' But told the team Pastor Don made it clear they could be dealing with this very thing.

She emphasized how intuitive the pastor was. "He used an example of a couple in the Bible who fell down dead after lying to Peter about an offering, Ananias and Saphira. We were both taken by surprise when he compared that to the news he heard this morning about Gunner Brown and his sister. Pastor Don asked if one of them had received an RA note! Max, Detective Malone, told him we were not at liberty to discuss that. But Pastor Don connected the dots. He got it."

At the mention of Ananias and Saphira, Dr. Brickman turned his head slightly, looked past Vince at Max. Max kept his eyes fixed on Hanover. Brickman got it. He knew whose handwriting was in his office. He knew why Max had to know. And who didn't need to know. Might never need to know. Brickman knew he was on the team.

"Wait a minute," the captain said. "Does Pastor Don believe these notes could be 'words of knowledge' written by six different people unconnected in any way but using the same wording in every note?"

"I asked him that exact question, sir," Max replied. "He thinks that's entirely possible."

"Lord have mercy," came right on cue from the captain.

Hanover summed up by saying, "I haven't run this by Detective Malone, but Pastor Don seemed to paint a pretty clear picture that we are either dealing with a group of religious zealots directed by a maniacal mastermind, or the notes are "words of knowledge" delivered by independent messengers, but the deaths are acts of God. Is that about right, Detective?"

"Yes, that's his view." Max concurred, but he refused to let the room drift in either direction.

"With all due respect to Pastor Don, as the minority skeptic in the room, may I remind everyone we have surveillance footage of three non-divine beings delivering written threats of bodily harm to people who shortly after lost their lives." He held up the packet. "What are we supposed to tell Ms. Jacobs? Your Ex was a stronzo, so God sent him a message, killed him and made it look like an accident?"

Vince interpreted in an exaggerated Italian accent, "'Stronzo' that's Italiano for 'jackass.'"

"Look, Max, no one's closing the book on this," the captain said. "We're going to review the evidence we've got case by case. And keep looking for those messengers. But I reviewed the statute, people, and without giving him any context, I confirmed it with Seneff in legal. If we can't tie someone to the actual harm, it's a Class A misdemeanor for harassment. That's why Dr. Guryon never pursues the threats he gets."

Hanover stood and went to the whiteboard. She flipped it over and erased the back side. As she wrote six names across the top of the board, the captain continued.

"Something about this one really spooked Clay. I've never seen him afraid of anything. And we know more than he does why this one is so serious. The life of the sixth name on that board hangs in the balance, people."

"And potentially one more," Thomason added.

"Exactly. Theo, would you put on a pot of coffee, please?"

"Yes, sir."

The next few hours produced enough unanswered questions and action items to keep them all busy for a month. They only had until 2:00 PM the next day, Sunday, before Dr. Guryon's plane left for New Orleans. No one said it, but none of them were convinced that leaving town was any safeguard for him. The looming seventh target was even more nebulous. All the skill, brains, experience, and expertise in the room couldn't mitigate the feeling of helplessness in the team. They could babysit Guryon till his flight, but against who? Against what? Discovering the MO had gotten them a front-row seat to the mystery, but not ahead of it. At 8:45PM the captain read the room and called it.

"Alright, people, this bayou is fished out for tonight. Choose your two-hour shift. I'll take til

11:00PM. Max, Hanover, the Pantry at 8:15AM. Clay's reservation is at 8:30. Dr. Brickman, you ever done a stakeout?"

"No, sir."

"He can hang with me a shift," Vince offered.

Brickman pushed back. "Thank you, detective, but I actually have some more work to do related to this tonight."

Max said, "Sure you won't reconsider, Dr. Brickman? Vince usually brings his ukulele on stakeouts. His rendition of 'Rainbow Connection' is classic."

Vince shot back. "It's hard being green with envy, isn't it?"

The laughter around the table was therapeutic. The captain always took banter as a good sign, but he kept them on task.

"Vince, you and Marvin tag team from the Pantry to the plane, right?"

Both acknowledged.

Max suggested Hanover take 11PM to 1AM to get some sleep before the breakfast. His hint of kindness was not unnoticed around the table.

Vince couldn't let it pass. "She's not the one who needs the beauty sleep, Max."

Inside he responded, *Indeed,* but knew that would only fuel Vince. He let it pass and took 1AM to 3AM, making sure he would see her at the handoff. Thomason offered to take 3AM to 6AM, an extra hour so Vince could be home with family most of the night.

"Thank you, Marvin, well done. So, we're covered," the captain said. "Dr. Guryon lives on Tyne Blvd. I'll send the address. Vince, thank Julie for all these crazy hours. Marvin, the same to Shannon. I don't know how our wives do it."

Both agreed and thanked him.

Leaving the room Brickman said quietly to Max, "I'll call when I find out something."

"Leave a message if you can't get me."

"Yes, sir."

In the parking lot, Vince asked Hanover where her car was.

"We left it at Cracker Barrel and drove together to see Pastor Don," Hanover said and quipped, "to save on fossil fuel."

"In Max's rig? Bet you had to stop and fill up both ways."

"No, just once. To free a Prius caught in the grill."

Max didn't say a word. He didn't have to.

Vince volleyed to her across five parking spaces. "I warned you about exceeding the humor limit, Hanover,"

As she climbed into the F250 she tossed him one last line. "I'll write myself a ticket, Barney Fife style."

The atmosphere in the cab suddenly became an oasis from the heavy business at hand. Hanover's quick wit and reference to Max's dad's favorite TV show expelled the blizzard of details and lifted the fog of the unsolved mysteries temporarily.

"Wow," he said to her, "People pay good money to see that. I would. Who writes your stuff?"

"Probably got it from my dad. He was a hilarious DJ. King of the comeback line. Drove my mom nuts sometimes. But kept us laughing."

They headed out of the parking lot. Max said something that as he said it, he wished he hadn't.

"I've heard a good laugh actually releases endorphins in your brain." *Damn, what a geek thing to say.* His endorphins plummeted.

"Yea, I've heard that, too. I used to wonder how many thousands of people my dad made laugh every day on the radio. Seemed like a really good job."

Somehow, he regrouped and responded spontaneously, "Well, don't sell cops short. Someone's got to create the stress people need relief from – that's part of our job, right?"

Hanover laughed. His endorphins rose markedly.

Max did something he rarely did, even with Vince. He reminisced. "The Andy Griffith show was my dad's favorite. Sometimes he called my mom Ellie Walker, you know, the pharmacist?"

"Yea, my dad still does a great Floyd the Barber."

Neither said anything for several minutes. Hanover made one call to her neighbor about her dog. But the silence wasn't awkward. Being with someone so comfortable in their own skin was… Max couldn't find a word for it. He settled on: *so not uncomfortable.*

As he pulled next to her 4Runner at Cracker Barrel, he managed the Max version of an apology,

"I know I put you on the spot there in the meeting. I should've given you a head's up..

Hanover looked away from him out the side window. "Yea, I'm pretty furious about it. But God's used anger in my life before."

It was his turn to laugh. She did, too. Endorphins flowed.

"Seriously, you really did great."

"Are you only saying that cause you know what a good shot I am?"

"Yes, indeed."

"See, sorry, I'm channeling my dad again. I could just say thank you, Max. Detective. Sir."

She reached for the door handle and said, "See you at the Pantry."

In his head Max started to say, "Why wait so long?." But he still had quick enough self-editing to actually say, "Don't you mean 1:00AM at Dr. Guryon's house?"

"O, right. Ships passing in the night."

"That's a poem by Longfellow."

"I was thinking Dionne Warwick, early 80s. I got to meet her with my dad."

"Get her autograph?"

"Yep."

She reached for the door handle again. "O, by the way, what's Brickman checking out for you?"

There it was again. In Max's head two roads diverged into the truth. Would he tell the whole or partial story? Out of respect for her relationship with Pastor Don, he chose the one more traveled by the masses of men, like him, leading lives of quiet desperation. He chose a partial story.

"I want him to take a look at whether the handwriting on Dr. Guryon's note resembled any of the other notes."

"Good idea."

Hanover took a road less traveled - transparency.

"I can't believe I'm saying this, but I had a strange thought today. What if Pastor G wrote one of the notes? Is that crazy?"

Max wanted to go back to the fork in the road and choose differently, but it was too late.

"Yea, well, maybe not so crazy. He said he's had some words of knowledge before."

"Yea, maybe that's it. Have a good nap, detective."

"You, too."

"It's not that long till 11:00. After I walk my dog maybe I'll catch a couple of Andy Griffiths to get some stakeout pointers."

"Nice. Lately, I prefer Wheel of Fortune to hone my decoding skills."

They ended the long day with a mutual chuckle.

Max waited till Hanover was in her car and pulling away, then followed her out. It was a courtesy his dad taught him. She took a left on Harding. He took a right to merge onto I-65 north. *Who is this woman? How does a person get to be that much... person?*

On the way to Love Circle, the blizzard of details and fog of uncertainly crept past the grill guard back into the cab. Amid all the unknowns, two compelling things made him want to get up the next morning: he was having breakfast with Hanover and then, of all the unimaginable things, meeting her at church.

By the time he poured a glass of Chianti, climbed the stairs to his music room, selected a song, cleaned the LP and sat down in his recliner, it was 10:15PM.

The captain texted the team that Dr. Guryon's private security company was aware of their extra presence under the guise of purported burglaries in the neighborhood. Max acknowledged, 10-4.

He set the alarm on his phone for 12:30AM. Hit play. Like Max, the singer wondered how much of his mother was still inside him. And if the feeling of never being enough would always be there. Max wanted to know, too, "Will it wash out in the water, or is it always in the blood?" *John Mayer, 2017, from The Search for Everything.* Max hoped some of his mother was still left in him, deep down. His dad's mental prowess and curiosity were still there, but his Irish cheerfulness, not so much.

Glancing at the row of books along the wall, his eye landed on several volumes of Yeats, one of his dad's Irish heroes. He could hear his mental giant dad recite a stanza to him in their workshop, and he muttered it aloud,

> "God guard me from the thoughts
> men think in the mind alone
> He that sings a lasting song
> thinks in a marrow bone."

William Butler Yeats, 1893, from The Rose Collection. His remembered his dad saying, "Shaemus, God gave you and I good minds, but your mother thinks in a marrow bone." For most of his life, Max had no idea what that meant.

As he drifted off, thoughts of his parents and Hanover mixed like the wine and exhaustion. For a brief window, he came unguarded. The longings he buried and smuggled out of site every day surfaced. Another nugget from his dad floated in about his mother, the woman Liam Shaemus Malone adored, "Max, she wears her soul on the outside." Now he understood. *I should write that down for a song.* But he didn't. He savored the revelation. *That's what Hanover does. That's why she's...* The last thing he heard from John Maher was: "I can feel the love I want, I can feel the love I need, but it's never gonna come the way I am."

CHAPTER 33

Early Sunday morning 12:50AM – Day 7

Max pulled alongside Hanover's 4Runner on Tyne Blvd. She rolled her window down and greeted him with, "Goober says, hey."

Max smiled and said, "Hey, to Goober. So, you really watched Andy Griffith reruns?"

"Yes, sir, I did."

Anticipating difficulty parking at the Pantry, Max suggested they park a block north at the bank which would be closed and walk to the back entrance.

"Sort of feels like a backstage pass," Hanover said.

"You would know. Anything shakin'?"

"Apparently racoons and possums don't know it's a pretty exclusive neighborhood."

"Yea, they act like they were here first."

"Good point."

"Before the rich and aimless," Max added, attempting to be clever.

"The what?"

"The rich and aimless."

"That's a pretty broad brush. You think money makes you aimless?"

"Well, not necessarily, but I…"

"You know, sir, some might say that about the neighborhood you live in?"

"I can see that."

"People might wonder how a cop can afford that new tall-skinny in that great location? Nipped some drug money on a bust? Or won the lottery? I don't need to know but some people jump to..."

"Inheritance," Max interrupted.

"Really?"

"My dad held a couple of patents on engineering innovations and methods."

"OK. Well, see, that's great. For the record, sir, I don't consider you rich or aimless."

"I appreciate that."

"Godless maybe. But not aimless," her smile held no judgement, "and I mean no disrespect by that, sir."

"Non taken." *How does she do that? Speak her mind so effortlessly, without rough edges?*

"Sir, I apologize. I've been drinking coffee for about eight hours now and..."

"No need. Your, uh, unfiltered way is refreshing, caffeinated or not."

"Thank you, sir. We good?"

"We're good." Max couldn't remember when he was this good. "You gonna be able to get some sleep?"

"Yes, sir." She held up a travel mug. "This is chamomile tea with cinnamon. Started drinking that about an hour ago. I'm good."

"Good. See you at the Pantry."

"At the bank first, right?"

"Right. A little after 8:00. Come hungry."

293

"No worries there. I love their Sugar and Spice pancakes. And between me and you and the raccoons, I'm a big fan of bacon."

"Copy that." Max added to her profile: big fan of bacon.

"Goodnight, sir. Like the captain says, 'be safe out here.'"

"You, too. Goodnight."

As Hanover's taillights turned the corner, a light rain began to fall. A familiar chorus kicked off in his head, "All by Myself" Eric Carman, 1975. He loved Celine Dion's version, *1996, from "Falling into You."* He had both the LPs. But Eric Carmen's voice from the Raspberries was the one in his head tonight. *I guess there are worse things than being alone, but it ranks way up there.*

Over the next two hours, the ghosts of the survivors from the carnage of the previous week visited him. Davidson, rich, divorced, daughter living far away with his Ex, his only son dead. Tony Armstrong's horrific reversal and what must be a fractured personal world. Jessie Bellaire's mother masking her pain in pursuit of someone to blame. Ms. Jacobs. Max couldn't remember her first name. Planning a funeral for the father of her children, a man reviled in life, uncherished in death. Sydney Sera's widow and children grieving their loss and grappling with a husband and father's moral crucible. The sudden end of Gunner Brown giving his family no chance for goodbye. His sister, the Senator, silenced and trapped in her own body.

He saw the justice in all these cases. Severe as it was. And the debris fields of agony surrounding them. Max considered himself more than a big fan of justice. It's what he did. It's what drove him. He couldn't help but see the justice in Jennifer divorcing him for his negligence, drinking and adultery. He owned the outcome. *I deserve to be alone.*

Billy Sprague

By far it was not the worst kind of lonely, but that didn't mean he was at peace with it or longed for different. John Fogerty sympathized as the rain fell steady. His record dropped in the jukebox in Max's head. *"Someone told me long ago/ There's a calm before the storm,"* 1971, Have You Ever Seen the Rain? Creedence Clearwater Revival from Pendulum.

Max looked at Guryon's mansion through the security gate. He became agitated. The irony of a professional in pursuit of justice losing sleep to watch over a rich prick who made his living from "death and despair" focused Max more than any amount of caffeine could. It pissed him off. *Hands that spill innocent blood* he recalled. But the anger blindsided him with an unexpected revelation: *If there's a God, I hate the same things he does.* On the heels of that, he realized why: the damage done. *The Needle and the Damage Done* dropped on the turntable in his head. *Neil Young, 1972,* from his "Harvest" record. He paused the needle with the thought, *There's already a song about everything.* That pissed him off, too.

He hated the damage done. Not just to the victims, David Davidson, Brie Batson, Ms. Jacobs and her kids and the rest. He hated the fractures radiating out in every direction, creating fault lines of insecurity for everyone. Behind his passion for justice, behind his ire at the bad actors and the damage done, Max cared. Deeply. In an instant, he became the interrogator and the suspect. The next question put him naked in the crosshairs of self-awareness: *Am I like Jessie's mom, masking pain in pursuit of someone to blame?* Before he could deflect or answer, Thomason pulled alongside. They exchanged a few words.

Max started his rolling fortress and headed to Love Circle for three hours of sleep. The thought of breakfast with Hanover

295

cleared his mind as Fogerty put it, like rain "comin' down on a sunny day." The thought of church clouded him over again.

The handoff at 6:00AM from Thomason to Vince was seamless. All quiet on Tyne Boulevard. Except for the muffled sound of Vince's ukulele.

At 7:45AM Vince observed Dr. Guryon's Bentley leave his residence. He tailed him.

8:01AM Guryon picked up his fiancé, Veronica, oddly enough, at the same apartment building Jessie Bellaire had lived. *How bout that?* Vince noted. *Much younger than Guryon. Beautiful. Birds of a feather? Guryon and Armstrong?* Then he impressed himself with a rewrite he knew Max would appreciate, *same bird of prey?*

8:12AM Guryon pulled into Richland Place, an upscale retirement complex off Westend. He went in and came out escorting his mother to the car.

8:15AM Vince called Max to say Guryon was on his way to the Pantry. Max and Hanover were already seated on the far side opposite the door. Max was just noting again how attractive Hanover looked in street clothes when Vince called.

"How's the breakfast date going?" Vince began.

Max responded in kind, "Can I call you back? I'm in the middle of the Heimlich maneuver on Hanover. She's inhaling a stack of pancakes."

"Anything to get your arms around her, right?"

"Right, we're ready on this end. What's his ETA?"

"About fifteen minutes. He drives a lot slower with his mom in the car."

"Copy that. Will let you know when they leave here."

Vince signed off, "Bon appetit, stronzo."

Max had the last word. "Vince, your French and Italian are really coming along. But remember. 'Bon appetit' is French. The Italian is 'buon appetito, stronzo.'"

"He hung up," Max said to Hanover. "He doesn't take correction well."

Their order arrived. Hanover lit up. "How beautiful!" she said. "Look at that golden color!" She picked up the plate and smelled the pancakes. "Oh, sorry, sir, I smell my food. My dad does. Part of enjoying it he says."

Her vitality enthralled him. It made him feel like he was living in slow motion, walking under water. *Wonder what she's like when she gets enough sleep?* He picked up the knife and fork, spread the butter around, poured a generous amount of syrup, and cut into the stack of pancakes. Hanover didn't. Max hesitated.

"Sir, would you mind if I say grace?" He laid the utensils across his plate.

"Uh, no. Go ahead."

Hanover bowed her head. And then she pushed Max even farther from his comfort zone. She reached one hand across the table, palm up. Memory bullets flew. How many meals did his mother reach across the table to him and Arianna and his father? Thousands. And just as many prayers. He looked at Hanover, her head bowed, eyes closed. His motor skills failed him for a moment. He commanded his hand across the Grand Canyon between them and set it on top of hers, knowing he didn't deserve to touch her. He watched and felt her grasp his hand gently. She prayed.

"Lord, our daily bread is extraordinary today. Thank you. We thank you, today especially, for the love of our dear mothers." She paused. Max fought back emotion and waited for an 'amen.' But

Hanover added, "And Lord, help Max not be too nervous at church. Amen." There it was again. Wearing her soul on the outside.

Hanover dove into her breakfast like an athlete carb loading. After the third bite, she said, "Now this is my kind of stakeout."

Max was speechless. He wondered why the food tasted so good. Why the people noise around them sounded so cheery. He wondered at the wonder silently invading Castle Malone. He tried to chalk it up to nostalgia from Hanover's prayer about their mothers. But it was more. He couldn't say what it was. But it smelled like cinnamon and felt like Aretha Franklin humming.

He did not wonder why there was a long line of people outside under umbrellas in the rain wanting to be in a place like this with those they love. He was not used to being on the inside of such a thing. He was used to standing outside the beauty, looking in. Now he was seated across the table from it. And Beauty held his hand.

Beauty spoke again. "Detective, I just thought of something. I hate to admit this but, I don't know what Dr. Guryon looks like. Not very professional. I hope you do."

He did. "Just look for Robert Redford with Elvis' hair walking like he owns the world."

Hanover made steady progress on her pancakes.

Max made a suggestion. "I don't want you to take this wrong, but maybe we should eat slower. We may be here a while."

"You can say it, sir. I'm eating like a horse."

"Ok, Black Beauty, yes, rein it in."

"I love that movie."

"The book is better."

"Maybe I'll have some eggs. Would you split another order of bacon with me?"

"Sure." He would have split for the Caribbean with her.

The manager who led them in the back entrance earlier came out of the kitchen leading three people to a booth in the corner farthest from the main entrance and twenty-first street. *He's pretty boxed in if anything happens. Can't be helped.* Max and Hanover were only three tables from them. Max texted 10-97 to Vince, "arrived on scene."

"She's very pretty," Hanover said, "and young."

"I'm sure she's saying the same thing about me. I mean, you."

Max's attempted compliment turned joke caught Hanover mid drink with a mouth full of orange juice. She sprayed some of it laughing, and grabbed her napkin. Several tables turned and looked.

"Was that a joke or a compliment?" she said.

Max lowered his voice and leaned toward her. "I'm not sure what I was going for there, but officer Hanover, I'm sure you learned from Barney Fife the object of a stakeout is not to be noticed?"

"Yes, sir." Another side of endorphins arrived.

Max got the waiter's attention, ordered eggs, scrambled, for Hanover and another side of bacon. And more coffee. He hadn't once thought how much better his own coffee was. A refill arrived. Hanover took a sip. The line came to him again, *I envy the rim of your cup.*

For a while the conversation turned to what an unprecedented week it had been. When that ran its course, Hanover surprised him again.

"If I may, sir, are you nervous about going to church?"

Hesitant, but prompted by Hanover's penchant for being straightforward, Max subdued his normal mental posturing. He quelled a bit of panic and simply said, "Honestly, yes."

She played the silent card. Waiting for more. Max knew that move.

He took a sip of coffee while forming a follow-up in his head. He was about to speak it when she said, "Thank you for not pleading the fifth chapter of hesitations."

A gentle wave of endorphins washed over them both. Like one of those Andes Crème de Menthe after-dinner candies that makes you want to keep eating more of them, Max could not imagine getting enough of her. An echo of another memory floated into his head.

The country singer he fell for many years ago came to mind. Back then, she persuaded him to go to church with her more than once. The first time he picked her up to go, she answered the door, looked at him and said, "I could eat you with a spoon." God failed to get his attention that morning because he couldn't think of anything else during the church service. The next time he came to her door, he had a tablespoon sticking out of his shirt pocket. They were late to wherever they were going. For reasons still a mystery to Max, they never made love, though not for a lack of mutual passion and close encounters. He was torn between the regret of having never shared that intimacy, and yet relieved he didn't have that memory bullet to wound him, and perhaps her, over and over again. More recently, Max repurposed her spoon line as part of his enticing repartee to the younger women he dated. Looking at Hanover across the table, he knew he would never use that line on her. She was worthy of original material.

To Hanover's witty remark, Max responded, "Well played." Instead of a calculated deflection, he went with a more honest yet press release type of response.

"It would be an understatement to say church has not been my natural habitat for some time."

"I can appreciate that. I spent a lot of unchurched years."

Max wanted to say *I'd like to hear more about that sometime.* So, he said it.

"I'd like to hear more about that some time."

"Alright. Some time. So, why are you going today?"

If Max could live with his soul on the outside, he would have said, "To be near you." But he was a long way from that after so many years spent denying the existence of an eternal soul to wear on the outside. He did the best he could do. He spoke without completely thinking it out.

"Well, out of respect for Pastor Giacinto, and your admiration for him, let's just say, uh, I'm trying to be more open, to make sense of this case, of course, by, uh, you know, to get a handle on it by, by being open to getting a bigger picture than, uh, well, than only looking through, say, just the keyhole of evidence, motive and physics."

Max couldn't remember when he uttered a more tortured sentence. In the wake of it, he thought maybe it was a two-for-one: affirmation without conceding his own long-held world view.

Hanover didn't seem to mind and simply said, "Thank you, sir, that means a lot."

He thought he should stop there but didn't. He pulled out one of his stock Maxims, "Besides, I've always believed in going where the evidence leads. Even if it goes where I don't expect, or rather it didn't go."

"That's one of the things I've learned from you, detective. Oh, hey, it looks like some of our evidence is headed for the exit."

They had temporarily lost sight of the purpose of the stakeout. Guryon was already across the room by himself, heading out the main entrance through the crowd waiting to get in, presumably to pull the Bentley around in the rain. Max assessed that was a highly vulnerable scenario. He phoned Vince, but Thomason was taking the next leg of surveillance. Vince said he would alert him. Their bill hadn't been settled. Intending to keep an eye on Guryon, Max put two twenties on the table, asked Hanover to square it up with tip, and make sure to get a receipt to be reimbursed by the department. Hanover added another ten and said, "I've waited tables. Let's go."

"But the receipt," Max said.

"I'll come back for it."

Vince called. Thomason was on Guryon.

"We can relax," Max said. "Thomason's got eyes on him."

"So, who was the frugal one, your mom or dad?"

"Dad. Mathematician. My mom would buy a flower for someone with her last dollar."

Before he inquired about when to show up at church, Hanover told Max the music usually ran the first fifteen minutes. So, a 10:45ETA would work; she was stopping by her house to let her dog out and would get there early to get two seats; if an usher tried to direct him to the overflow video room, he was to tell them someone has a seat for him; she would text him the seat location. She even anticipated Max wondering how long it would last.

"Normal service is an hour and fifteen minutes. Pastor G tends to go a little longer, but it never seems like it."

9:40AM. They hurried to the bank parking lot through light rain under separate umbrellas. He wanted to say "Get seats not too close to the front. On an aisle if possible." but didn't. All that came out was, "See you at 10:45."

She said, "You're really going to enjoy Pastor G. Benedicilo. Did I say that right?"

"Close enough." He climbed into the F250 and waited till she pulled out. *She is just the right amount of perfect. I should write that down.*

CHAPTER 34

Sunday morning 10:40AM – Day 7

Max couldn't believe he was turning into the parking lot of the Holy Mess Church. On a Sunday morning. He rolled his window down as the parking volunteer approached.

"Hey, good morning, detective. It's me, Officer Weber." Max didn't recognize him out of uniform.

"Good morning, officer." *Great, ten to one in ten minutes Vince will know I came to church.* The only spaces left were in the back of the lot.

10:42AM Hanover's text arrived. "Far left aisle, three rows from the back on the aisle." *How does she do that?* He made his own little joke: *Probably got a word of knowledge.*

10:45AM Max entered the building. He heard music still playing. He lingered in the lobby.

10:46AM The music ended. Max entered the auditorium, far left aisle. The band was leaving the stage. He slipped into the seat beside Hanover.

"Good morning again, sir."

"Good morning."

A youngish man came to the microphone. Jeans and black t-shirt.

"Happy Mother's Day," he began.

"Australian?" Max quietly asked Hanover.

"Yes. Everything sounds more sincere in a British accent. Don't you think?"

Max adopted his dad's Irish, "Aye, lassie."

The young pastor welcomed newcomers with a reminder, "Like the sign outside says, bring your tattoos, doubts, traditions, and bring your heart, your scars, come as you are, we're glad you're here. Let's stand and a take a moment to greet someone around you."

Clever, eloquent fellow. The couple sitting in front of them turned around, shook hands and introduced themselves by first names. Congeniality was not Max's forte.

Helen said to them, "Good morning, I'm Helen and this is Max."

Hearing her say his name again was worth the discomfort. Under the cover of the murmur in the room, he leaned toward Hanover.

He said, "Good morning, I'm Max, a doubter with tattoos and a prodigal from a Catholic tradition."

She held out her hand to shake his and responded.

"Good to meet you. I'm Helen, not of Troy, a believer with tattoos and a holy mess."

Max shook his head and laughed. A free, stress-relieving laugh. He marveled at how nimble she was and could not recall ever laughing in church, at least not without getting a corrective look from Sofia.

At 10:50 Max felt his phone buzz. A text from Vince. "Breakfast and church date? G dropped off mom. Then fiancé. 10-20 now his house."

The pastor spoke, "Please be seated. The one thing I know is true about each of you this morning is this: You wouldn't be here without your mother. Am I right?" Mild applause. "For most of us this is a joyful day. But for some, it's a reminder of loss. This may be your first Mother's Day without your mom, or she may have gone on to glory some time ago. For others, there may be a sadness about the state of your relationship with your mother. We grieve with you and pray for comfort and mending."

Max conceded the pastor didn't need the accent to sound sincere. As he spoke, a young woman walked on stage with an acoustic guitar. *Looks like a Taylor.* She adjusted a microphone.

The pastor continued, "Whatever your story, scripture calls us to honor our father and mother. To do that this morning we have a song from one of the outstanding songwriters around here. There are a few around town." Mild laughter.

As the woman started the song, Hanover leaned toward Max and said, "That's my friend I went to hear at the Commodore Thursday."

Max could not have prepared himself for what she sang. As she sang the lyrics appeared on the giant screen behind her.

> If I could show you the honor I owe you
> the Oscar would go to the part that you played for me
> It wasn't easy but you kept believing
> and loved me like breathing, So the envelope please.

Her voice reminded Max of the lilt of Joni Mitchell with the soul of Mary J. Blige. She launched into the chorus.

> I want the whole wide world to know
> your brave heart and your shining soul
> if not for you I would be only a dream still waiting for wings
> O, it's so true, now I can fly, thanks to you.

Pressure built behind Max's eyes. The distance between his head and his heart began to shrink. To combat it he mentally categorized and generalized what was happening. *What a Roberta Flack moment. She's killing us softly with her song. "Killing me Softly" 1973, won the Grammy for Record of the Year in 1974.*

The deflection worked momentarily, but he couldn't get out of the crosshairs of the song. The second verse nearly wrecked him. It described Sofia's love for him. The love that shaped him.

> Higher, you lifted me higher, and I'm still inspired
> By all that I learned from you
> Life is like dancin' You gotta take chances
> The sky is a canvas you taught me to use.

As the chorus repeated, Max fought the impulse to leave. A crushing weight came over him, that he had not flown as high as his mother hoped and equipped him to fly. He felt earthbound, wingless, trudging, certainly not taking chances and dancing through life. Max knew he played it safe in everything, except the way he drove and pursued bad actors. At that moment, Hanover leaned toward him. Her shoulder touched his. The aroma of White Linen and the sound of her voice kept him in his seat. "She's good, huh?"

"Better than good." Max said.

A short bridge followed, returned to part of the first verse, then a final chorus. It ended with the tag:

> O, it's so true, now here I stand, thanks to you
> I am who I am, thanks to you.

The auditorium erupted in applause. The singer walked off stage as the paster came out again. "Jenny Meadows." Applause continued. "Thanks to you - for that." Mild laughter. "What a blessing. And the blessing can go on. Jenny's song, "Thanks to You," is available all week as a free download on our website to send to your mom. Or to remember your mother and the love she gave you. The download is free, but if you would like to donate something for it, all your gifts will go to an organization we support, Hope Clinic for Women, who help with unplanned pregnancies. This great music can do great good. Thanks to you." The pastor applauded the congregation.

This guy is a natural.

The young pastor prayed briefly, then introduced Pastor Giacinto who was met with warm applause.

"Good morning. Happy Mother's Day. What a privilege to be with you today. I'm always honored when Pastor Ben asks me to fill in." Pastor G's smile reached the back rows. He dove right in.

"In your continuing series, Roads to Faith, I want us to look at a road most of us have traveled. Doubt. Why we doubt and how it doesn't have to be a detour." Opening a Bible he said, "Would you please stand for the reading of God's word?" This part of mass Max remembered. There was a lot of standing. The scripture appeared on the screen. Pastor G read it in his warm voice.

Now Thomas (also known as Didymus), one of the Twelve, was not with the disciples when Jesus came. So, the other disciples told him, "We have seen the Lord!"
But he said to them, "Unless I see the nail marks in his hands and put my finger

Where the nails were, and put my hand into his side, I will not believe."

A week later his disciples were in the house again, and Thomas was with them. Though the doors were locked, Jesus came and stood among them and said,
"Peace be with you!" Then he said to Thomas, "Put your finger here; see my hands. Reach out your hand and put it into my side. Stop doubting and believe." Thomas said to him, "My Lord and my God."

Then Jesus told him, "Because you have seen me, you have believed; blessed are those who have not seen and yet believe.

John 20: 24 - 29

"This is the word of the Lord. You may be seated."

He walked away from the podium to the edge of the stage and began talking, not teaching or preaching. Just talking. Like he did with Max and Hanover the day before.

"One of my fondest memories of my mother, who was German, by the way, is connected with this scripture. Obviously, my father was not German. Giacinto is very Italiano. Benedicilo. That means 'Bless him.' As in Bless the Lord. Can you say that? 'Benedicilo.'" The entire auditorium repeated it in unison. Pastor G responded, "Bellisimo, that was beautiful."

He really knows how to get the endorphins flowing. It's what these guys do. Sweet music, beautiful singing, good-natured eloquence, a little humor. Skepticism rarely took a break guarding Castle

Malone. Lately, Hanover made his defenses less vigilant. Pastor G had some of the same effect. But he was a preacher, after all. Max knew his ultimate MO.

"Early on, when my mother read to us about Doubting Thomas, I asked her why he had another name, Didymus. She said it was because he showed up late and asked, '*Did I miss something?*" He laughed and the entire auditorium laughed with him. He put both open hands over his heart and said, "Blessed woman. I wish I could send her that beautiful song we just heard. Maybe she's listening in."

Max used to wonder occasionally if his mother was watching or listening in from heaven or wherever she was. But it was better not to think so. He was not sure she would like who he had become. Besides, since he believed there was no hereafter, he considered it sentimentality and a moot point.

Pastor G began to teach.

"'Didymus' actually means 'twin.' My mother knew that. But she made a point I want to start with today." He returned to the podium.

"Thomas, Didymus, did miss something. Not just being gone when Jesus appeared to the other disciples. He missed what believing is all about. Leaning on, trusting in, sure of and hoping in something or someone you cannot see with your eyes."

I know where this is headed. But Max didn't.

"For Thomas, seeing was believing. I can relate. I spent some years as a young man doubting the faith of my mother and father. I was smart. I was a very good student and very prideful. I was going to figure things out my way, like most young people. I, I, I, I, right? Sound familiar?

"Thomas seems smart, certainly pragmatic, doesn't he? He was the "Show me the money" disciple. Anyone remember that movie? 'Show me the money, Jerry!' But Thomas was also on the outside looking in. He was too proud to take someone else's word for it. The other disciples had an unfair advantage. They had seen Jesus."

"Ever been there? Everyone else has something or knows something you don't. Thomas' intellect and pride kept him from believing. So did mine."

"I generally run into two kinds of Doubting Thomas. The 'Que sera sera' doubter, who lives in a fog of self-preoccupation, ignores evidence and the march of time. Is ready to party like it's 1999, which now, I guess, is so 'last century.' Then there's the obsessive-compulsive OCD doubter. Reads every book, knows every argument, asks a blizzard of questions. Did Jesus *really* say that? Who reported it? Did John have a beef with Thomas to paint him in such a bad light? Was the text found in the earliest, most reliable manuscript? Were the witnesses reliable? Who translated it? Did the translator have an agenda? How far removed was the writing from the source or actual incident? Was a competing or slightly varied account voted down at the Counsel of Nicaea in the third century?"

Max knew which kind of doubter he was. He rebutted to himself, arguing that asking a lot of questions is essential in his line of work.

"You get the point. Thomas and I were OCD doubters. The only difference is, he actually got to see Jesus in person the next week. I came to believe without seeing, like those Jesus referred to: 'Blessed are those who have not seen and yet believe.'" That's me. That's most of you. And billions of people in the last two thousand years. As Peter puts it in one of his letters, "Though you have not seen him, you love him; and even though you do not see him now, you believe in him and are filled with an inexpressible and glorious joy."

"So, what kept Thomas from believing? Intellect and pride. Intellect is a great gift, of course. It results in discoveries and advances that benefit the whole human race. But like a saw, it can help build a house or cut down the ladder you're standing on. And pride is like glaucoma of the soul. Nothing blinds us like pride. As the great Italian philosopher Mark Twain said, (mild laughter) 'Human pride is not worth it. There is always something lying in wait to take the air out of it.'"

"So, what's the remedy for doubt? Jesus said to Thomas, 'Stop doubting and believe!' Just stop? That's it? Easier said than done. So how do you do that? If Jesus walked in here right now, especially if all the doors were locked like they were that day, and he invited you to touch his wounds, you would probably believe. Anyone would."

"But without seeing Jesus in the flesh, how do we simply, 'Stop doubting and believe?'" Apparently, in the Lord's view it was possible. So, what's the big mystery?

"Consider this: We already know how to believe without seeing."

Here it comes. Radio waves. Sound waves. Probably the wind.

"Radio and sound waves. You can't see them, but you know their effect. Like music."

Called it.

"Ultraviolet light from the sun. You can't see it, but you know it's real by the sunburn that keeps you awake. And we can't see the wind, but you see the effects of it. And you believe in the wind."

Called it.

"In fact, Jesus used the wind to make that very point. John recorded Jesus describing the wind in chapter 3 verse 8 to make the same point." The scripture came up on the screen.

> The wind blows wherever it pleases. You hear its sound, but you cannot tell where it comes from your where it is going. So it is with everyone born of the Spirit.
>
> John 3:8

Max leaned toward Hanover and whispered, "That was before Doppler radar, so we sort of can see what the wind is doing."

The very next thing Pastor G said was, "The OCD doubter here may be thinking, 'Well, we have Doppler radar now to help us see what the wind is doing."

Hanover stifled a laugh. Others around the room didn't.

Pastor G took the wind metaphor in a direction Max's radar did not pick up.

"Dear ones, have you seen the effects of believing in the Lord? Do you know someone who carried heavy shame, but doesn't now?" Yes, and Amen rose from the crowd. One of them was from Hanover.

"Do you know a believer who was a 'bah humbug' Scrooge but is now a generous, cheerful giver?" More Amens.

"Has anyone here been addicted to something but is free now?" Hallelujahs and Amens.

"Anyone been a prisoner of grief, but now you have hope, even joy?" More yeses and Amens.

This was getting close to home for Max.

"As a result of believing in the Lord Jesus, have you seen hardness, bitterness and anger replaced by loving kindness and peace?" More Amens and affirmations traveled around the auditorium.

"We cannot see the wind of the Spirit, but we know its effects."

He left the podium again. And spoke like he saw a target on Max's chest in his aisle seat, third row from the back.

"Here's another thing even doubters believe but have not seen. We cannot see our own end. But we believe it will come, right? We hear of people dying all the time. Some of us have seen people die. I have. We know it's real. We know and believe we will take a last breath."

Pastor G took a big breath and exhaled slowly. His large hands against his chest rose and fell. He took another deep breath and exhaled. After exhaling a third time, he stood silent, both hands over his heart. Eyes closed. And didn't breathe. The seconds ticked. No one moved. Not a single person cleared their throat. Max gritted his teeth and swallowed hard.

"And there will not be another one. Some of you have witnessed that. I have."

Again, Max fought the urge to leave. Pastor G had just illustrated how Sofia died. Max was there, at her bedside, with his sister and dad. He saw her breathing slow down. Felt the pause lengthen between each one. And then there was not another one. At that moment, his heart broke. He would not let that happen again sitting there with Hanover at the Holy Mess church.

Pastor G continued, "Thank God we cannot know or see that day, but we believe it's coming. So, believing without seeing is really not such a mystery. By the way, some years ago, I asked the Lord to give me a full seventy years. He's exceeded that by more than a decade and a half. Benedicilo." The crowd repeated 'Benedicilo' adding applause. He returned to the podium.

"There's another reason doubters doubt. Granted, we don't know anything about Thomas' backstory. His intellect and pride were enough to make him doubt. We do know he was on the outside looking in on the exuberance of the disciples who claimed they saw the Lord. That couldn't have been easy. To be on the outside looking in. I know what that's like. Many of you do as well." He walked to the edge of the stage again.

"I mentioned my wonderful mother and father. And they were. But they were not my biological parents. They adopted me as a baby in Italy. As a young man I was unaware of the invisible, unspoken hurt I carried, the wound of being rejected by the woman who bore me and the man who fathered me. And not knowing why? I didn't realize then, but that hurt fed my intellect and pride. For the longest time, I refused to cozy up to a God who would let that happen to me. It took years to get that wound out into the light.

I don't have time this morning to tell you my whole story, but through a series of very humbling circumstances, I finally cried out to my Father in heaven, like George Bailey to the angel Clarence in the movie, It's a Wonderful Life. I got very honest with the one who knows everything already. In a field out under the stars, I got down on my knees and prayed something like, 'Father in heaven, I'm tired of this hurt. It has ruled me. It has defined me. I'm tired of carrying it. I've been angry at you. I don't have peace or joy and I know I won't till you free me from it. I want that. I want to be free. I want to live. I believe, Lord, help my unbelief.' And he did. He freed me. I stood up a different person. Benedicilo." The congregation repeated it and broke into loud applause.

"Many of you know that same experience." Amens all around.

"I believe every doubter is carrying deep hurt in search of someone to blame."

Max was stunned. He couldn't believe his same thought from the night watch came out of Pastor G's mouth. *How does he do that?*

"Let me say that again. I believe every doubter is carrying deep hurt in search of someone to blame. I was. Quite often that hurt becomes a gavel to judge God or a clenched fist raised against Him.

"There are many signs, but here's a consistent one. A hurt and angry doubter, which I was, is not likely to feel or show gratitude. Gratitude is evidence of the wind of the Spirit moving in a person." A quote appeared on the screen. "Dietrich Bonhoeffer, the great German preacher, said this to a group of mourners at a funeral:

"Gratitude transforms the torment of memory into silent joy. One bears what was lovely in the past not as a thorn but as a precious gift deep within, a hidden treasure of which one can always be certain."

Max's memories of Sofia always came mixed with thorns, reminders of his immense loss. Pastor G pressed in.

"I love that. 'Gratitude transforms the torment of memory into silent joy.' For instance, those of us whose mothers have passed on, though we cannot see them now, we still love them, still carry them in our hearts as a treasure. Because the love lives on. And so do they."

Soft yeses and Amens followed. Max thought his 'yes' was silent, but he had whispered it. In a rare sensation, Sofia's love felt close and warm, precious, with hardly a hint of torment. The softening influence of gratitude poured into his mind like honey as he remembered her beauty, kindness, joy and tenderness. Hanover placed her hand on Max's arm. Her empathy nearly undid him. It made Sofia's memory nearly tangible. *I gotta get out of here.* But he didn't.

"If you are a doubter here this morning, a 'Que Sera Sera' or an OCD doubter, your doubt does not have to be a detour. The questions you ask, the anguish you carry and acknowledge can be the very things that put you on the road to faith." He returned to the podium.

"Let me say it is not my job to convince you to believe. In John 16:8, Jesus makes it clear that it is the role of the Holy Spirit to convict and convince. I'm just a fellow traveler comparing notes. I have two more brief observations from Thomas' experience. And we'll wrap up."

A text from Vince gave Max a timely distraction. "G 10-20 still at his house. Assume will get fiancé en route to airport. Pastor Don rocking it?"

Max whispered to Hanover, "Guryon's still at his house."

Pastor Don pressed on. "Thomas didn't have to take much of a leap of faith, did he? Jesus was standing right in front of him. But for us, we will not be able to see and touch the wounds of Jesus. To have that irrefutable, tangible, flesh and blood evidence.

Thomas actually demanded it before he would believe.

"A couple of songwriters I know wrote a song to a doubter like Thomas." The lyric came up on the screen. "Here's the chorus:

O but you want to hold the intangible
Fashion the darkness into familiar shape
To see with your eyes to know in your mind
O, ye of so little faith, Only the heart can hold the intangible.

"Thomas wanted to hold the intangible before he believed. And Jesus granted him that. But even beholding the Lord in person, Thomas did something all believers do. He chose. He declared, My Lord and My God."

Max's vigilant wariness kicked in. *Here comes the closer.*

"Thomas exerted what might be the most powerful force in the universe, next to the love of God. It's more powerful than all the Titan rockets ever launched because it can give any of us the thrust to break free, at least we think so, to break free from the constant gravitational pull of God's love. That awesome, God-given power is free will.

"You see, dear ones, God has done a risky thing. He gave us free will, wings to fly to him or away from him. Thomas, in spite of his intellect, pride and whatever pain he had, chose to believe. The Lord's point was, how much more blessed to choose to believe without seeing?

"And here's my final observation."

Here comes the Billy Graham moment.

"I love this. Jesus did not need a door. Did you catch that? The door was locked. The disciples were in hiding. They were afraid of who might come knocking. Scripture says, 'Jesus came and stood among them.' Hello? He could appear here now, without using a door. But this is what he says to us today who have not seen him. What he has said to doubters for over two thousand years. The words appeared on the screen:

"Behold I stand at the door and knock. If anyone opens to me, I will come in and eat with them and them with me."Revelation 3:20.

Max's free will rallied his intellect, pride, and pain to barricade the door of Castle Malone for Pastor G's final pitch. But there was no forced entry. Just the warm voice and hard-won wisdom of a man who had walked a similar road. Pastor G walked to the edge of the stage.

"My intellect, pride, pain and free will set a course for me to outwit God and escape his love. But I couldn't see the bigger picture. No matter how far I ran the Lord was there before me. It was like I was on a Mobius Strip, on a perpetually circular road that always led me back to the Lord and the goodness of his love."

The image disarmed Max. His dad's wry joke of making a Mobius Strip from a Stop sign came full circle. Instead of still wondering why he agreed to come to this place this morning, he wondered about an inevitability in it, as if there was a conspiracy that even his mother was in on this Mother's Day.

"Dear ones, we cannot outwit or outrun God's love for us." Amens and Hallelujahs traveled around the room.

Max gauged his resistance would hold if Pastor G finished soon. His next words were familiar. They reached into a marrow bone awareness buried in Max but denied for many years.

"Just yesterday, someone told me a powerful statement with a remarkable image. 'Science is a keyhole. Belief is the key.'" It came up on the screen. "Take that in. 'Science is a keyhole. Belief is the key.'"

Wait till Brickman hears about this.

"Imagine how limiting and narrow the panorama is through a keyhole. How can you possibly get the big picture? How much are you not seeing? Imagine beyond that door is the answer not to what created the universe, but who created it. The One who created you. Standing there. Ready to come in. Sit down. Say 'Peace be with you.' And have dinner together. The doubters I meet are all looking through the keyhole of science and the distorted lens of their pain at what can be seen and verified with the five senses and Doppler radar."

"Here's the good news. If you're already kneeling to look through a keyhole, you're in the perfect posture to use the key. Like I was in that field years ago. All that remains is your willingness to use the key and open the door. You may not be willing yet this morning. Oh, I pray you will be sooner than later. Because we are not here for long, and what we long for most is not here."

That should be in a song. Probably will be by tomorrow with all the songwriters in this crowd.

"Did you hear that, doubter? We are not here for long, and what we long for most is not here."

He paused and walked to the edge of the stage.

"If you are willing, and the Holy Spirit is stirring deep in your own spirit," Pastor G placed both hands, fingers spread wide over the middle of his torso, "it's not me who is knocking at the door.

It's the Lord himself saying, 'Stop doubting and believe.'

The band began walking back on stage and took their places.

"How do you open the door? Pray. Like I did in that field but in your own way. The band is going to lead us in a short reprise of a song we sang earlier. I'll pray and then you'll be dismissed.

If everyone stands that's my cover to slip out.

"As we sing, if today is your day to open the door to Jesus, or for any prayer needs you have, make your way to the chapel. Former doubters will be there to pray with you. Let's stand and sing."

Max felt trapped. If he left now, people would think he needed prayer or even getting saved. He stood with Helen. She got a text as a man began strumming an acoustic guitar. Max got one, too. From Vince. "G on the move."

A lyric appeared on the screen. The guitar player began to sing,

Here's to the day love makes a way
and peace comes to stay between us.

The melody and Celtic feel in 6/8 perked Max's ear. He leaned toward Helen and said, "Vince plays this on his uke." It had the curious effect of easing his anxiety to leave. It reminded him of *Morning Has Broken, Cat Stevens, 1971, from Teaser and the Firecat.* Dozens of people began walking the aisles headed for the chapel.

Here's to the ones, coming and gone,
all finally home, O, here's to the day.

The singer's warm baritone had a hint of James Taylor. But the voice Max noticed was Helen's. It was beautiful. The song and her singing made staying palatable. The singing of the entire congregation grew louder.

> Here's to the time, all in God's time,
> We stand in the light together,
> And here's to the hope, then sings my soul,
> Till everyone knows. O, here's to the day.

The whole band kicked in on the chorus.

> Come help me sing Hallelujah now
> You see, that's the sound when that morning breaks
> Come let us raise a reunion song,
> For that sacred place where we all belong.

All the instruments dropped out. Twenty-five hundred voices sang the first verse again, a cappella. Hands when into the air. Whenever Max saw images of people worshipping with both hands raised, he sarcastically thought *they look like little boys and girls wanting their dad to pick them up.* This morning it seemed less like a group mannerism. The anthem, rich with harmonies, filled the auditorium. It felt like the finale of Les Mis. For a brief window, the distance between Max's head and heart disappeared.

> Here's to the day, love makes a way,
> And peace comes to stay between us.
> Here's to the ones, coming and gone,
> All finally home, O here's to the day,
> O here's to the day.

From the front edge of the stage, Pastor G said, "Let's pray. Father in heaven, we praise you. For making the world with a word to the deep. Lord Jesus, we love you. For all that your suffering and sacrifice won for us. Holy Spirit, we thank you. For never leaving us to walk alone or find our own way home." He raised both hands in blessing toward the assembly, his eyes closed.

"For all the mothers here and all our mothers, we pray bless them as they have blessed. Lord, where there is turmoil, bring your peace. Where there is sorrow, give comfort. For weariness - rest. For transgression – forgiveness. Where there is pride, humble us. For our pain, bring healing. Where there is heaviness, O Lord, bring the joy of hope. And where there is doubt bring faith, the substance of what we hope for and the assurance of what we cannot see. Here's to the day, Lord, when we stand in the light together, and see you like Thomas, face to face. In the blessed name of Jesus, our Savior and Lord, and all the people said..."

"Amen" the congregation responded.

"Benedicilo" Pastor G added. Every person in the auditorium repeated it, "Benedicilo." Except Max.

People began streaming out. Hanover turned to Max and said, "Pretty powerful, huh?"

Max didn't hesitate to calculate a response. "Indeed. I can see why the place is packed."

Then he surprised her and himself with a rare openness. "I wasn't sure I was gonna make it through the Mother's Day song."

"I thought that might be tough. But isn't Jenny amazing?"

"Yea, extraordinary."

They joined the flow of people filing out. In the lobby Max remembered Vince's text.

"Oh, Vince texted a few minutes ago that Guryon was leaving his house. Did you get that?"

"No, Jenny texted me to see if I want to go to lunch. Would you like to go? And meet her?"

"Can you eat again already?"

"Maybe something light. But you're probably exhausted."

He was. But if it meant more time with Hanover, he could risk nodding off on a salad.

"As my non-stop Irish dad used to say, 'I can catch up on me sleep when I'm dead, lad.' You and Jenny decide, and I'll meet you. Text me."

"Ok. Great."

They headed toward the parking lot in different directions under a light rain. Max hadn't gone twenty steps when his phone buzzed. It was a group text from the captain. "Guryon 10-46, I-65 and 440. Vince is 10-97. Stand by for update." He turned around and spotted Hanover hurrying toward him. There would be no lunch. Or rest.

CHAPTER 35

Sunday afternoon 12:35PM – Day 7

En route, the captain sent word he just arrived at Vanderbilt ER. Ten minutes later, Max and Hanover ran up as Vince walked out of the ER entrance. He was soaking wet. Blood stained his white shirt, suit coat, and sleeves.

"Are you hurt? Max said with genuine concern.

"No, this is Guryon's blood."

"Thank heaven," Hanover said.

"Is he alive?" Max asked.

"Barely, EMT said he lost consciousness on the way in. He was in so much pain that might be a good thing."

"Is he going to make it?" Hanover said.

"It doesn't look good."

"Is the captain with him?"

"He just left to let Guryon's mother know. Didn't want her to find out on the news."

"What the hell happened?" Max said.

"Still piecing it together. Captain sent Brickman and Thomason to the scene to gather intel with the crash unit. I couldn't keep up with Guryon coming up 65. He was doing at least ninety. In the rain! At the ramp to 440 West a couple of vehicles were pulled over. A guy was climbing over the barrier. The other driver said the Bentley tore around him as they entered the ramp. It swerved to avoid an old 50s pickup, hit the guardrail and went over sideways. When I go there Guryon's Bentley was upside down in a small stand of trees. I radioed an ambulance. Called the captain on my way to the car."

Vince described how he and a motorist found Guryon hanging upside down by his seatbelt screaming 'Get me out of here, dammit!' His airbags had not deployed. The driver's side was wedged against trees. Vince tried to get him to stay calm, told him help was on the way. He tried to break the window but couldn't. The front windshield and roof were caved in. Guryon's hands were pinned against the steering wheel and the dash. His wrists and head were bleeding badly. EMT Fire and Rescue arrived in minutes.

"They used the jaws of life to remove the passenger door, cut his seatbelt and got a long crowbar under the windshield. We were working him out feet first. Guryon kicked and screamed. 'Stop! You idiots! My hands are still trapped! My hands are my life! My hands are my life!' They had to use a couple of pusher rams to lift the car and pry the windshield enough to free him. Guryon kept screaming, 'Careful with that thing you'll rip my hands off!' When they gained some separation of the glass from the dash both wrists bled like crazy. Max, it took four of us to lift him out. That's where all this blood came from. They got tourniquets on him pretty quick, but he lost a lot of blood."

Always the detective, Max asked, "Did he say anything to the medics on the way in?"

"I know one of the EMTs. She says he kept asking about his hands. How bad was it? And just before he passed out, he kept muttering, 'They got me. They got me.'"

"If he survives, how bad are his hands?" Hanover asked.

"When I told the EMT Guryon was a doctor she said he would be lucky to wipe his own ass."

"What about the fiancé? Anyone told her?"

"No, she lives just a few blocks from here. Same building as Jessie Bellaire," Vince told her.

"No shit?" Max said. "Birds of a feather, you think?"

"Or maybe the same bird of prey," Vince had been waiting to use that.

"Indeed."

"Or maybe this one was the keeper," Hanover countered. "You never know."

"He may not have time to find out," Vince said.

Hanover volunteered to tell the fiancé. Max offered to go with her saying he knew the manager. Before they could walk away, the task force got a group text from the captain. "With Gs mom. Then to hospital. Will update. Max/Helen tell Gs fiancé Victoria ASAP. Brinkman/Thomason finish up. Then go home. All of you. That's an order. Vince lose clothes 4 Julie & kids sake. Get some rest. It's out of our hands. LHM"

Max gave Vince the key to his place. He headed there to clean up and borrow some clothes.

It stopped raining. The storm moved on, the third in a week, nourishing the planet's revival but leaving upheaval and uncertainty in its wake.

Max and Hanover made the tough visit. They found Victoria in the lobby with her bags packed.

Helen stayed longer with her. Max went on to his place. When he arrived Vince was just coming out the front door.

"That didn't take long. How'd it go?"

"Shock. Tears. She seemed genuinely shattered. But said she would go to the hospital after she made some calls. Hanover stayed longer."

Vince reacted, "Who does that? I love you and you may be dying, but I gotta make some calls?"

"Indeed. Can you say, 'strike four?'"

Vince tossed the house key to Max. "Thanks for the garms."

"The what?"

"Garms. Garments. That's what my kids call threads."

"You're the only one who still says 'threads.'"

Vince said what they were both thinking.

"That's six, Max. In six days."

"Well, Jacobs died two weeks ago, but yea, we got six on our watch in six days. Unbelievable."

"You know the next shoe is gonna drop, right? And we can't do a damn thing about it."

"Yea, it's like a ride you can't get off of till the end and you don't know when that is."

"Indeed," Vince agreed.

Sinatra crooned in Max's head. *That's Life," 1966, from the album That's Life.*

Max opined. "As Frank says, that's life, right?"

"Frank who?"

"da Vinci, seriously? Sinatra. Is there any other Frank?"

CHAPTER 36

Sunday afternoon 2:15PM – Day 7

Max grabbed an open bottle of Chianti and a glass and headed upstairs to wrap himself in music to try to sleep a few hours. He dragged more than the weight of the week up with him. The unprecedented caseload and weariness multiplied gravity. But the load he carried was more than that. Years of running on a Mobius strip treadmill, every waking moment exerting his exceptional mental faculties, angst-driven ambition and free will, had left him with what? Brought him where? Alone and hanging by a thread of defiance.

He filled the glass, walked over to the solar system sculpture, bent the rod supporting the red planet and sent it careening into the others. He sank into the recliner and watched the planets gambol in all directions.

Get some rest? Seriously, Captain? How do you turn off the shitstorm?

The only rest Max had known for the last few years was in a bottle or the arms of a string of lovers. Jennifer offered him harbor for a time. But even then, his poorly masked *inquieto* chaffed against the mooring of their marriage and her rekindled faith. Being prodigal Catholics had been common ground they shared, but even that went away. Since the divorce, isolation was his harbor. Music, literature and justice, his paramours. Ironically, the songs and books provided the soundtrack to his unmet longing for the real thing. But feeding himself vicariously on the passion of the singers and authors he loved was wearing thin. Pastor Don's words echoed, "We are not here for long, but what we long for most is not here." That rankled Max. It didn't take much wine mixed with exhaustion to set him off.

But some of it is here, Pastor! Wasn't it your God who said, 'it's not good for man to be alone?' Apparently, God himself was not enough for Adam! He poured a second glass. *What a shell game. Wire us for intimacy with another person only to say that's not what we really long for? What a con!*

Max, the logician and mental chess master, suddenly became conscious he was privately arguing with Pastor Don under the assumption God is real. He chided himself for allowing the charismatic pastor's presupposition to corner him into a false syllogism. He reasserted his fatalistic world view with a dash of cynicism. *If there were a God who wired us to long for himself most of all, that would be creepy on a cosmic scale.* Diana Ross backed him up. "I'm Gonna Make You Love Me" played in his head, *The Supremes, 1969.* "I'm gonna use every trick in the book / I'll try my best to get you hooked." *God, the ultimate control freak! If I could force Hanover to love me, that wouldn't be love.* On the heels of that checkmate move, another statement from Pastor Don obliterated his rant. "God has done a risky thing. He gave us free will, wings to fly to him or away from him." Bishop captured King Clever.

Max spoke aloud, "Oh shit. Free will." He raised his glass. "Touché, Pastor G."

The second glass of wine was gone, and he hadn't put and music on. As he started to push himself out of the recliner to choose some tunes, his phone rang. It was Hanover. He laid back.

"Hanover."

"Detective, is this a bad time?"

"No, I was about to listen to some music and try to crash for a few hours. What's up?"

"I'm about to do the same. I wanted to let you know Jenny Meadows, the singer from this morning, is doing some songs tonight at Scarritt Bennett with another songwriter. Just wondered if you'd like to meet us there, if you're up to it?"

"Who's us?"

"Dr. Brickman and his parents are coming."

Silence. Max went into mental battle mode. He had been to a couple of weddings and a funeral in the gothic style chapel at Scarritt Bennett. Being in a church twice in one day was not his idea of rest. And being there with Brickman and his charismatic Catholic parents was not his idea of a good time.

"Detective?"

"What time?"

"7:30. Please come, Max, sir. I think her music right now would do us all good."

He gave himself an out. "Thank you, Hanover. It depends on whether I wake up or not."

"Of course, sir. I'll save you a seat as long as I can. She's getting pretty popular."

"OK."

"I hope you can sleep. Sweet dreams, sir."

That phrase and the tenderness in her voice nearly undid him. Jennifer and his mother were the only other voices attached to that phrase.

"You, too."

He hung up and set his alarm for 6:15PM.

What is it about her? It's not just physical beauty. And Pastor Don, too? Maybe it's that they live their presupposition. I can respect that. I live my own. They live like God is real. Fine. He poured a third glass, emptying the bottle. *We're all free to live our presupposition. I live like God does not exist.*

The unsettled planets had settled into their positions. In a moment of honest curiosity Max wondered, *So what is it that makes them so damned enviable?*

Out of the silence the answer floated into his head like a flying iota, small in the distance, then grew until its bright yellow body and wings spread across his entire mind: *they care.*

Of course, Max knew God-denying people who cared. They were genuine and had causes they championed. It energized them and made them feel purposeful, significant and noble, even in the face of an otherwise meaningless, merely physical existence where this life is the be all, end all.

Max had his own cause – justice. It gave him purpose. He felt motivated and gratified to hold the dark side of humanity accountable and in check. But his presupposition, denying the reality of a Creator God, Father, Savior, didn't call or equip him to care. Helen and Pastor Don's belief in God did, or seemed to, even though he could see no practical or ontological benefit for them to care for him. *Still,* he rationalized, *maybe their belief is just another way of whistling in the dark to keep the fear of death at bay.*

Max, the detective, smelled something else though, another dimension to Pastor Don and Helen's caring. It didn't fit the viewfinder he chose long ago in college with the help of professors who considered science the only wide-open door, not keyhole, to comprehending existence. They helped him see that the traditional belief, at least in Western Civilization, that what a "mythical" God endowed to humanity, Darwin repealed and replaced with observable forces of the universe - evolution and natural selection. In their learned view, even in the social sciences, America was simply the latest iteration of a strong contender in the survival of the fittest idea for a social contract. In their grandiloquent view, it remained to be seen if other, stronger, perhaps more efficient and equitable, perhaps ruthless competitors devoured it. After all, history demonstrated that the eloquent, sly, brutal tyrants who cycle through history were always queueing up to commandeer the masses by any means.

Arrayed against the longstanding bulwark of Max's worldview, Hanover's caring and simple utterance, "sweet dreams," threatened to topple every buttress of the Atheist/Darwinian view he white-knuckled since college. It was like an incantation waking him from a spell cast years ago by grief and a cadre of jaded college professors. Even back then, he had asked penetrating questions: How do music and literature, any art form, assure the survival of the fittest? And what about humor? Make the bully laugh so he doesn't end you? What alchemy of force, matter and time transformed primordial ooze into a standup comic? His professors had sophisticated but less than satisfying answers, high-flying constructs like a collective unconscious of our species and archetypes of repeatable and predictable patterns of behavior mixed with instinct. None of them could with any clarity name what ignited the "Big Bang," though they adhered to it like cult followers. They espoused their a priori assumption that something can indeed come from nothing and defended it like witchdoctors with PhDs. Max had bought it all. Afterall, they were the experts.

He briefly considered the irony that the professors he so revered ultimately relied on belief, not science. That was quickly replaced by the sobering suspicion he had fallen prey to their sleight of hand, which was ostensibly "learn to think" when they really meant, "learn to think like me." Now, in the trenches of life and death they seemed pompous and flimsy. Their arguments non sequitor.

A new assessment dawned on Max. None of their pontification and erudite certitude seemed to make them caring people. In hindsight, Max knew they were arrogant sophists. More energized by the sound of their own voices and sampling their wine collections from around the world than helping the world. They had brains and nothing else. *Like me.* Billy Preston kicked off in his brain "Nothin' from nothin' leaves nothin' / You gotta have somethin' / If you want to be with me." *Billy Preston, 1974, from "The Kids and Me."*

Max knew Hanover really had something. And he had nothing.

He forced himself out of the recliner. Vince's inexcusable Sinatra faux pas guided his selection. *Nothing like Frank for perspective.* He chose an LP. He cleaned and loaded the vinyl. Hit pause. Downed the remaining wine. Settled in and pressed 'play'. The King of Croon and his orchestra poured out of the Genelecs. "That's life, that's what all the people say / You're riding high in April / Shot down in May." Max drifted as the Chairman of the Board counseled him about life.

Sweet dreams. If only.

"Some people get their kicks stompin' on a dream." Frank lamented.

Hanover is a dream. But fat chance.

"I've been up and down and over and out…"

Max was out.

He woke before the alarm went off. Groggy, in a thick fog. He decided to take 440 off West End over to 21st and then north. Maybe grab a taco at SATCO on the way to the concert. A quarter mile before he exited, an electronic message board across the freeway flashed, "Max Malone. Prepare to reap." He jolted awake in a panic. Still in the recliner. His phone said 6:40. By habit he had set it for 6:15AM. He saw he missed a call from his sister. She left a message. That would have to wait.

The lure of seeing Hanover again conquered his lethargy. He showered to wake up and try to wash away the bad dream. Hot water proved no antiseptic for an embattled psyche. Over the years, Scotch and sex had proven ineffectual as well. Listening to music was the closest Max came to relief, but even that was temporary. Besides, it often exposed his fractures, brought on the pain, and sometimes the source of it rose to the surface. Standing under the hot water the thought came, "*You can't conquer what you cannot name*". *Where did I hear that? Better write it down in case I thought of it. Maybe write a blues song with it.* Max found the Blues had good therapeutic value. Blues songs were often about the reality or fear of being alone. In his head SRV named Max's condition. "I am stranded, caught in the crossfire." And his craving. "I need some kind of kindness, some kind of sympathy." *Stevie Ray Vaughan, Crossfire, 1989, from the album "In Step" Last LP he released before his death in 1990.*

No time to eat. He grabbed a granola bar from the pantry. Apple cinnamon. Cinnamon made him think of Hanover, which sparked another thought. It was a small, simple gesture but a significant sign of otherness in lone ranger Malone. *I wonder if she had time to eat.* He grabbed another bar for her. At 7:04PM, he texted her to say he was on his way. She texted back immediately, "Midway back on left aisle. Glad UR coming."

Before he could back out of his driveway, a group text came from the captain. "G in ICU. Brutal bang on head. Induced coma. Brain swelling. No surgeries until stable. Odds not good." Driving down from Love circle near the red light on West End, it was followed by another text: "Fiancé no-show but 3rd Ex did. Still G's emergency contact. Go figure. Reporters, too. Damn. Regroup in AM. For God's sake be safe out there."

Max hesitated to turn right on West End to avoid taking 440 over to 21st. Choosing not to be intimidated by a bad dream, he said, "What the hell," and turned left. *New steps on old paths, right?* Rounding the curve of the on-ramp he regretted it. Traffic was bumper to bumper, crawling along. "Damn!" *At least it's moving.* He muscled his way into the flow. From the vantage point of the F250, he could see equipment and crews setting up arrays of spotlights to work through the night. *What a thankless job.* The electronic message board loomed just ahead, his exit not far beyond it. Some of the road workers appeared to be interacting with motorists in their vehicles. *Uh oh.* Max sensed friction. What he actually witnessed baffled him. There was fist bumping through open car windows and thumbs up back and forth between workers and commuters. A glance at the message board explained it.

Max fines! Prepare to stop.
Road crews working harder
than an ugly stripper.

Max burst out laughing. *Whoever posted that is either fired or promoted. Hell, I want to buy 'em a drink.* The positive PR was evident. The normal irritation of delayed commuters appeared to be transformed by the unexpected shot of humor. Max felt it, too. He rolled down the passenger side window, gave a thumbs up to two workers and said, "Hey, thanks, you guys keep us rolling!"

One of them volleyed back. "This is crazy! Maybe we should take tips in our tool belts."

Max exited at 21st. He chalked up the hilarity as more evidence undermining Darwin's theories. *Ain't no way natural selection made primordial ooze so funny.* He considered amending the sticker on his dash to: Survival of the fittest, fastest, funniest or least stupid. But the thought on the top of his mind was: *I can't wait to tell Hanover about this.*

He hesitated to call his sister in the rush to get to the concert. But he did. She didn't pick up. He left a message. "Hey, sis, saw you called. I was crashed out. Headed to a concert now. Heard a great Mother's Day song at a church today. I'll send it to you." It was out of his mouth, so he let it stand. "Yea, you heard that right. At a church. Don't get excited. Work related. Long story. Tell you later." He signed off the way Sofia always did. "Ti amo. Ti amo di più." Arianna and her kids were the only people on the planet he said those words to: I love you. I love you more.

CHAPTER 37

There was nowhere to park within a block of Scarritt Bennett. At 7:23 Max texted Hanover, "Just parked." Nearly running, he passed an old blue Chevy pickup parked on the street. He slowed enough to check the tailgate. The bumper stickers confirmed it. *Same stronzo at the red light.*

The chapel was a packed house. At the front Jenny Meadows was flanked by two other musicians. She held an acoustic guitar. The murmur of conversations told Max it hadn't started yet. Before he sat down Brickman introduced his parents. Max was nervous. A rare occurrence. To cover it, he nearly told them what happened on the freeway then stopped short, sensing the venue might not be an appropriate setting for an ugly stripper reference and make a less than impressive first impression on Brickman's parents. For a man who didn't give a damn what people thought of him it was an unusual case of self-editing. But it had been an unusual week. He sat down in the packed pew, his thigh and shoulder touching Hanover's. She tried to scoot over a bit.

"Do you have enough room?" she asked him.

"Yea, you?"

"Yes. I told you Jenny's popular. Do I smell cinnamon?"

"Oh, I ate a bar on the way. Brought you one in case you didn't have time to eat either."

Surprised at such a kindness from the normally gruff detective, she took it.

"Thank you, Max. Very thoughtful. I didn't. Slept till nearly 6:30."

Max did the math. *She got ready that fast and looks this great?*

This was the closest he had ever been to Hanover. The scent of White Linen washed over him like incense as the lights dimmed. He felt a tap on his shoulder. He turned to see Dan Greene from Gruhn's Guitars extend a big hand and smile.

The emcee rescued Max from small talk. She welcomed everyone and gave a brief description of the mission of Scarritt Bennett and a pitch for donations on the way out the door. *Of course,* Max thought. The host introduced Jenny to warm applause and let her introduce the other musicians.

Jenny won the crowd with her first remark. "I can't believe I get to be the ham and cheese tonight between these two slices of awesome." Laughter rang around the vaulted ceiling.

The much older writer, "seasoned" as Jenny put it, sporting a bill cap and five-day scruff was Will Barnes. The name sounded vaguely familiar to Max, but he couldn't name a song Barnes had written. *No one knows songwriters' names. Mostly an anonymous job, like that road crew.* He knew Nashville did better at honoring songwriters than most places. He revered some legends, Cash, Kristofferson and Haggard. And hall of famers like Bobby Braddock and Curly Putman who wrote "He Stopped Loving Her Today" *1980* by George Jones. He also admired some of the new wave of writers, too. Mike Reid, whose hit "I Can't Make You Love Me" by Bonnie Raitt, wrecked him for a week, along with the Scotch, when Jennifer left him. He followed the work of a few like Wayne Kirkpatrick, Gordon Kennedy and Tommy Sims, who collaborated on Eric Clapton's song of year, "Change the World." His recent favorite was Natalie Hemby, especially her song "Rainbow," because it reminded him how valiant and hopeful his mother was. He and Jennifer heard some of them in concert halls and some up close and personal at places like the Bluebird.

The other slice of awesome was Jubal Biggs. Besides being a multi-instrumental musician in great demand around town, Jenny described him as a master maker of recorders, flutes, and penny whistles. Jenny plugged his company, "BreathtakingPipes.com."

Max leaned toward Hanover and whispered, "Well, he hasn't mastered traffic lights."

"What? Do you know him?"

When Max turned his head to answer, their faces were only inches apart.

"No, tell you later."

Jubal sat on a cajon behind a single snare drum and high-hat. An assortment of pipes hung on a wooden stand next to him. A small accordion lay beside it. He called it a "squeeze box."

Jenny called an audible insisting Will begin the set. They had rehearsed a song that afternoon and she didn't want to forget the parts. He protested, but conceded. Their rapport was lively and full of mutual respect. It made Max think of Vince. He wished he were there.

Will talked about how most songwriter's favorite song is the one they just wrote and that's what he loves about Nashville. New songs and future hits are being written every day. He asked the audience if they didn't mind hearing a few new ones before he played a couple of his hits. Applause was his green light. He made a joke that singing this song in a chapel might qualify as a confession, since it was about lying, but for a romantic cause - to leave a party early with your darlin'. He credited his two co-writers by name. Jubal strapped on his squeeze box.

"This has just been recorded by a husband-and-wife duo who call themselves 'Rodeo and Juliet.' Jenny will be singing Juliet's harmonies."

"Hopefully," Jenny quipped.

Will's humility and authenticity struck Max. Jenny had both qualities, too. He got a twinge of that feeling he often had of being on the outside looking in on something alien and better than him.

Will said, "This is called 'Sangria Lies'," and kicked off the song. The feel, Will's country delivery, and pulse of the squeeze box transported everyone to a neighborhood party in a small town. Heads started bobbing with the swagger in the groove.

> Tonight this little town gets fancy
> Everbody's dressed to the nines
> Sippin' from tall, skinny glasses
> And tellin' Sangria lies

Max, the would-be songwriter, marveled at the vivid storytelling, "word painting," his favorite literature professor, Dr. Tom Copeland, called it. Jenny came in effortlessly on the harmony in the second verse. And they nailed the chorus.

> Sangria lies, they don't need to know why
> We don't need an excuse
> Say we wish we could stay, then slip away

And do what lovers do
Sometimes the truth goes down better half than whole
Sangria lies. Say your goodbyes. Honey, it's time to go

After the first chorus, Hanover leaned to Max and said, "That sounds like a hit for Rodeo and Juliet."

"Indeed."

By the end, the audience sang the hook with Will, "Sangria lies, say your goodbyes, Honey it's time to go." Under robust applause, Max leaned forward over Hanover and said to Brickman, "That'll sell a lot of beer in Texas."

"No kidding," Brickman agreed.

A split-second later Jenny said from the stage, "Sounds like a future hit to me. Whatever happens, it's gonna sell a lot of longnecks in Austin."

Brickman reached over Hanover for a fist bump from Max. He obliged.

It was Jenny's turn. She played a chord a progression and set up the song simply, "Speaking of Texas, since it's Mother's Day, I want to dedicate this to my mom out in Waxahatchie. This is called "Thanks to You."

Max was glad he already heard it that morning. He could enjoy it more, with less tension and more appreciation of the song, and his mother.

Jubal added harmony and perfect embellishments on a recorder. Will jumped in on a Taylor guitar at the chorus. It was masterful. It was Nashville. When it ended, the audience ate it up. Hanover was right. Max felt better already. He thought about telling her. So he did.

"You were right. I feel better already. Haven't thought about this crazy week once."

She responded, "I'm glad. Me, too. There's nothing like hearing a songwriter do the raw version in person."

"We live in the right town for that." It was Hanover's turn to offer a fist bump.

Max noticed Brickman put his arm around his mother and turn to Hanover. He said in their hearing, "That song is exactly what these two did for me." His parents beamed.

As sappy as Max, the cynic, thought that sounded, he felt the same about his own parents. A mix of envy, loss and gratitude rose in him.

Will was up again. He pulled out a ukulele to sing a whimsical song he co-wrote from a crazy middle of the night poem a friend scribbled down. Once again, he thanked the co-writer by name for letting him write it with her. He said the song is a reminder to enjoy life, like kids do. He taught the crowd a sing-along part, "La La La Lo Cheerio. La La La Giddyup, Let's Go," and then dove in. Jubal provided the backbeat on the high-hat and snare.

> I can see a Mona Lisa floating in the clouds
> Squirt the whipping cream directly in my mouth
> Feed my betta fish crumbs of chocolate cake
> Invite the Queen of England for a PBJ

Max looked around the room. The delight on the faces was like a field of sunflowers all leaning toward the sun. *How do songwriters do that? Take you somewhere you needed to go but didn't know or had forgotten how to get there.*

The chorus presented a way of living Max lost a long time ago.

I'm riding time like a steed
Headed for eternity
He's so sure footed I can fly
Hold my hands up high,
It's not a race, it's a ride, so I am...
Riding time with no hands!

When the La La section came, the audience joined in. Hanover, Brickman and his parents jumped in like school kids. Max nearly sang along. Nearly. Against the backdrop of the traumatic week, he couldn't go there. It was too happy. Too free. He hadn't felt those things in a long, long time.

The chorus came round, the La La part again, then a quick stop ending. The applause and jubilation felt like a rally for dreaming outlandish dreams and living worry free. Max thought if the emcee wanted to pass the hat it should happen now.

But again, he felt like a spectator. Only this time he could name what was out of reach across the distance. And it stung. Joy. He had white-knuckled the reins of his life for so long there was no access, no connection, no nerve endings left uncauterized to experience pure joy. He had known for some time he really was the desperado in the Eagles song of the same name. Losing all his highs and lows. And it wasn't funny how the feeling had gone away.

Hanover sensed his reserve. "You alright?"

By reflex he deflected, "Yea, just amazed at the power and range of music. Where it can take people. And really impressed."

As the room decrescendoed from applause, Helen cupped a hand at her mouth, leaned over to him and spoke his own hallmark word close in his ear with a smile in her voice, "Indeed."

It felt like a kiss without touching him. Her nearness and breath on his ear ignited a memory. He was almost fourteen. A school dance. Ariana told him her older friend Linda Clark, already fifteen, wanted to dance with him. The song was a slow one, "Cherish" *1966, by The Association. It went to number one on the charts.* "Cherish is the word I use to describe / All the feeling that I have hiding here for you inside." Linda was pretty and already very shapely. He took four of the longest steps of his life to that point and asked her to dance. They walked to the dance floor surrounded by couples shuffling in circles. Linda put both arms around his neck, pulled him close, and rested her head on his shoulder with her face against his bare neck. He felt her breath on his skin. His hands rested lightly on her waist. It was the first time he was body to body with a girl. That night he lay awake in bed knowing - slow dancing was his new favorite thing.

It was Jenny's turn again. She pulled out a ukulele as well and introduced a song called "Kinder," cowritten with two other writers she credited. She announced, to much applause, it would be released as a single on Friday of the coming week. Jubal started a medium groove on the cajon. Will moved to a keyboard. Jenny set it up by saying every generation has its turbulent times and now so does hers. She said she didn't think music was the cure, but it could move people toward each other, and maybe toward the cure. She hoped this song would help do that and began playing. After the first verse, Max thought it had a Jason Mraz feel with a Dolly Parton lyric.

What kind of world are we livin' in?
Judged, banned, bullied for the color of our differences

Raise your voice, shake your fist,

We can be better than this

A little bit of love could really go a long, long way

The chorus was a call to the whole world to treat each other better in spite of our differences. To

Max it was another reminder of how far away he was from doing that. Exhibit A was sitting on the other side of Hanover. He knew he had been anything but kind to Brickman.

Let's be a little kinder, colorblinder

Let your light shine a little brighter

Spread a little feel good, real good love to one another

It starts with you and me

Can't we all agree to disagree?

And be a little kinder

The song wrapped up with Jenny singing ad libs over Jubal's groove and snapping her fingers. Jubal stopped playing. Jenny kept snapping and singing. She ended the song with two finger snaps. The place erupted. Everyone stood. Hanover, Dr. Brickman, his parents did. Max stood, too. Reluctantly.

When the crowd settled back in the pews, Will Barnes said, "You know, Jenny, if you keep working on this songwriting thing, you're gonna wind up writing something people like."

Everyone had a good laugh. Including Max. He stole a couple of glances at Hanover. She was so free. And beautiful. It was like seeing Sofia laugh. His dad could get her going with his Irish stories till she rolled on the floor. The atmosphere in the room was something Max hadn't known since those days. It was like family. Like a reunion. But he still felt like the only non-relative.

Max's phone vibrated. *No. Not now!* It was only 7:59. He was tempted to ignore it to prevent the best half hour of the week from being highjacked by work. But Hanover and Brickman reached for their phones, too. Relief. A group text from Vince. Not the captain. "Hope you are all getting some rest. We'll get through this. Julie and I prayed for everyone just now. IB. Peace out."

Brickman leaned forward and asked Max, "What's IB?"

"Intermittent Baptist. And he suffers from JLS."

"Which is?" Hanover asked.

"Jargon lag syndrome. Only Vince says 'Peace, out' anymore."

Helen got tickled. She covered her mouth to stifle the laughter and her shoulders bobbed up and down. She took a few deep breaths like trying to get rid of hiccups, but the shoulder bobbing came again. Max thought he could get used to making her laugh.

Meanwhile, Will described his next song. It came from the most "panoramic and detailed" dream he ever had. It was called, "The Library of My Life.' In his dream, he stood under a high domed ceiling with long corridors fanning out in all directions. Everything that ever happened to him was stored in thousands of volumes on the shelves. He apologized that the song had nine verses and blamed it on growing up on Bob Dylan's music.

"Maybe you have some of the same things in your own library." Will played a crisp lick on the guitar to begin and Jubal added a fluid line on penny whistle for the intro.

Max leaned over to Hanover. "It has the feel of The Boxer by Paul Simon."

She whispered back, "I have his autograph."

"Of course you do."

Max listened as Will sang the breadth of his life and much of Max's. It began with the chorus.

> My life is hidden deep inside
> Written and recorded line by line
> In dreams a doorway opens wide
> And I roam the Library of my Life

The first verses hit Max square in his normally well-guarded heart.

> My mother's lovely voice calls for dinner
> My daddy's hand on the steering wheel
> His cigarette smoke pours out the window
> The highway hums to grandma's through star fields

> One row holds first and last things
> Climbing the high dive, slow dance
> Soft kisses and hard goodbyes knowing
> Heaven's where I'll see that face again

The chorus repeated. Max couldn't get out of the way of the song. It bore down on him like a train, and he couldn't get off the tracks.

> Friday night circling the boredom
> Driving slow one-handed down the road
> Laughter and young love fog the windows
> "Yesterday" is on the radio

Memories stampeded him. He missed at least a verse thinking, *Is this guy a mind reader? How can he write so personal, and it be so universal? A young man couldn't write this song.*

> There's an unfinished wing for dreaming
> Where Jack Nicholson is my therapist

That line got laughs.

> My heart drinks in like wine what he's saying
> Forgiveness should begin your bucket list.

Jubal repeated the intro figure. It gave Max's mind time to digest and catch a breath.

> In memories I play with my dear children
> I can make them any age I choose

Even that couplet carried some hurt for Max because he had no children. But what followed was very much his own storyline.

> Perfume draws me through sorrow and triumph
> Past wine and women to a row marked 'You'
> A record drops, Dean Martin sings Amore
> On my mother's Zenith stereo

Zenith was, of course, the brand on which Sofia played all her records.

You take my hand and whisper "forever"
The ceiling blooms the door begins to close

Will stopped the train feel with simple chord rakes.

I wake up in tears from the beauty
And from knowing more is past than lies ahead
You reach for me, and ink is flowing
By tonight I'll wanta dream again

The train left the station again for the chorus, now familiar. A repeat of the last line seemed like the ending, but Will said he wrote one more verse just for this occasion.

One Mother's Day in May at the chapel
We gathered round and fed our souls
On tears, laughter, songs and stories.
Wrote 'em on our hearts and took em home

The audience lapped up the personal touch like biscuits and gravy at the Loveless Café. Jubal reprised the intro figure and with the same guitar lick that began the song, Will ended it.

Once again, the audience lavished the kind of applause the song and songwriter deserved. Clapping enthusiastically with everyone else Hanover leaned toward Max and said, "That's his 'American Pie'"

"Exactly, Don McLean." Max was more than impressed. "Your dad raised you on the right music."

"At the risk of jargon lag, right on."

Max laughed and relished how sharp she was.

Only five songs in and Max felt stuffed. Every song was like an entrée.

Jenny moved to the keyboard. Because of the beauty of the venue and acknowledging so many friends from church in attendance, she wanted to do a worship song. She asked them to help her with the next song. The lyrics would be on the screen behind the musicians. She invited everyone to join in as they learned it or just soak in the sound in the beautiful chapel. The song was called "I Rest My Soul."

"I love this one," Hanover said.

Max prepared himself to endure it, trusting the levee of his unbelief and antipathy to church and all Christian music to hold. The simplicity of the piano part and warm, understated sincerity of Jenny's voice disarmed him. This was no grand Trojan horse meant to impress the audience or the Almighty, smuggling a clandestine agenda to capture hearts by stealth, ambush and musical prowess. It was a personal cry of the heart. From the opening lines the song poured like a stream of clear water over Max's defenses. He glanced at Hanover. Her eyes were closed. She sang softly along with Jenny, other voices joining in.

> Lord, you know where my desperate heart's been
> Because you walked there, and gathered my tears
> You know the unknown that lies before me
> And you whisper, "I will be near"

The natural reverb of the vaulted chapel resonated with the vulnerability of the song and singer. Max watched as head after head bowed like sunflowers at sunset. Jubal began playing a part like a string line on a long, wooden recorder. The sound grew as more people joined in on the second verse.

> Lord, your power flows in my weakness
> Cover me now, Come flood my soul
> In your presence my fears will perish
> And you will carry my heavy load

When Jenny floated to the high notes on the first two lines of the chorus with the support and harmony of three hundred voices, Max knew something transcendent was happening, something that couldn't be explained away by evolution or instincts or archetypes of the collective unconscious. His view through the keyhole could not take it in. It was happening on the other side of a door he closed a long time ago and refused to reopen. The united voices amplified by the architect's design created something bigger than the sum of its parts, an awe, a presence his mother called "la vicinanza di Dio," the nearness of God.

> O, God of glory, Friend of the broken
> The High and Holy come down so low

The dynamic softened and the range descended back to the verse melody.

> Here in this valley Your love was proven
> So, in your hands, Lord, I rest my soul

Max leaned back and turned his head to look at Hanover. He watched as she sang the next verse, her eyes closed, her hands clasped over her heart.

Let your voice be – my assurance
Nothing can take me - from your grace
Beyond this valley – you are preparing
A pilgrim's welcome - a spacious place

When the chorus rose again, she opened her cupped hands in front of her. To Max, in the dim light she looked like a Rembrandt of a praying Madonna, her face radiating tenderness and tranquility. He thought she might cry.

In that moment, Hanover was his church. A cathedral of his desire. But the fear of her knowing him, his past and the tangled, bitter cynic within swept in like a dark cloud against the luminous worship rising around him. And what if the impossible happened, she gave him a chance and he let himself need her, leaned his life on her, made her his everything? He knew he would never be her everything. She had a higher dependency and would grow beyond him and his darkness and need. Like Jennifer. Or be taken out by some heartless miscreant, a capricious accident or indifferent, ravenous disease. Like his mother. Where would he be then?

Max looked up. Listening to the voices fill the chapel, he understood for the first time why Sofia adored cathedrals. It wasn't the structure, the art, the reverence or majestic music. It wasn't the beauty, the height, the timeless solidity enduring as generations came and went. His mother adored the One for whom the cathedral was built. The One it pointed to. And revered. The God who helped her endure to the end. The same God Helen revered. Sitting next to her, he felt dirty. Unworthy. She was indeed a cathedral, but as Sofia taught him as a boy, she was God's temple. And he was a hollow shell on a shifted foundation, the roof caved in, unable to shelter him from the ravaging storms of futility and imminent certainty of mortality. He crossed his arms tightly against his chest. He could feel his heart pounding. Hanover's eyes were still closed. Maybe she wouldn't notice if he slipped out. As the chorus repeated, he did.

He was almost to the street when she called his name. "Max, wait up." He stopped and turned. As she approached, he stood still, but his mind raced around Castle Malone searching for what to say. Out of character for him, he formed a simple sentence his head. *I don't belong in there.* But she spoke first and made it easy.

"I'm really hungry. Want to walk over to SATCO?"

"But you're missing Jenny. And those other two are great, too."

"Yea, so you're buying."

He shook his head and laughed. *How does she do that?*

CHAPTER 38

Sunday evening 8:20PM – Day 7

The taco place was only one block away toward Vanderbilt University and the hospital where Guryon's life hung in the balance. A drizzly Sunday had turned into a clear night. As they walked, fireflies did their annual flash dance under the trees.

"What do you call those?" Hanover asked. "Fireflies or lightning bugs?"

"Fireflies. That's what my mother called them."

"My dad calls them lightning bugs. He told me they charge up like a battery every time lightning strikes."

"My mom said they were trying to hold back the dying day. To slow down time."

"Nice. Either way."

"Yeah." Talking about his mother with Hanover, the memory didn't come with the usual sting. He added to her profile, "easy to talk to." The present tense in which she referred to her dad prompted a personal question, "Where is your dad?"

"He retired near Springfield, Missouri. Likes to fish. But he still does a few hours a week on the radio, of all places on a local Christian radio station, Joy101.

"There's a story there. He still making listeners laugh?"

"Oh yeah. His tag line on air now is, 'Happiness is overrated compared to Joy101.'"

There was a lull as they placed their order. She ordered a longneck. Max abstained. He bought. They found a table outside to wait to be called.

Hanover made a suggestion, "What do you say we don't talk about the cases till tomorrow?"

"Fine by me."

Max's name came over the speakers. He retrieved their food. Hanover attacked the tacos with the same passion as the pancakes at the Pantry that morning.

"Just a guess but, you like to eat?" Max said.

"Doesn't take a detective to figure that out. And I like to cook. Because it leads to eating."

"Indeed. Vince swears this queso has medicinal qualities."

"Yea, it cures insomnia and skinny jeans."

"That's hilarious. Channeling your DJ dad again?"

"It's in the blood."

Another lull. Again, Hanover broke the silence.

"Rare day for you, I guess."

"What do you mean?"

"When's the last time you were in a church twice in one day?"

"Not since I was a kid. But with another cop? Never."

"God moves in mysterious ways."

Max reserved comment.

There was a longer lull. They ate. And watched the mostly younger crowd sharing buckets of iced longnecks with their friends. Hanover primed the pump again.

"This morning at the Pantry, you said sometime you'd like to hear about my unchurched days."

"Oh, that's right." He couldn't believe she remembered. "Is this a good some time?"

For the next half hour, Helen described her sex, drugs and rock and roll days with a candor that unsettled Max. He knew everyone has a story, but he was not prepared for this one, not from Hanover.

Because of her mother, Helen grew up as a Presbyterian. Nominal. Even less "intermittent" than Vince. In her teenage years and into her twenties, she dated mostly musicians. Credited her dad with that. After all, he was the power DJ with backstage passes. She got addicted to the lifestyle, mainly the rush of attention from anyone crowds cheered for, someone larger than the life she had. She said the boyfriends came and went like "hit singles." *That's so eloquent*, Max thought. She even went on tour with a famous rock band for a couple of months, as a "merch" handler, but mostly rode the bus and partied. It didn't take long to feel like an ornament. She had sense enough to avoid the hard drugs. She watched a musician and a groupie OD. Was helpless to help. Both died. From a front row-seat on the drug dealers, she saw their appetite for money and complete indifference to the damage done. That was the first time she remembered wanting to protect and serve. And bag the bad guys.

She saved the hardest revelation for last.

"I know we agreed not to talk about the cases, and I'm not, but the Dr. Guryon situation hit a nerve." She told Max at twenty she had an abortion. Didn't think twice about it. Didn't love the guy. Didn't know God. She described her younger self as a poster child for a 'truth is relative,' morally liberated member of the 'me-now' generation.

"I wanted what I wanted, and I wanted it now."

Max tried to cut her some slack. "Aren't we all born like that? Welcome to the human race."

"Yes, but some people never grow out of it. We can camouflage our selfishness with unbridled ambition or OCD, an enneagram profile or a hundred other things."

Max marveled at her honesty and thought processes.

"I'm a 2, by the way. Giver, without the codependency, with a side of 3, Achiever, minus the uncertainty of my self-worth. I bet you're a 5, Investigator with a side of 6, Skeptic, or 8, Challenger. For now."

"Why do you say, 'for now?'"

"People can change. Before I knew the Lord, I was a 7, Enthusiast, with a side of 9, Peacemaker."

"Fascinating." He had no idea what an enneagram was.

"Anyway, the first time I heard my dad play the song "Angel of the Morning" I said, 'That's my theme song. 'If morning's echo says we've sinned…'"

Max finished the line, "'well, it was what I wanted now.' The Merillee Rush version 1968?"

"No, the one by Juice Newton."

"Yea, I prefer that one. It was a hit for her in 1981. Reggie Young played guitar on it. He's the same guy who played on Dobie Gray's 'Drift Away.'"

A veneer of details was an attempt by Max to manage Hanover's vulnerability. His right foot bounced involuntarily. It shook the table, so he willed it to stop. She added to her profile of him: *Voluminous knowledge of songs. Deflects with minutia. Foot bounces when nervous.*

"I agree. And I really want to see your record collection sometime."

"OK, on one condition. You bring over your autographs."

"That sounds great, or raw, if that's still current jargon."

Max made the day even more rare. He apologized and confessed something about himself. "I'm sorry. You were saying. Sometimes I deflect with minutia. Investigators with a side of stronzo tend to do that."

"Is that Italian?"

"Yea, it means 'jackass.'"

Hanover smiled and added the apology to her list of firsts from the detective. "And your foot bounces when you're nervous."

He was more captivated by her than ever. "Vince noticed the same thing. Go ahead. Before it starts bouncing again."

Until that moment, Max did not know endorphins were on the menu at SATCO.

"Well, I didn't know it then, but I tried to ignore the damage to my soul by going back to school, transferred to Tennessee, new start, MTSU to study criminal justice. You know, get a cause?"

"Mm-huh."

She chronicled graduating, moving to Nashville, working as a waitress, assistant to a program director her dad knew at a radio station. Didn't date for a long time. Swore off musicians, but in Music City they were everywhere. Dated one. A songwriter. Married him. Went to Police Academy against his protests. How he divorced her, "Like I told you the other night, to follow his music dreams and his own "'truth.'"

What a bona fide idiot.

"As the songs says, I was bluer than blue."

Max knew the reference, of course. He owned the album. He even knew "Bluer Than Blue," 1978, Michael Johnson, was written by Randy Goodrum, but kept all that to himself.

"Not long after that, a friend invited me to hear Pastor Don teach. I kept going back. He kept talking about God's grace and how valuable we must be to God for him to sacrifice himself for us, you know, the whole gospel thing."

"Mm-huh."

"At that point I was two-dimensional. Like one of those cardboard standups in a record store. Remember, record stores?"

"Oh, yea."

"One side of me was all painted up and presentable to the world. The other side was all shame and hidden stuff. I didn't feel very valuable. To God or anyone else."

She described how one Sunday morning Pastor Don brought out a life-size, cardboard standup of a person and used it to describe exactly how she felt. Papa G said was a cardboard person, until someone told him and showed him in the Bible what God did for him and thought of him.

"He started naming by memory all the things God says about us and the scripture references. He went on and on. You met him. You know how he is."

"Mm-huh."

"After the service, he prayed for me to believe Christ and receive his forgiveness. The only way I've been able to describe it, Max, it was like God's spirit inflated me from cardboard into a full person. I took the deepest breath of my life. The only specific thing I remember about his prayer was, "'Lord, make what you say about Helen, what she believes about herself.'"

She pulled out her keys. Attached was a plastic label case. She read the handwritten message inside.

"Lord, make what you say about me what I believe about me."

There was a lull.

"And I do. More chips?" She got up to get them.

Max was speechless. The intro to "I Will" *The Beatles, 1968, from the White album,* kicked off in his head, but it felt completely presumptuous, so he willed it to stop. The moment was too momentous even for music. And the possibility of such a thing with Hanover more remote than the stars above his head. He had already waited a lonely lifetime. He knew the odds. Will Barnes had just sung it. "More is past than lies ahead."

What replaced the Beatles' song in his head was the Huxley quote above his LP collection, "After silence, that which comes nearest to expressing the inexpressible is music." Huxley was just one of the God deniers that mentored Max's world view. A handful of his books were on the shelves in the music room. He knew Huxley and his cronies revolted against religion, especially Christianity, because a world without meaning meant liberation from a system of morality, to do as they damn well pleased. Huxley admitted that himself. But Max's own revolt was to deny the inexpressible mainly out of personal pain, and certainly, to cast off Christianity's view that the inexpressible and the meaning of life are best expressed in Christ and God's Word. *"The high and holy come down so low"* from Jenny's song floated into his head. It was only in college that Max adopted some of his professors' philosophical position that religion is oppressive and arcane.

Unlike Sofia, who loved to be still in the woods after a rain or in the serenity of an empty cathedral, Max was haunted by silence. Music shielded him from it. The irony not lost on him was that music was the very thing that pointed him to the inexpressible, and just now drove him to leave the concert. Music was another inescapable Mobius strip.

And now, Hanover. She revolted and walked away from God, lived liberated from a traditional system of morality only to come full circle to God and found, it appeared, true freedom, and her truest self. He could not deny she was a full person any more than he could deny his own cardboard existence.

When Hanover returned with more chips, Max's demeanor had wilted. Sitting across from her, knowing so much of her story, seeing the fullness of her, how whole, though not unscathed from the scars of her life, and how transparent she was about it, all of that exiled him again to the other rim of the Grand Canyon between them. *Why didn't I tell her I went down that same road but driven by anger and bitterness.* It had come to mind, but he didn't say it. *Why couldn't I tell her I'm a card-carrying member of the me/now generation, too. And still am! I threw generalities at her reality, like an absolution, like some get-out-jail-free card from self-condemnation. Why do I do that?* He knew the answer. Because cardboard standups can't stand up on their own. By design or by choice, they have no guts or backbone.

In his reflex tug of war between fight and flight, Max mentally searched for a way to wrap up with Hanover and get back to the relative safety of the tower in Castle Malone on Love Circle.

But as usual, Hanover spoke first.

"So, that's my story. Some time, maybe, I'd like to hear yours."

"Hanover, I…"

"Helen. Tonight, we're just Max and Helen." She was making flight much more difficult. But he was an expert.

Max answered haltingly, like a stroke victim. "Helen, I, I am truly, uh, amazed at you. I mean, at your story and see, I can see how, how real it is for you, I mean, in you. How real it is in you. It's so obvious." He unwittingly latched on the very thing that would nearly make the inexpressible expressible. "Like Pastor Don said this morning about, about the wind. We can't see it, but we can see the effects of it." But the verbal meandering took over again. "And as I like to say, go where the evidence leads and I can see you've done that in your life, and that's really all we can do, so I guess…" The rambling, stream of consciousness, frantic feeling in his head was, *I guess you can see I'm still pretty much a cardboard standup who fears the wind that inflated you into a full person and I've denied that wind exists for so long that I'm screwed if I tell you, but clearly you are not blind to that, so in order to maintain at least my two-dimensional existence and composure I really need to go.* But what came out was, "So I guess, thank you for your honesty."

"You're welcome, Max. Thank you for wanting to know."

His next two thoughts were, *I'll never be able to look at her the same at work,* and, *She's even more amazing than I thought.* He was figuring out how to call it a night when Helen got a text.

"It's Jenny. The concert's over. She and the Brickmans want to know if we'll join them here at SATCO."

So, they assume we're together? Guess that makes sense.

"I think I'll wait on them, Max. You don't have to. I know it's been a very long day."

There was his out. "Yes, it has. I'm gonna go unwind and try to get a real night's sleep."

"Thanks for dinner. I hope I didn't twist your arm too much. Or bend your ear."

"No. Not at all. Really. You made it... it really was a rare day. Good night."

"Goodnight. Sweet dreams."

There it was again. *How can two words carry so much?*

"You, too. See you in the A.M."

To avoid running into the Brickmans, he walked north to the corner, which took him right under Jessie Bellaire's balcony. He looked up before turning right on Grand Avenue. The details of the evening and the cases began pelted him like rain. It was three blocks to his car. He passed a couple arguing and another trio. One of them said something about how that "Kinder" song should put Jenny on the map. *I guess kindness isn't in my enneagram.* A block farther, he walked up on Jubal Biggs loading instruments into the cab of his old truck. Max mustered some cordiality.

"That was some mighty fine playing with Jenny and Will."

"Thank you, sir. And thank the Lord. I just want to be his instrument."

Max had no response for that. He just kept walking. At his own truck, he rolled the windows down and sat for a minute. He could see Jessie's building and the top outline of Vanderbilt Hospital. The throaty rumble of an engine approached from behind, accelerated and shifted gears as it passed. Jubal Biggs. A memory bullet hit Max square in the chest. He could hear his father say, *Stick shift. Probably a 327 small block.*

Professor Liam Malone taught Max everything he knew about engines and how to keep them running. He told Max, "For cars I'm your huckleberry, but in matters of the heart, your mother is bang on." To hand his dad one more tool or talk to his mother about Hanover would be heaven. But when it came to cars and hearts, he had been on his own for a long time.

Back at Love Circle, the cork in a fresh Chianti fought him. It broke inside the bottle. He poured the entire contents into a pot, skimmed off the floating pieces, and refilled the bottle with a funnel rolled from a laminated menu from a barbeque place he loved. Having a frugal father like Dr. Malone and an Italian mother from Italian wine country, Max wasn't about to waste a bottle of wine. He trudged up the stairs to the music room like a solitary lighthouse keeper, poured a glass and stepped out onto the balcony. Overhead the stars shone steady and reliable like they had for millennia, guiding sailors to and from harbor. Down below, a few fireflies still danced, valiantly looking for any lovers left unchosen in the darkness. Music drifted from a house a few doors down. Country music. It sounded live. *Must be my country star neighbor throwing a wingding.*

Caught between the stars and the fireflies, listening to the sanguine pulse of a party from a distance, an all too familiar marooned feeling washed over him. The beauty of the Spring night drove him back inside. He pulled out the song he played most whenever he was bluer than blue, "The Long and Winding Road", *1970, The Beatles, released one month after the band broke up.* But slid it back into the row. Several records to the right he selected Jackson Browne, The Pretender album, 1976. As carefully as always, he set the needle on "Sleeps Dark and Silent Gate," poured a glass of wine, readied himself in the recliner and hit play. "I found my love too late," Jackson sang. The entire song was a biography of Max's condition. He waited for a particular line. In his opinion it tied for first place with a Paul Simon line - "and a rock feels no pain, and an island never cries" - for the lyric line with the most pathos in all the music of the sixties and seventies. On this night, on this rare day, it became the first raw prayer Max had uttered since Sofia died. "Oh, God, this is some shape I'm in."

He awoke in the dark. Still in the recliner. The music had stopped. The clock read 11:11PM.

Max forced himself downstairs, undressed and crawled into bed. A single clunking noise outside half opened his eyes. He listened. Nothing. *Probably a racoon. They were here before us.* He thought about Hanover. Her story. As he drifted away. The last thing he heard was the throaty rumble of an engine. *Stick shift. Small block V8.*

CHAPTER 39

Monday Morning 6:15AM – Day 8

The sound of the alarm started Max's daily routine. He sat up on the side of the bed. Felt for the slippers normally placed strategically where his feet first met the floor. They were not there. Slippers could wait. Coffee could not. Barefoot, he made his first stop in the bathroom, relieved himself, dutifully washed his hands like Sofia trained him and rinsed his mouth with a water pick like his father. He did not look in the mirror to check on the recent invasion of grey hairs. As usual, he went to the northeast-facing window to see what kind of day it was. Sunny and clear. That could change. It was Spring. He opened the window. A soft breeze greeted him. Birds chirped their morning correspondences. He lingered. *Yesterday really was a rare day.*

Coffee beckoned. He headed to the kitchen to start the brew. The early glow of morning sunlight bathed the room in golden hues. Max thought he felt the new creeping in. As the designer coffee maker began its familiar percolating sound, Max stepped to the front door. Behind it was indeed another rare day.

When he swung the door open, something fell on the floor from the inside of the glass storm door. A white envelope lay face down. He didn't reach for it. He froze. It had finally happened. His dark premonition. *I'm number seven. That explains the bump in the night.* He looked out on the flawless Spring morning.

Whoever delivered this opened the storm door. He looked into the distance like a man whose doctor just broke the bad news about a terminal, untreatable illness the patient suspected he had all along. His breathing shallowed to nothing. The comforting sound of the coffee maker turned to a death rattle. In a matter of moments, Max went from shock to surreal acquiescence. *Of course. Haughty eyes. That's me.* The only surge of protest was a thought of Hanover. *I knew it was impossible.*

A spark of Max, the detective, kicked in. He took care not to touch the door. *Could be fingerprints.* He recalled several neighbors had security cameras, including the country star. *I'm gonna nail this bastard.* He looked back down. The shape of the envelope caught his eye. It wasn't nearly square like all the others. And smaller. A long rectangle. No time to glove up. He went back to the kitchen and grabbed a pair of barbeque tongs.

He went down on one knee, picked up the envelope deliberately like a spent shell casing at a crime scene. It didn't appear to be actual stationery like the other RA notes. He turned it over. Handwritten in large letters was simply:

MM from HH

Reality stuttered. The unexpected whiplashed him mentally in slow motion, like a castaway adrift on the ocean unable at first to recognize the ship come to rescue him. "Hanover!"

Max laughed. He spun around and slid down on the floor with his back to the wall. He couldn't stop laughing. If anyone had seen him, they might be convinced he was already drunk this early in the morning. He took the envelope in his hand and slid the tongs across the floor into the kitchen. Upon closer inspection, he could see it was a bank envelope, the kind a teller put cash in for a withdrawal. He opened the small flap at one end. The double folded note appeared to be written on a sheet torn from a yellow pad. *Definitely Hanover.* It read:

MM, Good morning. Hope you slept well.
Jubal Biggs (musician) invited Jenny - Brickman and me
to a music Bash at country singer's place down the street.
We came by to maybe get you but your lights were out.
Thought I'd leave a note to read over your coffee.
Here's to a less rare week than the last one...
H2H Here to help. Ha.

Coffee never tasted better. His morning routine evaporated. Max leaned against the kitchen counter and watched the morning light crescendo outside. The bump in the night was her. *She was the racoon. And the sound of Biggs' truck wasn't a dream.*

Two songs about Monday came to mind. Neither fit this one. *"Monday, Monday, can't trust that day"* 1966, *Mamas and the Papas* and *"Rainy Days and Mondays always get me down,"* 1971, *Karen Carpenter.* Max, the would-be songwriter, wondered why writers wrote so much about Monday. *"Manic Monday",* 1986, *the Bangles; "Come Monday,"* 1974, *by Jimmy Buffet, from Living and Dying in ¾ Time. What a great album title. But that song isn't even in ¾ time, is it?* He started to sing a little of it to make sure.

Half a cup wasn't gone when his phone buzzed. Group text from the captain. The real world ran on its own time signature.

"Hope you all rested. Conference Rm B. 9 sharp. Guryon survived the night. Still in coma. Theo, more strong coffee, please."

Max didn't move. He took a sip. Another text buzzed in from Vince.

"Hear you were in church twice yesterday?"

Mas clarified, "Once. And a concert. CU at 9."

He read Hanover's note again. *Her handwriting's as beautiful as she is.* He filled a second cup and headed to get ready for work. In the shower, the details of the Red Angels cases washed over him as well. *What the hell comes next? We gotta find one of these delivery people.* Max sorted the Rubik's tiles in his head. He always shaved in the shower but locked in the RA zone he forgot to. *First thing – we all view the footage from Davidson's gate, Jessie's place, the Capitol parking garage and Guryon's office. Who collected his birthday cards? My first stop – the cleaning lady at Jessie's. Who got her to slip the card under Jessie's door? Find that person, get some damn answers.*

The thrill of the hunt awakened again in Max. Even with fifteen minutes on the elliptical he was ready and out the door at 7:30AM. Plenty of time for a bagel. Review the facts, and sketch a plan of attack for the team. He knew the captain would have his own directives, but always valued Max's input. Eagerness that the 'game was afoot' blended with anticipation of seeing Hanover. At least in his mind, their relationship had changed dramatically in the last few days.

He strode out of his front door, laptop case under one arm, coffee in one hand, keys in the other and a line in his head from a song he had just cranked up on the elliptical, "Carry On My Wayward Son," *1976, Kansas from the album Leftoverture:* "I set a course for winds of fortune." Rounding the front of his truck, he clicked 'unlock' on the key fob. Before he could reach for the door handle all the winds of fortune went out of his sails.

Taped to the driver's side window was a clear, plastic baggie. A red envelope inside. He could read the handwriting: "Max Malone." For a fraction of a second, he tried to trick himself into believing Hanover left him two notes. But he knew. He yanked the baggie from the window, opened the truck door, climbed in and shut it. This time, he didn't hesitate. *To hell with it.* Without gloving up he pulled out the note. The first line was the only unfamiliar one. But no surprise.

> You have sown arrogance and unfaithfulness.
> Prepare to reap. Put your affairs in order.
> Your life is required of you.
>
> The Red Angels

There was no panic. No rage. No questioning why. Just a hollow oddness. The sounds around him faded like the last E major chord on "A Day in the Life," by the Beatles. It rang for forty seconds. Max lost all sense of time. He sat stone still, but inside his chest the planets swung randomly out of orbit. His eyes locked on the word "Survival" in the motto stuck to his dash. Max lived knowing no one beats the odds. *But this is crazy. Somebody believes the maker of the universe wants me dead. I'm a nobody. Less than a nobody. Hell, in a way I'm on God's side. I go after bad guys.* He wanted to argue with someone. Plead his case. *Who should I call? Not Hanover. God no, not her. Maybe Vince. No way. He would hover like Barney Fife trying to keep me safe.*

Max sat immobilized in his driveway. In the back of his mind a dark comic irony percolated about death stalking him in the season as the whole world comes to life. He thought maybe that's how he could present it at the meeting. *Just throw the card on the table and say,* "What a beautiful day to get a death sentence." But hearing it out loud he reconsidered. *How can I go into this meeting?*

The death sentence, if that's what it was, sank in. Obviously, it had been for Abe, Jessie, Donovan Jacobs, Sydney Sera and Gunner Brown. It remained to be seen if Dr. Guryon succumbed. *Very likely.* For a moment he recoiled at the thought of being in the same company with them. But he was self-aware enough to know, if not in kind, then by degree. *I'm definitely on that list.* He couldn't argue the charges. He looked at the card again. *Arrogance? Guilty, your honor. Unfaithfulness. No question.* He had seen many guilty perps stand before a judge and plead their innocence with a straight face, when everyone knew, and the evidence was overwhelming, they were guilty as hell. There was no way he could grandstand a defense.

In his analytical mind, it struck him that arrogance was the lesser of the two charges. It seemed more general, and he rationalized, should be less condemning. *Doesn't everyone suffer from that, at times?* That defense turned flimsy in the self-knowledge that he was not intermittently arrogant, like Vince being a Baptist. For him arrogance was a lifestyle, a permanent parasite on his character.

But "unfaithfulness," when he heard it as the second of two capital offenses, it stung more. He couldn't deny it was an egregious, damaging offense against people. Jennifer. And against Liam and Sophia and the faith they nurtured in him. *Hell, I've been unfaithful to the family crest, Fidelis ad Urnam. Faithful to the end? Not hardly.* He had stored away the crest for that reason. He could never live up to it. And now the end appeared imminent.

Max did what he always did, lay out the options. One - Rage against the dying of the light. Two - Face it like a man. Three – Drive slower. Be the fittest, biggest and least stupid. Minimize risk. *Right, in my job?* Four - Try to change. Bargain with God. *After years of silence and belligerence? Strike a deal? NOT going there.* Five – Do a foxhole mea culpa, put his affairs in order and hope for the best.

Max Malone, the great detective, had all his cards on the table. He looked at the time. 8:05AM. The meeting was in less than an hour. He had no idea what to do. He buried his face in his hands. Out of sheer exasperation, without thinking it, he borrowed Jackson Brown's raw line and added one of his own, "O God, this is some shape I'm in. What the hell do I do?"

Silence did not express the inexpressible. If it did Max had forgotten that language. The beauty of the day remained. Birds chirped their correspondences, like nothing in the universe had changed. Monday ticked away. Oblivious and indifferent. Out of the silence a line from one of Jenny's songs from the night before floated into his head.

> You know the unknown that lies before me,
> and you whisper, "I am near."

Max fought back a question. He pressed his lips tightly together. Rubbed his unshaven jawline. His right foot bounced. Asking this question meant diverging completely from a worldview and compass heading he chose in college and followed to this moment. He took two deep breaths, collected himself, willed his foot to stop bouncing. With his head against the headrest and eyes shut, he spoke out loud, calmly, what he didn't like to think of as a prayer.

"Are you near?"

He waited. Waited some more. He had two more questions behind that one, questions he had asked more than once, but out of anger. Before he could ask them, his phone rang.

He didn't recognize the number. Out of irritation he answered it anyway, "This better be God or someone very important!"

"Max? well, I'm definitely not God. It's Pastor Don."

Max scrambled to sound composed. "Pastor, sorry. In the middle of something here."

"I can call back."

"No. No, uh, just a little surprised." He was more than a little surprised. "How did you get my number?"

"From Helen."

"Oh, right. Sure. What's on your mind?"

"Well, you are, Max. I've learned when someone comes to mind that's usually the Lord prompting me to pray for them or contact them. Or both."

Max had no response.

"And I saw you from a distance at church yesterday. I wanted to thank you for coming."

"Oh, yeah. It was, uh, packed, and good. *How lame was that?* He tried to recover. "And Jenny's song really got to me. My mom's been gone a long time."

"I'm sorry to hear that. Yes, Jenny is…"

"Pastor," Max interrupted him. "What are you doing right now? There's been a, uh, development in our case and…"

"I'm available," Pastor Don interrupted. "Where would you like to meet?"

"Somewhere private."

"How about Fort Negley? I'm not too far from there. It's a good place to get a longer view of things."

Max hesitated but said, "Yeah, that's in the direction of my work. But you OK with that walk?"

"Oh, yes, I'm a regular there."

"OK. Twenty minutes, depending on morning traffic."

"See you at the top."

CHAPTER 40

Monday Morning 8:05AM – Day 8

Hundreds of ghosts inhabit Fort Negley. Ghosts of liberated slaves, conscripted by force for the work. In life, they built it on their own blood, sweat, agony, and some on their own graves.

Two ghosts of more recent memories were personal to Max. Being a man from the "me/now" generation who cared more about his own history than that of Fort Negley, he proposed to Jennifer there, thinking it would be a place that would not change as Nashville changed around it. On two anniversaries, when they did not go out of town, they walked up to the fort with a bottle of Chianti, took in the view of the changing skyline and toasted themselves. The second ghost traumatized the first and changed the fort for him. The morning his lawyer texted to say their divorce was final, Max was sitting at a red light at Wedgwood and 8th Avenue, headed north. When he got to Chestnut, he turned and drove to the fort. He parked and walked up to the spot he proposed to her. He didn't feel liberated. Quite the opposite. He felt conscripted by his own demise to rebuild his life. To go there again now, as a dead man walking, meant facing another specter. Certainly, what he needed was a longer view, perspective, though under the current threat, how much longer was in doubt. *New steps on old paths* fell a little flat.

Cominciando dall'inizio. First things first. Max needed to text the captain he would be late, maybe very late, and why. He struggled for an explanation without lying. He considered three options: *chasing down a breaking lead; an unavoidable personal matter*; or much closer to the truth, *I've been contacted by one of the Red Angels.* He chose "Chasing down a breaking lead" and suggested the team concentrate on finding who delivered the notes; review security footage; that Vince go to Guryon's office to investigate who collected the birthday cards and he would track down the cleaning lady at Jessie's building. Before hitting send, a call came in from Hanover. He wanted to answer, to hear her voice, but couldn't trust himself not to telegraph his distress. She was too sharp. He let it go to voice mail. Then listened.

"Detective, I wanted you to know Pastor Don called me for your number. Hope that's all right. And hope you got my note. See you at the meeting."

To avoid the impression of ignoring her call he decided to wait to respond. The tinge of deceit unsettled him, but he considered that tension manageable compared to the rest of his situation. He sent his text to the captain and headed for Fort Negley.

Arriving before Pastor Giacinto, the walk to the top gave Max a few more minutes to choose how to reveal the note. Should he reaffirm the confidentiality of the information? Start with an overview again, but be more specific and lead up to the latest? Ask some more about 'words of knowledge' and whether they are always a hundred percent accurate? Or just come out with it. He reasoned Pastor Don was certainly trustworthy and at least as sharp as Hanover. He recalled from their last visit how discerning he was. In an attempt to deflect the gravity of his situation, he

had the wry thought, *no sense beating around the burning bush.*
That struck him as a way to break the news to Hanover and the
team, but on second thought, perhaps a touch of cynicism was
not what the situation warranted. *I bet he prays first anyway.*

Pastor Don walked up with a gait of a much younger man.

"Good morning, Max."

"Good morning, Pastor. Thanks for coming on short notice."

"Glad to. You come up here much?"

"No, it's been years. You?"

"At least once a month. I meet some friends here to pray for
the city."

There was a lull.

"In fact, do you mind if we pray for, well, for whatever brings
us here?" He didn't wait for Max's permission.

Called it. Out of respect, Max started to bow his head, but
Pastor Don didn't. He didn't even close his eyes. Max looked into
the distance with the pastor.

"Heavenly Father, good morning. We pause on this high place
to thank you for another day. Gracious God, what we know not,
teach us. What we have not, give us. And what we are not, make
us. For your Son's sake, Amen."

There was another lull.

Pastor Don spoke first.

"Let's sit." The pastor sat on the low rock wall and swung his
legs over facing the view of downtown. Max joined him.

"Max, how can I help? It sounded urgent."

All of Max's indirect approaches vanished. He reached into his
jacket and handed the envelope to Pastor Don. "This was taped
to my driver's side window this morning."

The pastor opened and read it.

"O, my Lord. So, this is the kind of message that's been delivered. To how many now?"

"Six. I'm the seventh."

Pastor Don closed his eyes and rocked gently forward and back like he was listening. Max thought he might pray again, but he opened his eyes and said, "What's happened to them, Max?"

"All of them have died within a week or so of getting a note. Except the sixth. He's in the hospital. And it doesn't look good." Max was surprised by how calmly he said this.

Pastor Giacinto sighed deeply, "Lord, have mercy on their souls." He studied the note, then looked out across the cityscape. A long space crept by before he spoke again.

"Max, I know this is terribly distressing, and don't take this as unsympathetic, but you've been given an awesome gift."

Stunned, Max said, "What? You can't be serious? This is a death sentence!"

"Bear with me. Have you ever heard the term, a 'severe mercy'?"

"No."

"Max, look out across this city. Every person out there is going to die. They all know it. In theory, but none of them thinks it's soon, certainly not today. You know all too well some of them will be wrong. Yet they all go on, get up and go through every day, most of them ignoring the inevitable. Almost everyone avoids the weightier matters. You don't have the luxury of ignoring it anymore."

"Pastor, pardon me, but don't see the mercy in this."

"You're a detective, Max. What does 'Put your affairs in order' imply?"

"Uh, choose or lose? Decide before you die?"

"Yes, it means you still have time. Remember Ananias and Saphira? They had no time to put their affairs in order. Boom. Done. The way I read this, you have a window to sort things out, give your stuff away, bless some people you care about. Time to make amends. You said the others died about a week after getting their notes?"

"Yes. So, you really think these are messages from God? And he wants me dead?"

"Most likely yes. And no. God doesn't want you dead, Max. God wants us fully alive."

"Even if it kills us?"

Pastor Don laughed. "I'm sorry, Max. But in a way, yes." His voice broke on the word 'yes' and suddenly tears hung in his eyes. The pain behind them, Max could only guess at.

Max softened a bit. "Maybe your experience with God is different than mine."

"How so?"

"I watched my beautiful mother waste away with cancer and if he was near, your God did nothing." That was the crux of the two questions he wanted to ask in his driveway before his phone rang. Was God near her at the end and if so, why didn't he save her?

"Ah, Max, I'm so sorry. I see. God let you down. He didn't do what you would if you had all that power."

"Exactly."

"I read in an old devotional last week, 'Death's darts are under the Lord's jurisdiction.'"

"Pastor, the miscreants I deal with didn't get that memo. Are you saying your God is in charge of death and dying and fired the dart at my saint of a mother?" He was getting worked up.

"Again, yes and no. He is in charge and clearly, if he knows every sparrow that falls, he allowed death by cancer to usher your mother into eternity. Tell me about her faith, at the end?"

Max fought the pressure behind his eyes. He looked away from the pastor. "She was... she was as valiant as ever. Faithful to the end." The last phrase was meant as an indictment of himself.

Pastor Don remained quiet. Gave both of them a moment.

"Did she have time to speak to you?"

"Yes."

Pastor G waited.

"She begged me not to be angry with God. That we would see each other again. Have a long hello. That this was only arrivederci."

"'Until we meet again' That's beautiful. And painful. Max, that's the blessing of a severe mercy."

Max muttered an inversion of this dad's junkyard axiom, "One man's treasure is another man's junk, I guess."

"What?"

"Nothing. It's just that what you see as a blessing feels, it feels completely hollow to me."

"I know. I've been there many times. It's grief and loss. The place we're sitting was built on grief and loss." His long pause seemed out of reverence. Max had nothing to say.

"Max, everyone down there in this city knows that hollowness. Without hope, it's cavernous. They try to fill it with all kinds of things and wonder why they keep running on empty. You know that Jackson Browne song?"

"Sure, 1977, recorded live in Columbia, Maryland. My parents were actually there."

"That's incredible. What an amazing song! It's an anthem for an empty soul and about time running out."

"Indeed."

"I love living in a music town."

"Me, too."

"You know the song 'Live Like You Were Dying?'"

"You would go there, pastor. Yea, 2004, Tim McGraw. It won song of the year."

"You should go on Jeopardy."

"That's what my partner, Detective Wilson says."

There was a lull. Pastor G broke the silence again.

"If you die in the next week, would you call first? Today?"

It didn't take long for Max to answer. "My Ex, Jennifer. Then my sister, Arianna."

Pastor waited. Max continued.

"I heard a song last night at a songwriter thing. It was called 'The Library of My Life'."

"By Will Barnes. He's a friend."

Max was not surprised. *Of course, he is.*

"Will has weathered some hollow times."

"Yea, you can tell in that song. Anyway, there's a verse in it about an unfinished wing for dreaming…"

Pastor Don finished the line, "'Where Jack Nicholson is my therapist.'"

"Yea, very funny, then another line that leads up to…"

Pastor Don knew the line, but he let Max finish it.

"'Forgiveness should begin your bucket list.'"

"That's strong stuff, Max. Strong truth."

"Indeed."

Max's phone started blowing up. He silenced it. Pastor Don had turned his off. He looked at the note again. "Max, have you been arrogant and unfaithful?"

"Yes. And yes."

"That's called confession. Agreeing with God's diagnosis. History is full of what God can do with a humbled heart."

"In a week?"

"In a moment. Do you want me to list them? Humbled Hearts for four hundred, Alex."

They laughed.

"Pastor, yesterday, in church, you said God stands at the door and knocks. If we open it, he comes in and dines with us. Is that about right?"

"Yes. Revelation 3:20."

"Then that means I would have to be willing to sit down and eat with the one who allowed my mother to suffer and die?"

"Yes."

Max flared. "Who does that?"

Pastor Don thought a moment, "The hollow. The humbled. Those in need of mercy. Who trust his goodness and see that he suffered, like them, died like them and beat death, like we cannot. Your mother did that, right? Clung to him even in her own agony and death."

"Yes, but…"

"Max, do you know the story of Job?"

"Sure. Supposedly, God allowed the devil to make Job suffer to prove his faith, a proposition I have big issues with. He lost everything in a sick wager. God did the watching from a distance. Job did all the suffering up close and personal."

"Sick yes, unless God is good and good enough to turn the

worst into our deliverance. And by the way, God isn't just watching us from a distance."

"Nancy Griffith, 1987. "From a Distance." Most people think Nancy wrote it. A secretary, Julie Gold wrote it."

"I prefer Nancy's version to Bette Medler's."

"Yeah, but I like both. I own both versions."

"Max, the point is Immanuel doesn't mean 'God watching us'. It means…"

"I know. God with us."

"Right, and God suffered, Max. In Jesus. Anyway, about Job. Do you remember what he said when all his friends told him to curse God and die? He said, 'Though God slays me, yet I will trust him.'"

"Yeah, alright. So, Job was a man of faith in spite of everything. Pastor, I am not that man!"

Pastor Don turned and looked Max in the eye, "Not yet. I guess we'll see."

They sat in silence. Max, the skeptic, was weary. But retained enough reserve angst to put up a fight like a cornered animal.

"Max, what if you could be a man of faith from this point to the end?"

"And prove to God I've changed? To get off the gallows at the eleventh hour?"

"No, to rely on his faithfulness. Gallows or not."

"That would be a slick deal. Live Godless like I have most of my life and then slip into heaven under the wire?"

"Exactly. That's what the parable of the workers in the field is about. They got hired at different times of the day, but all got the same wages."

"Who does that?"

"The owner of the field. He's not like us. Benedicillo."

"I don't deserve that, Pastor."

"No one does. By the way, that's humility. See, you're changing already."

Max laughed. "Right. I can just hear my mother, 'You and your father, always late, Maximillian.'"

"I can assure you she will be radiant with joy."

Another lull.

"So, if I only have about a week, what do I do, Pastor?"

"I believe you've been given time to put your affairs in order. Most people don't get that. *Cominciando dall'inizio.* Come to terms with the long view."

"Which is?"

"Here it is. The long view for a thousand, Alex. This is what I fill my cup with every day, whether I'm hollow or full of joy: If Jesus beat death in a hazardous world to give us a glorious life forever after this life, and if God is good and his will wise and perfect, then live or die it will be well with me."

"So, you hang it all on a couple of ifs?"

"No, much more than that, historical record, eyewitness accounts, divine revelation, the creation, 'the heavens declare his handiwork,' a lot of things. But isn't that what you've hung your life on? *If* God does *not* exist?"

"Touché."

"How has that worked for you, Max? How does that work with this note in your face?"

Max considered. "Honestly, I have to say that facing mortality with just a philosophy has always been like trying to swallow an elephant whole. It just doesn't go down."

"Mind if I use that? I'll give you credit."

"Be my guest. Looks like I won't be around to make sure you do."

Pastor Don chuckled.

Max said, "I can't believe I'm asking this but, on a practical level, how would I give my stuff away? To make sure it goes where I want? I did a simple will early in my marriage. The department required it. But that's been a while."

"Well, you could get a lawyer, but you know how much time they take. Or go home and handwrite it today, date and sign it. Choose an executer. Take a picture on your phone. One of the document, and one of you holding it. Send the pics to someone you trust who won't freak out. You can send them to me as a witness. I'll acknowledge I got it. That will legally establish your intent."

"Have you done this before?"

"Oh, my yes. Over the years I've chaperoned a lot of people near the grave."

"Hmm. 'Near the grave.' I've felt close to death a lot of times in my work. But never like this."

Both fell silent. They watched the busy city. It was 8:55AM.

"Max, are you familiar with the old Italian saying, 'La verità è più forte del tempo…"

Max finished the second half, "e il tempo è più breve dell'amore.'"

It was the pastor's turn to be stunned. Max pulled up his right sleeve. It took Pastor Don a few seconds to interpret the tattoo. His face lit up.

"No way!" burst from his lips and he laughed. He couldn't stop laughing. He clapped his hands and laughed some more. "Max, Max, I'm sorry. When did you get that?"

"When I was eighteen."

Pastor Don laughed again. "Don't you see? You've been wearing the answer all these years!"

"How so?"

"The truth your mother spoke with her life and on her death bed, the truth that love, God's love, is stronger than time, and the love she has for you, and you for her outlasted her life!"

"Yes, but..."

"Don't you see it? Love goes on. So do we. Jesus rose. So will those who open the door to him." Max watched Pastor Don's animation grow, like new lights were illumining ancient truths even to him. For a man in his eighties he was as giddy as a teenager.

"Max, I'm telling you, God writes the best stories, even if they don't end the way we want them to."

"All I know is, I don't want mine to end this way."

"But if it does, Max, if it does, will it be well with you? That's the question, my brother."

Max hesitated. "I can't answer that."

"You just did."

There was a lull. They stared out at the city.

"Max, let me say it straight up. I don't know any other way to be. I'm praying you will be reconciled to God and find your peace through Christ, come what may. Let me pray for you."

Pastor Giacinto reached over and put one his big hands on Max's shoulder. This time he bowed his head and closed his eyes.

"Gracious Heavenly Father, thank you for already beginning to answer our prayer earlier. For teaching us what we didn't know. Lord, give Max what he doesn't have. Make him what he isn't yet. And if the end is near, in your mercy and power, carry him from this moment till then and beyond. Grant him faith in you, Lord, for that long hello with his dear mother, all in your time. I place him in your much bigger hands. Amen."

Max sighed and said calmly, sincerely, "Thank you."

"Of course."

"So, that's it. Tick tock?"

Pastor Don nodded, "For all of us." He handed the card back to Max. "You've got some sorting out to do. Looks like some calls to make. You have my number in your phone now. Call me anytime. Day or night. As often as you like. Will you?"

"I will. I can't believe you called when you did."

"The Lord works in…

Max spoke the rest with him, "mysterious ways. Hanover's always saying that."

"She's remarkable."

"Indeed, and amen."

They stood. Max started walking down the hill. He turned back to Pastor Don.

"You coming?"

"I think I'll stay a bit. You go on."

Max headed down. He intended to go back home. He wasn't ready to face the team. As the road rounded the curve of the hill he looked back. Pastor Don was standing, facing downtown Nashville, both arms raised high, hands open. Max knew the pastor was praying, but to his mind he looked *like a little boy wanting his dad to pick him up.*

CHAPTER 41

Monday Morning 10:15AM – Day 8

Max sat at a small desk in his music room gazing north across downtown. Sometimes he counted the cranes. Their profusion testified to a thriving city. On this morning his focus went beyond those to the several slender overlays of hills north of the city, each a lighter hue of blue receding into the distance like waves on the ocean. The pages in front of him were as blank as the blue sky.

In the silence he could feel the pulse, the cadence of time, running without reins underneath him. A line out of a Will Barnes song from the night before came to mind, "I'm riding time like a steed, headed for eternity." Max had deleted the notion of eternity from his core lexicon so long ago, the thought of infinity now messed with the calculus from which he derived much of the passion for his work. Namely, if this life is all there is, a person murdering another, depriving them of their time here, is all the more villainous. Thus, murder rightly ranks as the most heinous of crimes and, in his view, murderers should receive the commensurate penalty, forfeiture of life, either physically or essentially by being locked away from enjoying life, liberty and the pursuit of happiness.

Staring into the distance, he recalled debating Vince about this many times. Vince also viewed murder as the most abominable act imaginable, but because every person was created in God's image. He believed Christ's coming and sacrifice confirmed that value. Max only agreed with him in the sense that "laying down one's life for a friend" was the noblest act possible because a person willingly forfeits the rest of their own unrepeatable, limited time here, in order that someone else may go on living. Vince conceded *if* Max was right, and there is no afterlife, that loss is "insurpassable." At that point they argued whether the word was "insurpassable" or "unsurpassable." as Max held. They finally agreed on "the ultimate."

Beyond the spelling contention, Vince always argued that *if* there is eternal life in glory for those who follow Christ, then the value of the afterlife far exceeds this physical life on earth, even though the Creator declared this life good, and Christ's incarnation validated that. Max contended *if* Jesus knew he was going to beat death, was it really a sacrifice, or just theatrics? At that point Vince went off on him.

"Max, you think after he died Jesus was in some off-stage green room on a smoke break saying, 'Hey, Father, get a load of my second act?' Max, let me beat you half to death, drive nails through your hands and feet and hang you up till you suffocate and see if that's just theatrics? The point is, he came back to life! That means he was not here, but somewhere else. In the *after* life. Get it?"

Max conceded the point *if* Jesus really did return from the dead. That teed off Vince even more.

"If? If? If he didn't, and there's no after life, we won't even have time to be pissed! But if he did, Max, wake up on the other side without Christ and you're screwed!"

Max remembered goading Vince and his response, "Either way, it's kind of a crap shoot, right?"

"What? Maybe for you, which, by the way, I would sincerely hate."

"Thank you, Da Vinci. I know you mean that."

"I swear, Max, that great mind God gave you lives in a cul-de-sac even you can't get out of."

Max, relentless, had responded, "Vince, that's brilliant. Thank you."

"For what?"

"For describing exactly what life is, a cul-de-sac in a cemetery. Only one way in and no way out but the grave."

His words haunted him now.

The empty page on the desk brought him back to the task at hand. He debated which to do first, call Jennifer and Arianna or write the will. A text from the captain intervened. The team was reviewing security footage. They planned to fan out in the afternoon in search of links to the delivery people. The captain asked Max to check in, "keep me posted on new lead and cleaning lady." And of course, "be safe out there." Max simply responded, "10-4."

He decided the will was more manageable. Staring at the blank paper, a memory bullet hit its mark. Sofia helped him memorize the state capitals by drawing a line down the middle of a long piece of butcher paper. She listed the states alphabetically on the left and the cities in random order down the right. With colored pencils and a ruler, Max had to draw a line between each state and the correct capital city. When he was done, it was a kaleidoscope of colored lines. *This should be easier. Fewer people. Less stuff.*

He drew a line down the middle of a page. The left column he labeled "People." The right column "Stuff." As he wrote Arianna's name to begin the left column, a text came in. Hanover.

"You OK? Anything I can do? Just ask."

He hesitated, but thought at least responding would bring less attention.

"Good. Got your note. Surprised me. In a good way." The one lie, 'Good', stuck in his mouth, so he deleted and wrote, "Hanging in. Got your note. Surprised. Thanks." He reread and amended to, "Hanging in. Got your note. Surprised. Heard the music. Thought I was dreaming." *No, that might imply I was awake when she came by.* "Crap!" *Keep it simple.* He went back to, "Hanging in. Got your note. Surprised. Thanks." And hit send.

In ten minutes, he had a list of names and stuff. The names included the obvious: Arianna, Jennifer, Vince, Captain Haskins. He felt an impulse to leave something to Hanover and Pastor Giacinto. Their names went on the list. To his surprise he added Dr. Brickman, Ms. Jacobs and Sydney Sera's wife. He debated if there is a God and if he is watching from not so far away, then adding those names might be a ploy to garner favor. But he genuinely regretted the way he treated Brickman and Adele Jacobs in her interview. He thought of her kids growing up without their father, despite his stronzo nature. He had not even met Sarah Sera, didn't know her health status, but would inquire. No matter how it looked to the investigation or to a near or distant God, he wanted to do something.

In the 'Stuff' column as he listed three song titles, he remembered a fourth, the one to the old flame, "The Way You Made Me Need You." Before adding her name to the 'People' column, he got a twinge about how that might hurt Jennifer, even after all the years. He debated briefly which he valued more: (a) the old flame finally hearing his heart or (b) not hurting his Ex over it. He chose (b) and didn't add her name and the song to the lists. He even chided himself for deliberating. A barely perceptible warming trend in Castle Malone caused him to wonder, *Maybe this mortality thing is really getting to me.*

Max looked at both lists. It struck him how few people were in his life and how all his worldly possessions fit easily on one page.

Arianna & kids	House, paid for
Jennifer	Truck, paid for
Vince & family	Record collection
Capt. Haskins	Book collection
Dr. Theo Brickman	One Martin D-35
Adele Jacobs	1 sculpture of the solar system
Sarah Sera	1 Weber grill and 1 Traeger smoker
	Glock 19, S&W 357, Sig Sauer 9mm
	1 elliptical machine
	1 coffee/latte maker
	12 framed concert posters
	1 framed family crest
	3 song titles (unpublished)
	Furniture
	401K,
	Savings account
	Quarterly royalties from dad's patents

Max was also not aware of the full magnitude of including Dr. Brickman, Adele Jacobs and Sarah Sera, that it showed an uncharacteristic degree of caring. He simply pictured it making

Vince speechless at the reading of the will. If, as Pastor Don put it, Max had already begun to change, and these choices were indicators, he was not stopping to "enjoy the new" or hold it up as a bargaining chip against the judgement the Red Angels delivered. The fact was, his check-the-boxes approach to life rarely included caring about others, especially strangers, except those who were victims of violence. He did not fully comprehend that his pit bull M.O. as an investigator was the warrior/advocate side of compassion.

He did notice his list lacked any causes.

Looking over the panorama of Nashville the question arose, *What do I care about?* The first two things that came to mind were cops and music. He knew the organization that supported the families of officers killed in the line of duty and donated some over the years. He searched online what C.O.P.S. stood for. "Concerns of Police Survivors." He added it to the left column.

"Music," on the other hand, was so general. He scanned the hundreds of LPs along the wall. It hit him: *Duh, it's Nashville - songwriters.* He found a website called "Music Health Alliance," read their story, purpose and services. It went in the left column.

Without laboring the 'why,' he took out a pencil and attended to what stuff goes to whom. At first it seemed clear cut. Start with the easiest. He drew a line from Capt. Haskins to the coffeemaker. *Lord have mercy, he will love that.* Next was Dr. Brickman. His line ran to the elliptical machine. *He likes to stay in shape. But Vince needs it more.* Vince's lines connected to the truck, grills, guns and Martin guitar. *Ten to one he has a fender bender in the first week.* It struck Max to leave some money for Vince's kids, *college or whatever. Come back to that.* He drew lines from Arianna's name to the family crest, their dad's planet sculpture, the 401K, and the house, *probably to sell*. He reasoned as a realtor she could pocket half the commission. From Jennifer's name, he drew lines to the concert posters, and the three songs. But he wanted to do more than that. *Come back to it.* Two of the songs were about Jennifer. The third, "Music City Mayhymn," he considered, should probably go to Vince. So, two lines connected to the songs with a note in the margin: Music City Mayhymn to Vince, *just to keep getting on his nerves.* He bogged down trying to figure how to distribute funds to the two causes and Adele Jacobs and Sarah Sera. It was getting complicated.

He took a break. Coffee called. Three steps down the stairs his heel slipped off a tread. In an instant, he was on his back. Both hands pressed against the walls but failed to catch him. His head slammed onto the hardwood stairs. "Dammit!" He lay there, taking stock. Rubbed the back of his head. No blood. He sat up. Everything worked.

He blurted out loud, "Trial run, Red Angel?" But the mocking tone dissipated in the realization that it could happen anywhere, at any moment. With one trip or in a breath, anyone can be launched out of the universe. *Like a flying iota.* He got up, grabbed the handrail, and walked carefully down to the main floor.

Leaning against the kitchen counter, over a double shot latte, he sorted how to split the assets on his list against the names. He pictured all those people in the same room for the reading of the will and how they would react. That helped make it real. In spite of the fall and considering the surreal sense of his terminal situation, he felt an odd buoyancy about giving everything away. He amused himself with the thought, *Too bad I won't be there.* It wasn't full blown joy, but a nascent satisfaction aimed in that direction.

He considered making the two calls, but decided to finish the will first. A picture on the refrigerator of Arianna and her family changed his mind. He pressed her number. No answer. *Probably showing a house.* When the beep came to leave a message, he fumbled a bit, "Hey, sis. Max. Duh, who else calls you 'sis'? I, I just called to say, to say I love you... Stevie Wonder, 1984. Ha. Give my love to the kids, and Sam. Ti amo di pui. Call me."

The other call took more grit. He paced the kitchen, hoping maybe Jennifer wouldn't answer, but panicked at the thought of saying what he wanted to say on voice mail. *What if her new husband sees my name on her screen. Or worse,* he thought, *what if I'm dead before she listens to it? Maybe she doesn't have my number anymore.* But she did. And she answered.

"Max. This is a surprise." Her tone was pleasant. But she added, "Did somebody die?"

His wit almost shielded his anxiety.

"Always. *And not yet.* Or I'd be out of a job."

"I'm sorry, Max. That was mean. Old habit."

"No worries."

"So, it must be important. You OK? Arianna OK?"

"Yea, O yea, it's just that, well, is now a bad time?"

"No."

"I won't keep you, I'm in the middle of a bunch of cases, as usual, and, uh, something about these got me thinking and... well, here it is... I was listening to 'The End of the Innocence' the other day and..."

"I knew there had to be song attached to this...sorry. Yea. Don Henley. Go on."

"Anyway, you know how it..." he took a deep breath, "how one song talks about the heart of the matter and..."

"Yes."

"Well, Jen, I got to thinking… how much I put you through and the drinking and working all the time and, well, how I hurt you… how I betrayed you…"

"Max…

"No, please, let me finish, Jen…" He took a moment.

"I'm listening."

"I really need to say, I need to say… how sorry I am about all that. You put up with a lot. My anger took a toll on you. On us. I was so… I was such a…"

"Stronzo?"

"Worse. And I guess what I really want, and you can think about this but, it would be, I mean, I don't deserve it but…"

"Max, just say it. Ask me to forgive you."

There was silence on the line.

"Max?"

"Jen, please forgive me."

He heard her clear her throat. In a calm, soft tone she said, "I already have, Max. But if you need to hear it, I forgive you." There was a brief lull. "I didn't want to for the longest time. Swore I wouldn't. Honestly, it nearly took me under.'

"I hate that."

"Hey, what did you always say about sad songs, 'they break you down to build you up.'"

"But I only broke you down, if only I…"

"Max, it wasn't the end of the story. What did JT say? if, if, if I'd not be on this road tonight."

"1981, The Lonesome Road, from 'Dad Loves His Work.'"

"You ever gonna tryout for Jeopardy?"

"Next life, maybe. I still have that concert poster. Remember?"

"Of course. You still love your work?"

"I enjoy putting bad guys away. But the bad guys seem worse every day."

"That sounds like a song, you better…"

"Write it down, yeah, maybe."

There was another lull. Jennifer asked him, "You still pissed off at God?"

"Ha. Let's just say he's got my attention."

"Negotiations. That's a start."

"It still feels like a hostage situation."

She laughed. "I get that. But remember the last hostage situation you were in? You got you shot."

"Are you casting God in the role of domestic abuser? That sounds more like me."

She laughed. "Max, your mind always was your best and worst ally."

There was a long lull.

"Thank you, Jen."

"I really wish you well, Max. I really do. I pray for you in that crazy world you live in."

"If you only knew."

"Tough case?"

"Toughest ever."

"Take care out there."

"You, too. Goodbye, Jen."

"Goodbye, Max."

The silence in the kitchen expressed the inexpressible. A clean, uncluttered space opened up in Max. Sadness, relief and reverence poured into it. It felt like the moment as a kid on a swing set, swinging all the way forward and up, leaning back, looking at the sky and hanging nearly weightless before gravity claimed you again. But it lasted longer. Before he realized it, tears filled his eyes and ran down his cheeks. He put both hands over his face and let them come. No hit song intruded. It was a space where songs come from, perhaps only instrumentals, a string quartet or a simple solo violin. Title: A Good Goodbye.

Max collected himself. It came to him what he wanted to leave Jennifer, and Hanover and the others. And someone else, as well. It was his stuff. He could do what he wanted with it. *Why stress about what anyone thinks? I'll be MIA.*

Back at the desk, he quickly drew new lines. He added a second line from Captain Haskin to the big Glock. *That will fit his big hand.* And notated: S&W to Vince. He split the sizable 401K evenly between Jennifer, Arianna and Vince; He left the house, record collection, books, furniture and Sig Sauer to Hanover. *She can't miss with that thing.* Lump sums from the savings account went to Adele Jacobs and Sarah Sera; a third of the patent royalties he directed to C.O.P.S., and a third to Music Health Alliance for their ongoing work; the other third he gifted to Pastor Giacinto for his ministry. At the bottom of the benefactor column, he added a name: Jenny Meadows and drew a line to the Martin D35. He marked out the line to Vince with a notation in the margin: "Sorry Vince, she'll get the songs out of it." Piggybacked on the guitar connection, Dan Green suddenly came to mind from the concert the night before. *Why not? I wouldn't have that guitar if not for him.* He added Dan's name and drew a line to $2000 from the savings account. Max hadn't had this much fun in a very long time. Standing so close to it, he didn't realize he was thinking in a marrow bone.

He reviewed everything. *What have I left out?*

The sound of a yard trimmer caught his ear. He stepped onto the balcony. His landscaper, "T" or "T-Lo" looked up and waved. Max waved back. *He's got kids.* He went back to the desk and added "Tifton Lowe" to the column of names, drew a line to the savings account and notated $2K. He imagined T getting the call to attend the reading of the will. He pictured the look on his face when the captain read the number, and T-Lo telling his wife. Delight, a first cousin of joy, made him laugh.

He reviewed everything again. A glaring omission occurred to him. The question in his head seemed like someone else asking it: *What will it cost to bury me? Where does that come from?* A sudden flash answered it. *My Roth IRA!* Seldom reviewing his finances, he had forgotten to add it to the Stuff column. He looked online at its current value. Like a man drunk on generosity, he increased the numbers for Adele, Sarah and doubled the numbers for Dan Greene and T-Lo. Based on his father's cremation cost he earmarked $2000 for that. In a moment of self-pity, he wondered if there would be at least a small sendoff. Just in case, and to motivate Vince, he designated $2500 to him for Martin's Barbeque and SATCO catering. And beer. He got a good laugh out of it.

Max felt the new – a completely new new - the joy of a renovated Scrooge.

It took him another twenty-five minutes to handwrite it all into a clear document. At the top of the page, he assigned Captain Haskins as executor, adding, "Thank you, Captain, for everything." He dated and signed it. Took photos of both documents. He struggled to hold each one and take selfies. Before sending them to Pastor Don, he sat back and looked out on Nashville.

Memory bullets flew - the original visit as a kid with his parents, his face glued to the window; the first milkshakes at Elliston Place Soda Shop; Dolly at the Ryman; after high school driving I-40 with his dad into town with all his stuff in the Wagoneer; graduating from the academy; falling in love; the incredible concerts; the miscarriage; making detective; partnering with Vince; the post 9-11 security vigilance; moving to Love Circle; sucking at songwriting; all the cases; getting shot; getting divorced. *The library of my life.* It had been a colorful ride. He knew the city would go on without him. He was good with that. Gratitude, the warm, steady alto to the soprano of joy, serenaded him. He felt another new. The sense of contributing to the growth and health of the people and city he loved. But now, more than ever, he didn't want it to end. *Cranes aren't the only things building this city.* That sounded like a line in a song. He wrote it down under the columns and lines.

Max looked at the time. Already 1:00PM. Jessie's building was the next stop. He sent the two pictures to Pastor Don. *Where should I put this will?* He looked around the room. *Of course.* He folded the pages in half and slid them into the LPs between Jimmy Webb and Hank Williams. *Vince will find it. And enjoy the hunt.* He left a clue in the desk drawer on a 3X5 card: "I never told you, my friends, but you were all gentle on my mind. Max"

A text buzzed in. Pastor Don. "Got it. Will not read beyond the executor you assigned. I am proud of you, Max. Steady on. Praying. The Lord is good. And near. Call me ANY time."

Despite the duress of the Red Angel sentence, Max felt a curious lightness having put his affairs in order. He hurried across the room.

At the top of the stairs he downshifted, used the handrail and descended deliberately like a debutant in high heels. On the main floor, an unexpected eagerness to do his job focused him on the next step - finding Jessie's cleaning lady. He swung the front door open, prepared to meet whatever kind of day it proved to be, ordinary or otherwise. His phone interrupted his exit. Vince. He answered it.

"Da Vinci. Have I got a…"

"Max, we've got a 10-62. Brie Batson just called. Two perps are harassing her about Abe's drug stash. Looks like the big fish."

"What makes you think so?"

"BB says they're from out of town and are determined to find Abe's inventory. They want to use her to get into his place."

"Where is she now?"

"They just broke in where she's at. She's hiding in a closet."

"I thought she was under surveillance?"

"She gave our guys the slip. She's laying low at a girlfriend's place, a Celia Patterson, a songwriter."

"Isn't everyone. She alone?"

"10-4."

"Address? ETA?"

"I just left Davidson's. She's in the Woodbine area east of Nolensville south of 440. Just sent you her 10-20."

"We got back up?"

"Captain assigned Hanover and Thomason. Their ETA two minutes. Other units converging."

"I'll beat you there."

"Code 3. But no sirens. And Max, armor up. BB says at least one is armed."

"Copy that. Rolling."

CHAPTER 42

Monday afternoon 1:20PM – Day 8

En route Max called Hanover.

"Three minutes out. What have we got?"

"Corner lot. White siding with black shutters. One car with out-of-state plates on the back of a side drive on the left. Backed in. Three exits, front, side porch and back. Perimeter and com established. Units blocking traffic to the area. Our 10-20 out of sight half a block behind the house. Another unit, Calton and Weber, half a block on the other side. Dr. Brickman a block away. One of his drones is monitoring the house. The app gives us all eyes."

"What app?" Max wondered.

"At the meeting this morning Dr. Brickman demonstrated it and linked us up."

"That guy is determined to make me like him. What about the girlfriend?"

"Located her at work. Officer detained her."

"Good work. Do not approach."

"Copy that, sir."

"Do we know Ms. Batson is in there?"

"Her phone for sure. Trace verified."

Max went silent.

"How do you want to play this, detective?"

"Any pets?"

Hanover had seen Max use this ploy before. Pet food delivery. He carried two bags behind his back seat. One for dogs. One for cats. Max would walk right up to the door with a bag of food and knock. If someone inside instructed him to leave it on the porch, he told them his boss wouldn't allow that because "Racoons make a mess." If the door opened, he assessed the situation and sometimes made a move.

"None. And no roommates. I had the officer ask Ms. Patterson, sir."

He wanted to compliment her instincts and initiative. But the urgency of the situation preempted that.

"We gotta draw them out, Hanover." Max's phone buzzed. "Vince is calling."

"Roger that, sir. Out."

"Vince, ETA?"

"Four to five minutes. Davidson's assistant just phoned. BB just called her to come get some things in Abe's place."

"Perfect. Have her call BB and tell her to come now, before Davidson gets home. Then verify the call with you."

"Should I let Vice know to back off?"

"No. We nab them here."

"On what charges, Max?"

"Kidnapping and assaulting an officer."

"Have they done that?"

"Not yet. Out."

Max drove by the house, past Officers Calton and Weber sitting in a black and white. He made a three-point turn and parked far enough behind them to act like he lived in the neighborhood. He doublechecked the com. Everyone had ears on.

He called the captain to bring him up to speed. The captain was monitoring visually from his office through the app.

"I see your truck, Max. Pick your moment. We only have Ms. Batson's call. No evidence to make an arrest yet."

"Yes, sir. Understood."

Max walked forward to the black and white and got in the back seat. He explained the ploy to lure the suspects out of the house to avoid a standoff. A visual of the house from the drone displayed on their computer screen with a view of the front and side door. Officer Calton said, "Pretty cool, huh? Dr. Brickman's a genius."

"Indeed," Max conceded, without an ounce of sarcasm in his tone.

Brickman's voice came through the radio, "Suspect one exiting side door."

The three watched as a man exited and got in the driver's seat of the car.

"It's going down," Max radioed to everyone. Hanover and Thomason exited their black and white and headed up the street toward the back of the house. Simultaneously, Max walked quickly toward the front façade under partial cover of trees and a hedgerow. The last forty feet, he was completely exposed, but still out of sight of the car and driver around the corner of the house. In his ears he heard Brickman's voice.

"Suspect B exiting with Ms. Batson. He has her by the arm."

As Max reached the edge of driveway the suspect descended three steps with BB in tow.

If I'm on my way out, might as well make it count. The sun was at Max's back. *It'll be in their eyes.* Perfect. Pulling BB by the arm, the man took two steps heading around the front of the car.

Max stepped out and yelled. "Where you going with my girl?"

Obviously surprised, the perp was still quick on his feet. With his right hand he shaded his eyes and said, "Your girl? She's got a video shoot. Tell him BB."

Countless pivotal moments in life turn on a single word or phrase. "Fire" in a battle or firing squad. "Four" just before a golf ball knocks a spectator unconscious. "Strike" when Detroit Tigers ace hitter Miguel Cabrera stared at strike three without swinging and ended their World Series bid to the Giants in 2010, or "I'm your Huckleberry," moments before Doc Holiday blew gunslinger Ringo away in "Tombstone."

Brie Batson, not as quick on her feet as the thug, blurted a single word that turned things dicey on a dime, "Right, everything's OK, *detective*."

The perp's pistol came out. He swung BB in front of him and put the muzzle against her ear. His left arm tightened around her neck.

Max pulled his Glock. In his periphery, he saw Hanover and Thomason getting a drop on the perps to his left on the side street concealed by trees. But his eyes remained fixed. He kept his pistol aimed at the potential harbinger of death using Brie as a shield.

"She owes us," the thug said. "We just want what's ours."

Max lowered his weapon. He began to walk down the driveway.

"One more step and she's dead."

"Hard to collect from her then. I know where Abe's stash is."

Max took more steps. Perp two squinted in the direct sunlight.

"So do we. How does that help us?"

"I can get you in there."

"So, can she."

"But not like a police escort."

Max stopped just past the corner of the house, twenty feet from the cornered bad guy. He said, calmly, fearlessly, against all protocol, "I'm going to holster my gun slowly," and he did. In Max's ear Hanover whispered, "Max, what are you doing?"

The captain broke in, "Max, back off! Let backup move up!"

Max turned off his com.

Vince heard everything going down as he rolled up and joined Calton and Weber on the street. At the captain's directive to Max, he headed across two yards, staying close to the houses. He crept to the corner of the house where Max stood with his back to him on the near edge of the driveway, not five feet from him.

"Back off or I'll shoot her," perp two said.

"Then what?" Max said. He made an unorthodox offer. "How bout this? Shoot me instead."

"What? Don't think I won't."

"I'm counting on it. I've been shot before."

"Apparently not where I'm going to shoot you. You still got balls." The perp swung his weapon from BB's face to point it at Max.

"Max, move!" came over everyone's com.

Maximillian Shaemus Malone stood his ground. Vince lunged at him.

Two shots rang out so close together it was anyone's guess who fired first. The perp or Hanover. Two bodies went down in sync as well. BB let out a scream to wake the dead. But she didn't fall. The perp's body collapsed at her feet. His blood and brain matter splattered on her face and clothing like a gruesome Rorschach image. Vince tumbled onto Max, then onto the driveway.

Hanover raced to them. Thomason secured the driver without resistance.

Hanover radioed, "Shots fired. Officer down! I repeat. Shots fired! Officer down! I need an ambulance at my location. Stat!"

A pool of blood expanded under Vince. The bullet struck him in the right groin. Max applied pressure with both hands. He shouted to Hanover, "No! Call LifeFlight! Now! What the hell, Vince! I had this."

"I think I peed my pants." Blood leaked through Max's hands. "Just breath."

Vince groaned and said, "Max, I'm gonna have to tell Julie you touched me in a way that made me feel uncomfortable." He laughed.

"Shut up and breath, Vince. Stay calm." They both knew what that meant. The lower the heart rate, the less blood loss.

Crucial minutes passed before they heard the approaching helicopter. Four other patrol cars rolled up to cordon the scene. The clock was ticking on what first responders call, the "golden hour," the critical window. Medical attention within that hour dramatically increases the chances of survival. Vince didn't have an hour.

"Max, my leg's asleep. Tell Julie and the kids I'll be late for dinner, and I love 'em."

"They know. Tell them yourself."

"She's a great cook, Max."

"I know. I love her lasagna."

Vince's eyelids opened and closed slowly. One hand searched for Max and found his shoulder.

"Max."

"I'm right here, Vince. Talk to me."

"Max, the word."

"What?"

"The word. You're right. It is unsurpassable."

The noise of the chopper landing in a vacant lot across the street made it difficult to hear each other. The medics took over. One checked the perp. Nothing to be done. The other two compressed Vince's wound. Started an IV. They loaded him in the chopper in under three minutes.

Max stood on the driveway beside a pool of blood much bigger than a dinner plate. He and the other officers watched the chopper lift off and move away toward Vanderbilt Hospital. Hanover pulled Max aside and ran water from a garden hose over his hands.

"Max, we need to get to the hospital. I'll drive your truck. Thomason, take over here."

"Got it. Go."

She took Max by the arm and walked him toward his truck. Distraught, his clothes stained in Vince's blood, Max fumed.

"That was my bullet! Dammit! Mine. Hanover, you're a hell of a lot better shot than God!"

DENOUEMENT

David Davidson – With Abe's death, the dream drained out of the mansion, the cars, the horses, along with the whiskey in his collection and the dalliance with Ms. Haley Andrews. The Dream Builders jingle, "Your Love Makes It Home," became too painful for him to hear. He commissioned a new ad campaign, "BYOD Bring You Own Dream - We'll build a home for it." Splits his time between Nashville and Hawaii hoping to redeem some time and relationship with his daughter.

* * *

Brie 'Bebe' Batson - Memorial Day weekend survived an overdose of cocaine laced with fentanyl. Hanover walked her into a rehab facility and came by to see her every day. Helen had a soft place for young women like Brie, dancing with the drug devil and addicted to and used by musicians. She told Brie her own story. Bebe revealed she became a Christian and was baptized at age twelve at a church camp. She was ashamed of how far away from God she was and knew he was disappointed in her. Helen reassured her God was not far away, not mad or disappointed and still saw the beauty in her.

On their next visit, Hanover gave her a key ring like hers with the handwritten prayer, "Lord, make what you say about me what

I believe about me." Hanover prayed for her. It surprised Brie that a cop would care like that.

In the middle of the second week of rehab, Hanover stopped by, but Brie had checked herself out. She left a short note for Helen. "Thank you for saving my life. Pray for my soul, Bebe." Alarm bells went off in Hanover's head. Brie couldn't be found. Two mornings later, a jogger reported a woman asleep in a car in the rolling estates south of Green Hills. Officers responded. It was Brie Batson, parked just outside the Davidson gate. She was not sleeping. Cause of death. Overdose. Oxy and meth. Captain Haskins broke the news to Hanover. She was devastated.

* * *

Jazmine Bellaire – Returned to Texas to bury Jesse. Came back once to Nashville to sue the city and the police department for negligence and unethical and unprofessional conduct. A judge threw the case and her out of his court. Currently back in Austin, engaged in an ongoing hunt to milk the sympathy and finances of another sugar daddy.

* * *

Tony Armstrong – Sold the country house on Arno Road. The ghost of that night made it uninhabitable. He suspended the divorce process and briefly pursued reconciliation with his wife. She filed. After much legal jousting, their divorce became official on February 14, Valentine's Day. His five-figure alimony payments are due the fourteenth of every month.

* * *

Adele Jacobs – After thorough investigation, Captain Haskins assured her no connection could be made between the Red Angels note and Donovan's death. That it was likely from a disgruntled churchgoer. Even if they could find the source, it was only punishable as harassment and a fine. To pursue it further would complicate her settlement. She left the note in the captain's custody. It took five months, but she won a sizable claim against the supplier who mislabeled the bleach. That settlement and another financial windfall out of the blue enabled her to quit her job. Adele works as an interior designer, a passion and path her late Ex resisted.

* * *

Sarah Serah - The court determined Sydney Sera's Red Angels note was part of an attempt to extort his false testimony. All defendants denied writing or delivering the note and it could not be linked directly to anyone named in the indictment. Sydney's well-documented evidence sent one developer and three contractors to prison, in addition to hefty fines. The three injured workers received high six-figure settlements. Sydney's widow was awarded an undisclosed figure from the insurer of the construction company found liable for improperly securing materials that led to his death. Like Adele Jacobs, she received an additional generous financial gift from an unexpected source. With those funds, Sarah continued her cancer treatments and is currently in remission.

* * *

Agnes Brown-Hyden - Her forced silence and long rehab from the stroke required her to resign the state Senate seat, but not without protest. Absent the flow of funds funneled from peddling influence, she could no longer afford the mansion in Germantown. Begrudgingly, she moved into the apartment in her former district, retired from public life, but not from complaining about it.

* * *

Clay Guryon – Future wife #4, Victoria, exited days after the crash. Wife #3 proved to be cut from sturdier cloth. In July she remarried Clay and cared for him through three more hand surgeries and the ongoing, arduous physical rehab. Dirk was also there every step of the way. Their friendship rekindled, though not without further challenge.

In early September, a man showed up on Clay's doorstep. Rugged good looks. Jet black hair. Guryon's son from a fling in college. Clay didn't know he got her pregnant. The man told him his mother kept it secret and took a break from college because she didn't want to derail Clay's plan to become a doctor. The son, J. C. Nolan, was an EMT in Little Rock with two kids of his own. Clay introduced him to Dirk. When the man said his mother was their classmate at LSU and spoke her name, Dirk had more to forgive than he knew. It was clear Clay cheated on Sandy during their engagement.

Dirk spoke a cruel truth to Clay, "If you had known she was pregnant you would have insisted on an abortion and that fine young man and his two kids would not exist!" He distanced himself from Clay until he witnessed the effect J.C. had on him.

In late July, after the second surgery, Dirk had introduced Clay to Pastor Don. The soul-searching Dirk urged Clay to do took root, under the watchful care of Papa G. On a cool October evening five weeks after James Clay Nolan showed up, Pastor G and Dirk walked to the top of the hill at Love Circle with Clay and Regina, wife #3 and #4. The colors of change were on the trees and in the air. In a torrent of remorse at the magnitude of the lives and destinies he clinically and dispassionately snuffed out, Clay threw himself on the mercy of God and fully embraced his swamp faith again. Regina joined him.

In the following months, Dr. Guryon divested from and tried to dismantle his clinics at great financial loss. To his dismay, new management did an end-around and relaunched the lucrative "health care" services. He and Regina became active in a group that prayed across the street from the main clinic Clay formerly ran. J.C. Nolan joined them on one occasion. The local media and a few regional film crews showed up. But only one national news service. No voice was more powerful or credible than Dr. Guryon's. Or more conspicuously ignored.

Clay currently drives a vintage '65 Mustang. Some things never change. 330 cubic inches. Dirk helped him install a Holley 4-Barrel carburetor. Clay says it will do "zero to 45 in 6 seconds, with Regina in the car." He serves on the board of Hope Clinic for Women and works part time at a walk-in health alliance. His physical therapy continues. One more hand surgery is on the calendar. He and Regina eat breakfast every Saturday morning at Pancake Pantry. They attend the holy mess church.

About the Red Angels note and the wreck, Dr. Guryon considers them both a term he learned from Papa G., a 'severy mercy.' He entrusted the note to his childhood friend, Captain Haskins. When Pastor Don invited Clay and Regina to record their story for the Sunday services, he made it clear, "I deserved the severe part, but not the mercy."

* * *

Officer Marvin Thomason - In June, Brickman's mother prayed with the Thomason's to conceive. In August, Officer Thomason made corporal. The following March, he and Shannon welcomed their first child, a son.

* * *

Joseph Theodore Brickman – Over the next year he proved to be invaluable to the department, bringing cutting-edge skills to forensics. His remarkable work contributed to solving more than a few difficult cases. By September he completed his outdoor "cathedral."

The Red Angels note found during Gunner Brown's autopsy rests inside a plastic picture frame on Brickman's desk behind the science and belief note from his parents. Per Captain Haskin's directive, only Dr. Brickman knows its 10-20. Always a by-the-book guy, Theo protested, insisting it was tampering with evidence and committed the same deceptive maneuver Mr. Brown had practiced, i.e., promoting an incomplete or distorted narrative, i.e., lying. The captain prevailed, arguing in deference to the grief of Gunner Brown's boys that it would do no good and possibly great harm to them. And besides, there was no actionable evidence of foul play. If any turned up, the note might become germane.

At Thanksgiving, Theo's romantic prospects took a happy turn when his fan status of Jenny Meadows upgraded to mutual love interest, and instrument valet for her many gigs.

* * *

Captain Dirk Haskins – Still captain. Still doing justice as his professional driving force. Still tempered by his characteristic kindness and humility. He is the keeper of five Red Angels notes, to Abe, Jessie, Donovan, Clay and Max. Should more evidence come to light about the authors and deliverers, he has sole access and knowledge of their 10-20. The note to Sydney Sera and his confession letter were sealed by the judge to protect Ms. Sera and her family from possible retribution. It is stored with the rest of the case documents in the evidence archives.

On the captain's birthday in August, the officers under his command canonized his verbal moniker, "Lord, have mercy," in a personalized license plate: LHM. He stretched the rule against personal displays on department vehicles, as he did for Detective Malone, by mounting it on the front of his suburban for two weeks. Thereafter, for as long as he was captain, it would speak his benediction for the department from above his office door. Hanover began the tradition of touching it as she headed out on patrol. Other officers followed suit.

* * *

Pastor Don Giachinto – Still teaching, pastoring, mentoring, praying for Music City once a month atop Fort Negley. Still befriending doubters. Still waiting for his Dad to pick him up.

* * *

Detective Max Malone –It took God six days to make the world. Seven to undo Max's. Longer than that to remake it.

The looming Red Angel countdown after the shooting began with the vigil at the hospital while Vince's life hung in the balance. The incessant threat in Max's mind about the death sentence hanging over him added to the trauma. He agonized over Vince's willingness to sacrifice himself. His own blind complicity in it withered him.

Nothing was certain. Could Vince survive the hours of surgery to repair the artery and wound? And more hours for an osteopath to remove bone fragments and stabilize his pelvis? Even though he went into surgery only thirty-eight minutes after the shooting, the doctor reported multiple organ dysfunction from the rapid loss of blood, including acute kidney failure and a condition called shock liver. It was indeterminate, but likely, Vince's brain suffered a degree of anoxic impact, oxygen deprivation. If he survived, the Vince they knew might not return even if his body remained.

The captain finally made Max leave the hospital and go home. He dragged his shame, regret, anger, pride and self-loathing up the stairs and collapsed in the recliner. He spent his last energy and outrage on God.

"I begged you for my mother. I will not beg you now for Vince. You're gonna do what you're gonna do. And we gotta live with it." With a snarl he added, "Thy will be done, right? But I'm the one who deserves to die. I'm the one. Me. Not Vince."

When the sun came up on Tuesday, the agony continued. He expected and even welcomed any event that might end his life, especially if Vince didn't make it. Two days dragged into a week.

The Red Angels harbinger dogged Max into the official inquiry about his tactic that day and whether Helen's risky, pinpoint lethal shot of the perp was justified. Some on the review board made the case that both Detective Malone and Officer Hanover needlessly endangered Detective Wilson and Brie Batson. Max was compelled to watch Brickman's drone footage and explain his actions. It was torture seeing Vince shot and fall. Managing the press, who were almost all in Vince's corner, fell to the captain. In the end, the testimony of the witnesses, the drone video and Brickman's 3D digital reenactment of the incident vindicated them both, though the report deemed Max's actions "reckless" and "unorthodox." This was no revelation to those who knew him. But once the task force became aware of the RA note delivered to Max that morning, they understood more had been driving him.

The captain became angry and stern. He ordered Max to take four weeks off, a paid administrative leave, and attend counseling sessions. Max protested the counseling until the captain told him his sessions would be with Pastor Giacinto twice a week.

Hanover was furious. Her reaction, visceral. She drove straight to Love Circle and excoriated Max for the crass disregard of his life and how he dared put everyone in the position to see him shot down right before their eyes! How dare he dishonor his fellow cops and friends and the memory of his mother and father and the faith they had in him! And how dare he think he could prove something or square his account with God in such a brazen, cavalier way. The deep care behind her anger boiled over in tears. She yelled and shook the entire Malone Castle with one broadside, "Dammit Max, Jesus already died for you!" She wept. He held her. And poured out a stream of sincere remorse and culpability.

Every day that first week, Pastor Don read Max like a book. He made himself available 24/7. They walked Love Circle, up Fort Negley, around Radnor Lake, to get Max away from the hospital and help him come to terms with his own actions. For not wearing his Kevlar vest. For trying to put himself in the direct path of death to martyr himself, since he felt doomed anyway. For believing he deserved it, that he was beyond redeeming, and that Vince took the bullet meant for him.

Papa G assured Max, God is sovereign, not captive to human choices or the forces of physics or ballistics. Ultimately, He writes the story. Free will shapes it, but God is the final editor. Case in point, the Lord spared Dr. Guryon's life, but not his hands. He assured Max God was still writing his story. He counseled, "We simply must learn to trust the author. Come what may. Like Vince. Like Hanover. Like Sofia did."

Eight days after receiving the note, Pastor Don reminded Max, he was still alive.

Nine days after the shooting, around 7:17PM in Max's music room, in the hands of Helen and Pastor Don, the walls of Castle Malone came down. Max cast himself on God's mercy. He opened the door to the One knocking. He went down on the floor a broken, empty cardboard man. God's Spirit inflated him.

Redimensioned him. He stood up a 3D human. A forgiven, unfrozen man. He felt the new. The change in the air was heralded by fireflies.

Every morning Max woke up and thanked God he was still alive to see another day.

May turned into June. The chatter of cardinals gave way to the jeers and whistles of blue jays.

Max's relationship with everyone metamorphed. Especially with Hanover. She brought her autograph collection over to his music room. Those music sessions and barbeque on his grill became a regular thing through the summer, as well as some evenings in Brickman's garden. Max was more amazed than anyone that he actually attended the holy mess church, almost always with Hanover.

Every week, he asked Pastor Don why he was still alive. His answer was always the same. Max could quote him. "All our days are written in his book before one them came to be. Psalm 139. His mercy triumphs over justice and his mercies are new every morning."

Hanover made Max a key chain with a quote from a singer she admired because he had lived what he sang. "Live like you'll die tomorrow, Die knowing you'll live forever." She told him the songwriter, Rich Mullins, died needlessly, in a car wreck. He was so free-spirited he refused to wear a seat belt. Max got the point and he care behind it.

Summer balked at autumn, reluctant to stop playing and come in for supper.

In the lovely days of Tennessee fall, Max helped Helen study to become a detective, preparing for the rigorous NDIT and

PDET exams, which included more than a few "study" sessions on the deck at SATCO.

In October, she and Thomason were shot at while serving a warrant. Max heard "shots fired" on his radio. He raced to the scene. Everyone was fine but Max. To calm him down, after her shift Helen met him for dinner and a drink at the Commodore Grille. New to the caring thing, he struggled to get out how it scared him to think of her getting hurt or worse.

She said, "That's what you get for having a heart now." He made a note of that in his phone.

They walked over to Centennial Park. Behind a column of the Parthenon, she pulled him close and let him kiss her. The Grand Canyon of impossibility shrunk to a crack in the marble under their feet.

In early November, Max got a call from Jeopardy. Someone anonymously nominated him to audition for Cops Week. He made it through with flying colors. In February, a week before Valentine's Day, he and Hanover flew to California for the taping. Max won the week with $206,000. Each cop played for a cause of their own choosing. Max played for two widows in Nashville. Alex Trebek Daily Doubled his winnings to $412,000.

Spring returned. Big change was in the air.

EPILOGO

One Year Later May 5

Four seasons since that dark Monday, the early glow of morning sunlight bathed the room in golden hues. No alarm went off. A soft breeze moved the sheer curtains revealing a view of rolling green and azure hills, like sleeping voluptuous goddesses. A church bell rang in the distance. In Max's waking moments the lingering jetlag disoriented him. A figure resembling the rolling hills lay next to him under the satin sheet. The waking goddess spoke. Max felt the new. It was righting his world.

"Good morning, Shaemus."

"Buon giorno, detective Malone."

Helen had made detective in March. That was a rare and brilliant day. Two months later, May Day, was even more rare and brilliant. In Brickman's garden cathedral, surrounded by cops, extended families, blossoming dogwoods, friends and guests, Pastor Don married them. Guests included Adele Jacobs, Sarah Serah, Dr. and Mrs. Guryonand and Dan Greene. Theo's fiancé, Jenny Meadows, sang "Thanks to You" in the ceremony. At the garden reception Will Baker performed a song co-written with Max called, "That's What You Get for Having a Heart."

That's what you get for having a heart
Shoulda known better than to let those feelings start

A raging fire just needs a spark

That's what you get, That's what you get for having a heart

Jenny surprised Helen with a song for their first dance, also co-written by Max, "Just the Right Amount of Perfect." As everyone predicted, Jenny's reputation as a songwriter had risen. The song was already on hold for Michael Bublé.

You're not some dream you're better than that

What's hard for most you're a natural at

You being you, and never needing to rehearse it

You're just the right amount

Just the right amount of perfect

After their first dance, Helen presented Max a wedding gift - a 1970 Gibson J-45 sunburst. Dan Greene helped her find it. It was not Max's original, but spectacular none the less, and more than ten times the cost of the stolen one. Overwhelmed, Max was reluctant to present his gift to her, but she loved it – a Sig Sauer P226 Legion 9mm with three magazines. Their other gift to each other was tattoos. On the inside of her right forearm Helen got the Italian saying, "Il tempo è più breve dell'amore." Time is shorter than love. In the same spot, Max added a second mathematical formula: MM + HH = 2 x ¥.

They spent their first night in a suite at Union Station Hotel, an unexpected gift from the Guryons. For their honeymoon, Helen insisted Max visit his mother's childhood home.

A long flight to Rome and picturesque train ride deposited them in Florence for two nights where they saw Michelangelo's

David. Viewing him from the backside Helen said she could see the resemblance and patted Max's backside.

A rented car, Alfa Romeo, whisked them through the oil painted landscape of Tuscany to a quaint inn in the ancient hilltop town Sofia grew up in, Montepulciano, home of the Chianti Max loved. Helen contacted Sofia's relatives before the trip. They greeted the newlyweds upon arrival, kissed both cheeks, presented wine and remarked how much Max looked like his mother. Even the sound of the language fed Max's soul.

Beyond all Maximillian Shaemus Malone ever imagined, he and Helen were husband and wife. For five days. Together, in the vineyard laced hills of Tuscany. In this dreamlike setting he turned to her on a glorious Tuscan morning and said, "Detective, Interpol policy requires me to strip search you."

"Again?" she replied, lifting the cover.

"Oh, I see you're already in compliance."

They spent the morning like newlyweds in Italy, celebrating anatomy, savoring a light breakfast on their terrace, local breads, olive oil and balsamic vinegar, cheeses, grapes, olives, prosciutto and strong coffee. They basked in the world renown Tuscan light on the vineyards and olive groves stretching into the translucent distance. To Max's eye, in that setting, were Leonardo da Vinci to capture Helen in that light, she would be the masterpiece and Mona Lisa a distant runner-up.

He said, "If I could only paint you right now."

"Oh, Max. Thank you. You should write that down. Later. First, let's take it from the top and start with what we've got." She led him back inside for more anatomy appreciation.

For a late lunch, they strolled to a classic outdoor Italian café, dodged a few mopeds and decided to rent one later.

"One?" Helen said. "What are you gonna drive, amore mio?"

While deciphering the menu, a song played in the background. Partly in English, partly in Italian. Max thought the singer sounded like Diana Krall. He asked the owner its title and to restart it, "por favore."

He responded, "Prego. Il nome di questa canzone è Cappuccino Love."

"The song is called 'Cappuccino Love,'" Max translated for Helen.

"That part I understood. I'm a detective, you know."

It appeared endorphins were on the menu in Italy, too.

They listened, holding hands, taking in the storybook view across the rolling hills. The song was about a couple who come to the same café, same corner table, same waiter, order the same cappuccinos. The sultry singer sang:

> Corner table once again - Face to face, hand in hand
> Our waiter doesn't say a thing- Always knows what to bring
> Your hands round the cup - the first careful sip
> Your smile, the foam on your lip
> There's nothing as warm or real as this
> How can I resist? - Our cappuccino love
> I love our cappuccino love

The second verse began in Italian. Max said, "I think we found our theme song for the trip."

His phone buzzed. He looked at the number, showed it to Helen.

"Of course, take it. I'm going to the bagno. Give him my love."

* * *

Detective Vince Wilson – When the LifeFlight medics took over that terrible day, Vince's pulse was beyond faint. By the time they landed at Vanderbilt Hospital, it was difficult to find one. His blood pressure bottomed out. Max, Captain Haskins, who called Vince's wife, and other officers arrived a few minutes before Julie and their kids. Vince was already in surgery. All cops know the pattern. If someone comes out with news in the first five minutes, it's rarely good. They waited. Max was highly agitated. He kept telling the captain and Hanover, "That was my bullet! It should be me in there. What the hell was he thinking?"

At fifteen minutes, an eternity, a doctor the captain knew came out briefly. Vince was still alive, but gravely wounded. The immediate objective was gettomg his vital signs stable.

At twenty minutes, Pastor Giacinto showed up. He prayed. Put Vince in bigger hands. They waited.

At thirty-five minutes, a different doctor came out. Pulse steady, pressure low but stable. They lost Vince once. But were able to restart his heart. The bullet was a hollow point designed to inflict maximum carnage. It shattered the ball and socket joint in his pelvis and nicked the femoral artery.

"Will he make it?" Max blurted.

The doctor wouldn't say either way.

Max walked away muttering to no one, "That was my bullet. What an idiot thing to do."

Hanover followed and pulled him down a hallway. She put a hand on his chest, looked him in the eye and said quietly, but firm, "Max, idiots don't save your life. That hero has a wife and kids in there. Breathe, Max." Looking up into his face, she took big breaths, saying, "Breathe."

He did.

Tender human touch was foreign to him. It was like soul-to-soul resuscitation. Then came the ambush. Helen held him. She lay her head against his chest. He had only imagined, and dreamed once, about being this close to her. But not like this. Not in that place. Before he could move his arms to embrace her, she released him and walked back to the waiting room.

Every hour Vince survived was a gift. Four hours in surgery to repair the artery and wound. Two more to remove bone fragments and stage the hip for replacement. Vince was too weak and the femoral repair too fragile for hip reconstructive surgery. That could wait. A medically induced coma and ventilator kept him motionless, to give the femoral artery time to mend and let his brain rest and heal. His multi-organ crash also needed constant care and monitoring. The head surgeon was certain the pressure Max applied immediately to the wound saved Vince's life. Even though the medics had the foresight to pack his leg in cold packs, there was some disagreement between the surgeons whether they could save it. The prognosis for full recovery of functions on many levels was uncertain. If Vince survived, he might never walk unassisted. Worse, he might not be fully Vince anymore. Whatever the case, the odds seemed high against ever returning to fieldwork as a detective. Max had not lost a friend yet. But their partnership was over.

Pastor Don immediately set in motion a prayer network. Brickman contacted his parents, who did the same. The usual media showed up pressing for answers. While Vince was still in surgery, at a 6:00PM briefing, Captain Haskins described Detective Wilson's selfless action and critical condition. He called on Nashville to pray for his survival and recovery. At one point he said, "With your prayers I am convinced, Vince will make it."

One media outlet led with the headline, "I am conVinced." It became a rallying cry. The next morning, bumper stickers with praying hands multiplied around the city. The proceeds turned into a GoFundMe campaign. Money for Vince's medical bills and recovery poured in. Electronic signs, message boards over the freeways and even Bridgestone Arena displayed, "I am conVinced." Nashville had rarely seen such a show of unity, especially in a time when people were divided over so many issues. In forty-eight hours, Vince Gill wrote and released a song with other artists called, "I Am ConVinced."

> I am conVinced heaven can be moved
> I am sure somebody watches over me and you
> I have no doubt God's good will will come through
> I am conVinced heaven can be moved
> Yeah, I'm content and confident to conclude
> I am conVinced heaven can be moved

Ten days after the shooting, the day after Max's awakening, Detective Wilson came off the ventilator. The next morning, he opened his eyes. Julie was the first person he saw. The second, Max. Vince blinked and looked around. A very long minute passed. The first words he managed came out in a hoarse whisper, a common effect of the ventilator. They were cryptic, "The shiny

one," a hard swallow, then he mumbled, "he let me come back."
Julie and Max looked at each other, uncertain what to make of
that. His second statement sounded like the old Vince: "Sorry,
did I miss dinner?"

The city went crazy! You would have thought the Titans won
the Superbowl. Drinks flowed. And so did money for his recovery.

The next night, Max and Julie were sitting up with Vince. Julie
asked him, "Honey, what did you mean when you said, 'The shiny
one let you come back?'"

Vince told them he had one of those out-of-body experiences
people sometimes report after "dying" in surgery and being
restarted. He remembered floating up out of his body, watching
the surgeons frantically working on him. He passed through the
wall outside the building and floated down onto a small grassy
area by the hospital. Four people met him. Three dressed in white
robes and one in regular clothes, but shimmering. The
shimmering one spoke to him in a warm voice, "Welcome. Come
with us." There was so much light shining from behind the
speaker he couldn't see his face. Or tell if the light actually shone
through him. At that point, Max asked if it was Jesus. Vince said
he thought so at first and then didn't. They began walking up a
wide path. There was darkness to the left. On the right, a beautiful
white and gold fence stretched ahead to a small gate. In the
distance to the right was a shining city. The speaker told him not
to listen to the voices on the left. The warmth and sense of peace
coming from the light were overwhelming. Everything in him
wanted to go there. Vince said, at one point he stopped and said
to his escorts, "Wait, this will shatter my wife and kids." The
speaker calmly told him he had a choice. The next moment he

was back on the operating table, knew he was badly hurt, but never more peaceful in his life.

Vince's story got around. The usual skeptics lined up to refute it, claiming the cause of such "visions" is merely a combination of nerve impulses and chemical reactions firing memories and connecting archetypes in the subconscious. For many years, Max had used the same argument viewed through the keyhole of science. He now held the key to a different view and had complete trust in the eyewitness.

Fifteen days after the shooting, Vince was stable enough and his wound sufficiently healed to undergo a complete hip replacement using the latest high-tech materials and design. All paid for by a generous city. Physical rehab would be long and challenging. Therapy also focused on his mental abilities and coordinating motor skills. Vince's speech pattern faltered. Sometimes he sounded like English was not his first language.

He told Max, "If I known all I had do was take a bullet for you to believe, I would of deranged it sooner." Max's return to faith was a prime source of inspiration and motivation for him.

Day eighteen, on Julie's birthday, the hospital staff helped Vince stand for the first time with a walker. The city went nuts again.

The next day, Julie wheeled him to the lobby of Vanderbilt hospital. The Governor presented him a Valor Award and Purple heart. Head coach and the quarterback of the Titans handed him a football signed by the entire team. Plus, season tickets. If he had not won every heart in Nashville, Vince did when he declared, "If you gotta get shot in the line of duty, my partner Max and Music City are worth taking a bullet for."

Progress was slow but steady. Max was his biggest champion. He often drove him back and forth to therapy. The first time he did, Max blasted Queen's "We Are the Champions."

Fall became a season of new beginning. On Thanksgiving dinner at the Wilson's, Vince confessed he was the one who registered Max for the Jeopardy audition.

By the new year, Vince's progress was remarkable. His speech patterns returned to normal. His humor, which never went away, shifted into high gear. Sometimes he faked a speech impediment just to rattle Max. New Year's Eve he sang, "May old atankens beez a lot, and neither bought to mind." He walked farther distances, first with a walker, then with a cane.

In spite of the progress, Vince accepted the obvious. He was no longer physically suited for the rigors of fieldwork. The captain urged him to apply for a position at the Police Academy. After some soul searching, prayer and consultation with Julie and Max, he applied and took the job, teaching a range of subjects, including ethics and community and victim relations. After years of uncertainty every time Vince went out the door, the new assignment was a great relief to Julie and their kids.

The day after the trip to California to flim Jeopardy, Max confided in Vince his intention to ask Hanover to marry him. The first advice Vince offered was, "Definitely NOT at Fort Negley." Max asked him to be his best man. Vince made a promise. "I'm going to walk in with you. No cane."

March 1, on Sophia's birthday, Max proposed to Helen on top of Love Circle. May 1, Vince walked in, took his place in Brickman's cathedral beside Max with Pastor Don and Captain Haskins. Without a cane.

Five days later, from the other side of the world, he was calling to brag.

* * *

Max saw Vince's name on the screen, "Cosa da, da Vinci? Or should I say professor?"

All Max heard on the line was a ukulele and Vince whistling a few bars of "That's Amore."

"Good one, Vince. Bon journo, it must be early in Music City."

"It's nearly 7:00," Vince responded. "Hey, I broke my record, Max. Walked a whole lap with the kids. No stops. First half without a cane. Second half almost without cussing."

"You really are the champion of the world."

"Intermittent for sure. How many laps you and the Ms. do around the room this morning?"

Max ignored that. "How are classes, professor?"

"Going really well. Unlike you, these future cops actually listen to me."

"What's that?" Helen returned to the table. "The beauty here is so distracting. And so is Italy. Helen says 'Ciao' and sends her love."

They spoke a few minutes, laughed some more. Max ended the call in Italian. "Arrivederci, da Vinci. Ti amo mio amico."

"Chicken catchiatori to you too, paisano. God bless. Love to Helen."

"Ciao."

"Peace, out."

"Vince sends his love and said, 'peace out.' Some things never change."

They ordered a bottle of Chianti.

Standing across the street from the café, a beautiful little girl in a bright yellow dress caught Max's eye. She was about ten years old. Cradled in her arms were two long loaves of Ciabatta bread wrapped in white paper and a bundle of pink lilies, no doubt from a nearby market. Max imagined his mother doing the same for her mother on these very streets. The girl stood looking at Max and Helen. She crossed the street and walked right up to their table. She was as radiant as the day.

"Novelli sposi?"

"Si." Max said and translated for Helen. "She wonders if we're newlyweds." He asked the girl in mixed Italian and English, "Come faccio? How did you know?"

"Bai tuoi occhi," the little girl answered, pointing to her own eye. Max didn't understand.

"Eyes. By - your - eyes." She handed Helen a pink lily. Max reached for his wallet.

The girl protested, "No. No. Prego. Benedicilo," and hurried off.

As she disappeared around the corner of an ancient stone building, leaving them in the wake of her blessing and the tranquility of the moment, something else disappeared, too. The last residue of Max's inquieto. The nagging unrest. Frayed threads of the knot in his chest, carried and guarded for so many years, untangled and fell away. He took Helen's hand.

"What is it, Max?" with her other hand she stroked the side of his face.

"Could this day get any better?" Max said.

"Perfect will have to do," Helen agreed.

"Indeed."

They talked and laughed and poured more wine. Helen brought up Pastor Don's request for Max to video his story as part of a message about the stubborn love of God.

"Are you nervous?" she said.

"Honestly, yes."

"Well, I have to say it." She raised her glass. "Look who's going to be the motivational speaker. 'Hello, my name is Maximillian Shaemus Malone. Are you living angry, bitter, pissed off at God because in your mind he's mismanaged the universe? Well, I've been there. And I'm here to help.'"

Max's laughter echoed down the stone street, blending with the sounds of daily life in a small Italian town. He clinked his glass against hers. "Touché."

"Seriously, what are you going to say? Have you thought about it?"

"More than a little. I want you there, of course."

"Where else would I be?"

Max told Helen his notes were a jumble of thoughts and quotes from at least two songs, "Desperado…"

"What a surprise," Helen commented.

"and "I Rest My Soul." He planned somehow to talk about Truth being stronger than time and time being shorter than love and how he wasted so much time in bitterness resisting the truth and what brought him to surrender to the love of God and urge anyone doing the same not to waste as much time as he did.

"I don't have the whole thing mapped out yet, but I know how I'm going to start."

"Fantastico. Can I hear it?"

Max raised his glass. He started to speak, but suddenly looked past Helen. The joy drained out of his face. He set down his glass and leaned forward. A distinguished, older gentleman at the next table was reading a newspaper. Max's Italian wasn't good, but he could read part of the headline:

Angeli Rossi: Sono Qui?

"Max, what is it?" Helen turned around to see what hijacked him.

Max spoke to the man, "Mi scusi, signore, parla inglese?"

"Si, a leettul."

Pointing to the headline, Max asked, "Does that say 'Red Angels?'"

The man bent the paper around to see where Max was pointing.

"Si," he said, "the rred-uh angels ar-uh here."

Helen and Max exchanged an incredulous look.

"Por favore, what does the article say? Please, tell us?" Max's intensity clearly surprised the man.

The gentleman smiled and translated slowly in a heavy Italian accent, "Eet sehzuh 'All citizenz of Montepulciano ar-uh, um, incoraggiato…'"

"Encouraged?" Max guessed.

"Si. All citizenz of Montepulciano ar-uh enkooradged to, um, voluntariato,"

"Volunteer?"

"Si, your Italian not so bad."

"Grazie, por favore, go on. What else?" Max's impatience showed.

The gentleman smiled again at Max and said in flawless English, "Respira, amico mio. Breathe, my friend. This is Italy.

Life is short, but in moments like these, we live like we have all the time in the world."

"Si, of course. Grazie." Max took a breath and forced himself to sit back in his chair. The gentleman continued to read the newspaper article in perfect English.

"All citizens of Montepuciano are encouraged to volunteer in the city center, tutta la settimana, all week, dare, to give, sangue alla Croce Rossa – to give blood to the Red Cross."

Max and Helen looked at each other. They started laughing. They couldn't stop.

The man wanted to laugh, too, but had no idea what the joke was.

Max finally regained control. He said, "Grazie, grazie mille, Signore."

"American?" the congenial man said.

"Si. Novelli sposi."

"Ah, you are felice di essere felice."

"What is that?" Helen asked.

"You are happy to be happy," the man said.

"Yes, we are. Thank you."

"You will do well here. Italy is gelato for lovers." He went back to his newspaper.

They poured more wine. Laughed some more.

"Where were we?" Helen said. "Oh, you were about to tell me how you're going to start your interview with Papa G."

"Right. OK."

Before Max could begin the waiter brought fresh glasses and a wine they had not ordered, a Montepulciano D'Abruzzo Reserve. He said, "Dal Signore," and pointed to the gentleman.

The old gentleman raised his glass. "From my vineyards."

"Grazie mille," they both said.

"Prego. Buon appetito."

The waiter opened the bottle and poured.

Max said to Helen, "OK, here's my opener."

"Grazie mille. Thank you very much, Pastor Giacinto, for this chance to tell my story and teach everyone un po Italiano, a little Italian. I'm Irish-Italian. By God's grace this is my nuova sposa, my new bride, Helen. Thank heaven for her part and Pastor G's in my story. Basically, I'm a detective who misread or ignored every clue God gave me for a very long time. But not anymore. My name is Maxmillian Shaemus Malone," Max raised the glass of new wine and finished with, "and I'm a recovering stronzo, Benedicilo."

la Fine (lah Pheeneh)

THE AUTHOR

William Luz Sprague was born in Tulsa, Oklahoma in 1952 to Bill and Oteka Sprague. He grew up in West Texas, in Amarillo and Borger. He was graduated from Texas Christian University, studied literature at University of Texas for two years before spending a quarter of a century writing songs and recording in Nashville. He is father to three children, his "muses with faces."

Mr. Sprague is an award-winning songwriter, recording artist and the author of LETTER TO A GRIEVING HEART, a best-seller for those facing grief, and ICE CREAM AS A CLUE TO THE MEANING OF THE UNIVERSE, later retitled, IS GOD REALLY THERE, AND IS HE GOOD?

His next novel, UNTAMABLE, will release in 2023.

Find other works at billyspraguemusic.com

ACKNOWLEDGEMENTS

Deep thanks to:

My Music City tribe, for being shelter in the storm and rebar in my life lo these many years.

My weekly bedrock boyz, Jim Weber, Michael Nolan, Dan Green, Greg Seneff and Jeff Large, for steady hands on the wheel.My weekly bedrock boyz, Jim Weber, Michael Nolan, Dan Green, Greg Seneff and Jeff Large, for steady hands on the wheel.

Michael Blanton, for lassoing me onto this creative road, convinced heaven can be moved and the world changed.

The gifted songwriters I have cowritten with, for making me so much better.

Steve Gilreath, for good counsel about birthing books and leading the way.

My Florida stalwarts, Ed and Mary Beth, for safe harbor and a dock o' the bay to write on.

Dr. Tom Copeland from my TCU days, for your contagious passion for literature and teaching me to think in a marrow bone. God bless you with a library in paradise.

Everyone who broke my heart, for the redeeming scars.

Every heart I hurt, for giving me grace to get free from myself.

My Dad in heaven, for telling me I could do anything I set my mind to.

My children, for making my heart soar.

Their mother, for them and the hard lesson in the freedom of forgiveness.

Karla, for fresh wind in my sails.

Jesus, for mercy instead of justice and a hand on the pen.

SONG CREDITS & HOMAGE

As a songwriter myself, I am a huge fan and supporter of songwriters. I acknowledge the creative role that the songs referenced in my story contribute to the character of Detective Malone and the fabric of the narrative. This music shaped my life as well. The vast majority of songs are referenced by title only or within the copyright fair use policy for minimal inclusion in works of fiction.

To honor and promote the songs and songwriters, all songs referenced are listed below to remind readers of their greatness and introduce them to new generations. Please support these great writers and artists by adding them to the soundtrack of your own life wherever you source music.

Chapter 1

Can't Buy Me Love	1964, by Paul McCartney & John Lennon, recorded by The Beatles on A Hard Day's Night, © Sony/ATV Music Publishing LLC
Part Time Lover	1985, by Stevie Wonder from On Square Circle, © Universal Music - Z Tunes Llc, Universal Music Publishing Canada, Internash Songs, Gangsta Gal Music, Jobete Music Co., Inc., Jobete Music Co. Inc.

Spooky	1968 by Tom Shapiro, Buddy Buie, Harry Brooks James Cobb recorded by The Classics IV, © Sony/atv Songs Llc, Bike Music
Til I Die	1971, by Bryan Wilson, recorded by the Beachboys, © Wixen Music Publishing
Baby, You're a Rich Man	1967 by Paul McCartney & John Lennon from Magical Mystery Tour, © Sony/ATV Music Publishing LLC
Lyin' Eyes	1975, by Don Henley & Glenn Frey, recorded by the Eagles on One of These Nights, © Cass County Music, Red Cloud Music
Victim of Love	1976, by Don Henley, Glenn Lewis Frey, Don Felder & John David Souther, © Cass County Music, Red Cloud Music, Fingers Music

Chapter 2

Human Touch	1992 by Bruce Springsteen from the album Human Touch, © Sony/ATV Music Publishing
Life In the Fast Lane	1976, by Don Henley, Glenn Lewis Frey & Joseph Walsh recorded by the Eagles on Hotel California, © Cass County Music, Red Cloud Music, Wow and Flutter Music
Wildfire	1975 by Michael Martin Murphey, from Blue Sky-Night Thunder © Universal Music Publishing Group
Red Rubber Ball	1966 by Paul Simon & Bruce Woodley, recorded by The Cyrkle © Universal Music Publishing Group

Chapter 3

Walk Like an Egyptian   1986 by Liam Hillard Sternberg,
                                           recorded by The Bangles
                                           © Peermusic Publishing

Chapter 5

Your Body Is a Wonderland   2002 by John Mayer from Room for
                                           Squares © Reach Music Publishing

Chapter 6

Walkin in Your Footsteps   1983 by Gordon Sumner recorded by
                                           the Police on Sychronicity
                                           © Gm Sumner
House of Gold   2013 by Tyler Joseph & Josh Dun
                                           recorded by Twenty-One Pilots on
                                           Regional At Best
                                           © Warner-tamerlane Publishing Corp.,
                                           Stryker Joseph Music
Walk Away   1971 by Joe Walsh recorded by The
                                           James Gang on Thirds
                                           © Duchess Music Corp., Home Made
                                           Music Co.

Chapter 7

Nowhere Man   1965 by John Lennon & Paul
                                           McCartney recorded on Rubber Soul
                                           © Sony/ATV Music Publishing LLC
Here's to the Day   2021 by Billy Sprague © Songwriting
                                           University 101
Free Fallin   1989 by Tom Petty from Full Moon Fever
Satisfaction   1965 by Keith Richards and Mic Jagger
                                           recorded by the Rolling Stones on Out
                                           of Our Heads, © Abkco Music Inc.

Feels So Good	1977 by Chuck Mangione © Gates Music Inc
Sounds of Silence	1965 by Paul Simon recorded by Simon and Garfunkel on Wednesday Morning 3AM, © Paul Simon Music

Chapter 9

Witchy Woman	1972 by Don Henley & Bernie Leadon recorded by the Eagles on their debut album, Eagles, © Cass County Music, Likely Story Music Co.
Lady in Red	1986 by Chris De Burgh © BMG Rights Management, Tratore
Will it Go Round in Circles	1973 by Billy Preston & Bruce Fisher from My Life Is Music © Almo Music Corp., Irving Music Inc.
Never Die Young	1988 by James Taylor live version 2007 One Man Band © Sony BMG Music Entertainment

Chapter 13

Questions	2005 by Tommy Emmanuel from Live One. © Tommy Emmanuel

Chapter 16

Like a Rolling Stone	1965 by Bob Dylan, from Highway 61 Revisited © Universal Music Publishing Group
Free Fallin'	1989 by Tom Petty & Jeff Lynn from Full Moon Fever © Sony/ATV Music Publishing LLC, Gone Gator Music

Chapter 17

Let it Rain

1971 by Eric Clapton, Bonnie & Delany
Bramlett recorded by Eric Clapton on
his debut solo album Eric Clapton
© Embassy Music Corporation,
Embassy Music Corp., Delbon
Publishing Co., E C Music Ltd

The Long and Winding Road

1970 by Paul McCartney and John
Lennon recorded on Let It Be
© Sony/ATV Music Publishing LLC

Chapter 18

Everything I Own

1972 by David Gates recorded by Bread
on Baby, I'm-a Want You
© Sony/ATV Music Publishing LLC

Chapter 19

What a Fool Believes

1978 by Kenny Loggins & Michael
McDonald recorded by the Doobie
Brothers on Minute by Minute, ©
Gnossos Music / Milk Money Music,
Kobalt Music Publishing Ltd.

Till There Was You

1950 by Meredith Wilson, Beatles
released it in 1963.
© Kobalt Music Publishing Ltd.

The Way You Made Me Need You

by Billy Sprague © Songwriting
University 101

Chapter 22

She Blinded Me with Science

1983 by Thomas Dolby & Jonathan Kerr
recorded by Thomas Dolby on The
Golden Age of Wireless, © Carlin Music
Corp

Chapter 24

Beauty and the Beast

1991 by Alan Menken & Howard
Ashman © Walt Disney Music
Company, Wonderland Music Co. Inc.,
Wonderland Music Company Inc.,
Wonderland Music Company Inc

Life is a Highway

1991 by Tom Cochran recorded by
Rascal Flats 2006 for the movie Cars,
but originally by Tom Cochran
© Universal Music Publishing Canada

All I Have to do Is Dream

1958 by Boudleaux Bryant recorded by
The Everly Brothers © House of Bryant
Publications USA, Acuff-Rose Music
Limited

Chapter 25

Deacon Blues

1977 by Walter Becker & Donald Fagen
recorded by Steely Dan on Aja, © ©
Music Corp. Of America, Inc.

Reelin' the Years

1972 by Walter Becker & Donald Fagen
recorded by Steely Dan on Can't Buy a
Thrill, © Mca Music Publishing, A.d.o.
Universal S, American Broadcasting
Music, Inc., Red Giant Music Inc, Red
Giant, Inc.

Chapter 26

Frozen Man

1991 by James Taylor recorded on New
Moon Shine © Country Road Music,
Inc.

Chapter 29

Can't Take My Eyes Off of You   1967 by Bob Crewe & Robert Gaudio, recorded by
Franki Valli and the Four Seasons ,© Sony/ATV Music Publishing LLC, Broma 16, Universal Music Publishing Group

Chapter 31

We Will Rock You   1977 by Brian May recorded by Queen © Sony/ATV Music Publishing LLC

You Must Be Evil   1989 by Chris Rea from The Road to Hell © Warner Chappell Music, Inc.

Grand Canyon   1992 by Wayne Kirkpatrick recorded by Susan Ashton on Angels of Mercy, © Universal Music Publishing Group

Chapter 32

Sometimes When We Touch   1977 by Dan Hill & Barry Mann recorded by Dan Hill on Longer Fuse, © Sony/ATV Songs LLC; Mann & Weil Songs, Inc. & Sony/ATV Tunes LLC

Rainbow Connection   1979 by Kenneth Ascher & Paul Williams recorded by
Kermit the Frog © Fuzzy Muppet Songs

In the Blood   2017 by John Mayer from The Search for Everything © Reach Music Publishing

Chapter 33

All By Myself   1975 by Eric Carman & Sergei Rachmaninoff, © Eric Carmen Music, Round Hill Works, Boosey & Hawkes Music Publishers Ltd

Have You Ever Seen the Rain?	1971 by John Fogerty recorded by Creedence Clearwater Revival on Pendulum.
The Needle and the Damage Done	1972 by Neil Young recorded on Harvest, © Broken Fiddle Music, Words & Music A Div of Big Deal Music LLC

Chapter 34

Thanks to You	2013 by Billy Sprague © Songwriting University 101
Killing Me Softly	1973 by Norman Gimbel & Charles Fox recorded by Roberta Flack, © Warner Chappell Music, Inc
Hold the Intangible	1993 by Wayne Kirkpatrick & Billy Sprague recorded by Susan Ashton on © Universal Music Publishing Group; Skin Horse, Inc.
Here's to the Day	2021 by Billy Sprague © Songwriting University 101

Chapter 36

I'm Gonna Make You Love Me	1969 by Jerry Ross, Kenneth Gamble & Leon Huff recorded by Diana Ross and The Supremes © Warner Chappell Music, Inc
Nothin' from Nothin	1974 by Billy Preston & Bruce Fisher recorded by Billy Preston on The Kids and Me, © Almo Music Corp., Irving Music Inc.
That's Life	1966 by Kelly Gordon & Dean Thompson recorded by Frank Sinatra, © Bibo Music Publishing, Inc.

Crossfire	1989 by Reese Wynans, Thomas Smedley, Bill Carter, Ruth Ellsworth & Chris Layton recorded by Stevie Ray Vaughn on In Step, © Universal Music Corp., Killagraham Music

Chapter 37

He Stopped Loving Her Today	1980 by Curly Putman and Bobby Braddock recorded by George Jones, © Sony/ATV Music Publishing LLC
I Can't Make You Love Me	1991 by Michael Reid & Allen Shamblin recorded by Bonnie Raitt © Universal Music Publishing Group, Amplified Administration
Change the World	1997 by Wayne Kirkpatrick, Gordon Kennedy & Tommy Sims recorded by Eric Clapton, © Universal Music Corp., Universal Music - Brentwood Benson Songs, Sondance Kid Music, Downtown Dmp Songs, Universal Polygram Int. Publishing Inc., Universal Music - Brentwood Benson Publishing
Rainbow	2012 by Shane Mcanally, Natalie Hemby & Kacey Musgraves recorded by Kacey Musgraves, © Warner-Tamerlane Publishing Corp., 351 Music, Smack Hits, Smack Songs LLC, EMI Blackwood Music Inc., and These are Pulse Songs
Sangria Lies	2021 by Joe Beck, Tracie Taylor & Billy Sprague © Songwriting University 101 & 102
Thanks to You	2013 by Billy Sprague © Songwriting University 101

Riding Time	2019 by Mary Beth Koplin & Billy Sprague © MaryBethMuse, Inc., Songwriting University 101
Cherish	1966 by Terry Kirkman recorded by The Association © Sony/ATV Music Publishing LLC
Kinder	2020 by Joe Beck, Eric Speigel & Billy Sprague© Songwriting University 101 and 102
Library of My Life	2012 by Billy Sprague, © Songwriting University 101
American Pie	1971 by Don Mclean, © Songs of Universal Inc., Benny Bird Co. Inc.
I Rest My Soul	2019 by Joe Beck, Brittney Morse & Billy Sprague© Songwriting University 101 & 102

Chapter 38

Angel in the Morning	1968 by Chip Taylor recorded by Merillee Rush and in 1981 by Juice Newton, © EMI Blackwood Music, Inc.
Drift Away	by Mentor Williams recorded by Dobey Gray © Almo Music Corp., Rondor Music (London) Limited
Bluer Than Blue	1978 by Randy Goodrum recorded by Michael Johnson© Let There Be Music, Springcreek Music, Inc.
I Will	1968 by Paul McCartney & John Lennon, recorded by The Beatles on the White Album, © Sony/ATV Music Publishing LLC
Sleeps Dark and Silent Gate	1976 by Jackson Brown from his Pretender album © Swallow Turn Music
I Am a Rock	1965 by Paul Simon recorded by Simon & Garfunkle on Sounds of Silence, © Paul Simon Music, Lorna Music Co Ltd

Chapter 39

Monday, Monday	1966 by John Edmund & Andrew Phillips recorded by the Mamas and the Papa,© Universal Music Publishing Group, Downtown Music Publishing
Rainy Days and Mondays	1971 by Paul Williams & Roger Nichols recorded by the Carpenters on the "Tan" album © Universal Music Publishing Group
Manic Monday	1986 by Prince recorded by The Bangles, © Npg Publishing
Come Monday	1974 by Jimmy Buffet from Living and Dying in ¾ Time.© Abc Dunhill Music, Inc.
Carry On Wayward Son	1976 by Kerry Livgrin recorded by Kansas on Leftoverture © Sony/ATV Music Publishing LLC

Chapter 40

Running on Empty	1977 by Jackson Brown on Running on Empty © Swallow Turn Music
Live Like You Were Dying	by Craig Wiseman & Tim Nichols recorded by Tim McGraw © Warner Chappell Music, Inc, Round Hill Music Big Loud Songs, BMG Rights Management

Chapter 41

I Just Called to Say I love You	1984 by Stevie Wonder on The Woman in Red © Black-bull-music, Inc.

The Heart of the Matter	1989 by Mike Campbell, Don Henley & John David Souther recorded by Don Henley on The End of the Innocence © Sony/ATV Music Publishing LLC, Warner Chappell Music, Inc.

Denouement

Live Right	1986 by Rich Mullins, Wayne Kirkpatrick & Reed Arvin recorded by Rich Mullins on his debut album, Rich Mullins© Universal Music Publishing Group

Epilogo

That's What You Get	2021 by Billy Sprague, © Songwriting University 101
Just the Right Amount of Perfect	2019 by Mary Beth Koplin & Billy Sprague © MaryBethMuse, Inc., Songwriting University 101
Cappuccino Love	2019 by Mary Beth Koplin & Billy Sprague © MaryBethMuse, Inc., Songwriting University 101
I Am Convinced	2021 by Billy Sprague, © Songwriting University 101
We Are the Champions	1978 by Freddie Mercury recorded by Queen on News of the World © Queen Music Limited
That's Amore	1953 by Harry Warren & Jack Brooks recorded by Dean Martin © Paramount Music Corp

Made in United States
Orlando, FL
26 April 2023

32481839R00275